PRAISE FOR SERENADE, BOOK

"It's been a long time since I've enjoyed a romantic suspense this much ... I'll be stalking library shelves indefinitely for this author - she had me hooked after the first page. Lifetime fan. SO good."
                    -JULIE BRANDENBURG, LITTLE MISS BOOKMARK

"The suspense is nail biting..." IN'DTALE MAGAZINE

"Female heroine. Check. Adventure with high stakes. Check. Strong and powerful story with intrigue and secrets. Check. I loved nearly everything about this story. It had everything I hope for and love in a YA book. The writing style and powerful way the author can showcase emotions makes me eager to read anything McKenzie will write next- fiction, nonfiction, picture books, or anything."
                    - RACHEL BARNARD, AUTHOR

"Heather McKenzie did an amazing job at keeping her characters reliable, plausible and, above all, unique."
                    -ZØE HASLIE, AUTHOR

"What was great about this book was the intense pace it kept. There were no lulls in the story or with the romance and the scenes were adventurous and exciting. McKenzie is a promising author that is going to give readers a powerhouse trilogy..."
                    - DANIELLE ROBERTS, THE PLUVIOPHILE READER

"This book really took me on for a ride. There was not a single dull moment and I will be waiting eagerly for the next one in this series!"
                    - POULAMI, DAYDREAMING BOOKS

"Amazing and outstanding and crisply written."
                    -SAMANTHA MCLAUGHLIN – GOODREADS

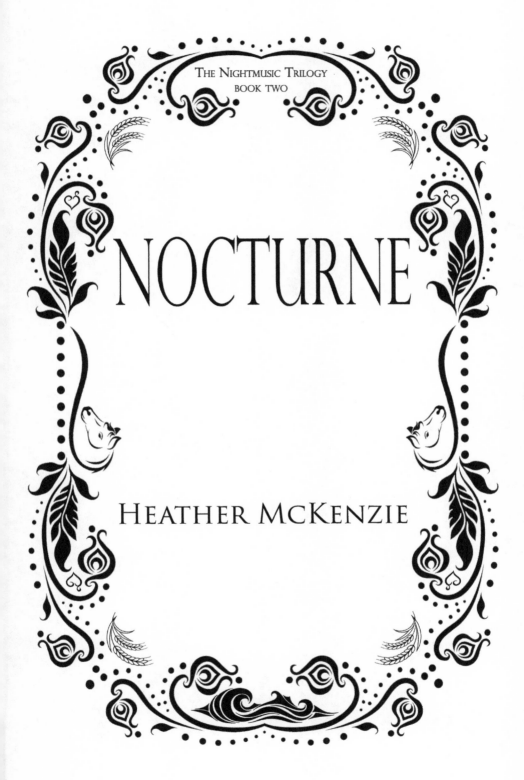

The Nightmusic Trilogy
BOOK TWO

NOCTURNE

Heather McKenzie

For Haley, Emily and Joshua

Play Amongst the Stars
-WISE UNICORN PENCIL

NOCTURNE
Copyright ©2018 Heather McKenzie
All rights reserved.
Printed in the United States of America
First Edition: July 2018

www.CleanTeenPublishing.com

SUMMARY: I am hunted. A pawn in a vicious game. The only way I can protect the ones I love…is to disappear. Kaya's perfect world is shattered when a deadly invasion brings an old ally to her rescue. Devastated to learn the identity of her attacker, she must do something truly heartbreaking in order to save the ones she loves.

ISBN: 978-1-63422-306-5 (paperback)
ISBN: 978-1-63422-307-2 (e-book)
Cover Design by: Marya Heidel
Typography by: Courtney Knight
Editing by: Cynthia Shepp

COVER ART
© ORHIDEIA / FOTOLIA
© EXTEZY / FOTOLIA
© BETELGEJZE / FOTOLIA
© YOD77 / FOTOLIA

Young Adult Fiction / Romance / Contemporary
Young Adult Fiction / Mystery & Detective Stories
Young Adult Fiction / Thrillers & Suspense

content disclosure

For more information about our content disclosure, please utilize the QR code above with your smart phone or visit us at www.CleanTeenPublishing.com.

KAYA

1

ℳusic over my ℋead

A fall heat wave blanketing the resort town of Radium made the normally cool, mountain air thick and heavy. Flowers had already bowed their heads and the foliage had long lost its color, but the air conditioners still roared through the rows of motels on the steep streets. Tourist season had come and gone, those seeking the hot springs and hiking trails now fewer than the vacancy signs that lit the night. The streets were quiet. The shops empty. And Luke and I found our little piece of paradise here, tucked away in a corner of the Lemon Tree Motel.

Our one-night stay had turned into a week before Luke finally started to relax. The blue of his eyes appeared lighter, and the dark shadows underneath them were gone. His forehead wasn't creased with concern, and an easy smile tugged at the corners of his mouth. He was beautiful. When he smiled, he was achingly so. I contributed these glimpses of his pearly whites and lazy shoulder shrugs to my fading bruises—which he inspected daily—and seven solid days in the company of new friends. They were a distraction from things we were avoiding, like the looming threat of my father, the email I'd been putting off reading from Stephan—and each other.

We had gotten to know the musicians staying on the second floor during a few late-night swims. Dustin, the singer for the band The Rain, loved to talk, and his personality was as big and bold as his bright green mohawk. Tonight, after his band played a show to what he'd called a 'festival crowd' at the local bar, he had Luke cornered in his room and was passionately recounting the musical highlights of his performance. While I sat next to his pretty blonde girlfriend, Dustin's raspy voice filled the room.

"The club felt like it was on fire, like... literally. All my fans were sweating buckets, every single one of them. I couldn't even wear my leather tonight. How can anyone not believe in global warming when it's like the freaking desert here in Canada? Geez. It's the middle of October, and I'm frying." Dustin fanned his face with silver-ringed fingers, and his girlfriend rolled her eyes. "I mean, look at me. I'm barefoot and shirtless... in the fall. I know the ladies dig it, but I hate to be ogled all the time. You know how it is. Right, Luke?"

Luke was half listening, as if lost in a daydream, when his eyes lifted to meet mine. "Oh, yeah, sure," he said with a grin and a wink. "I know all about that."

My heart did a little jump. It always did when he looked at me that way. Even in a plain white shirt and jeans, golden hair pulled back into a messy pony, he outshone the flamboyant singer. Dustin—decorated with tattoos and studded clothes—was bland next to Luke. Nothing could compare to the mesmerizing way Luke talked, the way he moved, and the way he took a sip of his drink.

Dustin's hair shook as he spoke, and he eyed Luke's glass. "Uh-oh, seems we have both run dry, my friend."

Luke shrugged his shoulders. "Ah, yes. For the third or fourth time."

"Fifth," I corrected, embarrassed I'd been keeping track. "I'll make the beverage run this time. More soda and ice on the way."

"That would be great, love," Dustin said. "The pop machine up here is empty, though. You'll have to hit up the one on the first floor by the pool."

Luke tensed and straightened his back. "I'll come with you."

Dustin pointed a black-painted fingernail at Luke's chest. "Whoa! Dude, you follow your girl around like any second, she's going to spontaneously combust. Let me tell ya, that's the fastest way to lose a chick. Stalkin' em ain't cool. I'm pretty sure your girl here can find the pop machine. Just sayin'."

Luke shook his head. "It's just that... there are people..." His voice caught and trailed off. When he stared at me wordlessly, I knew what he was going to say—there are people who want to kill my girlfriend.

I hated being the source of such worry.

"There are what?" Marie said, quiet until now.

Luke cleared his throat. "People around. You know... strange people around that..."

Dustin laughed while Luke was at a loss for words, and his stretched earlobes wiggled. "Stranger than me?"

Luke had no reply to that.

"Dustin's right. I don't need a stalker," I said.

Luke's eyes held mine from across the room, and butterflies danced in my stomach. Although I cherished every second alone with him, exercising my independence had become intoxicating. I felt bad about the turmoil he went through every time I left his side, but being free was a new thing for me. A few days ago, I went to the front desk, by myself, and paid the nice grey-haired man for another two nights. Then yesterday, I ventured to the little gift shop at the bottom of the hill and bought every kind of chocolate bar they had—just because I could. I talked to a stranger. I navigated the world on my own. It was a small accomplishment but one that almost made me cry with joy. I craved freedom, almost as much as I did Luke. And by some miracle, I had both.

I squared my shoulders. "Just stay here and relax, Luke. I'm only going down one flight of stairs. I might stop at our room to change into a cooler shirt on the way, but I can handle that on my own."

Luke was about to protest, but something made him change his mind. He leaned back on the bed and gave me a nod.

"Great! Don't forget the root beer," Dustin said triumphantly. "And, hey, there are snacks on the first floor too. How about some chips? There's some change on the dresser by my shorts if ya need it."

Marie stood, and I thought for a moment she might hit her head on the ceiling fan. She was tall and sturdy, body like a pro-wrestler and face all sharp angles surrounded by a halo of blonde curls. Her voice was deep and husky when she spoke, but when she sang…oh, the sweetest soprano voice poured effortlessly from her throat.

"Good Lord, Dustin. She's not a servant, and she can barely use one of her arms." Putting down a beat-to-crap acoustic guitar, she folded her arms over her chest. "Don't be a jerk."

"It's all right, I can manage," I said.

"No, I'll go with ya, Kaya. I need some air. It smells like ass in here."

"You mean it smells like successful rock star, yeah?" Dustin joked.

Marie grabbed the ice bucket from my hand. "If this is what success smells like, I'd prefer dating someone who reeked of failure."

The smile left Dustin's face. "Who says we're dating, Marie?"

His words stung. Marie seemed about to throw the ice bucket at his head until the door swung open. In the doorway was the spitting image of Dustin, grinning from ear to ear. Breezing into the room on a cloud of beer fumes with a girl under each arm, Rusty the drummer was ready to party. Marie took one look at him and then at the giggling girls before promptly handing me back the ice bucket—she wasn't about to leave her man alone with groupies.

I turned to Luke before heading out. "Like I said, I'll make the beverage run."

He was still staring, gaze so intense it made me feel like I was the only person in the room. "Don't be too long," he said.

Right. Ice and pop.

Music from the small room flowed furiously out into the starry night. It hugged the stifling heat as I made my way through it to our room. My shirt was sticking to me, and my heavy hair was turning my back into a furnace. I twisted it up, heading down the stairs barefoot, and decided I would cut it all off tomorrow. I could do that now—Stephan wasn't around to freak out.

Stephan.

I'd been putting off reading his email. It was ridiculous, but I was holding on to one tiny ray of hope that my father wasn't all that bad, and I knew that whatever was in Stephan's message would permanently snuff it out. For one more day, I would remain ignorant of whatever reality I would be hit with. I would read it tomorrow.

I slipped my key into the lock and pushed open the door. The room flooded with light, shimmering and dancing off the pool in the middle of the complex. It lit up the green shag rug, pine furniture, and clothes strewn over chairs. It was so cozy. So perfect. Except for the small table between the two beds where Luke and I slept. It made the distance between us at night as vast as the ocean.

For weeks, we'd wandered the world together in bliss. He'd held me in his arms all night long. During the day, there'd barely been a moment without his hand in mine. Every motel we stayed at was a fuzzy blur as our sights were only set on each other. While my body healed, his gaze smoldered with longing and I basked in his attention. Until suddenly, the second day here, things changed. He became withdrawn, kept his hands to himself, slept in his own bed, and only quickly kissed me goodnight. A tension built between us that didn't make sense, and I didn't know how to ask what was wrong. If it wasn't for the look in his eyes—the one thing that hadn't changed—I might have lost my mind.

There was a hint of music, and then stomping. Marie was strumming her guitar. Deep male voices were singing along, keeping time with their feet. The paper-thin walls rattled in the otherwise vacant building, and I wondered if Luke was joining in too… could he sing? Or was he politely smiling, tracking the time and wondering how long before setting out to check on me?

After tugging on a dry shirt, I scooped a handful of change off the dresser along with the room key and set back out on my beverage mission. The pop machine was on the opposite side of the pool, next to a massive 'keep out' sign. I circled the inviting water, sparkling and without a ripple in the moonlight, and cursed the red tape flanking the edges—it just didn't seem like a broken diving board was a reason to stay out. I believed in following rules, but it was hot, and how hard would it be to avoid that one area? Were all the warning signs and lounge chairs blocking the steps leading into the water necessary? A quick swim was all I needed to cool down. It wasn't dangerous.

Without second thought, I slipped off my jean shorts and top, then stepped over the red tape. A dip of my toes confirmed the water temperature was perfect. Soon, I was waist deep in the shallow end, inhaling the chlorine lingering heavily in the air. The heat in my cheeks started to subside. I moved farther, the gradual slope of the bottom of the pool bringing the tips of my shoulders beneath the water. I had only intended to wet my legs, but couldn't stop myself from pushing off. Relaxed, happy, and feeling a bit wicked for it, I floated to the deep end.

The music from upstairs had quieted for a moment, but then started again with roaring laughter and even louder singing. Another guitar had been added into the mix along with an unrecognizable, high-pitched female voice. Every window was dark except for the room Luke was in with our new friends. Shadows moved past the flimsy curtains, and I wondered if they were dancing.

I kicked my legs, propelling my body through the water while still favoring my arm. The skin around the burn on my bicep had at least lessened to a green-blue splotch, but the bone and torn muscle ached. Keeping it at my side as I went under, and coming up for air only when necessary, I savored the water's familiar comfort. At the bottom, ears popping and my body feeling weightless and heavenly, I crouched into an armchair position while the heavy suction of the drain tugged at my toes. There was nothing but silence here. Deep, thick in my ears, blocking out everything but my heartbeat. For a moment, the whole world went away.

With a quick straightening of my knees, I shot up to the surface to gulp in air and tilted my face to the sky and the stars twinkling like diamonds. There was still no breeze, and now, no music either. It was beautiful and quiet. Eerily so. I was about to dive under again when a shifting of light from the room Luke and I shared caught my eye. Damn it. He was looking for me. I swam to the edge and tucked up close, putting my head up enough to see the room go dark. Any moment now, he'd be calling my name. I had to get out of the pool and dry off without getting caught; I didn't want Luke to know I was swimming alone. It might add to the already strange tension between us.

I waited for his voice, straining to hear his footsteps. But there was only a weird silence minutes later. There was no one calling for me. Still no music. No shadows moved past the upstairs window —I could have heard a pin drop.

Something was wrong.

The chill of premonition rolled up my spine. I was about to launch out of the pool when a man's voice coming from overhead caught my breath. Throaty and gruff, it wasn't Luke, Dustin, or Rusty's voice, or the nice old man who sat at the front desk…

"There's no sign of her up here," he said.

My blood froze in my veins; the man was talking about me.

I swam slowly along the edge of the pool—grateful for the dim lighting and many shadows—and got underneath the broken diving board. The tip of it was skimming the surface, and it made a space dark enough for me to hide beneath. After pulling my knees to my chest, I slipped my fingers into the cracks in the plastic board above my head and held on. I watched two men take the stairs down toward the pool. One was tall and lean, scanning the complex, and the other—short and wide as an oven—kept looking at his watch. They kicked in the door of our room, and the wide man went in while the tall one stood by. Luke… Oh my God… Was he still in there? Had he turned off the light and gone to bed?

I held back a yelp of panic.

"Clear," the wide man said, exiting the room with the laptop we'd just bought.

The tall man fumed. "The front desk clerk confirmed she was here. She couldn't have gotten far. Search every square inch of this dump. If we go back empty-handed, Rayna will have our heads."

Rayna?

My heart stopped. Were they talking about the woman whose picture I'd found in the estate lobby? The woman who was related to me somehow? Our eyes were the same color, our smile and bone structure eerily identical. She was so familiar I was certain she was my real mother. Could she be searching for me just as I was for her?

I wanted to call out. The child in me was about to throw her arms in the air and holler. But the person who had grown considerably wary of others over the last few years thought better of it. When the motel clerk came shuffling out of his office in his slippers and housecoat and was shot in the chest and tossed into the shallow end of the pool, I figured I'd made the right decision.

"Boss lady is gonna be pissed about that," the tall man said. "She said keep it clean."

"Well, Rayna can suck it if she doesn't like how I do my job," the wide man said.

It was all I could do to not scream. The old man's body quickly sank to the bottom before it floated back up. A red cloud grew around him. It started spreading out toward my hiding spot. As the splotch neared, I fought to keep quiet. I watched and waited while the men searched one room, then another. When both disappeared at the same time into separate rooms, I snuck out. Hands on the ledge, I was about to pull myself up and out of the pool, but something caught my eye—there was another man. A figure crouched beside the towel bin with only his outline visible. Had he seen me, too?

The mouth of a waterslide was a foot away. I headed for it. As I wiggled my way into the red tube, my wounded arm throbbed and my legs quivered like jelly. Soon, it became too steep to climb and the slightest misstep would cause a loud shriek of my skin rubbing on plastic, so I froze with my arms and legs splayed like Spiderman.

The voices of the men grew louder. They were arguing about Rayna. One wanted to follow her orders explicitly—which was bring her my dead body. The other wanted to burn the whole place down and just get it over with. I was sure I misunderstood. Had to be hearing things. There was no way this Rayna was the woman I suspected was my mother.

They began circling the pool. My weak arm shook violently as I pushed harder against the plastic. A light passed across the bottom of the slide, just missing my toes, and I held my breath until the pain in my arm became unbearable. Suddenly, the torn muscle gave out and my feet made a horrific screeching noise as my legs crumpled beneath me. I tumbled down the slide and plopped into the water. When I came up for air, I was caught in the stare of the wide man, who was now grinning madly with a gun pointed at my head.

"Got her," he yelled, steadying a pair of dark, almond-shaped eyes on me.

His finger hovered over the trigger. Any moment now, my blood would mix with the old man's. Where was Luke? Should I shout and warn him to hide? To run? Or had they already found him? I eyed the clerk floating toward me. What if Luke was dead, too?

No. I would have felt that.

I braced, waiting for the bullet to end me, to see and feel the warmth of that beautiful white light I had been close to before...

But the wide man didn't make a move. He stood, staring, and something like sympathy came across his face. "You sure look like your mother," he said, head tipping to the side as he studied me. "It's too bad she wants you dead."

I could barely breathe. Should I scream now? "My mother?" I

choked on the words. "You mean… Rayna?"

He nodded. "Yeah. You're the spitting image of her. Damn, you've never even met her, have ya?"

He was confirming my suspicions about the woman in the picture. But I didn't like what I was hearing. She wanted me dead? "Rayna…" I repeated, feeling dizzy. "Your boss lady… is my mother? No. I've never met her."

I stared at the barrel of the wide man's pistol still aimed at my forehead.

"It's too bad," he said. The jowls under his chin shook. "You're so pretty. It's such a waste."

The world slipped away for a moment when the full force of reality kicked it in the ass. "There must be some misunderstanding." My legs were close to not holding me up.

The wide man laughed. "No, there sure isn't, Miss Kaya Lowen." He spat my last name like acid. "Rayna most certainly wants you dead. Don't worry. I'll make it quick and painless."

Behind the wide man, the figure crouching next to the towel bin stood. The shadows concealed his face, but something familiar about the outline of him tugged at my memory. This person moved like—

Suddenly, the man in the shadows lunged for the wide man's neck, getting hold of it with meaty hands and snapping it to the left. I heard bones break. The wide man's gun fell to the ground, then so did his body. And there, eyes wide and glaring, chest rising and falling with clenched fists and gritted teeth… was Oliver.

"Get out of the damn pool," he roared.

What? I was stunned. What was he doing here? How did he know where I was?

"Get out," he ordered again, barely able to get the words out.

I stared in stunned silence until another familiar figure emerged from around a corner, cheeks pink and blood on his forehead. I almost fainted in relief at the sight of him. "Luke, are you—"

Oliver cut me off. "It's about time," he snarled, turning to give Luke a sideways leer. "Did you get the other guy?"

"Yeah," Luke said, slightly breathless. "We've gotta get out of here, though, and fast. They've got backup coming. I know these guys, and they are ruthless."

Oliver's nostrils flared. He was vibrating with rage. "Damn Right Choice Group assholes. I can't believe you were a part of that crap. Did you know you were working for Kaya's mother? That's right, Luke. Rayna, your ex-boss lady, is Kaya's mother. For some reason, the bitch wants to put a bullet in her child's head."

Luke paled. He stumbled back as if all the wind had been knocked out of him. "I didn't know. Oh my God, I swear I didn't know."

I was freezing in the pink water while trying to make sense of the exchange between the love of my life and my ex-fiancé while a dead man who said I looked like Rayna—my now-confirmed mother—lay at their feet.

Luke crouched at the edge of the pool. His eyes, full of remorse, would have pulled at my heartstrings if it weren't for a whirlwind of fury building inside me. "Please believe I didn't know. Truly, I didn't," he said. "Let me help you out of the water, Kaya."

He HeH thrust his hand toward me.

My heart was pounding in panic to get out, but my mind raced with the realization I had been betrayed—on a few different levels. I waded to the other side and got out on my own. Picking up my discarded jean shorts, I yanked them up my dripping legs, hands shaking so hard I could barely get the zipper to function. The struggle with the shirt brought tears to my eyes.

"What about the others?" Oliver was saying as they rounded the edge of the pool toward me.

"The others?" My chest tightened in terror; were there more men here who wanted to kill me?

Luke's gaze met mine briefly before drifting to the second floor—where there was still no music. Then it hit me. Our friends.

I bolted for the stairs, taking two at a time and almost wiping out at the top, then ran toward the room where we'd sang and laughed for the last seven nights. Luke was yelling at me to stop. Oliver shouted for Luke to stop me. I ignored them and practically hurled my body at the door. It swung open.

"Kaya, please," Luke said. His hand caught my shoulder, stopping me from falling into the room. Into the chaos. Into the dead.

Luke was apologizing for not getting to them sooner while my heartbeat smashed in my ears and tried to drown him out. Marie was on the floor, her pretty blonde curls thick with red, and Dustin was splayed on the bedspread next to Rusty and the two groupies—their bodies riddled with bullet holes.

I stumbled backward, unable to look away. This was a nightmare, had to be.

"No… Oh my God, no. Because of me?" I choked out, feeling my stomach rise into my throat. The pulsing in my ears escalated into a raging storm. "Because of me they're dead?"

Luke pulled me away from the gruesome sight, his hand searing hot on my skin confirming I was awake and this was real. The sky shook, spots danced before my eyes, and then my legs gave out.

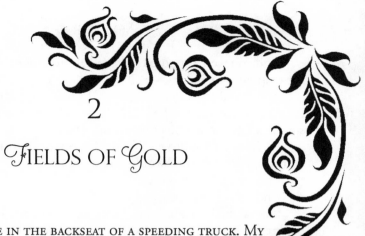

2

FIELDS OF GOLD

I WAS JARRED AWAKE IN THE BACKSEAT OF A SPEEDING TRUCK. My clothes were damp, my hair an uncomfortable mop around my head, and my chest ached from crying. The sun was just starting to come up and between heavy eyelids, I watched a deep magenta sky tinged with gold clouds come to life. The odd tree whizzed by. A bird or two. A telephone pole.

The window was down a crack. Cool air brushed over my swollen eyes, giving my bare legs goose bumps. I shivered, cold for the first time in weeks, and wondered where the warm air had gone. Where were we? By the rattling of the truck, it felt like a dirt road. I thought to ask, but then decided it didn't matter.

Luke was in the passenger seat. From my position, the golden stubble on his cheeks and chin and streaks of darkened blood on the side of his forehead was visible. Was it his or the other man's? It just didn't fit; his near-angelic appearance and ability to kill someone. I hadn't known he was capable of that, but then again, I hadn't known a lot of things about him.

But I knew exactly what Oliver was capable of. I'd witnesses it many times. I knew him. I could read him blindfolded. I didn't have to sit up and look to know his nostrils were flared and one hand was clenching the steering wheel while the other rubbed at his furrowed brow; I could tell that just from the tone of his voice and ice-cold replies to Luke's questions. So badly I wanted Oliver gone. Out of my life. Forever. The feeling was so strong I was tempted to throw myself out of the moving truck just to get away from him.

"Did you have to set fire to the place?" Luke asked him.

The truck accelerated. Oliver cleared his throat. "I couldn't leave behind any evidence she was there. So, yeah."

"She's shivering," Luke said, and the window was rolled up. "We've got nothing. You were supposed to at least grab some of her clothes out of the room."

"And you were supposed to keep her safe! I should pull over and beat the crap out of you."

"You could try, but you know I'd break your arms before you even touched a hair on my head." Luke wasn't being arrogant, he was just stating a fact—one Oliver wasn't okay with.

He let out a low growl. "You let her out of your sight. What is wrong with you? Why the hell would you do that?"

"She wanted to be alone."

"And you thought that was okay?"

Luke sighed. "Yeah. I did. I can't keep her on a leash, Oliver, nor do I want to. Besides, I knew you were watching. Nose out your window, binoculars in hand, or whatever your methods of spying on us have been for the last week."

"You better keep quiet about that, boy," Oliver warned. "She won't forgive you if she finds out you were working with her ex-fiancé behind her back."

Luke twisted around in his seat. His eyes were rimmed red. "She's awake, Oliver. Has been for a while. She knows."

I curled on my side and shut out what I was hearing. As the morning light increased, so did my anger at Oliver, and my guilt and sadness for my friends who lost their lives. It only multiplied the pain of being betrayed by the one person I thought I could trust.

"I'm so sorry I didn't tell you, Kaya." Luke's voice was full of sadness. "I'm sorry about everything."

Oliver said nothing, but the heavy, irritated breaths escaping his lungs were words to me.

"I have to pee," I said, now desperate to get out of the truck.

"We'll stop in a bit," Oliver said. "There's a town about fifteen minutes—"

"Now," I yelled so I didn't have to listen to him utter another word.

Luke pointed ahead. "Just pull over, Oliver. There, to the right. Take that road."

The truck slowed and then turned. My heart was pounding out a warning of an impending anxiety attack. We came to a stop. "If either of you follow me, I'll—"

I didn't finish. What I saw when I sat up made me forget my threat. After I pushed the door open, I stepped out onto a dusty road strewn with gravel. It stretched alongside a field where the most glorious breeze shook masses of flowers. Yellow and gold waves rolled atop tall green stems. The land sprawled beneath an endless blue sky that seemed to reach as far as the eye could see in every direction. It was so vast. There were no mountains or towers of rock obstructing the view. I'd never seen anything like it. My feet started moving, heading down a road so straight it seemed to never end. I inhaled the perfume in the air, so different from the pine scents back home. My anxiety started to subside. I'd never been anywhere else than the mountains. Never seen any place like this.

I picked up the pace. Before I knew it, I was running. Flat out. Flip-flops barely stayed on my feet. Crickets jumped out of my way, a hawk eyed me from above, and footsteps pounded behind me trying to keep up. Pumping my arms and moving my legs as hard and as fast as I could, I gave it all I had. When my lungs started screaming, exhaustion took hold and insisted I stop. Gasping for air and doubling over, I waited for my heart rate to slow. I waited for the heavy emotional turmoil welling inside to settle for a moment. I closed my eyes, took in a deep breath, then stood up straight and exhaled.

"It's mustard," Luke said from behind me, breathless.

I plopped down onto my butt in the middle of the road, not worried about getting run over. Luke sat down next to me, swiping away a curious bee. "All those yellow flowers are mustard plants. When the pods turn brown, the seeds are ready to harvest. You can eat the leaves too… or sauté them. Black mustard is awesome on hot dogs. Super tasty stuff."

"I don't eat hot dogs," I said flatly.

"Oh. Right." He reached for my hand, but I pulled away. "Listen, Kaya, I'm sorry. I should have told you about Oliver."

"Yeah, you should have," I said.

Guilt furrowed his brow. "I had a feeling he was following us. I caught him the first night we arrived at the Lemon Tree Motel. He made me a deal that just seemed, well, logical. I mean, I would love to hold him down and pound his face in—and vice versa—but knowing he was there, looking out for you, was comforting. I had back up if I needed it. And, apparently, I needed it. If he hadn't been there—"

"Would we have stayed for seven days at that motel if Oliver hadn't been lurking around?" I asked.

Luke shook his head. "No. It wouldn't have been safe. We would have kept moving. He told me he'd remain hidden and keep watch if we stayed put for a while."

"So, it's his fault, isn't it?" I seethed.

"What's his fault?"

"That our friends are dead!"

I leapt to my feet and headed into the field of mustard, the plants almost as tall as me, the humming insects fluttering my ears.

"I'm sorry," Luke said, marching behind me. "I doubted my ability to keep you safe. I have to make sure that nothing happens to you, and—"

I stopped short and turned to face him. "I want you as a boyfriend, not a bodyguard. There's a significant difference!"

He put his hands up. "There should be, yes, but when the love of your life is being hunted by her father and grandfather, those roles sort of merge together."

I swallowed hard, suddenly aware that although it was scenic, it wasn't all that warm, wherever we were. "Don't forget my mother."

"Rayna," Luke said uncomfortably.

"Yes. She wants me dead, too. Those men at the motel, I heard them talking. They said she wanted my body delivered to her. Why? Why would my own mother want to kill me? I thought that maybe…"

I didn't get a chance to finish. He lunged for me, pulled me tight, and cradled my head against his broad chest. "I won't let anything happen to you, Kaya, even if it means I have to endure your creepy ex-fiancé following us around. I won't take any chance, no matter how small, that I might lose you. Please forgive me for that."

His heartbeat crashed into my ears, soothing me and bringing the looming anxiety attack to a complete halt. I pulled back to peer into his glorious blue eyes that were the same color as the sky behind him, yet somehow more dazzling.

"Is that why you wouldn't touch me? You knew Oliver was around so that's why we slept in separate beds?"

"It was part of Oliver's deal that I kept my hands off you."

If anything, Luke was a man of his word. That's why there had been a strange tension between us. Why he'd kept his distance and tucked me in at night with a gentle kiss when the fire in his eyes said he wanted so much more.

"So, you still… want me?"

A devastating smile crossed his face. "Yes."

His mouth found mine, and his hands wound into my hair. Every single cell of my body lit up beneath his touch. He parted my mouth and moved his tongue across mine, the taste of him and the warmth of his glorious body thrilling all my senses. It didn't matter who I was, or where I was, I became lost in everything about him. He moved his mouth to my ear. A butterfly kiss on the lobe. I felt such love radiate through him it lit up my soul. He was the air in my lungs. The blood in my veins. Nothing else mattered.

"You have my heart and my body, Kaya, and I want to show you in every way more than anything in the entire world," he breathed. His pulse quickened at the base of his throat. "But I also want to wait until it's right."

I gulped, shaking from head to toe. "This isn't the Twilight movie, Luke. You aren't an old-fashioned vampire waiting for me to graduate high school so you can marry me first."

A grin stretched across his face. He leaned into my neck and gave it a playful bite. "Maybe I am."

My breath caught. I struggled to speak. "When do you think the time might be right then?" "Well, let's see… probably when your body is healed completely." His hand moved down my side before gently brushing over my stomach—which was now perfectly flat after the miscarriage. "And when Oliver isn't around, and I don't have to worry about one of your family members plucking you from my arms."

"That might not ever happen," I said, unable to hide my reddening cheeks and the need to kiss him. The breeze picked up. The mustard field swayed around us.

He cupped my chin. "Never? Well, in that case, how about tomorrow?"

All the air left my lungs.

"After you marry me, Bella," he said with a playful grin.

I detached myself and smacked him lightheartedly. "You're an ass."

His hands clutched mine, pulling me back in, face suddenly serious. "Honestly, Kaya, I've screwed up a lot in my life, and I'm not going to take a chance with you. I'm going to do things right whether it's old fashioned or not. You're not like other girls and I won't treat you like one. I don't want anyone for the rest of my life but you, and I want our first time together to be perfect. And, maybe I will put a ring on your finger first."

I shifted uncomfortably beneath his gaze while my heart thumped madly in my chest. "That's ridiculous."

But it wasn't. It was beautiful. It was perfect. It was Luke.

He lowered his mouth to mine again. For a blissful moment, everything bad in my world went away… until the sound of Oliver impatiently honking the horn pulled us apart.

3

MADE TO ORDER

WITH THE SUN DISAPPEARING BEHIND US, WE ENDED UP IN THE town of Rosedale, which was somewhere between nowhere and somewhere, in the middle of nothing. At the end of a field and the beginning of a gravel road, wheat and canola surrounded a place that resembled a set from a western movie. There was no one on the streets, only two trucks in front of the tavern, and the shops next to the gas station were closed. There were no trees. No busses, tourists, or signs posted everywhere—no chaos. It was nothing like the hectic and touristy Banff or cluttered and precipitous Radium, and that suited me just fine.

After much arguing—Oliver wanted to keep driving north and Luke wanted to head to a big city to get lost in—I insisted we stay. Mostly because spending another moment in the truck with Oliver was more than I could bear.

The Rosedale Motel had only one room available due to a rodeo event in the neighboring town, hence the 'crowd' at the tavern. We were told we were lucky there was a cancelation. I wasn't sure what the front desk clerk meant by 'lucky' when we opened the door to the dingy room. I'd thought the Lemon Tree Motel was a bit questionable, but this was nasty.

"Are they all this bad?" I muttered when the three of us entered the peach-painted room with matching threadbare carpet and curtains.

"Ah, this is actually rather luxurious," Luke said, flopping onto the only bed while Oliver peered out the window before shutting the drapes. "You're just used to life in a castle, princess."

That I was. And the thought of being back in my cage made the crappy motel room suddenly look like heaven. The only thing in it out of place was Oliver.

"Right. Well, you can go now," I said to my former fiancé. "Luke and I are just fine. Your services are no longer needed. Or wanted."

He flinched. I didn't care if I'd offended or hurt him.

"We need him, Kaya. He's trained for this sort of thing," Luke said gently. "There are too many people after you, and the two of us have better odds of—"

"If you say keeping me safe, I'll scream," I warned.

Luke cleared his throat. "We can keep the bad guys away."

Being in the truck with Oliver had been uncomfortable, but stuck with him in this tiny room? It was claustrophobic.

"So what's the game plan?" Oliver said, folding his arms across his chest. He glanced to where Luke sat on the bed, and then at me numbly standing next to a television that appeared as if it might explode if turned on.

"I have no idea," Luke said. "But we are all exhausted. Let's sleep on it and figure it out in the morning."

Oliver stared hard at me, and then at the bed. His teeth gritted. It was obvious what he was thinking. "If you think I am—"

Luke stopped him before he could go any further. "Kaya gets the bed. You take the floor on one side, and I'll take it on the other."

Oliver's shoulders relaxed somewhat. "Fine," he grumbled. "Let's order some food. I'll see if there's any place that delivers pizza out here."

"Or chicken," Luke said.

Oliver plunked in a chair next to the window. "Shows how much you know about her," he said with a sneer in my direction. "Kaya doesn't eat chicken."

"Yeah, she does," Luke said.

Oliver seized the opportunity to argue. "Born and raised a vegan. Never had meat in her life."

Luke moved to the edge of the bed, taking the bait. "Really? Because I'm positive what I tasted on her lips last night was honey-garlic sauce from a perfectly fried batch of chicken wings."

Oliver bolted out of the chair, and I leapt between him and Luke before fists started flying. I put my hands out between the two raging beasts. "Don't fight. Please," I begged.

"I should have killed you long ago," Oliver hissed at Luke.

"And I should have let you fall off that damn cliff," Luke replied.

The peach room was about to turn into a bloodbath if I didn't do something. My fingers grazed Luke's chest with one hand. The other was pressed against Oliver's shoulder. I stood my ground.

"Hasn't there been enough blood already? I swear, if either of you lay a hand on the other, I'm out of here. I'll walk out that door and never come back. Of that I can promise you."

Luke instantly backed away. But Oliver stayed put, stubbornly fueled by rage.

I glared. "Go ahead. Make a move. I would love an excuse to get away from you."

His arms dropped to his sides, and he backed away. I made the mistake of looking into his eyes, seeing a ton of hurt beneath the rage. I felt guilty. This was Oliver. The man who'd stayed by my side through thick and thin, saved my life again, and even now, when I was being awful to him, made no move to leave.

"I can't take any fighting between you two," I said, hoping my voice sounded firm. "Those people—Dustin, Marie, Rusty, and the others—are gone because of me. My dad is an evil megalomaniac, my granddad wants me dead, and my mom would rather have someone put a bullet in my head than even so much as lay eyes on me. You're all I've got."

You're all I've got.

As soon as it came out of my mouth, I regretted it. It brought me back to the Derrick Bar and the day Oliver said the exact same thing to me. Those words had changed everything between us. It was the moment I realized I felt something deeper than friendship for him. Judging by the look on his face, he was recalling the same thing.

Luke retreated to the bed while Oliver's eyes remained focused on mine, shining with something that made my chest hurt.

I pretended not to notice.

"I'm taking a shower." I had to remove myself from the room. "I'll eat whatever you guys decide to order. Even chicken."

Behind the safety of the locked bathroom door, I started to undress and let loose the tears that had been building up. I fumbled with the tank top, bra, and undies, remembering the blood of the dead man would be dried into the fabric. Suddenly, it became an act of desperation to get the clothes off. Naked and shaking with repulsion at the undergarments in my hands, I yanked open a crusty window and tossed them outside—I couldn't even bear the thought of seeing them on the bathroom floor. They joined the weeds, dirt, and beer bottles strewn against the back wall of the motel. I felt wretched. If I wasn't around, our friends would still be alive. Anne would be alive. Luke wouldn't have to be worried about me all the time. Oliver... could be free. It wasn't fair to anyone, this madness that was my life.

As tears flowed, I cranked on the hot water. Steam quickly filled the tiny space, and it sounded like a jet engine hitting the cracked tiles. I scrubbed madly at every square inch of my body, but all the soap and hot water in the world wasn't washing my self-loathing down the drain. Giving up, I wrapped a towel around my hair and dried off, now realizing I was an idiot for tossing my clothes out the window. All I had left were the jean shorts. I pulled them back on before trying to get my teeth clean with a damp cloth, cursing myself for now having to ask Luke or Oliver to go outside and get my clothes.

The tap squealed when I turned it off, and then I heard something like a heavy thud. A loud bang then caught my breath; the noise was coming from outside the bathroom door. Another crashing sound made the walls shake. There was struggling going on in the room. An unmistakable grunt came from Oliver—was he fighting someone? Luke, too? Who was there? Had Rayna found me? Or my father?

Panic consumed me. I froze, still as stone on the tiled floor as the thuds increased. What could I do? Stand there helplessly and let more blood be spilled because of me? Not this time. I had to swallow my fear and break through the paralyzing effects of panic. I had to move.

Opening the bathroom door would be a big mistake. Ambush was the only strategy that would work, so I crawled out the bathroom window, barely squeezing through the narrow opening. Jumping barefoot onto my discarded clothes, I kept a towel tight around my chest. A broken beer bottle was the best weapon I could find and I held it tight as I tiptoed over the garbage-strewn ground until I rounded the corner and was at the front of the motel. As I ran toward our room, every horrible vision imaginable flooded my mind. I couldn't lose Luke. I would die a hundred times over for him if I had to. And it hit me—as I stared at the door praying he was alive—that even with all the awful things he'd done, I couldn't lose Oliver, either.

It was too quiet. The thuds had stopped. In my experience, silence on these types of occasions usually meant one thing—death.

Not Luke. Please, Lord, spare him. Please let him be okay. Please let him be alive. I'll do anything…

With a deep breath, I turned the knob; it was locked. It was loose, though, like it had been broken a few times. I backed up, wielding the beer bottle, and then kicked with every bit of force I could muster. A searing pain shot through my foot and made the puncture wound from the Death Race start screaming again. I was sure I'd broken a few bones, but the door swinging open made me forget all that. I burst in…

The room was in shambles. A chair was upside down, and the TV was on the floor. A large dent was in the wall by the closet, and the bed was thrown off the box spring. But there was no blood. Luke was standing in one corner, breathing heavily, while Oliver was in the other with a cut lip. There was no one else in the room. With shocked faces and wide eyes, they said my name in unison.

"What the hell is going on?" I stammered, foot starting to swell as the beer bottle shook in my hand.

"You kicked in the door? How did you get outside?" Luke said incredulously. The guilty look on his face matched Oliver's. "And where is your shirt?"

I clutched the towel tighter, finding it hard to swallow. My throat was dry, body trembling. "I threw my clothes away. They were covered in blood from that dead guy. I heard struggling. I thought you and Oliver were fighting off attackers, and I wanted to help you. I could only find this beer bottle. I was scared that I was too late, and I—"

"Oh Kaya, I'm so sorry," Luke said, lunging for a sheet and draping it over my shoulders. He shoved the TV against the door to hold it closed before leading me to the trashed bed. Oliver just watched in detached silence. "Oliver and I were just figuring out dinner," he said sheepishly. "We couldn't quite come to an agreement, but I think we have now. Right, Oliver?"

Oliver nodded. A broken lamp dangled behind him, and the pages of Rodeo Weekly lay shredded across his feet. He and Luke had been fighting each other, and it hadn't been over dinner. It was over me.

But what if they had been fighting off one of the many parties eager for my death? A picture of that motel room—of Dustin and Marie bleeding out onto the carpet—flashed before my eyes. It could be Luke's hair bright red from a gunshot to the forehead, or Oliver's eyes vacant with death…

I had a tough time catching my breath. "I don't know what I'd do if anything happened to you," I said, staring into Luke's eyes to try to make the room stop spinning.

"Shh," he said, voice soothing as he pulled me close. He kissed the top of my head. "Nothing's going to happen to me, I promise."

I didn't believe him.

I loved him. I loved him so much my chest absolutely ached. The thought of this world without him in it caused such a constricting feeling it was hard to breathe.

"You'd be better off without me," I said. When he pulled away to look at me in shock, I took a sidelong glance at Oliver. "You both would be better off without me."

I was tucked into bed while both men quietly worked to put the room back in order. They were on their absolute best behavior, even faking the odd grin and attempting small talk for my benefit. I studied them, and they worriedly watched me. When they offered me drinks of water or bites of pizza, their eyes clearly said they were concerned about my mental state. They were scared that I truly believed they'd be better off without me.

And I did.

So I would disappear.

4

OUT OF THE FRYING PAN

I HAD NOTHING.

No identification, purse, toothbrush, jacket—nothing. Just flip-flops and shorts. I didn't have a plan either. I just knew I had to escape and run without second thought, because if I did...

I slowly sat up and moved to the end of the bed. Moonlight shimmering through the flimsy curtains cast shadows of grey and gold through the room. Luke was on the floor, flat on his back with a hand under his head. I could barely pry my eyes away from his chest rising and falling softly, his face in the relaxed serenity of sleep. He looked so peaceful. I wanted a life for him without worry, with days and nights of happiness. Oliver, too. He was on the other side of the bed, on the floor, in the exact position. Neither was prone to snoring, so I could only assume they were sound asleep. Neither would know I was gone for at least a few hours.

Luke's shirt was draped over a chair. It would be huge on me, but better that nothing. I carefully picked it up before noticing Oliver's wallet on the dresser. Flipping it open, I took out whatever cash he had and stuffed it into my back pocket.

He sat up. "Kaya?"

His voice created a huge lump in my throat. "I'm cold. Gonna have a bath. Go back to sleep."

Easing back down onto his makeshift bed, he mumbled for me to make it quick. I thanked my lucky stars there was no further questioning, but knowing he was half awake made my escape options minimal. I'd thought about simply going out the front door, but I guess my only choice now was the window in the bathroom.

Good Lord, I was doing this. I was really leaving. Through tears that had come on like a broken faucet, the room became a blur. I couldn't allow myself time to think. I just had to move...

But I took one last look at Luke on the floor. The light played in his mussed-up hair and illuminated the most beautiful parts of him—

which was everything. He was so perfect. He deserved better than this. Better than sleeping on a motel floor with his life in danger. He deserved happiness and peace of mind. He deserved something more than the life he would have with me. The scars on his chest, jagged wounds from that cat, were a reminder of the day I saved his life. By leaving, I was doing that again.

"I'm sorry," I said under my breath. "I love you. This is for the best."

I could have sworn he mumbled, "I love you too, Kaya," before turning over.

I had to go. It was now or never.

I locked myself in the bathroom, heart racing and tears pouring. Luke's shirt, heavy with his scent, came down to my knees. I knotted it at the side, and then gave up trying to figure out how to keep the neckline from falling off my shoulders. After turning on the water, I tossed my flip-flops out the window, squeezed my body through, and dropped to the filthy, weed-infested ground onto my hands and knees. The clothes I had tossed out the window were gone, but the garbage remained. Brushing off the dirt clinging to my legs, I stood. The foot I'd kicked the door with was swollen and ached, and the flip-flops made that awful thwap sound with each painful step. But I kept moving. After rounding the building, I came to the empty street and stopped.

Now what?

A cat tucked under a car meowed. The air was colder than I'd thought. I wanted to turn back... This was crazy! Running away from the person my soul was tethered to made my body lash out. It was hard to breathe. My arms and legs were like jelly. I was so torn over what I was doing I was sure I looked like a puppet on a string being pulled in a million directions.

"This is for his own good," I said to the cat, needing to hear it out loud. "If I don't leave, he'll end up missing or dead. Like Angela, Anne, Dustin, Marie, Rusty, that motel clerk..."

Soon, the sun would come up. Bands of orange and red had begun to streak the horizon. A cow mooed from not too far away. A chicken clucked, and I nodded at a man at the gas station who barely acknowledged me. In moments, I was at the end of the road and left with two choices: east to who knew where, or west the way we came. I picked east. Within minutes, I was out of town. Annoyed with the flip-flops, I took them off and carried them so I could go faster. My eyes were clouded and puffy, and when I wiped at them, tears turned the dirt on my hands to mud. I picked up the pace, ignoring the stinging throb in my foot. Move. Keep moving. Don't look back. This is for his own good.

The road seemed endless. As I walked, the cold asphalt became a wide band of sand that cut through fields lined with barbed-wire fences. There wasn't a person or building in sight, but the road had to lead to somewhere. I walked faster, afraid if I didn't, I might turn back. At a sign that hung limply from a post littered with bullet holes, I was faced with either going straight or turning, so I turned. The sound of insects humming in the fields grew louder as the sun grew brighter. I shivered as beads of nervous sweat rolled down my back and chilled my spine. My feet were assaulted by the gravel, and I wondered if I'd chosen the wrong way. I could be walking for hours toward nothing.

When the road began to curve toward the north, I was relieved to hear a horse neighing, because where there were horses, there were people. Something in the distance was moving, so I walked faster, breaking into a run. There was a clearing ahead with a few vehicles and trailers for animals. The shiny door of a polished white truck was opening, and a man emerged with a paper cup. He took a sip from it before stopping to stare at me. Ignoring common sense about approaching strangers and the dread over what I was about to do, I stopped to catch my breath.

"Mornin', Miss," the man said, tipping the front of his cowboy hat and leaning against his vehicle. Chestnut hair poked out from around his cowboy hat and framed his tanned face and sharp features. He was of medium build, wiry and thin, with a tough-as-nails exterior. He appeared to be in his thirties, but the sun could have aged him before years of living did.

There didn't seem to be anyone else around, so I moved a little closer. A massive black horse that was tied to a post pawed the ground. It tossed its neck around and sent clouds of dust into the air. My voice caught in my throat. I surveyed the distance behind me to see if I'd been followed, but the road was clear.

Nervously, I moved toward the man and the horse.

"What brings you out here—?" he started to ask, but then stopped when he got a better look me. I was sure I was quite a sight.

"I'm trying to... get away from..." I was shaking so hard I could barely speak. What the hell was I doing?

The man's expression changed from curiosity to concern. Regarding me intently, his eyes traveled from my swollen foot to my tear-streaked face. He tensed and seemed to carefully choose his words. "I'm headed home," he said, then nodded in the direction of the black horse. "Zander over there lost a horseshoe, so I'm pulling him from the rodeo. Figured I'd leave early and beat the traffic."

I couldn't imagine what traffic there would be around here. "I really need a ride to town." I looked behind me again, half dreading and half hoping Luke would be there. But the road was empty.

The cowboy pushed away from his truck and took a few steps closer. Instinct made me back away; he was taller than I'd thought, and his eyes were narrowed on me with an intensity that made the hair on the back of my neck stand up. He glanced suspiciously at the road behind me, then at the men's T-shirt that had fallen off my shoulder again. His expression darkened when I yanked it up and displayed my upper arm, scarred from burns and still badly bruised.

"Which town?" he asked.

"Huh?" I hadn't thought of that. "Oh, the next one."

"Okay… are you runnin' from someone, Miss?" he asked, scanning the dimly lit fields.

I couldn't answer. All the air left my lungs at the thought of Luke waking to find me gone. He would be hurt and horrified, and Oliver would be in a rage, putting on his shoes and bolting out the door…

"My name's Ben," the cowboy said, on edge now, apparently realizing he might have to defend my honor.

I could only stare. The realization of what I was doing almost brought me to my knees.

"You're safe with me, Miss," Ben said, opening the passenger door to the truck he'd been leaning on. He gestured me in. "No harm will come to you. On my honor. I'll give you a ride to town."

Although something about him was unnerving and rough around the edges, I made the decision to trust him. Besides, wasn't there some sort of cowboy moral code? This was probably the safest stranger to hitch a ride with.

"Please, get in," he said with a hint of urgency.

I inched toward the vehicle, the horse tossing its head up and down while the cowboy watched the road. I paused, hand on the seat, casting another glance behind me, half hoping Luke would come out of nowhere and stop me from what I was about to do…because what kind of idiot got into a vehicle with a stranger? Abandons the love of her life?

An idiot who wanted to save those she loved.

"C'mon now, darling. It's all right," the cowboy said.

I thought I detected alcohol on his breath, but ignored it. "Thank you," I croaked, and got in.

In a matter of minutes, Zander was loaded into the trailer. The truck headed away from the parking lot and moved in the opposite direction of the small town of Rosedale. I tried to stay composed, repeating to myself this was the right thing to do, but it felt like I'd ripped my own heart from my chest. The tears flowed in rivers now, threatening to drown me. And I wished they would.

Ben quietly drove, offering me tissues and bottles of water without asking any questions. Every stop sign, every turned corner, and every single mile that passed under the wheels of the truck took me farther away from Luke.

I felt like I was dying.

"CAN I GET YOU ANYTHING?" BEN ASKED.

I lifted my head off my knees long enough to see we had pulled up to a gas station. On the door was a sign that said, 'Live Bait, Fireworks, and Candy'. None of that appealed to me.

"No, thanks."

I dropped my head back down to hide my pathetic face from him and the sun that was now full in the sky.

"All right," Ben said.

I had a feeling there was something he wanted to ask me. Instead, he put on his hat and headed into the store. I watched him through puffy, dry eyes. There wasn't one tear left in my body, but my head throbbed, and my sinuses were packed full. I needed to get to a sink and splash water onto my face to bring down the swelling. Putting my flip-flops on and limping, I wandered to the side of the gas station, grateful the women's washroom wasn't locked. I'd heard about public washrooms being gross, but this was worse than I'd imagined. The floor was wet with what I hoped wasn't pee, the walls were covered in graffiti, and the lone sink barely clinging to the wall was caked with filth. I tried the tap, grateful at least for the water to cool my cheeks and pat against the back my neck. The sink threatened to spill over though, so I turned the water off and straightened up, unfortunately getting a good look at myself in the smudgy mirror. My eyes were a mess, nose red, and there was a look of sadness so heavy on my face it didn't budge even when I tried a fake smile. Luke's shirt hung off my shoulders and when I tugged it up, I got a whiff of him on it. I had to steady myself against the sink.

It was imperative I pull myself together and not think about Luke. Not here.

I assessed exactly what I had. Which, after counting the cash I'd stolen from Oliver's wallet, was only eighty bucks. What was I going to do? I could buy some food, but I didn't think I had enough to get a room for the night. I would have to take a bus somewhere…but where?

Where would I go? I had no one.

When I left the washroom, Ben was gone. The gas pump he'd parked the truck next to was vacant and the parking lot was empty. Now, besides feeling dead inside, I was scared to death. I didn't even know how to contact Luke or Oliver if I needed them. The full-on reality I was alone with nothing but eighty bucks and an empty stomach became all too real. I stood, staring across the street to where there was another gas station, a bunch of semi-trucks, and past that, nothing else. Rolling hills and miles upon miles of pasture surrounded this remote pit stop. When a car pulled in front of me with a license plate that said 'Wisconsin,' I realized I had absolutely no idea if I was even in Alberta. When the woman driving the car got out and protectively clutched her child's hand after eyeing me suspiciously, I felt even more wretched.

After I wandered away from the gas station, I headed toward the highway, leaving the paved area and not caring about the weeds and thorns attacking my ravaged feet. I didn't know what to do. Maybe I would just go and lay down in the middle of the highway. Get it over with. Let the wheels of one of those rolling beasts end this horrid feeling of despair. What did it matter if I lived? The only thing I wanted, the only person who mattered to me, I couldn't have. I had nothing. Nothing and no one.

A hand grabbed my shoulder. I froze. My heart jumped into my chest.

"Hey, you, I'm just parked around the corner over there. Had to check on the horse. Did ya think I left ya?"

Ben.

I gathered my breath. When I turned to face him, his eyes widened. Maybe he recognized my brief desire to end it all. He regarded me thoughtfully, taking a moment to find what he wanted to say.

"Don't let 'em win," he said after a very long moment.

Those words stopped me from fully submerging into the depths of the lowest point in my life. No. I wouldn't let them win. I wouldn't do Rayna and John Marchessa a favor by doing their dirty work for them.

"C'mon back to the truck with me," Ben said, trying to be lighthearted. "I got you a Gatorade. It's good for replenishing salts after… crying. And the store had fresh-baked muffins. Figured you might like blueberry."

His kindness pulled me back to earth. Grounded me. Ben had wandered across the weeds and thorns. He hadn't left me. Although I didn't know him, I at least felt I wasn't alone. For some reason, that meant everything.

The cowboy had saved my life. And I was sure tired of needing saving.

I felt my eyes well up again.

"It's okay if you don't like blueberry. I got chocolate and raspberry, too." He put out his hand, reaching carefully for me as if I were an easily spooked horse. "There's nothing around here but these two gas stations, Miss," he said. "At least let me get you to the next town so you can call somebody. Okay?"

Call somebody...

Ben's fingers wrapped around mine. He gently led the way back to the truck, me in such a daze I barely even registered the fact my legs were moving. I was safely belted in to the passenger seat. Gatorade, three kinds of muffins, and a T-shirt that said 'Rolling Meadows Farms' was placed on my lap. I tried to thank him, but my voice was so heavy with emotion it was nothing more than a whisper. With a nod and a tip of his hat, he fired up the truck and headed back onto the highway. I closed my eyes as soft air and country music filled the cab. When Hank Williams came on the radio pouring his heart into "I'm So Lonesome I Could Cry," Ben quickly turned off the song and gave me a friendly pat on the head.

LUKE

5

HEARTBREAK OVERLOAD

Luke,

I'm leaving, and I don't want you to try to find me. It's over between us. You betrayed me, and you are not the man I thought you were. I don't love you, and I am moving on. You should do the same.

P.S. I have not forgotten my promise; I will make Henry pay for what he did to your family.

I FOLDED THE NOTE AND SHOVED IT BACK INTO MY POCKET. I'D READ IT a hundred times, yet I had to confirm I was living my worst nightmare.

My heart was in my feet.

"Apparently the guy with the trailer is named Ben," Oliver said, jogging back to me over what he claimed were Kaya's tracks on the dusty road. "He was supposed to compete last night in the rodeo, but was disqualified for some reason. The woman I talked to doesn't have a last name, but thinks the horse's name is Kander, Zander, or something like that."

"Well, that's great. He should be easy to find. There can't be that many dudes named Ben with horses around here," I said sarcastically.

Oliver had used his bloodhound skills to track Kaya from the motel to this small holding lot where a few couples were getting ready to head back to the rodeo. My nightmare had gotten much worse if Kaya was in a truck with a stranger, going to who-the-hell-knew where. I felt sick.

"At least we've got something to go on," Oliver said. He was completely removed from all emotion, purely focused on the task at hand—finding his ex-fiancée. Sweating profusely even though the air was still cool, he tugged at the collar of his shirt. "Let's head to that rodeo in Larkspur. If Ben was competing there, someone will know him. Now we've got a bit of a lead, we gotta get on it fast."

"Yeah," I said sullenly, glued to a weathered fence post. Everything around me—the massive expanse of land between the towns, the endless stretch between cities, the countless gravel roads that led to more gravel roads—made finding Kaya seem impossible.

"Let's go, Luke," Oliver said. He sounded impatient, a foot from me but not meeting my eyes.

"You read the note, Oliver. She doesn't want to be found."

"Oh, get your head out of your ass," Oliver said, tone gruff. "Regardless of what that note says, we have to find her. If we don't, someone else will and she'll end up dead. Is that what you want?"

"No, of course not."

"Me neither. So man up. Unfortunately, we're stuck together, and if I have to look at your defeated, woe-is-me face for one more second, I'm gonna smack it right off your shoulders."

We knew that would never happen, but I'd give him an A for effort. He was right about one thing, though. I had to get myself together. Regardless of the note, I needed to find her. Then, when she said she didn't want me to my face, I'd leave for good. I'd walk away.

Yeah, right.

How the hell would I do that? How could I possibly tear myself away from her? She was everything. My entire world, my life. From the moment I first saw her, I'd known, and every second with her after only confirmed it tenfold. At one point, Oliver had felt the same. Or still felt the same. I couldn't imagine how he was still functioning after she'd displayed such hatred toward him. How had he walked away from her back at that ranch house?

Oh, right. He hadn't. He followed her—us—and dedicated his every waking moment to her safety.

I was screwed.

Straightening up, I took off down the road after him.

"And you can keep the shirt," he said, glancing back at me. "I probably wouldn't get the smell of lowlife kidnapper out of it anyway."

"Lowlife?" That stopped me dead in my tracks.

Oliver halted, turning to stare me down. He wanted to fight, and what a perfect place to do it—out in the middle of nowhere. We could muster up every bit of jealousy and rage we had toward each other and set it free... But it wouldn't do either of us any good.

I took in a few deep breaths and counted to ten, not wanting to hurt the only person who could help me find Kaya. Oliver's chest heaved, just waiting for an invitation to hit the go button. His dark eyes shone beneath a small cut on his forehead from where I'd hit him last night. His hands curled expectantly into fists, and the skin of his arms stretched tight over his ridiculously oversized biceps. Everything about him—from his posture and clenched jaw to the look of hatred on his face—was a cover up. He was a crumbling emotional mess just as much as I was. In fact, probably even more so.

"Listen, I'm sorry, Oliver," I said. "I wouldn't wish the heartache of losing someone you love on anyone. Even you. It really sucks."

Oliver started. He'd been expecting a different reaction. "Ah. You're getting a taste of your own medicine there, aren't ya? Except, your girl wasn't taken from you. She left of her own free will."

Keeping my composure, I looked him square in the eye, hoping he'd feel the honesty in my apology. "I know. And again, I am so very sorry for that."

The base of Oliver's throat moved with a heavy gulp and his jaw relaxed slightly. We stared each other down while bees buzzed around us, the wheat swayed in the breeze, and a mutual understanding momentarily suspended our hatred.

My apology was accepted with a slight nod. "Just get moving, golden boy," Oliver said gruffly. "We aren't going to find her standing here."

THE TOWN OF LARKSPUR WAS A MAZE OF BARNS, PENS, AND CORRALS stuffed full of people and animals. A large outdoor arena contained the most action as the crowd cheered for the dudes chasing down steers on horseback with ropes and incredible determination. I'd never seen so many cowboy boots in one place, and finally understood the appeal of them when my flat-soled boots became caked with muck.

Oliver and I scoured every corner, wandering past the action into a field where masses of trailers and trucks were parked. We searched the washrooms, the stands, the empty bleachers, the backs of vehicles—every corner of the place. Then we started asking questions. We quickly got nowhere. The sun was sinking low in the sky. Tired and sick of each other, we sat defeated on a bench in the arena while the announcer's voice boomed through the speakers. Oliver was scarfing down food while I bit my lip to keep from screaming Kaya's name at the top of my lungs.

"How can you eat right now?" I asked. Oliver was downing his third cheese-covered hot dog.

He wiped mustard from his mouth with the back of his hand. "Maybe you should try it. Eating, that is. When's the last time you put food in ya?"

Did I detect a hint of concern? I shrugged my shoulders. It had been a day or so, but I wasn't hungry. Nothing was appealing when my stomach was tied up in knots. "Maybe those prints we found weren't hers," I said miserably. "Maybe she caught a bus, hitchhiked out of town, or—"

"No," Oliver said firmly. "She left with that guy. With Ben."

"That could have been any girl. The couple saw a young brunette climbing into a white truck with a cowboy they thought might possibly be named Ben, with a horse that might have been named Lander..."

"Zander," Oliver corrected.

"Whatever. The girl they saw could have been anybody. I think we should go back, question everyone we can find, and see if we missed something."

"No."

"Good Lord, Oliver. You could be wrong. She could be—"

"Damn it, kid," Oliver growled, turning to face me, "I know her! You think because you spent a few weeks with her that you do? She would've started running without thinking things through. She knows how to survive in the wild, so instinct would have her head away from civilization. And then, when she realized she was all alone, she would have freaked out and searched for someone who could look after her. Now, you wanna go back to that town and waste your time digging for clues, then you go right ahead. I'm saying she left with the cowboy, and we are going to find him, starting right here."

I stared at my feet, fuming and trying to keep it together. Oliver tossed away the remainder of the hot dog, then reached into his pocket for a tube of pills. He popped some in his mouth and munched them violently while the loudspeaker announced an extensive list of competitors for the next event.

I was going to lose my mind.

"I can't sit here a second longer," I said. Oliver's implication I didn't know Kaya wasn't sitting right along with the echo of her words from the note. "I'm going back to that motel to search the room and—"

Oliver jumped to his feet and grabbed my shoulder, stopping me dead in my tracks. "What did the announcer say?" he asked, eyes widening and sweat breaking out on his forehead.

I shrugged him off.

"Alexander the Great, was that the horse's name... Is that what I heard?"

Before I could answer, he was off like a rocket, barging his way through the stands and seeking out someone with a clipboard. A poor beige-haired woman in head-to-toe denim was completely taken aback when Oliver practically lunged at her.

"The horse, Alexander the Great. Who's riding it?" he demanded.

The lady whose name tag said 'Lola' tried not to appear shocked by Oliver's looming presence and wild-eyed stare. He was a tornado bearing down on a daisy.

"You mean Zander? The rider is Ben Smith," Lola said, eyebrows drawing together as she inspected her clipboard. "They shouldn't have announced it over the loudspeaker, though. Ben pulled him from the event. Sorry about that."

My jaw dropped in astonishment. Oliver's clear head had picked up on the clue while mine was busy wallowing in doubt and misery.

"Ben Smith… where is he? Where can I find him?" Oliver asked far too forcefully.

Lola backed away, getting the attention of a few cowboys who were eyeing us. "Don't know," she said nervously.

She knew; she just didn't want to share. I put on my best smile and stepped in.

"Hey, Lola, is it? Nice to meet you." I offered my hand, widening my eyes a bit. "Sorry about my buddy here. He's a bit…" I leaned in to share the sensitive information. "He's a bit slow, if you know what I mean."

"Oh," Lola said, face softening with pity and understanding.

"Anyway, my buddy here likes horses. He also likes to keep track of things and gets a little worked up if there's a change. Know what I mean? He was rather upset when the barrel event with that poor horse that…uh…"

"Miss Lucky?" Lola said, eyes brightening as they met mine.

"Yeah. What happened with that was—" I was clutching at straws.

Lola suddenly became quite agreeable. "Awful. I know. Terrible thing to watch. It's a shame." She leaned in and whispered so Oliver wouldn't hear, "I hear they may have to put her down."

"Really? Oh, that is a shame," I said with a shake of my head.

A flirty grin crossed Lola's face. When I looked longingly into her eyes and returned it, her cheeks reddened. "Anyway, can you tell me if Alexander—Zander—is out of the rodeo completely? Or just for today? Forgive me, I'm a city boy and new to how this stuff works."

Lola's eyelashes fluttered. She gave me the once-over, which lingered a bit too long on my chest, then she gave Oliver a sideways glance of sympathy. "Ben packed him up to take him home. I'm sure he's not injured, though," she said with a motherly tone. "So don't worry about that."

"Ah, good to know. Thanks." I turned to Oliver. "Did you hear that, Samson?" I said loudly, giving him a pat on the shoulder. "Everything is just fine. You can write his name on your program and show your mom later."

Oliver forced the smile of a yawning gator. If he could have killed me right then, he would have.

I turned away as if satisfied with the information. Oliver followed my lead. I stopped, as if desperate for a little more small talk with Lola. "Oh, hey," I said, swinging back around to face her. She hadn't moved an inch, and her cheeks were even more flushed. "Where could I find Ben Smith? I'm thinking of buying a few horses. It would be nice to start off with some award-winning pedigree."

Lola smiled from ear to ear. "Oh, yes. Zander would be a good stud for sure."

"Certainly." I suppressed a snicker. "Can you share Ben's address or phone number?"

"Oh gosh, no. You know how it is, the Privacy Act and all. Besides, names are the only requirement to compete here."

"Oh, that's too bad."

"Yeah. I know he owns a ranch, not sure where though. Them small-town Saskatchewan boys keep pretty quiet."

I felt a slight surge of hope. "Thanks, beautiful." I smiled, giving her a wink.

"Anytime," Lola cooed, and handed me a slip of paper with her phone number.

Once out of the arena, Oliver and I practically ran to the truck. "Ben Smith from Saskatchewan. That will be like finding a needle in a haystack," I said under my breath, weaving through cowboy hats and plaid shirts while making sure to watch my step.

Oliver stayed close. "Samson? Really? And... slow?"

"I had to come up with something. You were attracting too much attention. You're a bull in a china shop with that aggression of yours. Ever consider anger-management sessions?"

By the way Oliver fake coughed, he knew I was right. "Well, good thinking, I guess."

"Was that a compliment?"

"Don't let it go to your head."

Oliver got in the truck, tossing me the keys since it was my turn to drive. He grew quiet, but I could tell there was something he wanted to say. Once we hit the highway, it came out.

"Are girls always like that around you?"

"Huh?"

"Do you always just bat your eyes like that and get what you want?"

I laughed, but then realized he was serious. Maybe he wondered if that was how I'd lured Kaya into my evil web, so I changed the subject. "Where to first?"

"Well, we need to find a computer."

"Okay...then?"

"Then we have to find every Ben Smith and pray one of them leads us to Kaya. I wonder if the rodeo keeps record of the horse of the year. What was the category he was in—tie-down roper? Whatever that is, maybe it will give us some leads. What I know for sure is Kaya is a runner. One wrong move on his part and she'll bolt. We gotta be fast about this, Luke. Got it? Or we really might lose her."

I nodded. The word 'we' wasn't lost on me. Neither was the fact he truly did know her better than I did.

KAYA

6

If I Could Drown

"Where are we?" I asked, waking folded up against the truck window with a dry mouth and stiff neck.

I must have been asleep for a while because the sun was low in the sky and Ben had turned on the heat. The landscape rolling by was identical to the scene I'd dozed off to. Flat. Vast. Miles of farmer's fields. I wondered if we'd actually gone anywhere.

"We're about an hour outside of Regina."

"Saskatchewan?" I said incredulously, doing the math in my head of how far I might be from Luke.

"Yeah. From there, it's about an hour and a half to my ranch. Got a place just outside of Radville. Nice, quiet town with good people."

His ranch? I almost dove out of the truck. "I can't go to your home," I said way too quickly.

"Oh. Right. No, of course not," Ben said. He took off his hat. After placing it on the seat between us, he ran his hands through his thick, chestnut hair, making it stand on end. He drove silently for a minute while I chugged the remains of a water bottle, wishing there was more.

"So, you wanna talk about it?" he asked carefully.

I feigned confusion as I stared at the empty ditches flanking the lonely highway. "It?"

"Yeah." He waited. Minutes crawled by. With a sidelong glance, I noticed his straight nose and strong jaw gave him a very pleasing profile. There wasn't an ounce of fat on him, but he wasn't skinny. He had the physique of a man who'd worked hard every day of his life.

"Tell me please, why, and who it is you're running from."

I shook my head with a gulp. "I can't."

"Must have been pretty bad for you to leave with no purse, proper shoes, or wallet while dressed in a man's shirt. Kinda seems like you had to escape with no time to grab anything."

I didn't answer.

Ben sighed. "At least tell me your name."

I wanted to confide in him, pour my heart out, and explain every-thing… but what he didn't know couldn't hurt him. "I can't tell you that either. But thank you for the ride," I said, feeling my throat constrict. "And the shirt and food. When we get to the next town, I'll call my—" I paused, my mind too rattled to lie quickly. "My sister. She will come and get me."

"All right." Ben clearly didn't believe me. "Listen, I don't mean to pry. It's just not often a guy gets to save a damsel in distress. The real story behind it might be better than the one I make up in my head."

"You have no idea," I mumbled.

Ben took his eyes off the road for too long, studying me. "I'm just a bit concerned for your safety. Maybe I can help you."

Helping me was a damn death wish. "Listen, I really appreciate your help, Ben. Who knows what would have happened if you wouldn't have been there for me. It's just that I have to get to somewhere."

He cleared his throat and turned up the heat. "Somewhere, eh? Fine. Well, I'm gonna stop at the next town for dinner. There's a bus depot and a motel there if ya need it."

"Sounds great," I lied, suddenly feeling anxious.

"Yep," he muttered.

Ben was a man of few words, and that suited me just fine. We didn't speak to each other for a long while, even when a couple of empty vod-ka bottles rolled out from under my seat—who was I to judge?—and we remained silent until he pulled up to a busy diner on the edge of a small town. Semi-trucks and trailers were angle parked out front, and the place churned with action. We exchanged a polite handshake and a tense goodbye, and then, clutching the new T-shirt to my chest like a lifeline, I walked in a daze toward downtown.

Five blocks of quaint buildings lined a spotlessly clean street. As I kept putting one foot in front of the other, the streetlamps came on. I found myself at the bus stop, but the doors were locked and it was closed until tomorrow. I walked back up the other side of the street, foot absolutely throbbing and that horrible feeling of panic creeping in. What was I going to do? I was alone with little money, no one to call, no place to call home… and now that unwanted, familiar feeling of the sky shaking had started up. No. I couldn't let my anxiety take over. Not now. Not alone out in the middle of—yet again, I had no idea where I was.

I ducked into a door with an open sign, getting some questionable glances from patrons in 'Charlotte's Internet Café'. As if waking from a bad dream, I headed for a booth in the corner next to a window despite the hushed whispers among a couple of blue-haired ladies. I heard the word 'tramp,' and quite possibly the word 'slut'. With a gulp, I sat and kept my eyes on the napkins. The whole place was polished to a high shine with thick wooden tables and mirrored walls, and it was almost impossible to avoid my reflection—which was indeed unsettling.

My heart was racing, but when I was handed a menu and given a friendly smile from a waiter with the worst bleached hair I'd ever seen, it slowed a bit. I forced a return smile at the young man whose name tag said 'Whitey'. His pasty white skin, white golf shirt, and bleached jeans suited him perfectly. My impending anxiety made my hand shake when I pointed to something on the menu called the Google Special. I knew I had to order something or I'd be asked to leave… and I didn't care what it was.

Within minutes, a cold glass of amber ale was set before me. Without thought, I practically downed it. Feeling eyes upon me, I looked up from the empty glass to see pity on the faces of the women. I couldn't imagine what story they were dreaming up as they snuck glances at me, filthy and covered in bruises. Runaway? Prostitute?

Whitey returned. "Another beer?" he asked, noting my empty glass.

"No," I squeaked out as my stomach twisted into knots around the brew.

"Well, ya got twenty minutes, then I gotta charge ya five bucks for every ten minutes after that, all right?" Whitey noticed my confusion and gestured at a computer he'd set down before me. "I'll be back with yer pie in a moment."

He left, and I stared numbly at a laptop he'd placed on the table. Apparently, the Google Special was beer, use of the internet, and the pie of the day—all for ten bucks. Good deal.

Please make sure your hands are clean and watch the time! Happy Googling, said a little sign taped to the lid. I opened it, and the screen sprang to life. For some strange reason, the familiar blue color was comforting. As the dark clouds rolled in outside, I felt the beer and the familiarity of the computer calm me inside. If I didn't look anywhere else, I could pretend Stephan was in the room with me and everything was normal.

When I took in a deep breath, the anxiety started to ebb. I decided to figure out where I was going. Wanting to search the bus schedules, I realized I still didn't know where I was. Whitey returned with a glass of water.

"What town is this?" I asked.

He eyed me curiously, setting down the glass along with two pieces of pie. "You look like you could use a little extra," he said, and triangles of pumpkin and what appeared to be apple pie were placed next to the computer. "I'm buying the extra one for you." He grinned, but it was kind of unsettling. "This is the town of Muldare. Oh, and I'm Whitey. I mean, my name is Whitey."

The town of Muldare… "Thanks, Whitey. That's very kind," I said, now getting a strange vibe from the overly attentive waiter.

Whitey broke out in the kind of wide toothy smile that had me tugging up the shirt over my shoulders. "We don't get many strangers coming in here, and I noticed you looking at the bus schedule. None comin' or leavin' until tomorrow afternoon just so you know. So, I assume you'll be staying at the motel? My buddy works at the front desk." Whitey lowered his voice, so he wouldn't be over heard. "He throws great parties," he added with a wink.

There was only one motel?

I wasn't sure if I should answer him. The eavesdropping ladies at the next table grew silent, trying to hear if I would. "Relatives," I blurted out. "I have an aunt and uncle here. I'm just waiting for them to meet me. Not staying." Damn, I was a bad liar.

"Right," Whitey said with another wink, and he strolled off to the back of the café.

With the waiter's eyes on me and whispers among the regulars continuing, I made a bee-line for the washroom and put on the shirt Ben had bought me. It was too tight and short, but at least it wasn't falling off my shoulders and didn't smell like… him. Gathering my composure and my hair into a ponytail with an elastic I'd found on the counter, I checked the clock and headed back to my table. With fifteen minutes left on the computer, I had to plan.

Searching the bus schedule for Muldare, I discovered there was only one bus leaving for Regina tomorrow in the afternoon. I googled motels in Muldare and found only one as well, and it was fifty bucks more than what I had in my pocket. Great. What on earth was I going to do? I could seek out some patch of grass somewhere and curl up for the night, but by the glances I was getting from Whitey, I didn't feel too safe about that. I had no one to ask for help, no one to talk to, and I yearned for Stephan terribly. Stephan. Maybe I could message him for help and he could send me some money.

And… maybe now was the right time to read his email.

With ten minutes left on the clock and no other options, I opened my secret Hotmail account that I'd used years ago under the fake name Chloe Alexandra. I pictured Stephan's face, beaming and eyes twinkling as he read my 'love notes to Prince Charming' in our email game. What

I wouldn't do to put my cheek against his beard and wrap my arms around him.

It didn't take long to find the newest message from 'Stevie Muffins'. The arrow from the mouse hovered over the subject line, and I had to steady myself before I clicked. What I'd been putting off reading sprang to life. My eyes welled up instantly at the comforting familiarity of Stephan's first few words.

MY DEAREST KAYA,

I LOVE YOU AND MISS YOU TERRIBLY. I HAVE TO TELL YOU A FEW THINGS AND I DON'T HAVE MUCH TIME, SO PLEASE FORGIVE THE SHORT EXPLANATIONS IN THIS EMAIL. I HAVE UNCOVERED A FEW THINGS YOU NEED TO KNOW, AND THERE'S NO EASY WAY TO SAY THEM.

YOUR FATHER KILLED LENORE. SHE DID NOT FALL, AND SHE DID NOT COMMIT SUICIDE LIKE HE HAD EVERYONE BE-LIEVE—SHE DIED BY HIS HANDS. HE THOUGHT THAT GET-TING RID OF HER WOULD GIVE HIM OWNERSHIP OF ERONEL AND THE ESTATE, BUT LENORE WILLED IT ALL TO YOU IN THE EVENT OF HER DEATH. HENRY'S ONLY BEEN WATCHING OVER IT UNTIL YOU COME OF AGE TO TAKEOVER, WHICH IS WHEN YOU TURN TWENTY-ONE. THIS IS THE REAL REASON WHY YOU ARE IN THE MIDDLE OF A WAR BETWEEN YOUR FATHER AND JOHN MARCHESSA. YOU ARE WORTH A FORTUNE.

Henry killed the woman who'd pretended to be my mother? I wasn't surprised. Something in my childhood memory confirmed this made sense. And as for the inheritance... that I already knew. I felt bad I hadn't told Stephan about the day Henry came to my room and made me sign all those papers—the day I'd vowed to never call Henry Lowen 'Father' ever again.

I took a sip of water and kept reading.

HENRY HAS BEEN CONCOCTING A PLAN FOR YEARS NOW TO GET CONTROL OF YOUR INHERITANCE, AND PART OF THAT PLAN INVOLVED OLIVER. AS IT TURNS OUT, MANY YEARS AGO, HENRY BECAME OLIVER'S LEGAL GUARDIAN. I AM POSITIVE OLIVER ISN'T AWARE OF THIS. SINCE OLIVER HAS NO OTHER FAMILY, THAT MEANS HENRY IS OLIVER'S ONLY NEXT OF KIN. SINCE AN HEIR IS WHAT HENRY NEEDS TO KEEP ERONEL AND ESTATE FOR HIMSELF, HE'S BEEN HOPING OLIVER WOULD GET

YOU PREGNANT. THIS WAY, BY GETTING RID OF YOU, THEN
YOUR CHILD, AND THEN OLIVER, ALL LEGAL BINDINGS TO
JOHN MARCHESSA WOULD BE BROKEN AND THE ESTATE, ERO-
NEL, AND THAT MASSIVE TRUST FUND OF YOURS WOULD ALL
BELONG TO HIM. THIS IS WHY YOU MUST HIDE AND NEV-
ER COME BACK HERE. YOU MUST NOT LET HENRY FIND YOU.
THREE YEARS MIGHT SEEM LIKE A LONG TIME, BUT IT WILL
FLY BY, AND THEN YOU CAN TAKE CONTROL AND SHUT HIM
DOWN.

ALSO, I'VE DISCOVERED OLD CARL WAS WORKING FOR A
WOMAN NAMED RAYNA CLAIRE GLESS, WHO IS THE MASTER-
MIND BEHIND THE RIGHT CHOICE GROUP AND THE ONE RE-
SPONSIBLE FOR ORGANIZING YOUR KIDNAPPING. STAY FAR
AWAY FROM THIS WOMAN. SHE ONLY WANTS TO GET REVENGE
ON HENRY BY USING YOU. UNFORTUNATELY, THIS WOMAN IS
YOUR BIRTH MOTHER. HENRY TOOK YOU FROM HER WHEN YOU
WERE JUST WEEKS OLD. I GUESS IN MY HEART I KNEW THIS.
I'M SORRY I DIDN'T LISTEN AND OVERLOOKED THE TRUTH FOR
SO LONG. SO VERY SORRY.

I WISH I COULD TELL YOU ALL THIS IN PERSON. JUST STAY
ALIVE AND COME BACK TO ME WHEN IT'S SAFE. DON'T TRY TO
CONTACT ME OR REPLY TO THIS EMAIL. DON'T TRUST ANYONE.

I LOVE YOU WITH ALL MY HEART, FOREVER AND ALWAYS
—STEPHAN.

Stomach churning and head spinning, I thought I could never have
felt more hate for my father than I did just moments ago, but now it had
escalated into dizzying heights. I fought to breathe as Whitey watched
me from the bar. Tears of anger hit the keyboard. I quickly rubbed them
off my cheeks before slamming the lid shut, startling the ladies at the
next table. I probably looked completely insane when I pulled money
out of my pocket and tossed it on the pie plate in a sudden rage. I wanted to scream, cry, yell at the top of my lungs, then smash the computer
to bits and push over the table. I barely held it together as I headed for
the door.

"Leaving so soon?" Whitey asked, getting between me and the exit
in the blink of an eye.

I bared my teeth at him. The sound that came from my throat was
a dog-like growl. He moved aside.

"Ooh, feisty. I like that. See ya at the motel a little later," he said
under his breath.

I flew out the door into the cool night, took four steps, then stopped—the latest enlightening news about my father had sent me over the edge. Tears burst from my eyes. The last shred of hope I'd been hanging onto that Henry wasn't all bad had been completely obliterated; he was an actual monster.

I dropped to the curb and put my head in my hands. The rain started falling, lightly dusting my shoulders at first, then becoming a downpour just to add to my misery. I became soaked head to toe, but I didn't care. I stayed where I was, wishing the rain would melt me into a puddle that would drain into the gutter and then just disappear into the earth…

"You left something in my truck," said a voice from out of nowhere.

At the edge of my vision was Ben, rain coming down even harder now and pouring off his cowboy hat in rivers. He was holding out a paper bag, which was now soaked. It was the muffin I hadn't eaten.

"I didn't want it to go to waste," he added, eyeing me with concern, then glancing at the café window where I could feel many sets of eyes on my back.

I dropped my gaze back to the gutter. My body didn't want to move, and I still held out hope that the rain might just wash me away. Ben said something, and then he hauled me up and turned me to face him. He lifted my chin, and I had no choice but to meet his eyes. The rain plastered my hair to my face, mixing with the tears that were spilling out of me with blinding force.

He gave me a weak smile. "I tried to leave. Got in my truck and was ten minutes out of town, but then I realized…" He paused, fumbling for the right words. "I could really use some help at my ranch. Now, the job doesn't pay much, but you'll have your own room and all the food you can eat. You'll be dry."

He waited patiently for an answer, but I was so grateful that all my words caught in my throat. He tossed the paper bag with the muffin into the garbage. After a quick glance at the internet café and the white-haired waiter watching from the doorway, his hand firmly latched onto mine. I had the sense I wasn't being given a choice, I was going wherever this cowboy wanted me to.

"I'm taking you home now," he said over the downpour.

Home. Home was in Luke's arms….

The rain was falling in sheets. Since I wasn't about to turn into a puddle and dissolve, I let the cowboy lead the way.

7

Don't Let Me Down

A GRAVEL DRIVEWAY FLANKED BY A WHITE PICKET FENCE LED TO A sprawling ranch house. It was after midnight, and the only lights were the ones shining above a wide porch and the sky full of twinkling stars. I couldn't see what animals Ben had, but the smell mixed with freshly cut hay suggested there were many. He parked halfway to the house, and the fattest cat I'd ever seen came to greet us. It skulked across perfectly mowed grass to circle my legs. I shivered from the bitterly cold night and the tickle of the cat's fur.

"That's Miss Halfhertail," Ben said, coming around to the passenger side of the truck to give the cat a pat on the head. "She guards the house. If she don't like ya, you aren't getting anywhere near it."

"Hello, kitty," I said, reaching down to stroke her, noticing that most of her tail was missing. "Ah… Miss Half Her Tail."

The cat purred, and the comforting sound made me suddenly acutely aware of how weary I was. I straightened up to take in my surroundings. "How much land do you—?" Suddenly, a wave of dizziness hit me like a hammer to the head, and I stumbled backward. Two nights of no sleep, not much food, and hours of crying had caught up with me.

"Whoa there, uh, girl," Ben said, lunging for me with outstretched hands.

"I'm fine." I backed away from him to lean against the truck. I didn't want him to touch me. If I was going to pass out, I'd rather hit the dirt all on my own.

Zander impatiently stomped his feet in the trailer. "Right," Ben said, rubbing his forehead. "Well, you wait here just one moment. I gotta get the horse into his pen and then we'll figure you out."

He spun around and marched off.

I contemplated running. I knew nothing about this man, yet here I was, at his house. Was there a town I could make a run for? Maybe I could steal the truck and…

The cat purring at my feet brought me back to reality; I couldn't drive, and running… seriously? It was all I could do to stand. I wasn't going anywhere.

So I watched Ben expertly tend to the massive horse, talking to him lovingly as he led him out of the trailer. With a light slap to the butt, he sent Zander through a gate and closed it behind him. When the sound of hooves trotting off faded away, he returned to me. I hadn't moved an inch. I didn't know if I could.

"I'll show you to your room, all right?" he said.

My throat went dry. "I could sleep in the barn, or in the back of the truck, or…"

"It's just up there," he said, pointing to the top left corner of the house.

The cat rubbing against my legs didn't calm my pounding heart. Ben was patiently waiting for me to move, but I just felt all the blood drain from my cheeks. I realized there was no way I could defend myself against him if I had to, and once inside, I would be trapped.

"Tell me your name," Ben said, the starlight giving his eyes an unnerving shimmer. I was at his mercy, and he knew it. He moved closer. "I need a name," he demanded.

"It's Kate Adams," I lied.

He shook his head with an amused huff. "No, it's not. But it's better than calling you girl. Anyway, it's late. I'm tired. Let's go."

He grabbed my hand, his grip far tighter and more insistent than it had been at the gas station. I wasn't being given a choice, yet my feet didn't budge willingly. I stumbled away from the truck, resisting as best I could.

Ben released his grip and sighed. Sensing my fear, he took off his hat and put it to his chest. His eyes settled on mine, and I hadn't the strength to look away. "On my honor, Kate Adams, no harm will come to you here. I promise."

A wave of relief washed over me. I could clearly detect the honestly in his voice. I was so tired, so mentally exhausted and overwhelmed, that when he pulled, I followed. With the cat leading the way, we passed an old dog that woke only to give the air a sniff. Soon, we were on the porch of his house. Again, I hesitated. Ben put a key in the door. This time, he didn't bother trying to comfort me when I held back. Instead, he threw open the door. With his hand still firmly around mine, he pulled me into a dimly lit foyer. He didn't even take off his boots before ascending a flight of stairs that felt like climbing a mountain. Finally, at the end of what seemed like the longest hallway in the world, a door was opened, and he let go of my hand. With a nod, he gestured me in.

"It's good and clean. There's a bathroom across the hall. Sleep. And when you wake, come downstairs for toast and coffee."

He flicked on the light. The entire room was done in flowers. Every square inch of it. I blinked a few times to see if I was still awake. The walls were covered in pink wallpaper bursting with red roses, hideous yellow curtains speckled in pink roses flanked the window, rose motif rugs, and even hand-painted rose-embellished dressers and chairs made the room a hideous bouquet.

"Yeah, Evelyn, my old cook, really liked the Victorian theme. She was always one to take things too far, though. Personally, I hate it. Just haven't had the time to give it a good paint job. It's not the Taj Mahal, but—"

"It's perfect," I said, eyeing the inviting bed.

Ben brushed past me into the room, appearing even more masculine than he already was among the visual onslaught of florals. His hat was gone from his head and the wooden heels of his boots clicked on the patches of bare hardwood. Pulling back the covers, he patted the pillow, then turned to look at me frozen in the doorway. I was upright, but dead on my feet. Even with his promise not to hurt me, I was still scared silly. He was about to say something, but instead crossed the room and picked me up like I was a sick calf. I was carried to the bed, the flip-flops falling off my feet, and then plunked down—not all that gently—and covered up. With a weary smile, Ben tugged the sheets under my chin.

"You need to get some sleep there, Kate. I don't need you passing out and smacking yer head or somethin'."

My eyes were closing even though I pleaded with them not to, the pillow under my head a heavenly cloud cushioning my cried-out skull. I wanted nothing more than to just give way to sleep, but my mind was racing.

The light had gone out, but Ben was still in the room, shuffling around. I held my breath, wondering what he was doing. There was the sound of a drawer being opened, and then a clinking of glass. I gasped when his hand found its way under my head.

"Scotch. Evelyn always had a stash," he said, lifting my head off the pillow. "She never bought the cheap stuff, either. I watered it down a bit since you don't seem like much of a drinker. Drink up so you can sleep."

I wanted to protest, but he'd put the glass to my mouth and the scotch was soon making its way down my throat. Five large gulps of liquid fire hit the empty pit in my belly. The smell of it reminded me of Stephan and the way his hands petted my hair soothingly after a good-night kiss on the cheek… the safety of his arms… the comfort of his soft beard on my forehead…

"You'll be all right," Ben said on his way out.

MY DREAMS WERE DISTURBING. VIVID. VISIONS OF LUKE WITH THE MOST horrific look of hurt on his face, yelling questions at me before doing an about-face and happily running off into the sunset with another woman. I was crying, calling his name, begging for forgiveness. So he came back, standing before me, fields of mustard flowers rippling in waves behind him. There was the wide man behind him, changing the direction of his gun from me to him. I was screaming before the wide man even sent a bullet through Luke's chest… screaming while Luke died and bled out in my arms, his blue eyes filling with tears as the light left them. And then there was Oliver. He was saying something I didn't understand. He was fading away, becoming nothing but a blur when he couldn't pull me away from Luke's dead body…

A sharp clanging sound jolted me upright out of the puddle of sweat and tears. Gasping for breath in a flood of sunlight, it took a moment to shake off the dream and then to recall exactly where I was—in a strange bed covered in rose motifs, without Luke. If I'd been questioning my sanity for leaving the love of my life, the dream only confirmed I was doing what was best for him. I'd long ago given up trying to do what was right.

My body ached from my hair to my toes. As I swung my legs over the side of the bed, I thought of my life back at the estate. Breakfast would have been on a tray on my lap, and I wouldn't have had to leave the bed for hours if I didn't want to. At the slightest wince from any sort of ache, Stephan or Oliver would have rubbed my muscles until they loosened up. Now I was on my own. I had no one to lean on, no one to pamper or protect me. It was scary, but somehow thrilling.

The décor of the room wasn't all that hideous in the soft light of the morning, but it was a bit much. A huge wardrobe lined the far end of the wall. Two very tall bookcases stuffed full of romance novels and cooking magazines were next to it. A dressing table held bottles of perfumes and potions, and a television from the seventies sat perched on a tiny table.

I climbed out of bed and tiptoed across the creaky floor to stand before a long mirror—I looked like hell. My hair was wild, and my eyes were puffy. The bruises on my arm were still prominent, and the one on my thigh from being slammed around in the falls remained an angry splotch reaching to my knee. My feet were a mess, too. The one I'd cut in the race and kicked the door in with was swollen, the toes purple. Even my lip was split, fingernails ragged from chewing them. I looked like I'd been beaten up and tossed in a ditch. And I felt about the same.

Turning away from my horrid reflection, I peered out the window; at least the view from the rose room was amazing. A massive expanse of land stretched out as far as the eye could see. Cattle, clusters of trees, green pasture with horses grazing, and small muddy patches circled a barn. There were sheds, shacks, squared-off sections of fenced land, and an overgrown garden.

I opened the wardrobe, hoping to find clothes that would fit. Unfolding a very faded pair of jeans, I discovered Evelyn must be a rather large woman—I could have fit five of me into them. The T-shirts were no better either and way bigger than Luke's. They kept falling off my shoulders and down past my knees. I found a drawer of undergarments—all massive—and stared in awe for a moment at a bra with cups as big as my head. My chest was ample, but not that big. What I wouldn't give for a bra that fit and some sweatpants...

There had to be something here I could wear. I hated digging through this woman's things—where was she, anyway?—but I was desperate to get out of my dirty clothes. A pajama top? Stretchy dress? Everything was size quadruple x and I was an extra small. Beautiful scarves in silk, some sequined, some covered in flowers—of course—and some heavy wool ones for winter caught my eye. I unfolded a cream-colored one made of light organza and speckled with little blue daisies. It was long and wide and could work as a shirt. I took off the kid's T-shirt Ben had bought me and put the scarf around my neck, crisscrossing it across my chest and circling it at my waist. It made a pretty top. But I was still out of luck in the bottoms department, so the jean shorts would have to do for now. I wrestled a hairbrush through my curls and twisted my hair into a long side braid, then patted the necklaces that were still safely against my chest for good luck; I was as ready as I'd ever be to face whatever was outside this room.

The smell of butter and coffee and something with cinnamon hit hard when I opened the door. My stomach growled in hunger. Following my nose down the stairs, past the front door and large foyer with more coats and pairs of boots than I could count, I began to hear voices from around a corner. I hadn't even considered there would be other people besides Ben, and I felt my pulse quicken. They were hushed, talking quietly, and I snuck toward them across a shiny hardwood floor in a hall lined with framed photos. Light poured out from the room ahead, along with mouthwatering aromas. I detected barbecue. That sweet sauce Luke liked on his chicken. How odd for breakfast. I moved quietly, getting closer to the voices, straining my ears and worried that my grumbling stomach might give me away.

"So, you just decided to bring her here?" someone asked.

"Yep. Awful things have happened to this girl. I'd never seen anyone cry like that in my life. And she's been beat up pretty bad. Covered in bruises. I had to do something. I couldn't just leave her." It was Ben answering, his voice low and somewhat defensive.

"Well, sure ya could have left her," a male who sounded quite young said. "You're not even supposed to be around women right now. Evvy said you are—"

"That's enough talk outta you, Hank," Ben hissed. "I don't want to hear one word about what Evvy said."

Another male voice spoke up. This one was deep, drawing out the vowels and oozing with confidence. "I'm surprised, Ben. I didn't think anyone would be able to tug at your rusty heartstrings. I assumed they'd broken off long ago."

Ben cleared his throat. "You would have done the same thing, Thomas. This girl was running for her life. Scared to death."

"As most whores are when running from their pimps," Thomas said coldly.

"She certainly ain't no whore."

"Oh, yeah? How do you know that?"

There was a pause. "When you meet her, you'll just know, too," Ben said.

There was silence for a moment. I stayed flattened against the wall, trying to decide if toast and coffee were worth going in there for, or if I should tiptoe back to the rose room and hide under the blankets forever.

"So what are you going to do with her? What if she's wanted by the cops or something? The last thing you need is more trouble," Thomas said.

Ben spoke quieter, and his tone suggested he was losing his patience. "The last thing I need is a young punk telling me what I need. And, if she is wanted by the cops, they can sort out their own business. I ain't givin' the girl up. I made a promise I'd keep her safe, and I'm going to keep it."

Someone I hadn't heard piped up. "You're doing the right thing. You can't go back on a promise."

"Damn straight, Mick," Ben said. "Anyway, I decided to put the girl to work at the ranch. Give her a chance to get on her own feet. No one touches her though, all right? Not one finger. I swear I'll beat y'all senseless if ya do."

"Whoa," Thomas said. "None of us want anything to do with some beat-up gutter baby you rescued from the dog pound. You can keep your little whore to yourself."

"Watch yer mouth," Ben hissed, and the sound of a hand slamming the table made me jump. I gave my presence away by knocking a photo off the wall. It crashed at my feet. The ancient thing didn't break, but it brought Ben flying around the corner.

He'd shaved—and it took years off his face. I noticed that his eyes were the color of butterscotch with flecks of light green. His mouth fell open slightly as he took in my tidier appearance, and he gave me a once-over from head to toes.

"You look better," he stammered.

"So do you."

"Sleep well?" he asked.

"I think so." I resisted the urge to run back to the floral room when the other men started chatting again.

Ben reached for my hand and enveloped it in his firm, slightly too-tight grip. There was no use resisting. He led me into the kitchen. The people he'd been talking to sat at a large polished wood table covered in food. He stood and waited for them to stop talking.

"This is Kate," Ben said loudly.

All eyes turned to me, and three strange faces morphed from smirks to shock.

"Hi." I smiled weakly.

Ben pointed to a large, baby-faced boy with a stack of food a mile high in front of him. Sandy brown hair and thick eyebrows framed his childlike, wide-set eyes, and full fat lips covered slightly crooked teeth. He had a bit of a pot belly and reminded me of an overgrown toddler. "That is Hank. He's my sister's kid. She caught him drinking beer in the garage and figured she'd send him to me for rehabilitation. Unfortunately, he's more hassle than he's worth. Thankfully, he's leaving in a few days."

Hank nearly sent the table toppling over to extend his hand. "Madame," he said politely.

"Oh, sit down for God's sake," Ben said irritably.

I smiled at Hank as he shrank back.

"Over there is Thomas. Mick is next to him. They're brothers. Been with me over a year now. Strong workers, good people, and they won't cause you any trouble. Right, boys?"

Thomas and Mick, probably in their early twenties, nodded in unison.

"Now, have a seat. Foods getting cold."

Hank pulled out a chair for me, so I sat next to him, forcing a polite smile at the brothers sitting across from me. They were built much like Ben... thin and wiry with ropy muscle and not a hint of physical weakness about them. They both had jet black hair. Mick's was shaved on the sides and the top of it pulled into a ponytail. The style made no sense to me, but it strangely flattered his high cheekbones and lightly bearded face. Thomas was clean shaven with a tidy haircut and smooth tanned skin. He poked at his food while eyeing me with laser focused deep brown eyes. He was striking; face shaped the same as his brother's but his features sharper, eyes darker, making him slightly more attractive. There was something very off-putting about him, though.

"So, who is Evelyn?" I asked.

Next to me, Hank spoke eagerly. "The best pie and carrot cake baker this side of Radville. She's got a free cruise somewhere in the Pacific, floating on a huge boat with a pool and restaurants. Imagine that! She's gonna see icebergs and get me some fudge. It's a long cruise, though... Ben says she could be gone months, years even. Think of it—floatin' on the ocean. Evvy will see sharks and whales. Dolphins, too."

"Years?" I said. By the look Ben gave me over his buttered toast, it was clear Evelyn was never coming back and he was protecting his simple nephew from some sort of heartbreaking news. "That sounds amazing," I said to Hank's beaming face.

Silence fell over the room. Coffee was poured. Mick got up to get a fresh bottle of syrup from a cupboard. The whole time, Thomas blatantly stared at me without blinking. I pretended to not feel uncomfortable under his scrutiny.

"So, what do you do here?" I asked, unable to avoid meeting his piercing gaze.

He put his fork down. "I work."

I gulped back the desire to run from the room. "What kind of work?"

"Before you interrogate me, how about you tell us about you, Kate... as if that's even your real name."

"Thomas," Ben said, coming to my defense.

I put my hand up. "No, it's okay. I know it all seems pretty strange. Just know I'm not running from cops or anything like that."

Thomas put his hands on either side of his plate and leaned in. "Boyfriend then? Husband?" I noticed he didn't say pimp. "No. I mean, well, sort of, but—"

"Are you after money? Because Ben doesn't have any, just so you know."

The meal came to a crashing halt. I fully expected Ben to speak up, but he remained silent, waiting for my answer.

"Money?" I said incredulously. I was worth a damn fortune... The thought hadn't even occurred to me that these people might think that I was the bad guy. I couldn't contain the look of shock that came over my face.

"Huh, I guess not," Thomas said, apparently satisfied with my reaction. "So, what then? Whatcha running from?"

I couldn't lie. I was terrible at it, but I couldn't tell the truth either. So, bits and pieces of information would have to do for now. I cleared my throat. "I had to get away because, well, you see, there are certain people that want me..." I pulled in air, not sure how to say my father wanted to kill me for my inheritance and my mother wanted me dead. "I just have to get away from people that—"

I couldn't finish.

"People, eh? As in, someone that makes money off you?"

I stared in shock. What was this arrogant cowboy accusing me of?

Mick spoke up. "You're being rude, Thomas."

Everyone at the table grew quiet. Hank was the only one smiling, oblivious to what we were talking about and only concerned with filling my plate with pancakes and steak. His elbow hit my arm on purpose. The coffee he'd poured into my cup sloshed about, and the pancake syrup toppled over.

Thomas just kept staring, trying to figure me out. Abruptly, he put down his fork. "Gimme names." His anger quickly transferred away from me to whoever he thought was responsible for my injuries. With his upper lip curled into a snarl and a muscle flickering in his jaw, he thought he had it all figured out. "My brother and I will solve your problem for ya."

Mick nodded in agreement, and the tension at the table became as thick as mud.

I shook my head. "It's not like that. You don't understand—"

"Uh, it's pretty easy to figure out," Thomas said, voice rising. "Look at ya! Covered in bruises." He was staring at my arm. "Heck, I know burns when I see 'em. Bite marks, too."

I covered up my scarred hand.

Thomas was fuming. According to the nodding heads, he spoke for everyone at the table now. "Some sadistic asshole took advantage of a pretty girl. By the looks of it, you got away before you ended up six feet under."

I had no reply. Why did this stranger give a crap?

"Just gimme names," Thomas repeated. "We will take care of whatever it is you are running from, and Ben can get you back to your family."

Mick's ponytail swayed in enthusiastic agreement. Ben muttered something indiscernible.

"It's not that easy." I was digging myself a hole for only imparting half the truth. "My family is not on my side. They are part of the uh… problem."

"They did this to you?" Ben said, pushing his chair back and rising from the table.

"No. Well, sort of, I mean I—"

"Boyfriend then. Has to be. There's no ring on her finger, Ben. She ain't married," Thomas said.

"Sick goddamn bastard," Ben replied.

My chest tightened, but I had to remain calm so the awkward conversation wouldn't escalate. "I just have to hide for a while until I can go back and make things right."

"Go back?" Ben said incredulously.

"Yes," I said, realizing how insane that sounded. "I just need time to sort things out."

"Time doesn't change the character of a man who beats a woman," Thomas hissed with a quick glance in Ben's direction.

Concerned faces regarded me over pancakes and bacon. "It's not like that. I just can't tell you all anything more. I'm sorry. I can't involve more people in my messed-up life." My chest grew heavy, as if the weight of the world was standing on it. "I won't let anyone else get hurt because of me."

Silence fell over the room, and the huge country kitchen suddenly became small as a shoebox. Ben was wringing his hands like he was ready to beat the world senseless. Thomas had turned to stare out the window. Mick hadn't said a word, but his cheeks were fire red, and Hank now sat still with his hands in his lap. I lowered my eyes to my cup of coffee; I thought all my tears had been cried out yesterday, but that familiar sting of them pushed against my lids.

Ben spoke, his voice cold and authoritative. "The weeds in the garden need pulling, and there's a ton of laundry that's backed up. Can you handle that?" He glanced at my injured arm.

I nodded anxiously.

"Meals need to be on the table at six, morning and evening," he added.

I nodded again, feeling overwhelmingly grateful for the tasks and an end to the line of questioning.

"Your pay will be room and board for now. We can discuss your wage after a two-week trial period."

There was an expectant pause from everyone at the table; I wouldn't stick around that long. I just needed some time to come up with a plan. "Thank you," I said.

"All right then." Ben thrust his hand across the table. His eyes met mine for a moment, then he blinked nervously and let go. "Okay. Well, dinner is over. Till tomorrow then."

Everyone stood, and though I was anxious to flee the room, I stopped in confusion. "Dinner?"

Ben forced a smile. "Yeah. It's seven thirty, Kate. I didn't wake you because you needed the rest. Make sure breakfast is on the table by six tomorrow morning. No later."

OLIVER

8

Hangin' On The Telephone

The hardest thing I'd ever done in my life was walk away from Kaya. At the time, Seth had a gun pointed to my head for encouragement, but it was the feeling of my heart being ripped from my chest that got my feet moving before I either blew up in anger or fell to her feet and begged her to take me back. At that point, I still had some pride. But now? If the opportunity arose, I'd beg. I'd plead. I'd make a damn fool of myself. Even though she said she didn't want me, didn't love me, and her green eyes flashed in anger when she shot out words like bullets, I loved her. She was still mine. And somehow, I would make her see that.

If only I'd found her sooner and hadn't held a knife to golden boy's throat. If only I hadn't shoved her down those porch steps. Since when had this rage inside of me taken control of my common sense? I was so wretchedly angry all the time...so...out of control. I'd even swung at Davis when he tried to rein me in. Swung at my best friend. I didn't blame him for leaving me and letting me wallow in my misery and anger. He tried to help, but I wasn't having any of it. When next we met, I was going to have a lot of explaining to do. And when I got Kaya back, I would apologize for what I did and then spend every second making it up to her. I would never let her out of my sight again.

That meant I would have to get rid of Luke somehow. Kaya would never fully return her heart to me with him around. The only reason I was dragging him along was to use him as an ice breaker. With golden boy at my side, I had a better chance of getting back into her good books. She'd only left to protect him; the note she'd written was complete bullshit. Even though I wanted to grab a handful of his hair to drag him out of this wretched bar and stuff him in a trunk, I had to play nice. Besides, as much as it pained me to admit it, he could beat the crap out of me if he felt like it.

"There are one hundred and twenty-seven Ben Smiths in southern Saskatchewan," Luke said, glancing up wearily from a laptop.

He guzzled back the remainder of a beer and wrestled to keep a brave face. He was so worried sick about Kaya I almost liked him for it—almost.

"Well, process of elimination it is then," I said, waving off a scantily clad waitress that was making her way back to Luke for the tenth time— the way chicks flirted with him was sickening. "We need to come up with a game plan before we hit the road."

"What do we do? Call every Ben Smith in the Saskatchewan phone directory and ask if he's picked up a young brunette recently? If we happen to call the right guy, he'd never say so. We need more info, Oliver."

"Relax, Luke."

"Relax? How can you say that? She's been missing for... how long now? Who knows if she's hurt or who she's with! You have no idea what it feels like to—"

His voice caught midsentence when he realized what he was about to say. I knew exactly what it felt like, and what he was going through. I watched him struggle with the things that torment a person's mind when the person they loved most in the entire world goes missing.

Basking in his pain was awesome payback.

"Get your head together, Luke. We've got a girl to find."

He nodded.

The waitress was back, a grin the size of Texas on her face. She had a notepad and pen in hand just in case she had the opportunity to hand over her phone number. When she asked golden boy yet again if he needed anything, Luke, oblivious to anything not Kaya related, rudely waved her off.

"Maybe you should order a sandwich or something," I said.

"Not hungry."

"You might not be hungry but remember, we are seeking info. Maybe someone in this bar saw her. Maybe Kaya came in here."

Luke straightened, his eyes widened, and he scanned the dimly lit room. "Damn it, you're right. I just can't think straight."

"Flirt with that waitress. I'm going to make a few calls," I said, standing and realizing I'd become numb to the cell phone constantly vibrating alerts in my pocket.

Luke stood from the table, then his hand lunged for my wrist—he was so damn fast I never even saw it coming. "We're on the same side. Right, Oliver?" he asked, staring hard at me for the truth.

We were, but I wanted nothing more than to grab his fingers and twist them into knots. I felt that sick feeling of rage seeping in. He was only asking a logical question, making sure I wasn't about to put Kaya's safety in jeopardy by calling the wrong person. But the desire to pound my fists into his face was at a constant, rolling boil. "I need to go outside," I said, trying to pull my arm free.

Luke's grip tightened, not letting go without an answer. "Oliver, she doesn't want anything to do with her father. You are his most loyal subject. You cannot call him. I'll ask you again—are we on the same side?"

"Yes," I hissed.

He let go and sat. How was he so trusting? I could have told him gators were falling from the sky, and he would have believed me. With a fake smile, he motioned for the waitress and I headed for the door.

Gritting my teeth so hard they hurt, I fished out my handy little pills. With shaking hands, I fumbled with the cap, popped two in my mouth, and swallowed, hoping they would douse the fire in my head— even the garbage can on the dirty street seemed to be asking for a fight.

Night had fallen over the town. I tried to take in a breath of the cool prairie air, but I was seeing red. I had such an intense desire to hit something. Anything. Two dudes smoking next to the exit gave me the once-over. My face morphed into a glare, needlessly baiting them. What the hell was wrong with me?

I reached for another pill, hoping to calm my Bruce Banner rage before I turned into a green monster. I ground the chalky paste between my teeth, counted to ten—fifteen times—and paced until my head cleared. Thankfully, the pills took effect quickly. My rage lessened, and I was brought back to the realization of my phone vibrating in my pocket.

I knew who it was. Last I checked, there were over a hundred texts and phone messages from Henry. All demanding, threatening, and yelling instructions to bring his daughter back. Now, for some reason, he wanted to make sure I destroyed that necklace she always wore. I hadn't replied yet because I knew there was no chance of having a civilized conversation with him. He was just going to have to trust I would do my job. But I was going to need more than golden boy's help to do that.

I dialed a number that was ingrained in my head. One I was only to use in case of an emergency. The only person I could trust that, like me, would one hundred percent have Kaya's best interest at heart.

"Hello?" a sultry voice said.

I took a deep breath. "Hello, Sindra." My jaw ached from clenching my teeth. "Is it safe to talk?"

Her high heels clicked loudly over a marble floor. "It is now."

I pictured her black hair, shiny like Kaya's, pulled tight into a braid and hanging down her back. She would be in her black business suit adorned with delicate gold jewelry. Henry would be yelling orders, and she would be following them, keeping him on schedule and planning his itinerary for the next day.

I took in a deep breath. "I need your help."

"For what, Oliver? We've had no contact with you for over two weeks now. Henry is losing his mind, and I've had to deal with it."

"I know. I'm sorry. It's just that, well… I've misplaced Kaya. She's, uh, run off."

A pause. "That's not good."

"I know. It's become complicated."

"Because she doesn't want to go back with you. Correct?"

"Yes."

"And you're playing Mr. Nice Ex-Fiancé and letting her exercise her free will?"

"Yes."

"Well, that just might get her killed."

The hair rose on the back of my neck. It started to rain. The veins at my temples throbbed. "I'm not going to let that happen."

Sindra sighed. "Well then, how can I help you?"

I started to pace, growling at the smokers. "Kaya got in a truck owned by someone named Ben Smith, a cowboy with a ranch in southern Saskatchewan. I'm hoping I'll find her with him. There are over a hundred people listed under that name and—"

"I'm on it. What else have you got?"

"He has a horse. Alexander the Great, sometimes called Zander. Competes in rodeos. I don't know if it helps, but he was 'horse of the year' for roping or something."

"I'll get on it."

"And Sindra—" I stopped pacing to stare across the street. "Please, just let me bring her back my way. All right? If I need more help, I will let you know. I promise."

Sindra cleared her throat. I imagined her dark eyes sparkling and her white teeth biting into her ruby-red lower lip. "You've got five days. That's all I can give you, Oliver. If Henry finds out I have information regarding his daughter's whereabouts and I am keeping it from him, he'll hang me. And not figuratively."

The pills had taken full effect now, and I realized, along with a heavy and calm head, that my hands were achingly cold. "I know. It's just that—" I sighed, never one to share anything personal with Sindra, but in this case… "I just need her to come to me on her own terms. What's the sense of bringing her back if she is only going to hate me forever?"

"Love has made you stupid," Sindra said bluntly. "If it was anyone else asking me to do this, I'd hunt them down and shred their insides"

"I have no doubt of that."

"Don't screw this up."

I was getting special treatment. I started pacing again, not caring about getting out of the rain. "I won't."

A heavy sigh. "Out of curiosity though, what made Kaya dump you so quickly? She was mad about you."

"She, uh…" It hurt to say it. "She fell for one of her kidnappers. Even though I knew that, I tried to slit his throat. I also pushed her down some stairs. Damn it, I didn't take the news of the pregnancy very well either."

Sindra gasped. "I hope the fetus wasn't compromised!"

I steadied myself for a lie. Kaya could share the truth when she felt like it. "No. It's fine."

"Good. I don't understand, though. It's not like you to act irrationally. I trained you better than that."

"I know."

"Oliver…are you still taking those pills I gave you for your ribs?"

I felt for the comforting plastic bottle in my pocket. "Yes."

"Oh, shit."

Sindra never swore. Never. She said swearing was for idiots who couldn't come up with anything intelligent to say. Hearing her curse was a shock.

"Why?" I asked tentatively.

"Well, I should have told you to only take a couple and then toss them. The drug is still in the testing phase. It's amazing for pain—targets the brain the same way antidepressants do—but it causes some significant side effects. We have discovered it is highly addictive. When leaving the system, it can cause extreme emotional fluctuations and incite uncontrollable rage and irrational behavior in certain individuals."

All the breath left my lungs, and I had to fight to get it back. "You're kidding me." I stared at the yellow bottle in my hand… no label, no warnings… just an impression molded into the cap that said Eronel.

Sindra cleared her throat. "Maybe you're one of those individuals."

I tossed the bottle into the garbage can and heard the plastic shatter.

"Anyway, I suggest you stop taking them before you do something you'll regret," she added.

"Yeah, ya think?" I hissed, putting four and nine together and coming up with the number one reason for my ridiculous behavior. "What, exactly, is Henry working on in that lab of his?" I spat, feeling the pulse of anger at my temple again. "Besides this crap you gave me, what the hell else has he got going on?"

"If I told you that, I would have to kill you," Sindra said flatly.

I had to laugh, even though nothing about this was funny. "Well, if I rip a small village to shreds and don't succeed in getting Kaya back, you can go right ahead and do just that."

Sindra maintained her professional tone. "Just don't stop taking those pills cold turkey, all right? You absolutely must wean yourself off them or you'll have one helluva wild ride for a few days from which you might never recover. We've had cases of brain damage… stroke… I think we had four or five people die from some sort of lung complications. At the very least, you might get uncontrollably angry."

I dove for the garbage can.

KAYA

9

Strawberry Wine

I woke in a cold sweat. A restless sleep full of nightmares brought about the morning like a slap to the face. Somewhere outside, a rooster was yelling at the world to get up and the clock at my bedside said five. No point staring at the ceiling.

Pushing away the rose blankets, I hauled myself out of bed. I was still wearing the clothes from the day before, which made it rather easy to get ready for the day. Tiptoeing down the stairs, I headed toward my first task as an employed person—getting breakfast on the table in an hour.

I had to admit, it did feel good to wake with a purpose. All my life things had been handed to me, and for once, I could do the handing. There was something powerful in the feeling of being needed, being useful. For a moment, it increased my self-esteem tenfold... only to have it crash to the depths of hell within seconds of stepping foot into the huge country kitchen.

The room with the gleaming white countertops and countless cupboards suddenly became the most foreboding place I'd ever been. I knew nothing about cooking. Absolutely nothing. I could peel apples and make tea, but I assumed Ben would be expecting something a little more elaborate than that.

I searched for cereal; I could put that in bowls and have the milk ready... but the only cereal I found was something called Sunny Boy, which apparently had to be cooked on the stove for twenty minutes. I didn't know how to turn the stove on.

Toast. I could do that.

I searched for bread, but all I found was some silver contraption that said Bread Maker on the lid. The inside of it was empty. There were brown packages of meat in the freezer. In the cupboards, there were bags of flour, sugar, bottles of spices, and dried herbs. There were loads of eggs and apples in the fridge, and a whole shelf dedicated to an assortment of cheeses... but nothing that was already formed into a breakfast shape.

I started to sweat. I needed to make this breakfast thing happen so I could stay here for a while. The thought of that gas station, the weeds under my feet, the utter despair and sadness and the desire to wander out onto the highway and end it all…was not a place I wanted to go again. And, I didn`t want to disappoint the man who saved me from becoming roadkill.

I had to do this. I could do this. Coffee—start with that.

I found a can of it. The uplifting smell was encouraging as I poured some shiny brown beans into the top of the coffee maker. I filled the pot with water, then placed it back in the device and flipped the on switch. Well, that wasn't hard. Now, the bread maker; I would put in some flour and water in it and turn it on, too. The toasting part when the bread was done would be easy.

The flour was in a sack in the cupboard just over my head. I reached for it, not thinking it would be as heavy as it was. It started to tip toward me, and there was no stopping it. My injured arm was still too weak to do much good, and the heavy bag toppled out of the cupboard to land with a loud thud at my feet. Of course, the top of the bag was open. White flour spewed into the air and covered everything within a five-foot radius. Including me.

"Need help?"

I turned to see Thomas in the doorway. He was freshly showered and dressed in a clean plaid shirt and jeans. His dark hair was damp, and it shone like the gleam in his eyes.

"No. I'm fine," I said, tasting flour in my mouth and trying not to cough.

He sauntered into the room toward me, smirking. He'd shaved. "You look like a ghost."

"The flour bag slipped. It's a little heavy."

He eyed my arm, and the smile left his face. "Yeah, for sure. So, what were you going to use the flour for?"

I coughed, trying to wipe the front of the scarf I'd borrowed from Evelyn. "Bread. Got the coffee started so all is fine. I don't need any help." I reached for a cloth on the sink before getting on my knees. I wiped and scrubbed, but I only managed to spread the mess around.

Thomas watched, amused. His eyes darted from me to the coffee pot. "The coffee doesn't seem to have worked. The water is… clear."

Indeed, there was nothing going on in the caffeine department. I was starting to feel frazzled.

Thomas went to inspect the coffee maker. "You didn't grind the beans?"

"Grind them? Oh, uh… no. It's better that way," I said, feeling like an idiot.

He stifled a laugh. "Oh, is it? About the water, though. It's supposed to go in here." He pointed to the top of the machine.

"I just haven't gotten around to that yet."

His grin stretched ear to ear. "Ah, I see. And, the flour… where were you going to put that?"

"Why are you so interested in what I'm doing?" I barked, feeling my pulse race in anger.

"I'm just curious because breakfast is the most important meal of the day. I'm worried you don't have a clue how to even turn on the stove."

"Yes, I do," I said defensively.

"Then show me."

I stood and marched over to the foreboding appliance, flour drifting around me and feet skidding on a pile of it on the floor. There were dials and buttons everywhere, so I picked one of them and turned a knob to something called broil. I placed the frying pan on top of the element closest to the knob. I hoped I'd done it right, but one look at Thomas's face told me I hadn't.

"What?" I said angrily.

He doubled over, and a silent laugh stole his breath. I wanted to kick him in the face.

"Listen, you need some help." He gathered his composure before turning the broil button off. "No offense, I think you could probably figure all this out on your own, but you might burn the house down in the process." He was tipping the coffee maker upside down to shake the beans out, and then poured the water in. "I'll help you. I'm handy in the kitchen… and in so many other ways if you're interested." He winked.

"You're disgusting," I said.

But he wasn't. As I watched him dig out a small hand broom and dustpan from under the sink, I realized everything about his physical appearance was perfect. He looked like he'd walked out of an advertisement for men's cologne. As he swept the floor, I was kicking myself for briefly admiring him.

"It's okay to admit you're infatuated with me right now," he joked, and his dark eyes flashed at me as he cleaned around my feet.

I felt like a kid caught with her hand in the cookie jar. My cherry-red cheeks had to give me away. "Don't be gross."

I got back down on my knees, determined to ignore him and his inflated ego, and used my hands to push mounds of flour toward his broom. When most of the mess was under control, I reached for the flour sack, and he took it from me.

"I got it. By the looks of it, you should probably not use that arm of yours."

I sneered. "Don't tell me what I should and shouldn't do."

We stared each other down, bulls about to butt heads, cats about to claw, both on our knees in the middle of the kitchen floor...

But instead of arguing, he smiled. "Do you like waffles?"

It completely caught me off guard. "What?"

Thomas stood and motioned with his chin to a clock on the wall. "Waffles. I have a great recipe, and it's fast. We could probably get a ton of 'em on the table with bacon and eggs in a half hour if we work together."

I refused his outstretched hand. As I wrestled into an upright position, I avoided his piercing eyes. I didn't want help, but I didn't have a choice.

"Fine," I said.

"Just don't be staring at my butt." He grinned, "I know it looks great in these new jeans, but we'll never get anything done if you're just admiring me the whole time."

He took the cloth from my hand. The expression on his face changed from teasing to caring. He reached out to rub flour off my cheeks, but I shoved his hand away.

"Man, you sure would look terrible as a blonde," he said with a chuckle.

I shook my hair and released another cloud of flour, some of it settling on top of his head. "Well, you'd probably look better."

Thomas snorted. "Touché."

AFTER CAREFUL INSTRUCTIONS ON HOW TO POUR THE BATTER INTO THE waffle iron, I was left to do it on my own while Thomas tended to sizzling bacon and the eggs he'd cracked into muffin cups.

"Five more minutes in the oven for these bad boys and I'm done," he said. "And you?"

"One waffle left."

I had to force back the smile that kept trying to creep in. Here, in the quiet peaceful morning, stirring batter and hearing butter sizzle on the waffle iron, I felt, for a moment...soothed. Thomas's patience while teaching me how to light the stove burners, grind the coffee beans, and measure the ingredients for waffles was a great distraction from the turmoil in my head.

"You're doing a pretty good job there, Kate."

"Thanks," I said, cringing at the sound of my fake name. I turned a perfectly browned waffle out onto a warming plate among nineteen others.

"You catch on pretty quick, too," he said proudly. "Maybe tonight for supper, I'll show you how to make beef stew. I have a recipe for gravy that will blow your mind."

Stew... An echo of a perfect moment circled back into my mind—the cave, sitting next to the bubbling pool, and the look in Luke's eyes when he put a cube of beef in my mouth. All of a sudden, I felt like I'd been punched in the gut; I missed him so bad it hurt. I had to steady myself against the counter.

"Everything all right?" Thomas said, coming to my side.

It was Luke I should be cooking with, stirring things with, smiling with...

"I'm fine. You don't have to baby me," I barked.

Thomas's dark eyes narrowed, and the smile left his face. "Because you've been babied your whole life. Correct?"

I glared. "What? No!"

"Oh, come on. I mean, what kind of girl doesn't even know how to make coffee? Or turn on an oven? You'd think you were a damn princess judging by your lack of domestic knowledge. You've been coddled. Waited on hand and foot. I'd bet my life on it."

I couldn't stop my eyes from widening as he hit the nail on the head.

"Ah, I'm right," he said, noting my reaction. "I don't get it. What kind of princess is beaten in her own castle? Your family... your boyfriend... what did they do to you? What's got you running? It must have been bad. So tell me about it. Who are you running from?"

He was throwing questions like darts. My chest grew tight, my mouth dry. What was I doing in this strange kitchen trying to make breakfast with this overly curious, extremely intuitive, and arrogant cowboy? I made a move for the exit, but was blocked.

"Whoa, stop. Hey, listen, I'm sorry," Thomas said, backing away and putting his hands up defensively. "I just thought you might like to talk about it."

"There's nothing to talk about," I said, choking back tears.

He nodded. "Okay. Whenever you're ready, I'll be here. Ready to listen. All ears. Just for you. Got it? No more questions for now, I promise. There's nothing to get upset about."

He seemed genuinely concerned, and he was being more than helpful when he certainly didn't have to be. I'd still be cleaning up flour if it wasn't for him. I had nowhere to run, and I needed the job. So…

"I'm not upset. My arm is just sore is all," I said, which wasn't exactly a lie. It was throbbing.

"Oh. Right. It looks bad. What happened?"

Shaking my head, I glanced over at the burning waffle.

I could feel his eyes follow mine. "Right. No more questions. I'll finish making breakfast. You go over there and sit down."

I was marched to the kitchen table and directed to relax into a squeaky chair. As Thomas got back to cooking, I tried to keep Luke's eyes from flashing through my mind. The emerging blue sky visible out the lace-curtained window reminded me of how they shone when we shared our first meal. How they focused on me in the hot spring and the desire in them after that first perfect kiss…

I might never see those eyes again.

That thought spun around madly. I took deep breaths and counted to twenty; the floor started to shake. I squeezed my eyes shut tight, and then my fists, digging my fingernails into the palm of my hand as the chair swayed beneath me.

I might never see those eyes again…

"Ever had chocolate chips on your waffles?" Thomas asked.

I felt stunned by the mundane question, but it forced me to breathe to voice an answer. "No."

Thomas maneuvered hot dishes onto the table and filled cups full of coffee. Setting out bottles of ketchup and syrups of all kinds, he was so graceful. So assured. I felt my mind drift away from the impending anxiety to settle on him.

"You'd think that whipped cream would be the obvious choice, right?" he said with an easy grin. "But heck… give me chocolate chips and raspberry jam any day. That's the bomb. You gotta try it."

He seemed to not have a care in the world besides the task at hand and sharing his ideas for waffle toppings. Now that he wasn't pelting me with questions, I realized he wasn't all that bad. At least his presence was comforting.

My anxiety drifted away.

"Hey, stop that," he said, spinning around from where he was now slicing oranges.

I gave my head a shake, meeting his sparkling dark gaze. "Stop what?"

His grin stretched ear to ear. "Admiring me from behind."

"**MAN, I'M SO** HUNGRY I COULD EAT THE ASS END OUT OF A LOW-FLYING duck," Hank said, diving into his breakfast.

His appearance suggested he'd been dragged out of bed. His hair was a brown mop on his head, and there were sleep marks on his chubby cheeks. A striped pajama top was half tucked into a pair of faded Levi's and his feet were bare. Mick and Ben were at the table, too, bright eyed, showered, and reeking of too much cologne.

"I gotta admit, Kate," Ben said, biting into a waffle, "I never expected you to have breakfast ready. Maybe coffee and toast, but not this. Your waffles are almost as good as Thomas's. I mean, I hate to say it, but for some reason, I didn't think you could actually cook."

I couldn't help but smile at Thomas when his eyes met mine from across the table. "Well, I had some—"

"Good teachers?" Thomas said, finishing my sentence for me.

"Yes. And lucky for me, that teacher had—"

"A good waffle recipe?" Thomas added.

"Uh, yes," I said.

Ben reached for the plate of bacon. "Thank heavens. A girl who can't cook is pretty much useless. Cooking and cleaning… if you can't do that, then what good are ya? I certainly wouldn't hire anyone without those basic skills."

That was why Thomas kept interrupting me. The smile left his face. "Not knowing your way around a kitchen doesn't make you useless, Ben."

Ben sighed, clearly used to Thomas challenging him. "Ah, you're always up for a fight, ain't ya? Jumping down anyone's throat who dares to say something you don't like. Now, you know I didn't mean to offend the weaker sex."

"Weaker sex?" Thomas said with an exasperated exhale. A look of utter disgust came over his face. "You really wanna go there, Ben? Do I need to remind you of the definition of the word 'weak'? Or could you just look into your past for a few examples?"

Ben's eyes lowered into a glare, and his hands curled into fists. A low growl came from his throat. "Watch it," he warned.

Mick attempted to prevent the destruction of breakfast. "I think Ben was just joking around there, Thomas. Let's not ruin the day right off the bat, all right? Besides, we don't want Kate to feel more uncomfortable than she probably already does."

Ben's fists uncurled, and Thomas took in a deep breath.

Crisis averted. The corners of Mick's mouth lifted. "What's on the agenda today?"

Ben raised his cup to his mouth, sipping the coffee slowly. It was impressive how quickly he'd calmed down. It was strange for a boss to take such sass from an employee. Maybe Thomas had some dirt Ben didn't want shared. Otherwise, wouldn't he fire someone who talked back and gave him such grief?

"I got a call from Jeb late last night," Ben said, reaching for a waffle. "The Carlsons need our help. They bought a couple of hundred head of cattle at auction, and they gotta brand 'em. I figured we'd head out around noon today."

"You're leaving?" I said before I could stop myself.

Ben put down his fork. "Yeah. You're coming with us, though. Mrs. Carlson will need some help in the kitchen making meals. We'll spend the night there, or maybe even two—there's a ton of work to be done. Lots of cows and calves to separate and brand."

"Brand?" I said.

Hank got excited. "Oh, yeah! It's crazy cool. Your gonna love it. They stick a red-hot iron to the cow's butt. Man, it stinks! It's like animal tattoos, but without needles and stuff. Ya dig? My ma told Ben I wasn't allowed to witness such poor treatment of animals, but Ben's gonna let me go anyway. Right, Ben?"

Ben shook his head in annoyance. "It's not poor treatment of animals, and you're sixteen for God sake. You can do whatever you want. Just stay the hell outta my way."

I suddenly dreaded the day. "I don't know if it's a good idea for me to—"

Thomas cut me off. "We'll have to make a stop in town on the way. Kate needs a proper shirt."

Ben nodded agreeably. "Yeah, for sure. She can't be wearing that scarf. She needs something warmer."

"I totally dig the scarf," Hank said, cheeks turning scarlet. "I think it's pretty."

"It's not practical," Ben said. "There's a Wal-Mart in Ginsburg. We can stop there, and she can pick something out."

They were talking like I wasn't even in the room, as if my opinion didn't matter. I was about to be upset about that, but then what they'd suggested hit me. Shopping—in public.

My breath caught. "I can't do that."

Ben smiled. "Don't worry, I'll take it out of your pay."

"No, it's not that. I can't go into a store," I said, feeling anxiety creeping in.

Henry would be searching for me, along with Rayna and Oliver… and what if I saw Luke? Would I run? No. I would probably turn into a puddle and melt right at his feet. And besides, being in public? I'd gone to the corner store and the front desk at the motel in Radium, but this was different. My sixteenth birthday had pretty much stolen any desire to be around crowds ever again; I gulped at the memory of it, and my hand instinctively went to the scar at my neck.

"Kate. Everything all right?" Ben asked, putting down his utensils.

The blood drained from my cheeks. "It's just… I like this scarf. I'm fine with wearing it for now. Besides, I still have that blue T-shirt you bought me. It's comfortable, in style, and—"

"You need shoes, though. Flip-flops ain't gonna cut it on a ranch. It's October. The weather can, and will, change in the blink of an eye."

Thomas was staring hard at me, as if trying to put the pieces of my crazy puzzle together. "Most chicks love to shop," he stated.

"I'm not most chicks," I replied.

I hadn't realized my hand had started shaking until the coffee cup I was gripping tipped and spilled hot liquid onto my knuckles and the table. The room fell silent. I set it down, about to try to come up with some sort of explanation, but a ringing telephone stole through the quiet room.

"Ah, I'll be damned. That'll be your mother, Hank." Ben sighed. "No one calls this early but her. Tell her I've gone fishing. Indefinitely."

Hank took his time getting to the phone, which was an ancient green thing attached to the wall. There was dread in his tone when he answered. "Hello?" he said tentatively, but then his posture changed, and he straightened up. "Nope. There's no Ben Douglas here, only a Ben Smith. What? No, this isn't an office…. Accountants? Hell, no. We got lots of horses and cows, though."

Ben rose from the table, his eyes wide. In a blur, he dove toward Hank and snatched the phone away. "Who is this?" he demanded of the caller. "What do you want?"

Judging by the glare Ben gave the phone before slamming it down, whoever it was had hung up. "Prank call," he said, giving Hank a slap to the head before storming out of the kitchen.

Apparently, breakfast was over. I forced my legs to hold me up; whoever had called had been looking for me. I knew it, and so did Ben. As I headed up to the floral room, stumbling past Thomas in the hall, it was obvious he knew it, too.

"Don't worry," he said. "Whoever it was won't find you. We'll be far away from here in an hour."

10

BLING THING

I FELT PAINFULLY HOMELESS SITTING IN THE BACKSEAT OF THE truck sandwiched between Thomas and Mick. They had backpacks with spare clothes and phones, and I had nothing. For the first time since leaving the estate, I longed for my possessions. The things I'd collected over the years—my shells, stones, zombie movies, and comfy sweatpants... even the jewelry in the safe that I never cared about. There was no buffer between the world and me, nothing comforting to hide behind or give my attention to. I stared at my hands the entire thirty-seven-minute trek to the city while Hank described the world rolling by outside the window.

"What's your favorite color, Kate?" he asked after counting a flock of geese heading south.

I'd never heard anyone talk so much in my life. I didn't even have a chance to answer.

"Blue? Red? I'd bet you'd look good in blue," he said, twisting around to face me, beaming. "Ya know, cause of your dark hair and all. Maybe I can find us all matching T-shirts in your favorite color. Then we'd be a team, right? We could show up at the Carlsons all dressed the same. Some would think that was weird, but I like it. Thomas? Mick? You into matching shirts? Oh... and they have McDonald's in Wal-Mart. You like chicken nuggets, Kate? I do. Not the sauce, though. I prefer ketchup."

"What the heck is a chicken nugget?" I asked before I could stop myself.

"Whoa, dude! You don't know?" Hank said, his voice rising in pitch. "They're awesome, breaded, nugget-shaped bits of mouthwatering—"

"All right!" Ben yelled, his hands clenching the steering wheel in agitation. "You are—" He was about to tear a strip out of Hank, but his eyes met mine in the rearview mirror. He paused. "You are in dire need of a new iPod and headphones, aren't ya, Hank? How about I foot the bill for that. Huh?"

Hank's jaw dropped. Thomas and Mick's did, too.

"Whoa! Hey Unc, that's wicked! Ma won't let me have one," Hank squealed.

"Today is your lucky day." Ben pulled the truck off the highway into a massive parking lot packed with cars. "You go on ahead now and pick out what you want while I check on Zander. Thomas will meet you in there with my credit card. Now get moving before I change my mind."

As soon as Ben brought the truck to a stop, Hank was running for the store.

I sank lower into the backseat. There were people everywhere. It was complete chaos. All sizes and shapes of characters pushed carts full of stuff and kids and babies crying, and the sliding doors of the store moved back and forth every second letting more people in and more people out... The parking lot was like main street Banff in the spring except no one looked happy or had cameras hanging from their necks.

"I'm not going in there," I whispered.

Oddly, no one argued.

"What size are your feet?" Thomas asked.

"Seven."

"And jeans?"

"Probably a two."

After an uncomfortable glance at my chest, Thomas was out the door with Mick in tow, leaving Ben and me alone. Ben wanted to check on his horse, but he seemed worried about leaving me alone even for a second.

"Do you know how much an iPod is?" he asked, attempting small talk.

"Sorry, no idea."

"If the kid returns with matching T-shirts, I'll kill him."

"No, you won't."

Ben sighed and took off his hat to run his fingers through his hair. "Yeah, you're right. I love Hank, but I hate him at the same time."

"I know that feeling," I said, Oliver's face flashing through my mind.

There was an awkward silence. Ben's eyes caught mine in the mirror, and he finally said what was on his mind.

"Whoever you're running from might have been calling the house."

He was right, but I didn't want to confirm that. "There's no way they could have found me. It would be impossible. You know that."

"They? So, you are running from more than one person?"

I sank a little lower in the seat, not wanting to think about who it might have been. "Listen, I'm not worried about it," I said, hoping to ease his mind.

"Let's just say, by some stroke of luck, they were able to track you to my house…wanna tell me what I'm up against?"

His question gave me an unshakeable chill. What he was up against?

I had to get away from him. Had to get out of this truck and not involve him, baby-faced Hank, too-quiet Mick, or arrogant Thomas in my messed-up life. Just as I'd done with Luke. "I should probably go and help the boys," I said, wondering how fast I could get to the highway. "Thomas will never know what size shirt to get me. I'll go help him and be right back."

I pushed open the door and jumped out, but Ben was already there, blocking me from going anywhere. His eyes lowered onto mine. "There is no goddamn way you are running away from me," he growled.

There was something very menacing about him. Something dark he struggled to keep in check. It made my neck hairs lift and my spine tingle. Female intuition said run, but I tried to be casual. "What? I just thought I'd go and pick out my own clothes."

"Bullshit," he said angrily.

"I can't involve you and your family in what I've got going on." Could I shove him out of my way without causing a scene?

"You already have."

"Well then, I really do have to leave."

I tried to move past him. Zander stomped around in his trailer, and Ben crowded closer to me. I could feel the heat from him on my bare legs, see the pulse of his heart race at the base of his throat.

"You don't have to protect me, Kate," he said. "I made a choice to get involved with whatever you got going on when I went back for you at that diner. You've got nothing. Not a cent to your name and obviously no one to help you. Did you figure you'd just take off in a pair of flip-flops, wearing only a scarf and shorts all covered in bruises? Goddamn it, girl, you are stunningly beautiful. Don't you realize that makes you more vulnerable than you already are? And on top of that, you're extremely naive."

"I am none of those things," I said defensively, backing up until I hit the truck.

He came closer. There was a whiff of alcohol on his breath, but no. He wouldn't be drinking and driving…

The veins at his temple bulged. "Did you even realize the white-haired boy at the diner was checking you out? He was reading over your shoulder, staring at whatever was on that laptop that was making you cry. Yeah, that's right. I was watching you, too, but for the right reasons.

That kid started texting madly the moment you got up to leave. Now, if I hadn't been there, you would have been followed, probably raped, and then tossed in a ditch somewhere. Or worse. Do you really want to repeat that situation again? Because I can't see it being any different for you. It's evident there's going to be some implications for me, but I'm prepared for that. You need to decide if you want to take your chances with a cowboy who has your best interest at heart or run off again and end up dead."

End up dead. Without Luke, I pretty much felt dead. But the idea of it happening didn't sit very well. That would mean either Henry, John Marchessa, or Rayna would have won—and like Ben had pointed out—I couldn't let them win.

My delayed response made Ben's face soften and his words catch in his throat. "Kate, you might not care what happens to you, but I do."

He was telling the truth. His chiseled features and gruff manner made him appear incapable of warmth, but the concern he had for me was genuine. He pushed himself closer. Too close.

"Don't run from me. Okay? Please promise me that."

Luke had made me promise that same thing. I imagined it was him standing before me, blue eyes flashing with that mind-melting smile on his face. His hand reaching for my cheek, gently pushing back my hair and making my skin tingle head to toe.

"Promise?" Ben said again. When I blinked myself back into reality, it was his hand on my cheek.

I recoiled and crawled back into the truck. "It's not a good idea to be around me," I warned.

"I'll be the judge of that," he said, firmly shutting the door.

NO ONE SPOKE THE REST OF THE DRIVE TO THE CARLSON'S RANCH. AFTER an unmarked turn off the highway and another onto a lonely gravel road, we made our way down a long drive flanked by fences and horse corrals. At the end stood a pink and white two-story house with a porch running along the front and overflowing window boxes beneath each sill. To the east and west were nothing but miles of flat land and bands of trees. Barns and outbuildings with well-trodden trails linking them together sat to the south. I caught a glimpse of a garden stretching almost all the way to a long band of silver birch trees that bordered the entirety of the property. Everything seemed immaculate and cared for, from the manicured lawn and freshly painted fences to the many cats and dogs with shiny fur and sparkling collars.

"We got ninety-five acres next to government land and over six hundred head of Red Angus cattle," Mr. Carlson boasted.

I instantly liked him. Kindness resonated in a voice as big as he was while he told me about his prized mini-pigs and his wife's prized pies. Tanned and weathered skin crackled around his eyes and a white beard floated around his face. His coveralls and rubber boots were spotless, and I suspected he had multiple pairs of each.

He pointed to one of many outbuildings. "The boys can have the bunkhouse. I've got the heat on in there, so they won't freeze. You best not be sharing a room with the likes of them, though, eh? I've got a spare bedroom in the main house—"

Ben butted in, clearing his throat. "No thanks, Jeb. Kate's an employee. She bunks with us."

Mr. Carlson crinkled his nose, his brow furrowing. "Uh, are ya sure that's a good idea, Ben?" he asked, and I noticed Thomas shift uncomfortably.

"She stays with me," Ben repeated.

Mr. Carlson and Thomas exchanged a glance I couldn't decipher. Ben stood tall, defiant. Why did it matter where I slept? I certainly didn't care.

Mr. Carlson mumbled something that sounded like 'all righty then,' and Thomas shook his head. We were led to the bunkhouse, a small structure painted deep red with white shuttered windows. Set atop a slight incline, the land stretching out behind it swayed with beige and gold grasses bordered by the line of silver birch. From the front porch, I could see the pasture speckled with low-lying bush and small patches of blue far off in the distance. I stood in awe of the landscape while Mr. Carlson whisked Ben away to show him his newest horse.

I was an outsider here, but the land was welcoming me. It was so different than the view I'd experienced a million times out my bedroom window back home. It was freeing to be able to stare at the horizon. I could live on a ranch with wide skies and seemingly endless land.

"The southwest section is where the cattle roam. Over there is Lake Diefenbaker," Thomas said coming up beside me. He leaned forward on the porch rails and pointed. There was a large scar on the back of his hand, and it reminded me to cover mine. "It's really beautiful, and the water is incredibly clean. Sometimes we go there for midnight swims. It's probably too cold for you, though, eh princess?"

"I grew up swimming in mountain lakes so I'm pretty sure I can handle it," I said.

Thomas raised an eyebrow. "The Rocky Mountains?"

I nodded. "The most beautiful place in the world."

"Must have been great growing up in your castle there."

"It could have been if I wasn't—"

Damn it, Thomas was good. I pressed my lips together for fear of saying anything else personal.

The corners of his mouth lifted. "Well, if you're up for a swim, you just might get to see me in a speedo. You think my butt looks good in jeans? You just wait…you won't be able to keep your hands off me," he said, grinning.

I wanted to smile, but couldn't allow him the satisfaction. "You're such a dickhead."

"Nah, I'm not," he said, his grin even wider. "Anyway, did you pick out your bed yet?"

I shook my head.

"C'mon inside. Your palace awaits."

I followed him into the bunkhouse, which was a long and narrow room without any decoration. Bunk beds with heavy grey blankets lined the walls, and a couple of chairs sat next to a cracked mirror. The windows were murky and the curtains thin. The room could sleep twelve people, but there wasn't room for anything but sleep.

"You can wash up over there," Thomas said, tossing the bag of clothes he'd picked out for me at the Wal-Mart onto a lower bunk before pointing to the corner of the room.

Once back there, I discovered a locker-room style shower. Wide open. No doors. Only tiled floors and walls with four spouts that stuck out of the walls next to hooks for towels. I grew up surrounded by guards and nannies and pretty much never had the option of being modest, so this didn't bother me. I'd bet by the way Thomas was quietly waiting for a reaction he suspected I would freak out.

"This place is…"

"A dump?" Ben said, suddenly behind me. I hadn't even heard him approach, even with his loud stomp-like walk and wooden-heeled boots.

"No, I was going to say it's great."

His hat was off and gripped tightly in his hands. "This place is clean and warm, but not much else. After a full day of work, though, you won't care what it looks like. As for showering? I'll make sure you have some privacy."

Thomas sidled past us with soap and towels. "Maybe Kate isn't all that shy," he said with a wink.

Ben ignored him. "Go change into some decent clothes and meet us outside. And hurry up about it."

Thomas whipped around to face Ben, soap dropping to the floor. "Why are you ordering her around like that?" he asked, challenging his boss with a bold stare.

I braced for another argument. Thomas and Ben's head butting wasn't about me, I suspected. There was a history between them, and I was just a catalyst to dredge it up.

"It's okay, I'm—"

"Used to it?" Thomas finished. "Yeah, we can see that. So Ben, how about treating her with a bit more respect, considering how she's been treated before... us."

Ben stood firm. "I'm just treating her like I would any other employee, because that's what she is. Same as you, Thomas. So remind yourself who signs your paycheck and get the hell out so the girl can get changed."

Thomas fumed, his cheeks turning red. I could see there were many things he wanted say, but he held back.

"I really would like to change. In private," I murmured.

Thomas gave Ben a glare, then in a huff, marched off.

"The only reason that boy hasn't been fired is because he's a hard worker," Ben said. My lie detector went off; there was definitely a different reason. "Stay away from him." His stomping shook the hardwood as he headed for the door. "He goes through women like toilet paper."

"I—"

The door slammed, and I didn't get a chance to explain how incredibly uninterested I was in Thomas. Self-assured, full of himself, hot-headed, and extremely good looking, he was irritating. Although, he somehow made me momentarily forget about the things in my life I was angry about. As I dug through the clothes he'd picked out for me, I was astonished he'd accurately guessed my bra size. The black lacy fabric fit perfectly and felt good against my skin, so did the jeans and the soft blue sweater. It was amazing to be fully dressed. It boosted my mood and made me feel not quite as vulnerable.

I glanced in the mirror. The clothes were nice, but I looked painfully thin in them. My hipbones were sharp, and my face seemed drawn. I appeared haggard. Sad. I was about to turn away from my horrid reflection, but a thin ray of sun straining through the curtains caught the gold of the maple leaf and silver of the pendant hanging around my neck. It stopped me in my tracks, shedding light on the most obvious solution to my problem—DNA.

I had it. Encased in resin in the silver pendant. The drop of Lenore's blood that was proof I wasn't her biological child. She had left it to me, giving me the means, the power, to break my ties to the inheritance and get my life back. All I had to do was get John Marchessa to believe me and analyze it—without him killing me first. I just needed time. Time to figure out how to do that...

"C'mon, Kate, hurry up. There's work to do," Ben yelled from outside on the porch.

I tucked the necklaces safely underneath the sweater, then pulled on a pair of comfy black boots. I felt better knowing I had a way out of this mess, and a second glance in the mirror reflected that.

"For God's sake, Kate, while I'm young," Ben shouted.

LUKE

11

Countdown To Launch

THE LAST TWENTY-FOUR HOURS HAD BEEN A NIGHTMARE OF DEAD ends and disappointment. Being stuck in a motel room with Oliver was the last place I wanted to be. Instead, I ghosted the streets of town—some butthole not worth knowing the name of—and tried to calm my head. Worry was eating me alive. I paced, stomped, and got curious eyes from the townsfolk going about their business. Hours rolled by. And when my feet couldn't take any more and my eyes would barely focus, I headed back to the motel.

Strange sounds greeted me the moment I entered the parking lot. There were a few people gathered outside their doors. Judging by a shirtless and angry man, it was obvious most had been rudely awoken. The crowd's anger was directed at Oliver's room. Coming from it were thrashing sounds as if a raging bull was trapped inside.

"He's probably on dope. Somebody call the manager," a woman said. "Or the cops."

An orange-haired lady poked her husband in the arm. "Just go in there and shut him the hell up! I need my beauty sleep."

The shirtless man had a phone in his hand, and I knew what number he was about to dial. I sprinted toward him with the room key in hand.

"Whoa, hang on…don't call the cops," I said breathlessly. "That's just my little brother in there. He's…uh…" I scrambled for a lie. "He has epileptic seizures. I'll get him calmed down, all right? I've got his meds."

The shirtless man puffed up his chest. "You better shut him up or I'll have to do something about it."

I nodded agreeably and waited for the crowd to dissipate before opening the door.

What I saw didn't make sense.

Oliver was in the middle of the room, swinging at the air. His fists were bloody, and he was swearing at someone…but there was nobody there.

"Oliver?" I said carefully and shut the door behind me.

My voice startled him. He turned to face me, eyes rolling around in his head. He swayed, then stumbled backward and crushed the neck of a fallen lamp. Was he drunk?

"Oliver?" I said again. "Everything okay there, dude?"

He blinked rapidly. Seeming confused, he glanced wildly around at the thrashed room. The bed was sideways and sheets torn off, the TV was on the floor and upside down, massive dents in the drywall were marked with dabs of blood—damn. I used my credit card to pay for the room. The cost for damages were going to be rock-star worthy.

Oliver's chest heaved with ragged breaths. "What the hell is going on?" he asked, voice breaking.

"I don't know. But, holy crap, I sure wouldn't want you as a room-mate."

"Luke?" he asked, as if he didn't recognize me.

Was he having a stroke? There was something wrong with him. His eyes narrowed. He gritted his teeth, lip curling into a snarl. "Yeah, it's me. Your favorite guy, Luke. Should I call you a doctor or something?"

He straightened his shoulders before puffing out his chest. "I hate you," he said, lunging for me.

I could have moved out of the way, but then his stupid head would have met the doorframe with full force and he would have knocked himself out. Instead, I stood there like a human pillow—which wasn't so good for me. The bloke winded me and threw a fist at my face.

"Oliver, get a hold of yourself," I yelled. "We're a team now, remember?"

He pulled back his arm to hit me again and I caught it, surprised it wasn't much of a struggle to hold him back. I knew what kind of strength Oliver was capable of, but he was strangely weak. Yes, my cheek was stinging, but not throbbing like it should have been. I pushed him away, sending him stumbling backward onto his butt as if the bones of his legs had turned to dust.

"We are a team?" he said, shaking his head as if trying to remember our mutual bad dream.

There was the tang of blood in my mouth. "Uh, yeah. We have to find Kaya. Remember her? What is wrong with you, Oliver?"

His eyes fluttered madly. He'd cut his arm on something. A large gash ran from his elbow to his wrist, bleeding onto the beige carpet. It was bad. I carefully sidestepped around him to the bathroom.

He was sweating. Spitting words. "Pills. I need them. Right now."

At least the bathroom remained intact. I took in a deep breath, hoping the man with no shirt wasn't calling the cops. "You mean those yellow things you keep munching on?"

"Yes. Get me some, Luke."

Oliver was a drug addict, but nothing about it seemed fitting. "I don't even know what it is you are hooked on. I can get you an aspirin if you want in a minute. But for now, here's a towel for your arm. You're bleeding all over the place."

Ignoring me, he struggled to his feet. "Get me those pills! Now," he yelled, then dove at me again. This time, I got out of the way and let him vault himself into the closet. When he stumbled back out of it, he left behind a completely crumpled plastic door. It only stunned him for a second.

His eyes were wide as plates. "Oh my God… she told me this would happen. I tried to wean myself off them, but I can't. My head hurts. The anger is consuming me…I have to get some more…"

"Who told you this would happen?"

"She did," he yelled.

"Whoa, calm down… judging by the looks of ya, I'd say getting off those pills is probably a good idea." I picked up a glass from the floor, keeping my eyes on him the whole time.

"Some more pills… I need them… And… I hate you, Luke," he hissed, his eyes clouded over. His arms started swinging, and he barreled through the room toward me. Avoiding his slow-as-molasses attempts to strike me was easy. Waiting for him to tire out so I wouldn't have to hurt him wasn't. Whatever was making him rage uncontrollably had also made him exceptionally tenacious. After ten minutes of dancing around the destroyed room, I had no choice but to give him a shot to the head or risk an unwanted visit from the cops.

"I'm sorry," I said, winding a telephone cord around his massive wrists when he collapsed into a heap onto the floor. I got the mattress back on the box spring and struggled to get him on it, then tied his feet together. The cut on his arm didn't look too deep, but it had bled enough to turn the sheets into something out of a horror scene. I ripped them, wrapping his arm carefully with shreds of the cheap linen, and then put a pillow under his head. His eyes flickered open, and he watched me silently.

"It seems as if you are having a bit of withdrawal," I said casually. There was no sense poking the bear.

His lip was bleeding and his voice now sounded like the Oliver of yesterday. "Yeah, I'd say so."

"What are you hooked on?"

"Painkillers. Some experimental Eronel crap. I've got a couple of busted ribs. When I was searching for Kaya, they made the pain bearable." Panic and fear shone in his eyes. "Listen, you can't untie me, Luke. I think I might try to kill you. Or anyone who comes near me."

"Yah, I kinda figured that. I just hope you get your head together soon. We've gotta find… her."

His brown eyes blinked rapidly. "Just go then," he said.

"And leave you alone?"

His eyes rolled back slightly, and he labored to re-focus them. "Yeah."

As enticing as that thought was, Oliver probably needed me more than Kaya did at the moment. Besides, she'd never forgive me if I just walked away. So, here we were again, him hanging from the edge of a cliff and me not able to let go. Fantastic.

"I'm gonna stick around, Oliver. I'm kinda getting a kick out of watching you suffer."

"Great," he said, then his eyes shut.

A phone softly buzzed from somewhere. Dumping Oliver's backpack, I found his cell. "Sindra is calling you…"

He was out cold. I held his phone in my hand, wondering if I should answer it. I knew about Sindra and guessed she was probably who Oliver had called back at the bar. Maybe she had information about Kaya.

An involuntary shudder rolled down my spine when I pushed the answer button. "Hello?" I said quickly.

There was a pause. "Where's Oliver?" said a cold and professional voice with a slightly British accent. It fit Kaya's description of Sindra.

"He's, uh, having a nap."

Another pause. "Is he acting a bit… strange?"

"Yeah. You could say he's not quite himself."

"I see. Am I to assume I am speaking to Luke?"

I cleared my throat. Obviously, she knew about me, too. "Yes."

"Well, Luke, Oliver is going through withdrawal. He might start getting very sick. Will you look after him?"

I detected desperation in the question. "That depends. Do you have any information for me?" I asked, hoping to barter Oliver's well-being for any clues to Kaya's whereabouts.

"Yes," she said. "I know where Kaya is. For the next two weeks, you must take care of Oliver. After he's better, I'll share her location."

Now the shudder rolled down to my toes. "Two weeks?"

"Yes. If Oliver lasts that long, he'll be in the clear and I'll tell him personally where to find her. But if he dies…"

"Whoa lady! What do you mean if he dies? Should I take him to a hospital?"

Sindra tried to hide her concern with a flat tone. "No. There's nothing they could do there. Just give him orange juice, lots of it. Dramamine and alcohol to sedate him, too, but not mixed together. Keep him restrained so he doesn't harm himself. Oh, and put him on his side when he blacks out to reduce the risk of him choking on his own vomit. If he quits breathing… Well, you could call an ambulance, but they won't be able to do anything. Just please, don't leave him alone."

"This is insane. I'm not a nurse."

"Listen, Oliver's health in exchange for Kaya's whereabouts or you will never see her again. Got it? She is as safe as she could possibly be for now, of that I can promise you. But it won't last forever. I wish you good luck. You're going to need it."

She hung up.

I went to the bathroom to try to settle my raw nerves by splashing water on my face, and then filled up a glass of it for the beast. I lifted his head. His eyes sprung open when I put the cup to his mouth.

"I hate you, Luke," Oliver sputtered after guzzling greedily.

"Yeah. So you've said."

His eyes met mine, faced twisted in pain and desperation. "But we need each other."

"Appears so."

"I hate that, too."

I agreed. "It's not ideal."

"Was that Sindra?" he asked. "Did she find Kaya?"

I nodded. "Yes. Can she be trusted?"

Oliver dragged in a labored breath. "Sindra's word is concrete. She is the only one we can trust. Did I tell you I like donuts? Maple glazed. Kaya doesn't. Oh my God! We have to find her. Luke, help me find her!"

Oliver was drifting back into his crazed state. "I will. It'll be easier if you stop trying to kill me, though."

"I can't guarantee that."

I moved the glass a safe distance away.

"I feel it… my head spinning out of control again," Oliver said sadly. "I can tell I'm drifting into that red zone, and I don't want to go there."

I made sure the cord was still wrapped tightly around his wrists and ankles. "I'll keep you under control."

"Thanks," he said, eyes rolling around in his head. "Oh, and one more thing…"

I braced for an onslaught of cruelty. "What?"

"I… I'm going to throw up."

KAYA

12

BRANDED

I WAS STANDING BETWEEN A STEAMING STOVETOP AND A COUNTER covered with enough pie dough to bake an entire orchard. I was in hell—also known as Mrs. Carlson's kitchen.

"Good Lord, dearie, have ya never baked a pie before?" she said, coming to inspect my progress.

Her apron and her hands were stained pink with beet juice. When she rubbed her sun-spotted forehead, she left behind a smudge. Her appearance suggested a sweet grandma from the movies with grey hair piled up into a bun and a twinkle in her eyes. She'd welcomed me into her home with open arms. But now, she was ready to boot me out the door. I had pie dough stuck to my hands and the kitchen counter, but nowhere near the pie plates. Worse yet, the pot I was supposed to mind was now bubbling over and splattering all over the place.

"I haven't really cooked much," I confessed.

Mrs. Carlson dove for the chili and took it off the heat. "And Ben hired you as his housekeeper?"

"He felt sorry for me, I guess." I wrestled with the sticky dough, making a bigger mess.

"And why is that?" she asked, lowering her shiny pink glasses to look at me, suspiciously eyeing my stomach.

My mind raced for a reason that wouldn't have Mrs. Carlson asking questions or thinking I was knocked up. "I'm saving up money for school. For college."

Her face relaxed. "Ah, that's admirable. Still, I'm surprised Ben would hire someone like you."

"Like me?"

She cleared her throat and lowered her voice. "Yes. You know… someone who can't cook."

"Huh," was all I could think of for a response.

"Well, ya must be real darn good at cleanin'." She pulled a knife from the kitchen drawer and approached me a little too fast. I froze in terror at the shiny blade heading in my direction.

"Whoa… I'm not that upset you ruined the pie dough." Mrs. Carlson laughed. "Lord thunderin' Jesus, you're a skittish filly. I just want to get the mess off your hands and the counter."

My past had made me irrational, and justifiably so. Obviously, this woman didn't want to kill me. Still, I trembled through a forced grin while she gently scraped over my scarred hand. Though she paused to give the bite mark a closer look, she brushed it off as nothing. But when her eyes caught and centered on the scar on my neck, she gasped and struggled to hold her tongue. Some story brewed in her head, which probably wasn't nearly as awful as the actual truth.

"Dog attack," I said.

"Uh-huh," she said.

Turning away, she pointed out the window, thankfully with no questions. "See that girl there, digging a hole? That's my daughter Marlene. She prefers gardening over horses and cattle, and Lord knows she ain't of any use in the kitchen, so you two will get along fine. I'll make quiche with the pie dough, it's too roughed up for fruit pies now, and try to save the chili you've managed to burn." After pointing to a cooler by the door, she headed back to the stove. "Get Marlene to drive you and the sandwiches out to the boys in the field. Take 'em lots of beer, too."

I felt like a putz. Cooking with Thomas had been a breeze compared to this. "I'm sorry. I'm sure I can figure out how to do this."

Mrs. Carlson regarded me with a motherly kindness. "My neighbor Bess is on her way over. She can chop and peel with lightning speed. So, get going now and don't worry about a thing, all right?"

Still digging pie dough out from under my nails, I headed outside and approached the young woman named Marlene. She was tall, probably close to six feet, and had the slim figure of a supermodel. She wore a black shirt tucked into a pair of tight jeans, and auburn hair grazed her shoulders in soft curls. She was singing as she drove the shovel into the earth. I paused and watched her for a moment. She seemed so… content.

"Hi there," I said.

She froze. The singing stopped. But she didn't raise her head or turn to look at me.

"I'm Kate. Your mom wants you to help me take food out to the men in the field."

There was no reaction.

I spoke a little louder. "She said you could drive me?"

Still nothing. I stared at the side of Marlene's face while she eyed the ground. I tried again.

"If you're busy, that's fine. I can carry the food out there myself…"

"Ha!" she said with a laugh. "You've got one useless arm, have no idea where to go, and by the looks of ya, an hour in the sun would turn you into nothing but a raging blister."

How would she know? She hadn't even looked up from her shovel.

I was about to protest, but she straightened up and turned toward me. My breath caught; one side of her face was pretty with lightly tanned unblemished skin over a high cheekbone and a piercing hazel eye, but the other side was disfigured. The skin covering the right side of her face was dark purple, as if a football-sized blueberry had hit her hard and left a stain.

"Nice, eh?" she said bitterly, holding the shovel like she wanted to drive it through my face. "It's a birthmark. I was born with it," she said with a growl. "God gave me a punch to the face. I've lived with it now for eighteen years and don't care what you think of it. So go ahead and stare. I don't give a shit."

I gulped hard, feeling sorry for her, and knowing that was exactly what she wouldn't want. I kept my eyes level, not shying away. "All right then," I said, hoping my voice sounded firm but friendly. "Thanks for the info. So… will you help me out? I don't want to get in trouble with your mom. I already ruined the dessert and burned the chili."

Marlene's eyes lit up. "On purpose?" She seemed hopeful.

"Ha. No. I'm a complete wreck in the kitchen. I mean, what the heck is a ladle? And why does it matter what temperature your hands are when you're 'turning the dough into pea-sized crumbles'? And what on earth does simmering even mean?"

Marlene marched across the potatoes to stand before me, startling me out of my kitchen nightmare reverie. She rubbed her palms on her jeans, which didn't do a thing to remove the dirt, then stuck out her hand.

"I hate cooking," she said, her serious tone an invitation for a hand-shake.

I stifled a giggle, mostly to cover my discomfort at her proximity and intense grip around my fingers. "But eating is good," I said, giving her hand a pump.

A genuine smile brought a blush to the white side of her face. I met her eyes fully and took in her features. A perfectly straight and tiny nose, full mouth, and high cheekbones… the birthmark that covered her eyelid and reached far down her neck was the only disfigurement. She was waiting for me to be bothered by it, but I wasn't.

"Sandwiches. Can't go wrong," she said.

"Damn straight," I agreed.

"Pickles and mustard on rye with pastrami."

"Plain old cheese and lettuce for me."

"Mayo is gross."

I nodded. "Yep. Eggs sitting in a jar on a shelf that can last for years? It's just not logical."

She nodded. I motioned to the cooler of food and cases of beer Mrs. Carlson was now putting on the porch. "So, whadya say?"

Marlene was eager to help. She tackled the heavy items, shrugging me off when I tried to help. It became obvious she hid whatever insecurities she had about her face behind brute strength. With the truck loaded and her at the wheel, we ambled across a freshly cut field with the food and booze. Minutes into the bumpy drive with the heat of the sun filling the cab of an ancient green truck, she decided to talk.

"Where ya from?" she asked.

"A small town out west," I said, bracing myself as we went through a rough patch.

The truck jolted, and Marlene swore under her breath. "Stupid gophers…. I keep shootin' em but they keep coming back and digging their holes. I like the cute little buggers, but they wreck everything," she said angrily. "So… boyfriend?"

Thinking of Luke, I gulped. "Not anymore."

"Parents?"

I liked that she was satisfied with short answers. "Dead," I said, wishing Henry and Rayna actually were.

"Mine, too," she said without sadness.

"Oh, I thought Mrs. Carlson was your mom?"

The field stretched out flatter now with only the odd strip of skinny trees obstructing the view. Cattle started to be visible just over a small ridge, and Marlene slowed the truck for a stray cow being urged back to the herd by a speckled dog. "My mom died giving birth to me and my dad died of a heroin overdose soon after, so I never knew them. Mrs. Carlson—Kay—took me in when no one else wanted the baby with the purple face."

I had a jealous pang at the thought of growing up in Mrs. Carlson's care. "You're lucky you have a mom."

"Yeah. But the insufferable woman thinks cooking and cleaning and sewing are the only things a 'God-fearing Christian woman' should do. The church has her brainwashed into believing all sorts of archaic bullshit. They've lured her and all the women around here into their lair, filled their heads full of stories, taken their money, and then sent them home to pass judgement and be jerks to all the 'non-believers' under the pretense of being forgiven for their actions on Sundays. So, while I'm home looking after the animals and making sure the garden doesn't get overtaken with weeds and bugs, she's spending hours praying for whatever sins I did to get myself this ugly face."

She inhaled deeply, now seeming embarrassed of the rant I suspected she'd been holding in for a long time. I studied her as she drove, the disfigured side of her face plain to see. "You're not ugly, Marlene," I said, "just lovely shades of purple and cream."

She bristled. "How can you say I'm not ugly? Look at me."

"I am. And what one person thinks is ugly, another might find beautiful. I see a strong, vibrant person who is intensely passionate about the things she believes in. To me, that's just as beautiful as your physical appearance. Ugly is such a stupid word anyway. It means nothing. I've seen art worth millions I think sucks, and stones at the water's edge of a lake that are more stunning than diamonds. Beauty is subjective."

She pursed her lips and gave me the oddest glance. Then, as if I hadn't even spoken, she cleared her throat and pointed ahead. "There they are."

We drove into a mass of cattle. When the truck stopped, the first thing I noticed was the sound of restless animals; it was a loud drone. A hum like nothing I'd ever heard before. Men on horseback had separated the calves from the cows, and an elaborate system of fences and riders were keeping them organized. The animals didn't seem upset. It was as if they were 'talking' to each other as the humans kept them calm. The smell was rank—grass, crap, and burning hair. I followed Marlene toward a makeshift pen, seeing two men holding down a calf and another pressing a scalding iron to its rump. The calf barely struggled as its hair and skin smoked, but I instinctively clutched my wounded arm. Luke had done the same thing to me, cauterizing my wound.

"It doesn't hurt them," Marlene said, misunderstanding my discomfort. "I mean, they don't love it, but they're fine."

"Why do they do it?"

"Lots of cattle roaming around out here. No one wants to argue over whose animal is whose. Every cow marked with CC is Carlson's property."

In the middle of the pen, Ben rode Zander. He perched majestically atop the shining black horse. He rode in a wide circle, rope in hand, and when a calf was let in to the pen, he maneuvered Zander into a gallop behind it before tossing his rope and catching the calf by the hind legs.

Thomas was on another horse and swiftly roped the calf's neck. In unison, they pulled their rope taut and brought the animal to the ground. Within seconds, two other wiry cowboys were wrestling the calf onto its side and holding it down while Mr. Carlson applied the hot branding iron. Vaccinations were administered by identical blond women moving perfectly with each other, and then the animal was castrated. There was no one yelling, issuing orders, or any sort of chitchat. This was efficiency at its best, and it was mesmerizing.

I got lost in the action. Entranced, my body glued to the fence and all senses captivated as I watched Ben and Thomas, their movements a predictable dance for my mind to surrender to. The repetition, the animals, the people, the pen, the pasture beyond it, and the expanse of blue sky so blindingly bright...

And a familiar figure off in the distance...

My mind caught, as if snagged on a hook. I zeroed in on the shape of a thin female with dark skin, hazy in the field. The pit of my stomach danced; I knew that person.

Marlene tapped me on the shoulder and handed me a sandwich. "Cheese and lettuce. No mayo."

"Do you see that person over there?" I asked, ignoring her outstretched hand and pointing to the lithe shape now moving toward a truck.

Marlene spun around in the direction of my finger. "Kind of..."

"Do you know who that is?" I asked, feeling the blood drain from my face.

"Uh, nope. There are all kinds of people here today. Neighbors and friends of pals, and who the heck knows who else. Lots of peeps I don't recognize. Why?"

It couldn't be. There's no way. Not in a million years would Sindra know where I was. It was impossible... but I sensed her. My hand instinctively flew to my chest to make sure the necklace was still there; the familiar pendant was safe and warm against my skin.

I jumped when a hand tapped my shoulder.

"Kate? Everything all right?"

I turned to face Ben. Face glowing, hair slicked with sweat and flat to his head. I noticed Marlene's shoulders slump at the sight of him, and I caught the sandwich she'd been holding out to me before it hit the dirt.

"I'm fine. It's all good," I said a little too quickly, then tried to be casual by taking a bite of gummy white bread and trying not to gag. My stomach was churning as my gaze wandered back to the truck in the distance with the familiar figure getting inside.

"Is she bothering you?" Ben asked.

The question caught me off guard. "Is who bothering me?"

It pained him to acknowledge Marlene, who was doing her best to ignore him, too.

"Her. Marlene. Is she—"

I stopped him. "What? No, of course not. Not at all."

"Good." His voice lowered into a whisper. "Why aren't you in the house? I told you to stay there."

The truck was moving away. The hazy field swallowed whoever was at the wheel. I had to be imagining things. That was the only explanation. No way was that Sindra.

"Kate?" Ben said, becoming irritated. "Why are you out here?"

I tried to get the bread down my throat to speak. "Oh. Mrs. Carlson had some neighbor named Bess coming over to help her. They wanted rid of me. So I offered to help Marlene instead."

Ben shook his head angrily. "That girl doesn't need any help."

Marlene continued to stand there, staring at her feet. "Uh, do you have a problem with her?" I asked quietly.

Ben spoke with venom. "She's tough as an ox, stubborn as a mule, and nothing but trouble. Stay away from her."

I felt I needed to defend my newfound friend. "She's been very kind to me."

"Kind? Not sure that's in her nature," Ben said, loud enough for Marlene to hear. "Anyway, get her to take you back to the house and stay there. Make yourself useful with the women somehow. You'll only be in the way out here, and I don't need the distraction of worrying about you."

Marlene's head snapped up. "You're a chauvinistic asshole, Ben," she spat.

And before I could agree, her hand latched onto my mine and she pulled me away.

Marching alongside Marlene, I watched the truck with the familiar figure become a dot in the distance.

As Marlene and I pulled up the last of the carrots from her precious garden, the men started to trickle back in. Soon, the farmhouse doors were flung open and tables of food were set up outside next to three massive barbecues smoking with thick slabs of red meat. I avoided the chili and the quiche and was teased about the lack of animal on my plate by a loud-mouthed man attacking an almost-raw portion of cow. I proudly told him it was my decision, my choice—one I'd made after looking into the eyes of an animal like the one on the barbecue—to follow a vegetarian diet whenever possible. Then the teasing began. I ignored it. Thomas ended it by firmly telling the man that only an asshole or someone with a guilty conscience about what he himself was eating would make an issue about what someone wasn't eating. Loudmouth had no reply to that.

Conversations swirled, the beer flowed, and when the sun went down, a massive bonfire was brought to life. Loudmouth became too drunk to talk. Hank entertained us with a song he'd written. Mick told lame jokes, and I often glanced up to see Thomas's eyes settled on me. There was something about his self-assured, blatant stare that was infuriating. It made me want to slap him and made my spine tingle at the same time. I kept telling myself I didn't like him. But every time I allowed myself to stare back to glare, or at least make him feel uncomfortable, he smiled and made me forget why I'd ogled him in the first place. So I did my best to avoid giving my attention to anything or anyone in his direction.

As the heat of the bonfire increased, so did the drunkenness. The twin sisters who had been administering vaccinations were arguing with Mrs. Carlson and her neighbor about carrot cake. Mr. Carlson and Ben, along with the wrestling cowboys and a veterinarian so skinny he looked like he'd break in a breeze, talked about ranching—of which I barely understood a word. When the Hericksons, the Greys, and the Franklins showed up with more food and booze than was humanely necessary, the laughter escalated. Everyone seemed happy.

Except Marlene.

She never said a word. She barely looked at anyone—and no one paid attention to her. I felt Ben's eyes burrow into my back when I left his side to sit next to her by the fire.

"Is it always like this?" I asked, referring to the increasingly intoxicated state of the group of people around us. Loudmouth was now out cold on the grass with a mini-pig curled up next to him.

Marlene tucked an auburn curl behind her ear. "Yep. My family loves any excuse to party," she said dismally.

Ben stared. Although the heat from the bonfire blurred his image, his gaze was intense and unavoidable. Mr. Carlson was leaning in to him, re-counting some horse tale, but it was obvious Ben's full focus was on Marlene and me.

"Your dad looks like Santa Claus," I said to Marlene, pretending not to be bothered by Ben.

Whatever she'd taken a sip of shot out her nose with a laugh. "I love Santa Claus. But I hate Christmas."

Oddly, I agreed.

She perked up, turning with a lopsided smile and a gleam in her eye. She was about to say something when she realized Ben's glare was now solely focused on her. Suddenly, she bolted from the bench.

"This is bullshit. I'm out of here," she said, storming off.

I leapt to my feet and Ben stood, too, his back rigid. Thomas sprang upward as well—they were way too concerned with what I was doing. Marlene was right; this was bullshit. I cast a warning glance at both to leave me alone.

"Wait up," I called after Marlene.

I practically had to run to keep up with her long, determined strides toward the barn. The structure stood not far from the house, and it was painted the traditional red and white. Wide doors on the bottom and loft windows made it look like a face, ominous and spooky under the full light of the moon. Moths were circling the lanterns. Inside, hay, freshly tossed into the horse stalls, made it smell clean and green. The air was at least ten degrees colder, and I was instantly chilled to the bone.

"So, what's with you and Ben?" I asked, shivering.

Marlene went to stand before one of the stalls. A beautiful white horse reached for her, and she stroked its muzzle. "He caught Hank and me smoking pot a couple of years ago."

That wasn't the answer I was expecting. "You and Hank? Hank doesn't seem like the type—"

Marlene turned to face me, the dim light in the barn making the purple side of her face almost black. "Oh, Hank is the type, but believe it or not, I'm not. Never touch the stuff."

"I don't understand."

Marlene peered around to make sure we were alone. "I was just hanging out with Hank to watch over him because he does such stupid things all the time. I took the blame for it because Ben hates the kid enough as it is. I told Ben it was my weed."

"Whoa. That was pretty nice of you Marlene."

Her affection for the boy was obvious. "Hank gets treated badly sometimes because he's, well… you know."

"Special?"

Marlene gulped. "Yeah. I know what it feels like."

"Of course." I nodded, feeling horrible for her. The heels of her boots clicked over the barn floor to the stall where a massive Clydesdale horse was penned. The sheer size of the beast was terrifying, but I suspected there wasn't much that would intimidate Marlene. "Is that the only reason he dislikes you so much?" I pressed.

She sighed. "No… I shot Zander in the butt with my slingshot once."

"What?"

"While Ben was riding him. He got bucked off."

I pictured that in my head and stifled a laugh. "When was this?"

"A long time ago."

"And… why would you do that?"

Marlene's face grew stern. "I was trying to help him and Dad with branding. Ben told me I was in the way and to get back to the kitchen where I belonged."

I laughed. He'd pretty much said the same thing to me. "Well, he deserved it then."

"He also called Hank an idiot."

"Well, that's not very nice."

"No, it's not. So I may have put a decaying fish under the seat of his new truck. It was hot outside. He was pretty mad."

"Oh?"

"And once, when the vet was taking horse piss samples, I may have served some to him as apple juice."

A snort of laughter almost escaped, but Marlene's serious expression kept it contained.

"I also buried his favorite hat next to the raspberries. And replaced his shampoo with the grease Mom keeps under the sink. Oh…. and I might have sprinkled an entire package of turmeric onto his pillow and sleeping bag one night before a rodeo."

My face contorted as I tried to contain my laughter. "Turmeric?"

"Yeah. The spice. Ben went to bed drunk and sweaty and woke up the color of mustard. It didn't wash off."

"Marlene, remind me to stay on your good side!"

She grinned, but there was sadness behind it. "He deserved it."

There was something she wasn't telling me. "So, you did all that because he told you to go to the kitchen?"

"Uh, yeah. But I'm over it. I won't torment him anymore."

But she wasn't over it. I could tell by the way she twirled a lock of hair with flared nostrils and gritted teeth. There was more to this story, but I wouldn't press. I'd give her the same respect she'd given me.

"Yeah. I think you got him back," I said. Reaching for a horse's nose, I forgot about my stupid arm and winced from the pain.

"I told you something. Now it's your turn… What's with the arm?"

Marlene asked.

The cold was making it ache even more than usual. I wandered to the stall where Zander was, his regal black coat shining, nose tipping to my hand for a treat. I wrestled to get control of my voice. "Well, since we are being truthful with each other... I was in the mountains. When I tried to save a friend from getting shot, I fell into some rapids. I got impaled on a tree, and then my boyfriend—" The thought of Luke almost doubled me over, the longing for him so painful. "—my friend rescued me and had to cauterize the wound with the blade of a knife he'd heated up in a fire."

Marlene was completely unfazed. "Cool," she said flatly. "You've been branded. Does that mean you belong to your, uh... friend?"

Her eyes met mine, and I instantly knew I'd made a wise decision in choosing her for company. "Yeah. You could say that."

"Where is your friend now?"

Luke. Thinking of him made every part of my body ache more than a million of those puncture wounds all at once. It stole my breath.

"Kate?" Marlene prompted.

I cleared my throat, hoping my voice wouldn't sound pathetic. "I had to leave him to keep him safe. My family is nothing like yours. If we stayed together, he would probably end up dead because of them. I couldn't take that chance."

"Tell me about him. What does he look like?"

I couldn't stop myself. I described him head to toe, recounting every detail as if to confirm in my mind that he was real. When I was done, Marlene didn't say a word.

The oats in her hand remained at her side while the Clydesdale bobbed its head impatiently. My mind spun madly. Had I said too much? Of course I had. Why on earth had I told this strange girl I barely knew my secret? Hadn't I already made this mistake with Angela? Angela... my first female friend who disappeared because I got caught sneaking out of the estate to see her at the Derrick Bar. What happened to her? And why was I putting Marlene at risk, too?

I couldn't trust anyone with who I was.

"Hey," Marlene said fiercely, demanding my attention. "Your secret is safe with me. I would do anything to protect those I love. I get it."

I stood before this strange girl in the freezing barn, suddenly wanting to cry my eyeballs out. I sniffed back the onset of tears.

"Buck up, buttercup. A girl like you has to stay strong," she said.

"A girl like me?"

"Yeah. Viewed as weak. Pigeonholed into some stereotypical bullshit because you are pretty and delicate looking. If you can be selfless enough to leave the love of your life for his own good, you can do anything. That is strength. That is power. Pull from it to get you through. Don't do none of that darn cryin' nonsense. That doesn't do anybody any good."

Marlene's gruff advice startled me into standing a little taller. She was right.

Zander put his nose to my ear. His hot breath made little clouds of steam around my cheeks. With a huff, he seemed to convey he agreed with Marlene.

"Let's go get some cake," Marlene said, finally giving the horse the treats in her hand. "My mom makes the best angel food, and if that doesn't make ya forget your troubles, nothing—"

She didn't finish. Suddenly, the power went out. We were instantly enveloped in the thick black of night. The air in my lungs caught.

"Ah, crap. Not again," Marlene said.

My heart rate quickened. The music that had been reaching us from the fire pit had abruptly ended, so did the buzzing sound of overhead lights. I swallowed hard when I realized I couldn't even see my own hands.

"Ya okay?" Marlene asked.

I mumbled something as my eyes adjusted to see moonlight making silvery waves on a few tufts of grass just outside the open barn doors. In the eerie quiet, Mr. Carlson's booming voice almost made me jump out of my skin.

"Marlene…" he yelled. "Try flipping the breaker in the utility room."

"I'm on it, Dad," she called.

I remained frozen where I was, relieved when Marlene's rustling produced a flashlight. The comforting flood of light reminded me to breathe.

"Dad's gone and rewired the whole ranch just so those darn mini-pigs can live in the Taj Mahal," she said. "The power is always going out now. C'mon, the utility room is just outside the back of the barn."

I tentatively followed her past the stalls of horses, their eyes lighting up in the flashlight beam like pairs of floating aliens. My chills multiplied, and I paused at the exit.

"You're not scared of the dark, are ya?" Marlene asked intuitively.

She shoved open the heavy barn doors, leveling her flashlight on a small coral where a metal shack stood in the corner. Ominous and creepy.

"No," I squeaked.

"Ah, heck. Yeah, you are. It's just dark, Kate, that's all," she said confidently. "Nothing is gonna happen. Here," she said, putting a cell phone in my hand. "Use the light on this, ya scaredy cat."

I eagerly switched it on and followed Marlene toward the shack. The metal door squealed loudly when she pulled on the handle, which brought forth a few restless sounds from the horses in the barn. I followed her into a small square room filled to the rafters with bottles of cleaning supplies, boxes, and shelves of scary-looking metal instruments. Marlene headed to the back where there was a massive panel on the wall covered in buttons and snaking multi-colored wires.

She cursed under her breath. "I don't remember which breaker it is.'"

I reached for a white plastic bottle, one of many on the shelves. It was decorated with skulls, crossbones, and warnings of every sort. Next to the words weed killer, it said, safe and effective.

Marlene kept muttering. "If I flip the wrong switch again, Dad will have my head. Last time this happened, I turned on the sprinklers and the irrigation system…ruined his new stereo."

I wasn't listening. I was about to put the bottle back on the shelf, but words on the side of the container caught my attention. Eronel Pharmaceuticals. I felt sick. Dad's precious company name was proudly emblazoned on this jug of poison. I recalled Regan patiently explaining to me how Eronel offered a cure for the very disease it had created. The company responsible for some of the most damaging toxins in history, specifically pesticides linked to infertility.

I knew that now, but I'd yet to have concrete evidence of it in my hands.

All Henry's ranting over eating organic and never letting me have red meat burst into my head as I held the jug in my hands. He most surely knew the connection between plant, animal, and human, and how it affected the chain of events that prompted childless couples to seek out his medicine. Regan had explained it all to me, and I'd understood it then. But now, being here in a place where I'd seen the cattle grazing on the pesticide-covered grass and watched the people chow down on those cattle, the connection snapped so vividly in place it was like a slap in the face. The lights came on—in my head that was—bright as the sun on a summer afternoon.

And then they came on in the metal shack.

"Got it," Marlene said triumphantly. A wide smile stretched over her face, which caused her right eye to almost disappear against the purple birthmark. The smile was short-lived when she caught a look at me. "Geez, you look like you seen a ghost, Kate. What's up?" she asked, turning off the flashlight.

I put the poison back on the shelf, and then moved to pick up another jug of something with a long name I couldn't pronounce. I recognized it from the table where the twin sisters had been delivering vaccinations earlier. It had Eronel Pharmaceutical prominently displayed on the lid. "Does your dad use all this stuff?"

"Well, yeah. That's why it's here."

"Do you put the pesticide in your garden?"

Marlene grew defensive. "Well, yeah. I don't need bugs and weeds taking over. Besides, it says it's safe."

I nodded, not wanting to upset her. "Right. Of course." I did my best to mask the hatred and disgust I had for my father. It was all I could do not to let loose a scream of rage from my throat. He was killing people, and he knew it.

"I'm cold and tired," I said.

Marlene asked no questions as she led the way to the bunkhouse. I was thankful for not having to fully explain my sudden need to go hide under blankets. With a pat on my shoulder, she left while I climbed onto the top bunk bed I'd claimed and continued to shiver, mostly in anger over the horrid things my father had done. I wondered what else he was up to. I couldn't possibly imagine what his power-hungry mind, endless resources, and love of genetics was stirring up now.

I tried to sleep, but my mind raced. I was still awake hours later when the boys came in. Hank, being loud, was promptly scolded by Ben and told to shut up. I felt the metal structure shake when Thomas silently flopped onto his bed, and I was grateful it wasn't Ben beneath me. Twisting in and out of a fitful sleep, I continued to shiver into the wee hours of the morning. It was only when Thomas got up and placed an extra blanket over me I fell fully asleep. Our eyes met when he pulled the grey wool up to my chin, but I was too tired to thank him.

KAYA

13

ẞINK ỢR ẞWIM

THE DAY WAS A BLUR; PULLING WEEDS, DIGGING HOLES, DELIVERING food out to where the men were still branding cattle, sweeping out the barn, trying to catch a horse in the pasture that didn't want to be caught, and washing the prized mini-pigs that squealed so loudly my ears would probably ring for days. I gave my mind over to the tasks, doing exactly what Marlene asked. By the time supper was over and the bonfire was lit, I realized I hadn't shed one tear the entire day. But now that the chores were done, the pain of missing Luke came back with crushing force.

"Beer?" Thomas said.

The sky was twinkling and clear, the evening air cool. He plunked down between Marlene and me on a wobbly bench, and flames from the bonfire reflected in his dark eyes. He'd shaved and changed into slim blue jeans and a soft grey sweatshirt, the smell of soap and spicy cologne on his skin mixed nicely with the wood smoke.

"I don't really drink," I said.

He grinned. "Maybe you should. What do you think, Marlene? Should Kate have a beer?"

Marlene's eyes grew wide, flattered Thomas was talking to her. "Personally, I think drinking is stupid. But if it prevents her from working herself into the ground as a distraction from what's bothering her, then I say go for it."

"Am I that obvious?" I said miserably.

Thomas laughed. "Here." He put a silver can in my hands. "You look like you need one."

One beer turned into two. When I started on my third, Mr. Carlson opened a bottle of what he called 'his finest hooch' and passed it around. It was disgusting. It was worse than the gin Angela had shared with me in her apartment.

Angela… She'd been fiercely independent with her wild-colored hair and tattoos. What advice would she give? And, what happened to her? After that night at the Derrick Bar, she went missing. Davis had tried to find her and came up empty-handed. I had to put all the scenarios I could imagine of where she ended up out of my mind. Because the outcome of each one ended with her dead.

Country music blared, the booze kept flowing, and when a freshly cracked bottle of liquid fire landed in Ben's hands, Mr. Carlson tried to take it back but Ben held on to it for dear life. He guzzled it greedily despite glares from Thomas and Mr. Carlson's pleading. I recalled the vodka bottles rolling out from under the front seat of his truck. It became glaringly apparent Ben had a drinking problem.

The wind picked up. We pushed the benches back from the flames and tried to rescue the roasting marshmallows. I'd never had one before. I thought they were disgusting so the pigs got the ones I didn't eat. People milled around, chatting, laughing, dancing, and among all the merriment, I felt horribly alone.

"Are you one of those sad drunks?" Thomas asked, taking the half-empty beer can from my hands and setting it on the grass.

"I don't know what that means," I said, noting the slight slur of my words.

"Some people get sad, some get happy. That's all."

I shrugged my shoulders. "I dunno. Which are you?"

"Well, first, I'm in too much control to get drunk, but if I did, I would be happy. I've got nothing to be sad about."

The music was turned up. Hysterical giggles came from somewhere behind me in the trees, but it was what Thomas said that captured my attention. "Really? You've got nothing at all to be sad about?"

"Nope. Why, is that shocking?"

"I just didn't think that was possible."

Thomas looked puzzled. "Sure it is."

"C'mon. Do you have a parent you mourn? A girlfriend who dumped you? Did something horrible happen in your childhood that haunts you? Did you ever lose lots of money? Or suffer from debilitating athlete's foot? There must be something."

He moved closer, his muscled thigh now touching mine on the bench. I should have cringed or inched away, but I didn't.

"I mean, there are things in the world to be sad about, hungry kids… war… you know, that sort of thing," he said, firelight in his eyes. "But for me, personally, I got nothing. My mom and pop are alive and well, and so are all my sisters and their kids. Mick is great… a best friend and a brother. I had a storybook childhood growing up on a ranch with lots of friends, and I've never had a girlfriend long enough to feel anything but relief after a break up. And athletes foot? That's funny, Kate. Look at me; I am perfect. Rock solid, strong as an ox, and drop-dead gorgeous. But I didn't have to tell you that, did I? So really, with everything I've got going on, what would I have to be sad about?"

He was being serious. He really was that happy. "That's amazing," I said, silently agreeing he was gorgeous—but certainly not my type. "It's refreshing and rare to meet someone like you."

"It is? Look around ..." Thomas made a sweeping gesture.

There wasn't a sad face on anyone. Even Marlene was grinning as Hank's hands flew to emphasize some story he was telling her. Out of the thirty or more people partying in the Carlson's front yard, there wasn't one sad face.

"You know, you're safe now, Kate," Thomas said, so close to my ear I could feel his breath. It gave me a slight tingle. "Don't worry about anything tonight. I got yer back. Just have fun; there's nothing wrong with that."

His hand moved to my leg. With what I could only describe as a brotherly touch, he gave me a gentle pat. It didn`t feel wrong, or like he was coming on to me or anything like that, but within seconds, Ben was looming over us, unsteady and slurring.

"What's going on here?" he demanded, blocking the heat of the fire.

"Just trying to get Kate drunk is all," Thomas replied in a tone meant to antagonize.

Ben leaned in to Thomas, his breath foul with alcohol. "I thought I told you to stay away from her," he hissed.

I was expecting an argument or some posturing like there had been yesterday in the bunkhouse, but Thomas spoke gently. "Uh, how much have you had to drink, Ben?"

Ben snarled an unintelligible response.

"You're not supposed to be doing that," Thomas said.

"Ah, mind your own business." Ben was loud enough for everyone around us to become quietly interested.

Thomas took in a long, deep breath. "Chillax. Settle down, Ben. I'm not making moves on Kate. Just trying to convince her to have some fun is all."

"Fun?" Ben's jealous glare turned into a mischievous grin. He lunged for my hand, captured it in his, and then yanked me off the bench. Thomas didn't stop him, and Marlene shot him a glare for not jumping to my defense.

"Fun is exactly what the docta ordered. Let's dance," Ben said far too enthusiastically.

Instant panic. "Oh no… no, no, no," I muttered, wobbling on my feet. "I don't dance."

"Ah, bullocks. Sure ya do." Ben's grip tightened.

"I can't," I said in desperation. "Last time I danced, there was a huge fight and my bodyguard almost killed a guy—" Idiot! My alcohol-infused brain was letting things slip. Ben was unfazed by what I'd said, but Thomas's eyes lit up like a Christmas tree.

"It's just dancing," Ben slurred, dragging me toward the patch of grass otherwise known as the 'dance floor'. He was insistent, and he wasn't letting go.

A surge of anger shot through me. No. No way was I going to allow this man to treat me this way. I didn't care if he fired me or dropped me off in the middle of a field of snakes; it was time to stand up for myself.

I gathered up my courage and pulled my hand free of his grip, my arm screaming in agony.

"Let me go. Now," I hissed. "And don't ever grab me like that again!"

Ben's arms dropped to his sides. I could have sworn the music quieted as well. A mixture of regret and sadness seemed to sober him up for a moment, forming deep lines between his brows. Mr. Carlson and Thomas exchanged a look of concern while they waited in the wings.

"Oh hell, I'm sorry, Kate. I didn't mean to be so forceful," Ben said remorsefully. "It's just that most girls like dancing is all."

I suddenly felt like an ass. "It's okay. Don't worry about it."

The smile returned to Ben's face. The shoulders of Mr. Carlson and Thomas sagged in relief. "All right then," Ben slurred, the volume of the music increasing. "But this is a good song. Are ya sure?"

I backed away, hands up in defense, and he started swinging his hips and throwing his arms out like he was roping a cow. The blonde twins joined in, swirling around him with giggles and whoops of laughter. Ben twirled them and moved maniacally to the music, then circled back to me. "Offer is still open," he slurred, then he stumbled, fell onto his butt, and flopped backward on the grass with his arms and legs sprawled out like a snow angel.

Then he passed out cold.

I stared in shock for a moment, then kneeled and pressed my fingertips to the heartbeat at his neck. "Oh my God, Ben… Ben, are you okay?"

I expected the music to cease completely and a rush of cowboys to come to his aid, but the only person who appeared and showed concern was Thomas.

"He'll be fine. Don't worry," Thomas said, picking Ben's hat up with care and hanging it on a fence post. "He does this all the time. In a few hours, he'll get up and wander off to bed."

"Are you sure?"

The twins kept dancing, the music kept blaring, and no one was even remotely fazed by the passed-out cowboy.

"Yeah. I'm sure," Thomas said, with a comforting pat on my shoulder.

Mr. and Mrs. Carlson began singing, and the neighbors started swinging each other around in some choreographed dance that made the ground shake. Ben lay there amid it all, unmoving, seeming dead to the world, and a cold chill ran through me as I backed up to the outskirts of the action.

"So, bodyguard?" Thomas said, unfazed by the increasing two-step fury.

"Please, don't ask me about it," I said anxiously, and was bumped into by a man in leather who smelled foul with huge sweat rivers running across his cheeks. He reminded me of the waiter on my birthday with his sweaty cheek against mine, his damp arm across my chest while he held a knife to my neck... I froze. Thomas said something, but I didn't hear him. The memory had me in its grip. There had been people dancing that day, too, so much noise, then death, and blood...mine running out of my veins onto the pink carpet...

I suddenly longed for Oliver. He'd saved my life that day. And if he were here he would have protected me so fiercely that not even an unwanted look would have come my way. I missed that safe feeling I had with him. The familiar comfort I could sweep my worries under...

The pounding of my heart stole my breath when the big, sweaty guy spun toward me again.

Thomas misunderstood the look of terror on my face. "Kate, honestly, this is a pattern with Ben. Pretty much the norm, and it isn't gonna change. I promise he's just sleeping off a binge. Now c'mon, let's get out of here before someone else asks you to dance."

I was stuck. Stuck to the grass and stuck in the memory of that horrible birthday. Thomas tentatively reached for my hand, and I let him take it. As if in a dream, I followed him past the fire, away from the house, and over to a bare patch of grass under the biggest tree in the yard. Lanterns hung in the branches and mixed a golden glow with silvery moonlit shadows. I pulled cool air into my lungs, trying to calm myself.

"All you all right?" Thomas asked, cracking a fresh can of beer and leaning against the tree.

"Of course. Why do you ask?"

"You have a look of terror about you. Are you that worried about Ben? He's just drunk is all."

"No. I'm just not used to crowds."

Thomas laughed. "Fifteen people dancing outside a ranch in the middle of nowhere is a crowd?"

It was to me.

Thomas took a long swig of the beer and then set it down at his feet. "Is that why when Milton Pickard bumped into you—who, by the way, is harmless—you squealed like he'd turned into a brain-eating zombie?"

"Stop trying to figure me out," I said angrily.

Thomas nodded, then bent to retrieve his beer. "Sorry," he said softly. "I'll mind my own business."

I thought he might walk away, and I desperately didn't want to be alone. "It's just I have an anxiety disorder and sometimes panic attacks just come out of nowhere. They used to be only triggered by storms, but lately it seems just about anything can bring them on. Seeing Ben on the ground, and then the sweaty guy bumping into me... I..." A shiver completed my sentence.

Thomas rubbed his chin. I stared at my feet.

"Thanks," he said.

"For what?"

"For actually sharing something honest about yourself. It's good to know. And now if I see your face turning white and your eyes as wide as a fox`s caught in a trap, I'll know why."

"It won't happen again," I said hopefully.

Thomas stood where he was, hands in his pockets and lantern light in his hair. That cocky grin played on his face, but now it didn't bother me. The music blaring from the house momentarily stopped, and the only sounds in the dark were restless animals and an axe chopping away at more logs for the fire.

"Anything else you'd like to share?" he asked.

It was innocent. Friendly. And it was the calm in his voice and kindness in his eyes that made my heart rate slow—I could breathe again.

"No. I guess I better turn in," I said.

Thomas laughed. "It's only ten, Kate, and we have this dance floor all to ourselves."

It was true; no one was paying any attention to the two people under the tree. "I can't dance," I squeaked.

"You mean you are scared to dance, because of something that happened in the past. Heck, it's just me and you, in the middle of nowhere, with nothing better to do. What's the worst that can happen?"

Armed guards opening fire. Oliver appearing from nowhere and choking the life out of him. "You have no idea," I said dismally.

Thomas took a step closer, faced me for a moment, then moved to my side. "Put your left foot out... like this," he said. "Now, step this way."

"I can't—"

"Please," he begged.

Against my better judgement, my feet started moving, the sound of autumn leaves crunching under them. I did as he instructed, putting my arms this way and that way, turning to the side, stepping forward and stepping back. Soon, the two of us were laughing madly as the tempo of the music picked up. I was clumsy while Thomas was graceful and practiced. I couldn't help but smile when after the tenth attempt at a swirl, I got it right. When my feet started moving automatically in sync with his, I realized that somehow, I was having fun.

When was the last time that happened?

We kept dancing, caught in the music and the moment. Laughter came easily, and I welcomed the heat it put in my chest. It felt magical, giving in to the demand of the beat, the tingly feeling of the beer, and Thomas's gentle, guiding hands. When a slow song started up, he carefully pulled me close until we were chest to chest.

"Oh, I can't..." I started to say.

"Why?" he asked.

Being next to him felt good, and it surprised me. "You're a stranger. I know nothing about you. I don't even know how old you are."

He sighed. "I'm twenty-one. Old enough to know better, and young enough to pretend I don't."

I stayed where I was, body wanting to be held and brain yelling at my body to hit the road. Thomas took my stillness as an invitation. His hands let go of mine and found their way around me, and I couldn't help but work my arms around him, too. His body was firm. Warm. He wasn't as tall as Luke and smelled and felt much different, but that comforting feeling of heat and safety had me melting into him more than I should have. We swayed to the music. I began to imagine it was Luke I was slow dancing with under the moonlight, and it was his arms tightening around me....

"Who are you thinking of right now, Kate?" Thomas asked.

I was startled out of my daydream and pulled away to look up into a beautiful face, but not the face of the man I loved. It hurt to say his name. "Luke."

"You love this guy?"

"Yes."

Thomas flinched slightly. "Is he the one who hurt you?"

"He would never hurt me."

I expected more questions, but Thomas remained oddly quiet, studying my face with an intensity that gave me shivers. His arms moved back around me, and he pulled me close again. I could hear his heart in his chest, beating as fast as mine, and we were swaying even though the music had stopped. Something was happening between us. I felt it. He felt it. And what it was, I had no idea. Underneath the old tree with him, I felt a sense of calm blanket my gloom and despair. My body relaxed. My mind eased. Our heartbeats slowed, becoming perfectly in sync with each other.

"This isn't right," I mumbled into his shirt. Happy to stay where I was, but realizing we'd been dancing for way too long.

"You know what you need?" he said, breath hot on my cheek.

I needed Luke. "I actually do know what I need, but I bet you have an interesting suggestion," I said.

Playfulness pulled at the corners of his mouth. "You need to see my butt in a Speedo. Then all of your heartache will be replaced with good old-fashioned lust. Up for a swim?"

LAKE DEIFENBAKER WAS A LONG, SNAKE-LIKE SHEET OF SILVER WITH TALL prairie grasses flanking the shoreline and a wide patch of sand for a beach. The light of the moon was uninterrupted as it settled around us, making the earth shimmer. It was far different from mountain lakes back home. A fingertip in it assured me it was much warmer, too.

"There's no weeds, not one. In case you were worried about that," Thomas said. The air was cold enough we had put jackets on over our sweaters, and he remained fully dressed. "No sharks, piranhas, or bloodsuckers. Just pike, but they don't bite. Hey, can you even swim?"

"Of course," I said, undoing my jacket.

"Whoa, not yet." Thomas turned and pointed to a tiny shack a few feet from the water's edge. "First, we heat up the 'poor man's sauna' and light a fire on the beach. We gotta get hot and sweaty first, then have a way to warm up after. Otherwise, we'll turn to popsicles."

"Pansy," I teased, although grateful for the idea of heat; I was cold already.

He shook his head. "You were just gonna dive right in there, weren't ya?"

That was exactly what I was going to do, just to prove… something. "Of course."

"Huh. The entire walk here, I kept expecting you to fake a stomachache or come up with some excuse to turn back. You constantly surprise me."

A smile crossed my face. "I can out-swim you, outrun you, and outsmart you, Thomas," I said, mimicking his cockiness.

"We'll see about that."

He grinned. His teeth were perfectly straight. Although he'd shaved in the morning, there was the shadow of stubble on his chin. Why was I noticing this?

I followed him to a circle of rock containing the remains of a dead fire. As he poked at the ashes, an owl hooted from not too far away. I scanned the thick band of trees for its glowing eyes, but saw only darkness.

Thomas gathered kindling from a wood pile stacked against the shack. In three small trips, the fire pit was stacked full.

"Ben and Mr. Carlson built the shack for Marlene," he said, motioning to the creepy, windowless structure that would probably topple over in a breeze. "Apparently, she wanted to be an Olympic figure skater and was really good at it. He cleared the lake every winter and kept the fire going in the shack so she could warm up. Marlene was out here every chance she got, then, one day, something happened that made her quit. Hank remembers her marching into the house one afternoon, throwing her skates in the garbage can, and never going back to the lake. She refused to give an explanation why. Anyway, now the shack functions as a good old-fashioned sauna."

Thomas was flicking a lighter to the edge of the dry firewood. The flame would catch for a moment, then fizzle out.

"I like Marlene. You could tell her all your secrets and know they would be safe with her," I said.

Thomas nodded. "Yep. She's the weirdest person I know, but as loyal and dependable as the sun rising." He was flicking the lighter again, bent over with knees in the sand, now blowing on the wood.

The damp air was messing with his horrible technique.

"Want me to show you how it's done, cowboy?" I said, feeling the effects of the beer loosen me up.

Thomas sat back on his heels. "You just go right ahead, Princess Kate. You can't even flip a pancake or turn on a stove, so this should be interesting."

I removed the wood he'd dumped into the fire pit and set it to the side, then I gathered up some dry grass and rolled it into tightly packed balls to make a tinder nest. Small twigs and dry reeds were plentiful, so I collected some and placed broken bits of it around the grass. While Thomas watched, amused, I built a small teepee structure with the wood he'd collected over top.

"You figure grass balls are gonna get the party started?" he said with a laugh.

"Nope, but pussy willow fluff will."

I marched over to the foliage next to the shed, grateful for the flashlight Thomas had given me to light the way, and nearly jumped out of my skin when the owl hooted again. Sprigs of pussy willows, almost as tall as me, were in full bloom. Mounds of what looked like exploding cotton balls came easily away from the stems. Soon, I had handfuls of the stuff. I returned with nature's best fire starter and packed the cotton next to the grasses. With one touch of the flame, the fire burst to life.

"Unbelievable," Thomas muttered. "How did you know how to do that?"

The light and heat from the fire was always comforting. "Survival training. Apparently, I was actually paying attention once in a while."

"What on earth would you need survival training for?"

"My extremely overprotective father had some very strange… uh, views on my education. Some courses were ridiculous, but that one sure did come in handy a few weeks ago."

"Oh yeah?" Thomas's eyes shone in the flames. "Did you have to live in a cave and fight off cougars and bears in those mountains you call back home?"

He was joking, but I shuddered at his ridiculously accurate guess. "Yeah. Something like that."

When he realized I was serious, he changed his tone. "You're not gonna tell me about it, though, are ya?"

I shook my head.

"All right. I'll go get the shack heating up. In the meantime, you crack this bottle open for us. We'll need warmth on our outsides and our insides after we swim."

He tossed me a plastic bottle of vodka. Just looking at it made me feel a bit queasy, but I nodded and twisted off the cap as he disappeared into the shed. Maybe a sip would do me good. The moment my mind was unoccupied, my thoughts drifted to Luke. Maybe I could dilute those thoughts with booze.

I heard strange rustling noises from behind me. The owl? I waited for that eerie hooting sound, but the trees had grown quiet. I shone the flashlight, aiming the beam at the tree trunks, the tall grasses, and then the small path we'd come out of, hoping for a brief second I might see Luke. But there was nothing. There was no sound. And no one.

I reminded myself it would be virtually impossible for anyone to find me out here. Even Ben didn't know where I was. It was just Thomas and me.

Thomas and me. What on earth was I doing? Apparently drinking made me stupid.

I shivered despite the fire. What would Luke think about what I was doing? What was he doing? Had he taken my note to heart and moved on? Gone back to Lisa and Louisa to begin starting a new life without me? Had I hurt him?

I took a swig of the vodka. My throat instantly caught fire, and it took all my strength to suppress my gag reflex. Luke... I took another sip.

"The stove is lit. It should be good and hot in the shack real soon. And look what I found." Thomas was grinning with two large wool blankets in his hands. One look at my dismal face made his smile disappear. "Hey, what's up?" he asked, dropping to his knees before me.

My chest hurt. I swigged more vodka, and Thomas gently took the bottle from my hands. "I don't know what you've got going on, Kate, but for tonight, try to forget about it, all right? We aren't gonna fix things, but we can distract you from it long enough to give your heart a break."

I wanted to cry but didn't. "Sorry, I'm just—"

"Hey, nothing to be sorry about."

Thomas took a long drink, then pulled me to my feet. "C'mon, let's turn that frown upside down. Let's get sweaty."

"Your pick-up lines are horrible."

"Oh, darling, pretty little Kate... You ain't seen this body yet in all its glory. I don't need pick-up lines."

HE WAS RIGHT.

In the heated shack, he'd stripped down to a pair of red swim shorts that left pretty much nothing to the imagination. I had a tough time keeping my eyes averted from his bare skin. Any girl not dying inside from heartache would have been all over him. Lean and muscled, perfectly tanned and smooth... he was rather captivating. But he was wrong about something—not one part of my longing for Luke was replaced with lust for him. In no way whatsoever was I attracted to Thomas. But,

I certainly could admire him—like one would an incredible piece of art that wouldn't match the décor if taken home.

I'd stripped down, too, leaving on my undies and bra—garments Thomas had picked out at the Wal-Mart that he quite boldly pointed out fitted me perfectly. On a bench opposite from him, I watched as he splashed water onto heated rocks, sending clouds of steam into the air. It was hot as blazes. I was starting to sweat. Rivers were running down my back and seeping under my hair. Thomas was glowing, his dewy skin glistening in the soft light of an old kerosene lantern and the fire crackling in the wood stove. The shack smelled of cedar and the spicy cologne coming from his pores.

"What is that you're wearing?" I asked, breathing in the steam and his scent, realizing I'd had too much vodka.

Thomas stood proudly and splashed a few more drops on the rocks. "You mean this little number?" he said, referring to his little red shorts.

My head felt a bit dizzy, but my body was so gloriously hot. "No, the cologne."

He ran his fingers through his dark hair, flattening it to his head, which brought out the angular features of his face. "Oh, that heavenly smell… It's 'Eau de Hot Guy', mixed in with a little Old Spice from the dollar store."

I laughed. It sounded way more boisterous than I'd intended. "Oh. I thought it was 'Eau de lonely cowboy who has no chance whatsoever with the girl in the sauna'. Mixed in with a sprinkle of desperation."

Thomas howled. He laughed so hard I couldn't help but join him. When he finally caught his breath, his cheeks were red and streams of sweat poured across his muscled stomach. I could not look away no matter how hard I tried.

"Sense of humor, too. Who knew?' he said. Suddenly, he sprang from his side of the shack and was before me. He planted his hands on either side of my thighs and leaned in, face inches from mine. I didn't flinch as his eyes took in the damp display of my chest. Boldly, with his fingertips, he grazed the skin at my collarbone. I should have felt scared to death, but I wasn't. Not in the least. Picking the necklaces up from my skin, he regarded them curiously. I stayed put under the inspection. I could have pushed him away, but there was no need to.

"Such odd choices," he muttered, fingers grazing the maple leaf, tooth, and pendant.

"What are you doing?" I asked a little too flatly for what was happening.

"You remind me of my sisters. Too trusting," he said, face as serious as a heart attack.

Our knees knocked together. And now I gulped, not from possibility of what he might do to me, but from the proximity of his skin. I told my hands if they moved from my lap, I'd cut them off.

My throat became painfully dry.

"Look at me," Thomas said. I forced my eyes up, and he grabbed my chin to hold my gaze. "I'm not the kind of guy who would take advantage of a girl. Not ever. Do you understand?"

I knew that already, but I nodded anyway. His hand fell away. This was a brotherly, alcohol-fueled bout of schooling, nothing more. He was trying to scare me, but he was a bad actor.

"But, as you know, there are many who would," he continued.

I nodded again, looking directly at his bare chest and feeling my heart rate speed up a bit—from the heat of the room, though, not him.

"I could do whatever I want with you," he said, trying his best to look villainous. "Tie you up… beat you…force myself on you… and there would be nothing you could do about it. No one would hear you out here."

I sighed. "Yeah, yeah. Thing is, for some reason, I know in my heart you would never do that. So quit trying to teach me a lesson. I've had enough of them in the last month to last a lifetime."

We were nose to nose. "Just don't go for midnight swims or hang out in creepy shacks with anyone but me, all right?"

I giggled nervously, because I had the strangest urge to run my hands over his bare shoulders—a side effect of the vodka, obviously. "No one but you," I said.

Satisfied with my reply, he stumbled away, and the mischievous smile came back over his face. He took another sip of the vodka. "Good. Now that we have that business out of the way… are you ready to race?"

My limbs felt like spaghetti, and I was so hot I thought I might pass out, but I stood and got eye to eye with the weird, cocky cowboy who soothed me, intrigued me, pissed me off, and made me laugh all at the same time. I grabbed the bottle from his hands and tipped it to my lips, forcing back another couple of gulps. "Last one in the water makes the waffles in the morning," I said, then bolted for the door.

I GAVE MYSELF OVER TO THE COOL LAKE WATER CARESSING MY OVERHEATED body, letting it numb my emotions and senses until things became a blur. The lake stretched out in a seemingly unending expanse. When I tried to swim across it, Thomas dragged me back. I felt myself laughing as we dried off, giggling madly at the difficulty of getting dressed and tying shoes while damp and exhausted. Next to the roaring campfire, we sat on the blankets and howled at the moon, hooted like the owl, and told each other stupid jokes. There was a smile on my face and sounds of happiness coming from my throat, even though I knew it was a cover up of how I was really feeling; Thomas was an excellent bandage over my gaping wound of heartache.

Flat on my back with Thomas on one side and the fire raging on the other, I finally had to close my eyes and block out the starry sky that was starting to spin a bit too fast. My thoughts tumbled downhill into a void, and my body became part of the sandy beach. I couldn't have moved or even opened my eyes if the world was blowing up around me. When I felt something on my neck, I was powerless to do anything about it. A hand was drawing down the zipper of my jacket, and the frigid air of the night hit my bare skin. What was Thomas doing?

"Get off," I hissed and tried to raise my hand to push him away, but it was held down at my side, and my wounded arm was too weak to lift. Between heavy eyelids, I caught a glimpse of ebony hair hovering over me. I swore—at least, I thought I did—and then the zipper of my jacket went back up. The skin at my chest became warm again. Within seconds, I heard Thomas snoring and I gave myself back to the night, passing out completely until waking up to the rising sun—and Marlene's disapproving glare.

"What are you dumbasses doing?" she demanded.

I answered by throwing up on her boots.

14

SHOOTIN' FISH IN A BARREL

I WOULD NEVER, EVER DRINK AGAIN.

After a full day of chores, the silent treatment from Ben, and the lingering effects of the vodka, I figured a shower might make my head stop throbbing. I turned the water on as hot as it would go, steam filling the bunkhouse. Thomas was right, laughing had felt good and temporarily absolved all my problems, but now I was so tired and hung-over my emotions were hard to keep in check. At dinner, I hadn't been able to sit through another minute of Ben's death glare, so I feigned having a stomachache. Now alone and close to tears again, I took my time scrubbing and lathering.

I hoped Thomas wouldn't be mad I used up more than half his bar of soap and washed my hair four times with one of his manly smelling shampoos. Inhaling the heavenly scent of pine and mint, I stood under the flowing water as the bubbles collected around my feet and spun around and down the drain. I was about to shampoo my hair again, but the light shifted and there was a slight creaking sound of weight on the floorboards...

"Who's there?" I asked.

There was no reply.

Thomas had probably come in to get something and left. He'd promised to keep everyone out of the bunkhouse while I cleaned up. And by everyone, I knew he specifically meant Ben.

I faced the hot water, letting it blast my cheeks and chest until I turned pink and the water turned cold. Toweling off and squeeze drying my hair as best I could, I smoothed some lotion into my skin that I suspected was Thomas's. It smelled like his skin in the poor man's sauna, and the memory of us laughing and howling at the moon put a smile on my face. Suddenly, I feverishly hoped there would be more moments like that between us. Then I mentally kicked myself—those should be moments spent with Luke.

The floorboards creaked again. "Hello?"

No answer.

I held the towel tight, waited for a moment, and heard nothing. No. Thomas wouldn't let anyone in. I was hearing things... I really was that tired.

I tiptoed over the cold floor, eager for some warm clothes, but stopped dead in my tracks. Ben was sitting on one of the bunk beds. His hat was off and next to him. His cheeks were shadowed with heavy midday stubble, and the death-glare that had been in his eyes all day was replaced with a look I could only describe as... hunger.

"Feeling better?" he asked.

I clutched the towel tighter, wishing it was longer. He was directly between me and my clothes. "How long have you been in here?" I asked, realizing he had a pretty good view of the showers from where he sat.

He stood. "I wasn't watching. Swear. Didn't see nothing. I was just check on you is all."

He was drunk. His cheeks were as red as I imagined mine were. I marched past him to my bunk as I felt his gaze on my exposed skin. I grabbed the first item of clothing I could reach and kept my voice calm—Ben looked unstable.

"You couldn't have waited until I was done showering?" I said, trying to remain neutral.

"Thomas wasn't..." Ben's eyes slowly scanned the room before they settled on me and narrowed. "At dinner either."

"So?"

"So I thought... he might be in here. With you."

The accusation in his tone made me angry. "And what if he was?"

Ben's eyebrows drew together, and his cheeks grew even redder. I saw his pulse quicken at the base of his throat. A muscle bulged in his jaw. "Then I would deal with him," he hissed.

"Deal with him?" I felt my heart race. "Listen, I have no interest in Thomas except as a friend. None. But if I did, it sure as hell wouldn't be any business of yours."

Ben's hands balled into fists. "Everything you do is my business, Kate," he said, voice a low roar. "From the moment you came to me for help, scared to death and runnin' like you were being chased by the devil, you became my business. When I found out Thomas was trying to get Jeb Carlson to hire the both of ya, I knew what he was up to. But I'm not gonna let that happen. I'm certainly not going to let him take you away from me." He stumbled back a bit as if pushed, but then righted himself.

"Listen, Ben, I don't know what Thomas is up to, but I—"

In two large strides, Ben was before me, breathing heavy, every corded muscle in his arms tense. I backed away and found myself against the bed frame, dropping the dress I was going to change into in order to keep the towel secure.

"Back off," I warned.

His body was now too close to mine. His hands took hold of my shoulders, and I got the distinct whiff of alcohol on his breath. He wasn't just drunk; he was dangerously drunk. Every bit of female intuition I had sent off warning bells to run.

"I can't back off," he breathed, fingers digging in a little too deep. "Don't you get it? Can't you see that fate brought us together? Finally, after all these years of waiting and giving up on ever finding the one... you fell into my lap."

I tried to stay calm as he stared at me like he might devour me whole. "You're a sweet guy, Ben, and I'm grateful for all you've done. But I don't feel that way about you."

His breathing sped up and his eyes danced in his head. I could feel this wasn't the Ben who had carried me to bed, tucked me in, and so gently cared for me. Alcohol had brought out something dark in him. It had taken over his mind.

"Ben..." I said, hoping to snap him out it, hand on his chest to keep him from getting closer.

His gaze moved from where my hand rested against him, and then traveled up my bare arm to the edge of the towel to stop and linger on my mouth. Before I could react, his lips were on mine and his hands were firm at the back of my head. His mouth was searching, searing, and the heat coming off him was like a roaring bonfire.

I turned my face away. "Stop it," I yelled, holding the towel with one hand and pushing him away with the other.

"Just lemme," he slurred.

"No—"

My words were muted when his mouth covered mine again. I struggled against him, but my resistance only seemed to fuel him more. He was tight against me, relentless and crushing. I fought harder, but this just seemed to incense him. So I became perfectly still, trying the opposite approach, hoping this would douse his flames.

"Ah. Kate...my beautiful Kate..." he said, hand traveling down my shoulder and across to my chest. He paused, then tugged on the towel to expose my breast. He gritted his teeth before gripping it possessively.

I attempted to shove him away, but he latched onto my wrists. I was no match for his physical strength. It was effortless for him to restrain me while his mouth moved across my cheek and down my neck. I struggled, panic starting to blind my thoughts. I could barely breathe. "Stop it Ben, please, you're drunk. Stop...stop..."

But my pleading fell on deaf ears. He swung me away from the bed and pinned me against the wall, both wrists secured behind my back in his unshakable death grip. I wondered if he even knew what he was doing now; his eyes had become nothing but black holes.

"I don't want you to touch me," I said firmly, hoping the tone of my voice would snap him out of it.

His free hand began reaching under the towel.

"Don't you dare..." I hissed. "This isn't you, Ben. This is the booze. Please let me go. You don't want to do this!"

He was panting hard and prying my legs apart with his knees, intent on getting what he wanted. I fought like my life depended on it, which made him more aggressive... more determined. As his teeth grazed my neck and his calloused hand roamed across my body, panic took hold. When his fingers found that place at the apex of my thighs, every muscle in his body grew rigid. From deep in his throat came a predatory moan. I screamed. I put all my strength into my voice...

And I was heard.

Ben didn't even register Thomas storming into the room until he was pulled from me and slammed to the floor. Thomas spun to face me giving me the once over with wide, wild eyes. "Kate...?"

The question on his lips was answered with one look at my tear-streaked face and the towel that had dropped to the floor. He yanked a blanket from one of the beds and wrapped it around me while I stood in shock over what just happened. I tried to breathe as I stared at Ben, now struggling to his knees.

"Are you hurt?" Thomas asked.

I shook my head. "No...but he... he tried to... he was going to... I said no, but..." I couldn't finish what I was trying to say. And I didn't have to.

Thomas threw his hat to the ground. He turned his attention to Ben in a complete rage. "I'm going to kill you..."

Thomas drove his knuckles into Ben's cheek, sending him flying backward, then ascended without missing a beat, fists connecting with Ben's ribs and face. I had to dig deep to find my voice.

"Stop. He's drunk, Thomas. Stop hitting him."

Thomas got one more in before he hesitantly backed away. Blood spurting from Ben's nose pooled onto the floor.

"What the hell is the matter with you, Ben?" Thomas roared.

Ben muttered something incoherent and stood, assuming a defensive stance, feet wide apart and hands up. His eyes shifted in and out of focus until the bunkhouse door swung open and Mr. Carlson, shotgun in hand, stormed into the room. Then Ben's eyes grew wide and his hands dropped to his sides.

Mr. Carlson's anger over having his dinner interrupted dissolved when he saw me shaking like a leaf. "Oh, shit," he said.

"Yeah. That's right. You know what happened, Jeb?" Thomas roared. "Exactly what I told you would happen."

Mr. Carlson let out a heavy sigh and lowered the shotgun. He rubbed his chin before speaking. His voice was too low and calm for my liking. "Did he, uh… hurt you, missy?" he carefully asked.

I knew what he meant. "No."

"Do you wanna press charges against him?"

I shook my head. There was no way I could get the police involved.

"Well, I'm sorry, Kate. Ben don't mean to do what he does; it's the booze-devil in his veins. He needs help. Let's just keep this between us, all right?"

Thomas was shaking harder than I was. "There's only so long you can keep making excuses for him, Jeb. Kate could have been… She was almost…" Thomas didn't finish.

Jeb Carlson put his hands up and nodded sadly. He shook his head at Ben, and turmoil creased his weathered face. "I'll get him fixed up," he said to Thomas. "I promise. In the meantime, you can have the job and stay here as long as ya like. We'll work out the terms later." He cleared his throat. "You get on now and look after the girl. I'll look after the idiot."

Thomas seethed. "I should beat the fuck outta the idiot."

"I think I'll leave that to his sister."

Ben's shoulders crumpled at the mention of his sister. A feeble no came from him, cowering as the floor shook with Mr. Carlson marching over and pulling him into a head lock.

"You'll get what's coming to ya," he said, and dragged Ben from the room.

Thomas's chest rose up and down in an attempt to take in even breaths. "Get dressed," he said, turning his back to me.

I picked the sundress off the floor and wrestled it on, arms shaking so hard I could barely manage.

"Did he—?" Thomas asked, his back still to me.

I fumbled for words. "He…tried to. I said no. I told him to stop, and he wouldn't listen. How could he do that? What if you hadn't stopped him?" My stomach flipped with the 'what-ifs'. "I'm gonna puke."

Thomas lunged for the trash can by the door, getting it to my lurching body just as my stomach brought up everything in it. He paced the floor until my retching ceased.

"I'm so sorry. I was only gone for a few minutes helping Marlene in the barn. I didn't think he was that drunk. I didn't—"

My throat burned. "I should be able to look after myself, Thomas," I said. "Anyway, it's over and it's not your fault."

Thomas was visibly fighting to remain calm, just as I was. There were beads of sweat on his fresh-shaven cheeks, and he rubbed the split knuckles on his hands. As the room started to spin around me, I held his gaze, which seemed to be the only stable thing in my life.

"You're safe now, Kaya. I promise," he said.

And suddenly, as if things weren't bad enough, the room froze into a panicked focus. "Uh…why did you just call me Kaya?"

Thomas crossed the room to pick up my discarded towel to hang it over the edge of the bed. He took his time answering. "Because that's your real name. You told me."

Bits and pieces of conversation we had on the beach suddenly drifted back in. "I told you?"

He reached for a soft blue-knit sweater, one he'd picked out for me at the Wal-Mart, and pulled it down over my stunned head. "You told me everything—family hunting you down, ex-fiancé bodyguard, crazy revenge-seeking mother, and that kidnapper dude… You literally told me your whole life story. That's why I asked Jeb Carlson to hire us, so we can stay here on his ranch where no one can find you. Well, that, and now my suspicions are confirmed that you can't be around Ben… ever."

I ran for the bathroom, my stomach now intent on bringing up all my internal organs. Yet again, I involved someone in my messed-up life. I had told Thomas everything. What was wrong with me?

I got to the sink first and held onto it for dear life. Dry heaving, I shook off Thomas when his hand attempted to rub my back. Ben's touch had rubbed my nerves raw… his hands had been all over me, down between my legs, and…

I heaved again, stomach trying to purge the trauma.

"Kaya, look at me," Thomas said.

I took in a deep breath. Steadying myself against the sink, knees shaking like a leaf, I lifted my head to see him in the mirror standing stoically behind me.

"You don't have to worry about a thing."

If my stomach would settle, I could make a run for it. Get the hell out of here and…

"Kaya," Thomas murmured.

My real name spoken out loud was good to hear, but it also felt like acid pouring into an open wound. I couldn't hold back the tears. "I have everything to worry about."

"Ben will leave. You will never have to see him again. And regarding everyone after you, I know if they can't find you, you'll be perfectly fine. I'm not going anywhere, and I'm not going to breathe a word of what I know about you to anyone. Trust me. You don't have to worry about a thing. Now, if you go running off again—which I can tell is what you want to do—then you'll be found for sure and that won't end well for any of us. Know what I mean?"

I sure did.

"We're in this together, whether you like it or not. So stand straight, put on your fiercest face, and let's get through this. Take comfort in knowing I have a plan," he said.

I forced myself upright and couldn't ignore my pathetic appearance in the mirror.

He was right. I had to man up. I needed to take care of things myself. I didn't want to be weak. I didn't want people to have to look after me. I didn't want to miss Oliver every time I felt unsafe. I wanted to be strong.

And I knew how to start doing that.

Because I, too, had a plan. And the first part was to get away from here, get the necklace to John Marchessa, and end all this.

As Thomas watched, a smile of pride tugged at his mouth when I smoothed the hair away from my cheeks and took in a deep breath. I straightened my shoulders, mustered up what inner power I had left, and forced it to show on my face.

I had a plan, too…. My insurance would get me out of this mess, get Luke back, and save everyone whose lives had become tangled up with mine.

I patted the preserved drop of Lenore's blood nestled in the silver pendant resting against my chest—

It was gone.

15

TURNING POINT

I SEARCHED LIKE MY LIFE DEPENDED ON IT. BECAUSE IT DID.

The barn, the bunkhouse, the showers, the pig Taj Mahal, the kitchen, and the garden… the pendant wasn't anywhere. At the lake, I scoured the beach, the poor man's sauna, and the bushes where I'd gathered pussy willows. I searched through every patch of grass lining the sand and shoreline. After digging through the cold fire, only ash in my hands, I gave up.

The necklace was gone. And it was the only necklace that was gone— the tooth and maple leaf still hung side by side on the chain fully intact around my neck. It didn't make sense; how could only one go missing?

Thomas took finding the silver pendant as seriously as I did, although he didn't know why—I guess I'd missed out telling him that part of my 'life story'.

Standing at the water's edge of Lake Diefenbaker, the air warning of an impending storm, he shivered as he pondered the gleaming expanse of water. "Guess I'll go in." He began taking off his jacket.

"No, Thomas. It's gone," I said dismally.

He paused, one arm removed from the sleeve of his jean jacket, and stared at me. His eyes were brimming over with compassion for my plight. This beautiful man who barely knew me was ready to dive in to a frigid lake to find my necklace without even knowing why it was so important.

"I'll go in if you want me to." His breath made little white clouds in the air.

I shook my head. "It's okay."

The wind picked up. A slap of cold at the back of my neck and bare legs made the shiver in my bones so deep my teeth hurt. It increased the familiar sting starting in the back of my eyes.

"Don't cry, Kaya—or, should I keep calling you Kate? Anyway, it might still turn up."

Don't cry, Kaya… Don't cry, Kaya…

Don't. Cry. Kaya.

Weak!

My shivers stopped. Something dark came over me. It crawled over my skin and slipped beneath it, expanding my anger, sadness, and misery, pushing against my insides as if I might explode from the pressure. My heart thudded, threatening to slam me to the ground, then gave me a jolt.

I didn't want to be weak.

Never would any man use me.

Never would any man take advantage of me ever again...

Never.

The dark thing spread, picking up pieces of me and building them into a tower... climbing higher and higher, the pain of absolutely everything reaching upward to dizzying heights... until... I just stepped off. Took the dive. Plummeted off the peak into a dull void of... nothing.

Snap.

I didn't need the necklace. Or Oliver. Or anyone. I had myself.

I blinked away tears—out of habit because there were none. Thomas stood watching me intently, waiting for me to say something, so I said the only thing that came to mind. "Thomas, I'm glad I chose you as a friend."

The base of his throat lifted with a gulp. "Well, I'm honored to be chosen," he said sweetly.

Waves started rolling onto the beach, almost touching our toes where we stood. "Can I ask you for a favor?" I had to yell to be heard over the wind and the horse that was neighing anxiously behind us, wanting to head back home.

Thomas considered me with curiosity, putting his freezing hands in his pockets. "Yes, anything."

The wind let out a frightening howl, and I waited—waited for the anxiety to surge in because of the impending storm and steal my breath and turn me into a quivering bowl of jelly. But nothing happened. My head stayed clear. My heart just pulsed in a nice even beat. I could hear it in my ears, feel it steady in my chest. I had become emptied of the relentless assault of my emotions. I'd turned them off.

"I want you to teach me, Thomas. I want you to teach me how to... how to not be weak."

Thomas grinned. It was a smile that would have melted my heart if it hadn't just turned to stone. "I think you're figuring that out for yourself," he said.

Yes. Yes, I was.

Now it was my turn to smile. I took a step into the waves, letting the frigid water soak my shoes as I put my arms out to my sides. The wind rippled through my hair, lifting it and dropping it madly, but instead of fearing it, I spun with it, moving with its biting sting, twirling as it nipped at my bare skin. I beheld the sky, shifting and foreboding, and challenged it. I felt a sense of power like nothing I ever had before, and it increased with the howl of the storm. I realized I had everything I needed to get my life back—me.

LUKE

16

TRICK OR TREAT

OLIVER WAS DELIRIOUS. I PUT A COLD CLOTH ON HIS FOREHEAD, hoping to cool him off. He was burning up. Red hot. Frighteningly hot. Hours ago, I'd sat on his chest, pinning his arms to his sides with my knees and forcing orange juice and dramamine down his throat—which was like trying to hold down a raging bear. Occasionally, there were moments of lucidity when his eyes were clear and focused, and he apologized for trying to bite me or for throwing up on me. That I could deal with. Even his rage was something I'd figured out how to handle. But this phase? It was vastly different. Now he was subdued. Barely conscious. And this seemed much worse.

He moaned and kept calling for Kaya. Her name spoken in the completely thrashed motel room was like knives hitting my chest. His anguished voice—rising in pitch when he announced vehemently how he would never let her go and would never stop loving her—mirrored my own feelings.

Days passed.

I stayed close while Oliver purged whatever Eronel Pharmaceutical had been brewing in him. The damp towels didn't seem to do much to cool him down. His shoulders radiated heat like a furnace, and even the air around him was hot. I forced him to drink. Bought a bag of ice and placed mounds of it under the pillow case cradling his neck. The fever was making him confused and his face contort in pain. Coughing fits lasting almost fifteen minutes resulted in bloody gobs on the shredded carpet.

I found myself praying Oliver wouldn't die.

And not just because I needed him to find her.

Oliver was different. There was an intense sense of loyalty about him I couldn't help but admire. He wasn't a quitter. He would do anything for his family, anything to protect those he loved—and I knew that feeling all too well. Unfortunately, his family was Kaya. The person I had taken away from him. So, I owed it to him to stay by his side. I had a connection to this man Kaya had loved—and probably still did—and hated to admit that even in his sickly state, occasionally I caught a glimpse of what she saw in him.

More days passed. I lost count of time.

I was half asleep in the chair by the window when Oliver shifted uncomfortably on the bed, shirt off and damp stains on the sheets around him from his skin and the wet towels. His cough pulled me out of my favorite daydream, the one with Kaya and me living in some cozy little house somewhere, surrounded by a family we'd created… that was the dream that kept me upright. Kept me hoping what I was doing was the right thing. Kept me breathing.

"There's someone here," Oliver said.

His voice was croaky. Dry. He was burning up again. I put my hand under his neck, lifted his head off the pillow, and put a glass of water to his lips. "Drink," I said. "If ya don't, by the amount your sweating, you're gonna shrivel up into a raisin."

His eyes were closed, but he took a few sips. For the first time, he didn't try to push my hands away. "Don't hurt them, please…." he said.

"Them?"

The tone of his voice had become infantile. It caught me by alarm. "Please… don't hurt them," he repeated.

"I'm not going to hurt anyone."

His eyes flashed open, but they were looking past me. What was he seeing? His forehead was beaded in sweat and his gaze distant. I eyed the phone, but who could I call for help?

"Mama? Do you know that man?" Oliver said. His pulse raced at his temples. He was pointing behind me. "No…. stop! Please not my mama… Stop…."

I shook him gently. "Oliver, it's me. Luke. Your family is fine. You're just delirious from the fever. Relax."

"Maisy… no. Stay where you are! Don't go to him." Oliver's voice became strained and his body shook. He was gripped with terror, and tears streamed down his cheeks. "Stop! You're killing them! You're killing all of them. Stop! Not my mama… Maisy… please stop… please!"

Choking back my desire to run from the room, I replaced the cloth that had fallen from his forehead. I tried not to look at the pain, clear in his eyes, when he'd started sobbing over his parents' dead bodies. It was heartbreaking. Whatever was going on in his mind was so vivid he then tried to hide from it. He mumbled and thrashed. He had three sisters. He had two brothers. They were murdered, and it was by someone he knew. A man his father owed money to—a man whose name would forever be locked in my head.

I had to pin him down again. His fevered mind was reliving his childhood, and I was dragged along with it. He recounted everything he'd seen and the horrible guilt he placed on himself for not stopping the death of his entire family. He'd been just a kid, so scared all he could do was hide under the bed. The days afterward were just as bad, roaming the streets alone until Henry and Sindra hauled him into a limousine. What happened after that didn't seem much better either. He recalled memories too horrific for my exhausted emotions to handle. With the sun full in the sky and the temperature of his skin remaining the same no matter what I did, I finally had to stretch out on the floor and shut my eyes, hoping he would come back to reality. He coughed between words, and a full hour later, he finally stopped talking.

I tried to sleep, but Oliver's story was keeping me awake. His whole family was murdered. Murdered. My mom had taken her own life and that was bad enough. What Oliver had gone through was unthinkable. He made sense to me now. His insane possessiveness over Kaya was still wrong... but I understood why.

"Luke?" he said.

I lay completely numb on the disgusting carpet using an empty pizza box as a pillow. "Yeah?"

"If you give me more orange juice, I'm gonna rip your heart out."

I laughed. The Oliver I now knew and didn't hate so much anymore had returned. "Go to sleep, asshole," I said.

"I think the fever broke. How many days have I lost?"

I didn't want to upset him. "Just a few."

He sighed. There was so much emotion in that one breath, it caught mine. "Thanks for looking after me," he said sincerely. "You don't have to anymore, though. You should go. Find her."

I cleared my throat. "Don't get mushy on me. I don't like you all that much, but I'm not leaving you. So, shut up and go to sleep. I'm too tired to listen to your whining."

His reply was a weak cough accompanied by a painful moan he couldn't stifle. He turned over in the bed, the springs groaning under his weight, and I thanked the Lord above he was still alive.

"Honestly though, thanks Luke."

"You're welcome," I said, and was surprised I actually meant it.

A KNOCK AT THE DOOR PULLED ME OUT OF A RESTLESS SLEEP. EVERY ACHE and pain my body had collected over the past few weeks had multiplied from lying on the floor. "Don't need room service," I yelled.

Whoever it was, they were persistent. I'd paid the maid well to not come anywhere near the room, but the sharp rap of knuckles hitting the flimsy plywood wouldn't let up. I sat up to blink back the sun pouring in through the murky window.

"Please. Open the door," a female voice said.

"Who is it?" I asked, looking behind me at Oliver. His eyes were shut and beads of sweat still clung to his forehead, the sheets around him shredded underneath his fingertips—he was useless if this person was a threat.

"I spoke to you on the phone," the female said.

Sindra. I was fully awake now, and glad there was a gun at my waist and a knife strapped to my ankle. I removed the chair I'd shoved under the knob and undid the deadbolt, pulling the door open a crack to peer into the dark eyes of a caramel-skinned woman with polished, shining black hair. She had an exotic aura even though she was all business in a form-fitting pantsuit. The way her head tipped to the side, studying me as I did her before looking past me into the room, put me on edge.

"I'm Sindra."

I hesitated. "I know who you are."

"Let me in," she ordered.

I had nothing to lose. I pulled the door open and moved aside. "Welcome," I said, making a sweeping gesture into the disgusting room. Her musky perfume hit my nose as she sidled past.

"Yeesh. What a—" Her breath caught when she noticed Oliver on the bed. Her stiff posture crumpled, but she quickly corrected it. "You've given him orange juice?"

"Yup." I nodded, motioning to five empty cartons piled into the wastebasket.

"Dramamine?"

I nodded again.

She marched over to the bed and sat down, not seeming to care about the nastiness of the linens encountering her expensive clothes. She lifted Oliver's hand and took his pulse, holding his wrist long after thirty seconds had gone by.

I cleared my throat. "He's been on a pretty wild ride. At first, he tried to kill anything and everyone around him, and then a fever took hold with some gnarly coughing fits. I'm not gonna lie. I've been pretty worried about him."

"Me too," she said softly.

The polished beauty rose from the bed, trying to not seem affected by Oliver's appearance, but her voice had given her away, I could hear a tremble in it.

She extended her hand to me, her grip firm. "Nice to meet you," she said, looking me straight in the eyes. "I work for Henry Lowen, but I have come on my own. He does not know I am here."

"I'm Luke," I said, tentative to shake her hand. "I'd say nice to meet ya, but I'm not sure about that yet."

"You're the man Kaya left Oliver for, correct? You are working with The Right Choice Group?"

I realized I felt embarrassed about my previous employer. "I've since resigned. Kidnapping isn't my thing."

Sindra studied me, pursing ruby lips. "Yes. I can see where it would probably be detrimental to a kidnapping mission to fall for your target. It's amazing you took Kaya right out from under my nose, though. Your scheme was well executed. If you are ever looking for work—"

I cut her off. "Why are you here?"

She put a manicured hand into her pocket and produced a bottle of pills. "Oliver was unable to complete his duties, and I am supposed to retrieve him."

I was pretty sure there was no way Oliver wanted to go anywhere without finding Kaya. I was also pretty sure he wasn't going to be given a choice; I'd heard all about Sindra and what she was capable of.

"You don't own him."

She laughed. "Ha. Yes, I do."

My hand went to the gun at my waist.

Sindra noticed the threat but appeared unaffected. "But," she said, holding my gaze, "I have a different plan."

"I seriously don't care about your 'plans'. I kept Oliver alive, so now you tell me...where is Kaya?"

She put a couple of pills on a spoon she'd plucked off the floor, and then began to grind them with the butt of the TV remote. "Don't worry, she's safe. Under the circumstances, I think it's best we leave her exactly where she is."

"Which is where—with that Ben Smith?"

"Hmm... not really. But sort of."

I pressed. "And under what 'circumstances'?"

"Well, I have come to realize she's no longer pregnant with Oliver's child, so that part of Henry's plan has been obliterated. By the looks of you and the effects of Oliver's poor decisions, the chance of that happening organically again is slim to none. So, that means Henry would have to resort to medical intervention to get an heir from Oliver and Kaya, and I don't agree with the ethics of that."

First, I was surprised this woman had ethics, but then I realized what I was hearing. "Whoa… wait a minute… Kaya's pregnancy was planned?"

"Yes. Well, orchestrated might be a better word."

"Why?" The thought of Kaya being manipulated twisted my insides into a swirling rage.

Sindra kept crushing the pills on the spoon, adding a bit of water. "I guess there is no harm in telling you since you have Kaya's best interest at heart, as do I. You see, Luke, Henry is Oliver's legal guardian. If Kaya and Oliver give him an heir to dispose of, Henry has the means to inherit all that belongs to Kaya."

I felt sick. "Dispose of… as in… kill?"

"Kill. Murder. Whatever you want to call it," Sindra said flatly.

"He would do that? To his own grandchild?"

"Yes. And his child. And… Oliver."

Ah… the part that wasn't sitting right with Sindra; she had a thing for Oliver.

"What exactly belongs to Kaya?" I asked, then wished I hadn't.

"More than you could possibly imagine." She parted Oliver's lips, her voice soft as a kitten as she put the spoon to his mouth. "Oliver is oblivious to all this by the way. He's suspects he's been used, but he doesn't know why."

An unsettling thought rattled my mind. "Oh my God. Doesn't that mean Kaya and Oliver are brother and sister?"

"Yes."

Holy shit. "And Kaya…does she know?"

"She didn't—obviously—but she might now. We think one of her handlers found out and sent her an email. But no amount of torture has prompted him to divulge any specifics."

"Torture?" The room suddenly grew very hot and I didn't want this strange broad sitting next to Oliver. She talked about torture and murder so casually it made my hair stand on end.

"This is insane. What part do you play in all this?" I asked, wondering if I might do a little torture of my own if that was what it took to find Kaya and keep her away from these crazy people. Apparently, to protect Oliver, too.

Sindra put water to Oliver's mouth. Her hand grazed his cheek in a show of affection I suspected was being greatly suppressed. "I've watched Kaya grow up," she said softly. "I've played a part in the lockdowns and the fake abduction attempts that bonded her to Oliver. I've organized her security and followed every instruction Henry has given me to keep her safe from his enemies—real and fake. I know who Henry Lowen is—sick, twisted, ruthless... and I still have more loyalty to him than I have to my own mother. But the murder of a baby, his own child, and... Oliver? No. That's where I draw the line."

"But torture and manipulation are okay?"

Her gaze on me was unsettling. Cold. "Of course," she said and rose from the bed. Smoothing the front of her shirt, she headed for the door. "Thanks for the chat, Luke. The medicine I gave him should help, but don't leave him alone for a few more days yet."

I was so stunned by what I'd heard it took a second to gather my thoughts and get my feet moving. Lunging for the door, I blocked the exit. "You're not going anywhere until you tell me where Kaya is."

Her eyes lowered into a glare that actually made me uneasy. "She's safe. That's all you need to know."

Before I could stop myself, my hand was around her neck, not cutting off her air but squeezing just enough to let her know I was serious. Could I hurt a woman? Probably not, but I felt crazed and desperate enough to try to scare her. "Tell me," I hissed, feeling the world slow down, hearing her breaths become long inhales as the blinking of her eyes took moments to complete.

Oliver muttered her name. He told me to let go. Sindra had remained completely calm and unaffected by the threat to her life, staring me down like at any moment she might rip my eyeballs out, until her name passed Oliver's lips. Then a tremor of weakness ran through her.

Oliver struggled to sit up. "Please, Sindra...tell me where she is." His voice was frail. "And Luke, back off."

Oliver seemed clearheaded. I didn't want to upset him, so I released my grip.

Sindra backed away, rubbing her throat with hatred in her eyes. I expected a fight. For her to lash out and show me why she was so intensely feared. Her feet were spread, muscles taut in her neck. Damn it, I couldn't hit a chick.

"Sindra. Tell me," Oliver begged.

His desperation made her shoulders slump. She sighed heavily, and the desire to fight left her eyes. She straightened up and turned to face Oliver, valiantly trying to maintain her composure. "Trust me. You don't want to know."

Oliver tensed. "Why?"

"Because—" Sindra paused, as if what she was to say next would hurt him. "She's happy."

All the air left my lungs. Oliver's, too. It was like we were punched in the gut at the same time.

"Lying. You're lying," Oliver spat, and I quickly checked to make sure those phone cords were handy if I had to tie him up again. "Either you have no idea where she is, or you are going to take her back to Henry without me. Is that it, Sindra? You want me out of the picture now? How dare—"

A cough stole his words. When he finally got his breath back, his hand came away from his mouth with splotches of bright red. This made Sindra fold. It took her a while to put her cold and unfeeling expression back on.

"I hate to do this," she said.

From her pocket, she withdrew a familiar object—Kaya's silver pendant. The strange red gem caught the sun as it dangled from her fingers, swinging like a pendulum on a clock.

"I took this from Kaya while she lay in the arms of another man," she said flatly. "I watched her, happy and carefree, and I realized that's how she should be. So I've decided to let her go. She's never had a life, Oliver, none. And now she's living freely with people who care about her and will protect her without bars on her windows or intentions of killing her for money. She doesn't need you. Or... you," she said, pointing a finger at me. "You're nothing but a two-bit criminal, and not even a loyal one at that."

My damn knees just about gave out.

Oliver lunged for the necklace in Sindra's hands. He held it for a moment before slamming it on the nightstand. With the TV remote, he began to smash at it madly. His arm delivered such force the top of the nightstand broke in half and began to crumble. Fists flying, he was a madman again. I was about to get the phone cord...

"That's enough, Oliver. Stop it," Sindra said calmly.

And to my surprise, his hand froze in midswing.

"Put your hands in your lap."

He did.

"Now, breathe."

Oliver drew in raspy breaths. He sat frozen in place, chest heaving, limbs hanging at his sides, more confused than when he had a fever. Among the thousand other questions raging through my mind, now I wanted to ask what sort of hold this woman had on him.

But enough talk.

I steadied my gun on her.

"Just tell us where she is," Oliver hissed. "Tell us or I'll have Luke shoot you."

"Ha!" Sindra laughed. "You know, I could demand you leave Kaya alone and then just kill your new pal Luke and be done with this mess. But the bloke kept you alive, and I'm feeling generous today. How about I just give you proof why you should stay away from Kaya?"

Sindra held up a cell phone, and then pushed play on a video. She angled the screen, so Oliver and I could see...

And there she was. My dark-haired beauty. Half-naked. On a beach. A moonlit lake shone in the background and a campfire roared on a beach. A man put his arms around her after draping a blanket around her shoulders, and she was laughing like I'd never heard her laugh. There was a big smile on her face as water dripped from her skin and hair to her feet. She fell to the sand with this man, both laughing. Wrapped in each other's arms.

Sindra was right. Kaya was... happy.

My chest caved. The walls closed in.

"Kaya deserves a normal life," Sindra said, brushing past me toward the door. "Here is your chance to give it to her. If the both of you stay away from her forever, it would be the best, for all of you."

She smoothed the front of her shirt and squared her shoulders. "Oh, and Happy Halloween."

Then she was gone.

17

BED, BATTLE, & BEYOND

KAYA WITH ANOTHER MAN WAS AN AXE TO MY CHEST. IT HACKED my heart to pieces. I was in actual, physical pain.

Barely aware I was even going through the motions, I found a different motel, dragged Oliver out of the truck, and got him onto a clean bed. Exhausted, I sank into a chair by the window. I stared out at a parking lot, a bleak highway on the edge of a small town, and day turned to night.

I couldn't block out the images on Sindra's phone, or the words on the note that were now repeating endlessly in my head. Kaya was happy. It was obvious on her face and in her voice. I wanted that more than anything for her. And if I had to let her go so she could have that, I would.

But it would kill me.

I shuddered. A violent tremble shook my soul at the thought of not having her in my life, because it would be meaningless if I had to go through it without her.

"What time is it?" Oliver asked.

Snow sparkled under the sparse streetlights and icy breaths of wind crept through the edges of the shoddy window frame. I pulled my eyes away long enough to look at my watch. "Four in the morning," I replied. My throat hurt.

The floor shook. Oliver forced himself off the bed. "We're getting a storm. Damn it," he said, the deep timbre returning to his voice.

I knew what he was thinking—who was soothing Kaya? Holding her through an anxiety attack?

"Did the video give you any clues to where she might be?" he asked.

I squeezed my eyes shut. The room spun madly; the chair beneath me became a roller coaster and I was about to derail.

"Luke?" Oliver's voice had lost all the aggression it once had.

I couldn't answer him. My throat had tightened up, along with the desire to either curl into a ball and die, or start swinging madly at everything around me.

"Geezus, kid, you don't think what Sindra showed you in that video was real, do ya?"

I couldn't nod my head. It was cemented in place to my shoulders.

Oliver sighed. "Kaya was drunk. I could hear it in her voice. That's why she was laughing. She's not happy, nor has she fallen for some other bloke. I know this girl. I sat at her bedside while she was sick. Nursed her through fevers, chicken pox, and deaths in the family. I've watched her grow from a kid into who she is now. I know her. What you heard was her scared to death, trying to cover it up with a few giggles induced by a lot of booze. That's all."

Oliver was giving me a ray of hope. But it wasn't bright enough. "What if…. what if she really is better off where she is? What if the best thing we could do for her is give this all up and just leave her alone?"

Oliver winced. "No. She needs us. I don't believe she's better off, Luke. I can't believe that. Because then… I'd have… I'd have…"

He paused. I finished his sentence because I felt the same. "Because then you'd have nothing to live for."

Oliver's hands dropped to his sides. He stared out the window, too. I could see his reflection. The muscled, stubborn beast was crumbling, just as I was.

The snow fell harder, whipping around in the sky. I didn't move. Neither did Oliver. For what seemed like an hour, all we did was breathe.

Then Oliver finally broke the silence. "Sometimes, I wonder if everything I feel for Kaya is… completely real."

I turned to look at him, shocked by what seemed like a painful confession. "What?"

"I mean, I love her. I would do anything for her—die for her—that I know deep in my heart. But this extreme, all-consuming addicted feeling I have for her… is that all me? Or did Henry create that somehow?"

Oliver's question dangled precariously in the motel room. I knew what he meant; I watched how Sindra controlled him with nothing but a simple command. I recalled her words—Oliver is oblivious to all this. He suspects he's been used… Now for me, personally, if someone could give me a reason why the crushing pain in my chest should let up, I would want to hear it. Oliver could have easily had his feelings orchestrated.

But, we both felt the same way. And my all-consuming desire for her wasn't courtesy of Henry Lowen.

It took every bit of energy left in my body to answer Oliver. "I don't think it matters. You feel what you feel, and there's no changing that. I mean, yeah, by the things Sindra was saying, it sounds like you were heavily manipulated. I mean, fake abduction attempts? Wanting you to get her pregnant to use your child to get control of whatever it is the sick bastard wants control of?" Oliver's eyes widened and his jaw dropped—he didn't know that. "Henry Lowen is sick enough to abuse your love and loyalty—which most certainly is real—and use it to his advantage. All I know is you're a good guy, Oliver. You don't deserve to be used for any reason, and you don't deserve to doubt or question your very reason for living."

Oliver took a moment to process this. A rogue morning ray of sunlight peeked through the clouds and into the room, then disappeared back behind the grey. "I think you need some rest," he finally said, and reached for the blister pack of dramamine on the table. Popping two caplets into his palm, he held them out to me. "Take these. It will help you sleep."

There was strength back in him. I stared hard at his outstretched hand, too weary to argue, so I just shook my head. I would stare out the window until my eyes melted out of their sockets, and maybe the axe in my chest might obliterate me completely.

The storm raged.

My eyes throbbed.

Another hour passed.

As my body began to melt into the abyss, two massive hands found their way under my armpits and I was lifted. With no strength or fight in me, I was removed from the chair.

"Guess it's my turn," Oliver said. With a not-so-gentle toss, I was deposited onto the bed. "Now, lay down," he demanded.

It went against every manly instinct I had to obey him, but weeks of worry and no sleep had left me with nothing. I had nothing left. Even the daydream of Kaya at my side, the two of us old, grey, and happy, was becoming impossible to conjure.

I fell backward, head hitting the pillow. Oliver shoved the dramamine into my mouth and insisted I chase it with warm orange juice.

And then it was him who sat in the chair by the window, watching the sky.

LISA

18

ᏔWO ᏔOO ᎭANY

I was Louisa's first outing since I'd rescued her at the train station. I'd run out the door with her the day I'd rescued her from Claude, worried she might make strange with me and try to squirm out of my arms. But now, on this sunny afternoon in the near-vacant produce department of the local food mart, she held my hand tightly and wouldn't leave my side. She looked so cute in her mermaid dress and princess shoes, giggling at Seth's attempts to use vegetables as puppets, grinning madly at all the junk food he was sneaking into the cart. I pretended not to notice that underneath the potatoes and apples were cookies, licorice, and a massive bag of gummy bears, but Louisa practically squealed with delight when she saw the Rice Krispie treats he'd hidden under the lettuce.

"Seth, really. You're not going to eat all that garbage, are you? It's so bad for you," I said, adoring the mischievous look on his scraggly, weathered face.

We were so different. I was a health nut, and he was content to eat everything deep fried. I wore my heart on my sleeve, my feelings and intentions obvious, and Seth was reserved. Sly. Crafty. Always seeming up to something. I had youth on my side, endless energy, and the desire to know everything. Seth was older, wise already, and content to sleep away the day. Sometimes these things made me crazy, but I was falling hard for him regardless. The hurdles in our blossoming relationship weren't going to be about secrets or our age gap; it was going to be the fact that he used to be a cop and my experience with police was the stuff of nightmares.

He kneeled before little Louisa, tenderly tapping her nose with a grin as wide as the ocean. "All kids need to have some fun foods. Treats are good for the soul. Right, Louisa May?"

Louisa grinned with the innocence only a child can possess. "I like treats," she said in her heart-breakingly sweet voice. Head tilting, lashes fluttering, she sought my approval. "But... if Lisa says they're bad, maybe we should only have five."

"Five?" Seth stood and laughed. It was a boisterous, hearty laugh that made a lady squeezing melons speed off with her cart. "I guess I'm fine with five. It is an excellent number."

"Or maybe we should get eleven. Cause Regan will want some, too," she added.

Luke's little sister had taken it upon herself to care for Regan. At the house, she played nurse while he remained immobilized with his leg in a cast, bringing him food and taking his temperature with her plastic thermometer. Regan talked incessantly about medicine, his school days, his family, and his deep hatred for Henry Lowen, and Louisa pretended to listen while she decorated his cast with her crayons and brushed his lust-worthy red hair. It was amazing to me that after all the child had been through, she still found it in her heart to be nurturing to a stranger. To be trusting.

She was just like her brother.

"What should we get for Regan then?" Seth asked with a bag of candy in one hand and a pomegranate in the other.

"Let's get him some cake. He likes chocolate," Louisa said, and she started to wander toward the bakery.

Her hand left mine. She took about ten steps forward while Seth and I watched wordlessly. She seemed like any other kid eager to get their hands on a cookie until a large man with a cart headed her way. It was then her cheeks paled, and a look of terror came across her face. She ran back to me, crying. The scars of Louisa's past were still so horribly fresh, and I could relate. Mine still felt like gaping wounds sometimes.

I held her tight and wished I could bring Claude back from the dead to kill him. And then kill him again, again, and again... and I'd make sure each time was more horrifically painful than the last.

The drive back to the ranch was peaceful. Country music softly played over the truck stereo, and Louisa slept in my arms. I admired Seth while he drove. He was different now. His gaze softer, his words kinder, and his actions now his own. Not like before. Not like when we planned Kaya's kidnapping and worked together in the Death Race. Back then, I had admired the strength and masculinity that emanated from him in the purest form—but he was mean. His heart was cold, and his mind was controlled by a woman who had used him for years to nurture hate and revenge. Rayna was just as evil and cunning as Henry Lowen. She'd taken over his mind. Dominated him.

I liked to think I was the reason Seth came to his senses. That I was the one who brought about the change in him and made him stop taking orders from her and her Right Choice Group minions. But if I recalled the expression on his face when he brought Kaya into the house that day, her limp body in his arms as he yelled at the doctor on call to tend to her immediately... I wondered.

"Whatcha thinking bout, Lees?" he asked, catching me staring.

I didn't want to talk about Kaya because that would lead to a discussion about Luke, and that would just reinforce the pain of how much I missed him.

"Just thinking about dinner," I said.

The truck rattled onto a secondary road. "I like how your mind works," he said with a wink.

The sun was just going down. Soon, it would disappear behind the golden mountains. It hit me suddenly, as the car inched through the picturesque valley, that I felt like I was going home. And then it hit me that I'd never, ever, felt that way before. But as we approached the house, my warm fuzzies were replaced with dread. Someone had been here while we were out; Brutus didn't come running to the truck, the front door was wide open, and tire tracks had gashed through the grass and flung dirt onto the porch.

"Oh my God. Regan..." I muttered.

Seth had his gun out of the glove box as soon as we stopped. I carefully pried Louisa off me, laid her down on the seat, and hoped she wouldn't wake up. Heart pounding, I imagined the worst. Seth and I exchanged glances; we knew who had been here and what the insufferable woman was capable of.

"Keep the truck running. If I'm not out in five minutes—"

I didn't let him finish. "Then I'm coming to get you."

He was about to argue, then changed his mind and bolted for the porch. I watched him swing open the kitchen door before tentatively going inside.

I waited.

I studied the child on the seat next to me. Her golden hair hung in loose curls around her face, her heavily fringed eyelids were shut, and her berry-red mouth slightly parted... she looked so much like Luke. God, I loved her. Loved her like she was my own child. If anything happened to her, I would never forgive myself. And if anything happened to Seth...

It had been two minutes and there was no sign of him. A bee buzzed past the open window. The grass rustled in the breeze. The heat of the engine waffled the air above the hood.

Another two minutes. Still nothing.

I was going in.

I locked the truck and pocketed the keys. Bolting across the lawn to the porch where we'd sat every night taking in the sunset, I could smell the blood before I even saw it, before I even pulled the squeaky door open and took a step into the kitchen…

It was everywhere. Red streaks of it running down the walls and the cupboards, splatters of it on the fridge and lace curtains. My stomach came up into my throat. Was it Regan's blood? I took in a breath and gagged. Then I noticed the source; the remains of a mutilated rabbit artfully displayed on the kitchen table. The innards very clearly formed the letters RCG.

"That bitch," I said.

Clumps of hair and skin were impaled to the drywall with steak knives. The head of the rabbit, eyes missing, was perched atop my favorite teapot.

"Seth?" I called, feeling my veins pulse with anger.

His voice drifted to me from the other end of the house. "I'm in my office. Regan's here. It's all clear."

In the living room where we'd left Regan asleep in his recliner, the curtains were completely shredded, the couch slashed to bits and everything else that could be smashed or thrown was. The first bedroom was empty but destroyed, and the second one contained an agitated Brutus—thankfully unharmed—waiting patiently to be let out. He bolted past me and headed for Seth's office, sniffing out where his master was. I followed. When I saw Seth kneeling before Regan, I breathed a sigh of relief.

"Is he all right?" I asked.

Regan was tied to a kitchen chair in the corner of Seth's office. His head hung forward, and his thick red hair blanketed his face. The cast that ran from his toes to his thigh made his leg stick straight out. Seth was on his knees, knife in hand, working frantically at a zillion knots binding his cast leg to the other. Both of Regan's feet were frighteningly purple.

"I don't know what happened. My dog didn't get slaughtered, and Regan is still alive. But my gun stash is gone," Seth said, hands steady but anger shaking his voice.

"Man, he's really out of it." I put a hand under Regan's chin and lifted—not a scratch to his gorgeous face, thank heavens—but his eyes were rolling around in his head and the tape that Seth had peeled from his mouth had left behind patches of red skin. "Can you hear me, Regan?"

He moaned.

"Get his hands untied, Lees."

Seth had left that task for last so that the barely conscious Regan wouldn't fall over. I circled around, getting behind the kitchen chair while gently patting Regan on the shoulder. What had they done to him? Was he drugged? Why was he so out of it? "It's okay, you'll be fine," I said, trying to be comforting. But when I looked down, my feet were in a pool of blood. My breath caught.

"Oh my God," I said, now dizzy.

Finally freeing Regan's legs and standing, Seth's eyes grew wide at the horror on my face. "What is it?" he asked.

I gulped back the vomit rising into my throat. "She took two of his fingers."

My explanation to the very intelligent doctor about how a man in a cast from his ankle to his hip had an accident with a table saw wasn't one of my better lies. Luckily, the doctor eventually lost interest and decided he didn't care how Regan lost his fingers.

I breathed a sigh of relief when we left the dismal building into the fresh morning air. Regan would never be the same; his ring and pinkie finger were gone. But as we maneuvered our way through the parking lot with him complaining about the state of the crumbling pavement, I wondered if I was more upset about it than he was.

None of us had slept—except Louisa, who was quite happy dozing in my arms—and tension was high. We hadn't spoken of Rayna. Not in the hospital room, the crappy café with the burned coffee, or in the slowest elevator in the world. But now that we would not be over heard, Seth let loose. He started swearing like a sailor while he helped Regan into the backseat of the truck.

"I'm sorry that bitch did this to you," he said, adding in extra expletives under his breath.

"Yeah, whatever. Not your fault," Regan said nonchalantly, wincing as he got comfortable. "I don't get it, though. Why didn't Rayna kill me? She just trashed the house, chopped up some poor bunny, and left her mark everywhere like a pissing dog. Doesn't make sense."

"She's just trying to mess with me," Seth said, starting the truck.

There was a nervous tick in the corner of his eye. A tremble in his voice. I was surprised how much Rayna had gotten under his skin. The sun shone as we headed out of town toward the mountains posing in the distance, lighting up his hands gripping the steering wheel like they were gripping her neck.

"I mean, really," Regan slurred from all the painkillers pumped into him. "If she really wanted to get back at you Seth, she could have shredded Brutus. Spread his guts all over the kitchen table. Or at least done something a little more sinister to me besides taking two fingers. There are ways to torture somebody that could have made a much bigger mess for you to clean up."

The child in my arms was thankfully still asleep and not listening to this. "Maybe Rayna has a soft spot for you, Regan," I said. "Or for the both of you."

Seth laughed, but it was nervous. "Not in a million years. Even as cute as Doctor Death is back there, that woman is fueled by hate and revenge. She's playing mind games. She wants me to be on edge and waiting for her next move. Trust me, the only soft spot on that woman is…" I raised an eyebrow at Seth, imagining him thinking about Rayna's gorgeous body. "Well, nowhere."

Regan squirmed around, trying to get comfortable. "Well, she didn't even ask me any questions. Just had her goons tie me up and then sat at your computer while they trashed the house. I figured I was in the clear until she pulled out the metal cutters. She did it herself, too, smiling the whole time. See what Henry Lowen does to people? He poisons them. He turns them into crazed, hate-fueled demons."

"Not Kaya," I said softly.

Regan let loose a long breath. "And that's a bloody miracle."

"She's caught up in this mess, and it's not fair. Does she even know who we were working with? Does she know Rayna is her mother?" I said, feeling horrible we'd kept that from her.

Seth fidgeted with the heat and kept quiet. I couldn't read him. There was something he was keeping from me; I could just feel it.

Regan piped up. "I hate Henry Lowen as much as the next guy, but I can't believe we all worked for that bitch. It's probably best if Kaya doesn't know her mother likes cutting off appendages with metal cutters."

My stomach churned. I'd gotten involved with The Right Choice Group for Luke. As a means of getting his sister back. As a means of seeking justice for his mother's death. I had never given much thought about who was calling the shots or the innocents who might end up involved. But now it was eating away at me like acid. I wouldn't change what I had done—as I gazed at the child in my arms, I certainly had no regrets—but I would make things right going forward. Louisa was safe now. And I would make it up to Kaya for all the hell we put her through.

"...I heard the bone snap before I passed out the first time," Regan was saying.

I put a hand over Louisa's ear. "How can you even talk about it, Regan? Aren't you kinda freaked out?"

I twisted around to look at him. His freckles stood out even more against his pale skin. To a stranger, he probably appeared the sweetest boy in the world. His attractive exterior was an incredible cover up for a ruthless, cold, calculating, and brilliant mind.

"Bloody right I'm freaked out," he said slowly. "But I'm high on revenge. It's my dream to watch Henry Lowen suffer, even though that dream cost me a few things I'll never get back. It's a small price to pay, and it's nothing compared to what I've lost that was dearer to me than anything in the entire world. I'll get revenge for my sister's death, and for all those women who died taking drugs they thought were helping them. I'll get revenge for Rayna, too... It's not her fault her mind has been poisoned by him. I get it. I'd take a couple of fingers, too, if I had to."

The conviction in Regan's voice gave me the shivers. I remembered him talking about injecting Kaya with Cecalitrin. Filming her while she lost her mind and then handing her a knife to end it all. Now there was no doubt in my mind he would have done exactly that if it hadn't been for Luke.

I held Louisa a little closer.

Regan kept talking. "I can't believe you were married to her, Seth. I'm surprised she didn't cut off your ba—"

"Whoa," Seth interrupted, clearly uncomfortable. "I didn't know what a good woman was until I found one." His calloused fingers reached for my hand. "And now I do. I'll never let her go."

The truck hit a bump, and Regan groaned. "Right. Well, we better let Luke know Rayna is on the warpath. Have you guys even heard from him? Have any idea where he is? If something happens to him, I'll—"

"He's fine," I said quickly.

Truthfully, I only had a couple of very quick calls from Luke checking in on Louisa. I could tell he was hiding something from me, too. His voice was strained and his answers vague when I asked about Kaya. He was always in a rush, having to go without answering any of my questions. I never told Regan this because his worry didn't mix well with mine. When it came to Luke, he got very worked up.

"Good," Regan said with a cough. "I'm hungry. And thirsty. Got any sandwiches, Lees? Coffee? I think I need to lie down; my head is a bit fuzzy. And where is Luke? Where is he?"

The painkillers were messing with him now. "We will be home soon, and you can lie down. There are no sandwiches in the truck but I will make you the best grilled cheese you've ever had soon, okay? As for Luke, like I said, he's fine. Seth's keeping track of his whereabouts by his credit card purchases. Apparently, he's in a motel in Saskatchewan, of all places. I thought he'd take Kaya out west to see the ocean or something... that's what I would have done."

Regan, in his foggy-minded state, muttered something about wanting parmesan on his sandwich and insisted the house be sanitized before he stepped one foot in the door. "I sure hope you don't keep track of those credit card purchases on the computer in your office, Seth. There's no password protecting it." He was slightly breathless now, eyelids barely open. "Only an idiot would do that. Rayna would have figured that out and be half a day ahead of us on her way to revenge-execute her daughter and my best friend by now."

Seth almost ran the truck off the road. "Oh, crap."

19

EASTBOUND

IT KILLED ME TO LEAVE LOUISA BEHIND WITH REGAN AND HIS brother Ellis, but I knew the child would be in good hands. Ellis was doting and loving, and Regan was fiercely protective. Still, I worried. As the sun left the sky and the mountains slipped away behind us, Seth reached for my hand. His skin, covered in scars and sun spots, was so weathered and aged compared to mine. I loved everything about it.

"Don't worry, Louisa will be doctoring up the doctor and bossing around the nanny," he said, turning on the truck's headlights.

I nodded, checking my phone again for the hundredth time to see if there had been any calls.

Seth smiled. "Ellis is strange, but we know there's not a better babysitter in the world than him. He'll have that house cleaned up, supper on the table, and keep a game of Barbie going on the whole time. And don't forget about Brutus and Regan—both excellent guard dogs."

That didn't stop Rayna, I thought.

"She won't strike twice," Seth said perceptively. "She'll be off sniffing after Kaya like a dog on a bone. Louisa is safe, I promise."

I didn't want anything to mess up the life I pictured with Seth and Louisa. Family suppers, back-to-school shopping, first dates, and vacations… I wanted that more than anything. I finally had a taste of a life that felt normal, and it reeled me in hook line and sinker.

"We'll stop at the next town. Get some gas and burgers," he said, giving my fingers a squeeze.

I gave him a disapproving glance.

"Or salad," he said, rolling his eyes. "We just gotta keep it quick, Lisa. We have to catch up to Luke before Rayna does. No doubt she will have an army with her that he won't be expecting."

"Why no cell phones?" I asked, still confused as to why this incredibly easy sort of communication was lost on everyone but me.

"Dunno. Never thought about it to be honest. Things just moved too fast to get Luke set up with one, and I never bother with the damn things. I don't want people being able to contact me twenty-four hours a day. That would be a bloody nightmare."

"Right. All your friends would drive you nuts," I teased.

He gave me a sideways sneer.

"So, what are we going to do when we find Rayna?" I asked, eyeing the glove box rattling with ammo.

Her name made him grit his teeth. "Blow her a kiss, and then blow her to bits. No sense leaving her alive."

"You know that's, uh... murder, right?"

"And you know she won't stop until an innocent girl is dead, and every second leading up to that death will be horrific. I know this. Her. All she talked about for years was how she would mutilate Kaya when she got a hold of her, and then send her in pieces back to Henry. There is not one single bit of doubt in my mind that's what she'll do."

The hair on the back of my neck rose. "Why did you marry this bitch?"

Seth let out a heavy sigh. "Truthfully, I had no choice. Old Carl dumped her on my doorstep one day. He said he was cashing in on a favor I owed him and if I didn't take Rayna in and hide her from Henry, he would have to murder her. Obviously, I couldn't have that on my conscience."

"Oh?" This was the most information he'd doled out on his ex-wife. "And?" I pressed.

Seth shifted around uneasily. I let him. It was time he gave me some sort of explanation—we were sharing the same bed, so he could also share his past.

"She was so pretty," he said, staring straight ahead at the desolate highway. "So... innocent and heartbroken. Devastated her child had been taken from her and the man she thought was the love of her life wanted her dead. I'm sure she sobbed for three weeks straight. Anyway, Old Carl was a scheming bastard. He got into Rayna's head. He visited her twice a week, showing her pictures of Kaya growing, of Henry with other women, of the life that should have been hers...and it broke her completely. There was nothing I could do to pull her out of her misery, and believe me, I tried. Old Carl had her where he wanted her. She was an empty shell he filled full of hate, nurturing and feeding and grooming it into something so wicked and sick Rayna became barely recognizable. I stood by and watched while this young woman, once kind and innocent, became solely focused on one thing—destroying Henry Lowen. It completely consumed her, which was exactly what Old

Carl wanted."

"He sounds like a great guy."

Seth shook his head. "I used to think he was. We were best friends. Fishing buddies for years. He just seemed like this grumpy old dude who liked to drink beer and complain about his job. I never imagined he was capable of the things he did."

It was pitch black outside now. Seth turned up the heat. "What else?" I asked, hoping he would continue.

"Well, then came the money. Old Carl started showering Rayna with whatever he could steal from Henry. He filled her pockets and her head with the power that money could bring. That's when things backfired on him. Rayna was smart. She payed Lowen employees for any information she could get on Henry, squirreling cash away to invest in her dream of creating The Right Choice Group... and suddenly, she didn't need shelter under my roof anymore. She didn't need Old Carl, either—and she made sure he knew that.

"So, just to make a point, and to make sure she didn't go anywhere, Old Carl marched into my kitchen one Easter Sunday when I was out tending to a sick cow, and plucked her right off a kitchen chair. One minute, she was in my house, the next... gone. For three years, I searched until I eventually found her in a cellar in an abandoned house. Old Carl had kept her alive, of course, but whatever bit of soul she had left, whatever pieces that had remained before this, were obliterated. There was no light in her eyes, and there never was again. I blamed myself for a long time for not stopping Carl back in the beginning, for not torturing him into telling me where she was. And then, I lived in fear he might march into my house and take her from me again. So I did the only thing I could to keep her safe; I married her. I figured I at least owed her that."

I couldn't believe what I was hearing. I'd thought theirs was just some twisted love story... not this. "Why did marrying her keep her safe from Carl?"

"Ah. Well, me and Old Carl had an agreement; no matter what we were using each other for, whether it be hauling in a fish, smuggling drugs, or plotting to murder someone, our family must never be hurt or involved. And that would include my wife."

I suddenly questioned Seth's judgement. "And you were friends with someone capable of locking another person in a cell for three years? And... underground drug connections? You were a cop. I don't—"

"That's in my past, Lisa," he said hurriedly. "I promise on my mother's soul I am not that person anymore."

I stared at him. Hard. His wool coat collar flipped up around his ears cast a shadow on the claw marks from Kaya's fingernails on his cheek, scars that would forever brand him. I'd seen a change in him since then. Felt it. But knowing what I did now and realizing he was probably leaving out much more, I wondered if I could trust him. I wanted to with all my heart, but—

"Lisa? You understand why getting rid of Rayna is what we have to do, right? She will never change."

I nodded, feeling the pit of my stomach churn. "Yes. I just don't like the thought of spending more time behind bars is all."

Seth laughed, and his hand moved back to mine, patting it soothingly. "I promise that won't happen. All you have to do is help me find her and then leave everything else up to me."

"I know what I signed up for. I'll do what I have to do for Kaya."

"You mean... for Luke," Seth said intuitively.

"Uh, yes. Him, too."

Seth became lost in thought before pulling out into oncoming traffic to pass a slow-moving motor home. "Your turn to talk. How long have you known him?"

"Since high school. He uncovered my secrets, and I uncovered his. It connected us. I'd patch him up after fights and sometimes put makeup on his bruises. He'd hide me in his bedroom or come to my rescue when my dad was raging and out for blood. We tried to date, but it never worked out. There was too much 'life' getting in the way."

Seth nodded like he understood. "Was Luke always uh, you know... so fast?"

"Yup." I remembered fondly the times it had been lifesaving. "The only way you'd get to him first was if he'd been drinking. A lot. One night when were out trying to be boyfriend and girlfriend, there were a couple of dudes he'd beat in a fight sitting a few tables away. They kept sending over drinks, pretending to be buddy-buddy, and I kept warning Luke they were up to no good. Luke, in his ridiculously trusting nature, figured they were just trying to be nice. Fifteen shots of tequila later, when he stumbled out in the parking lot, they tried to take him. When it became clear Luke was not going to win, I stepped in. But I might have stepped in a little too much."

"And that's when you landed yourself in jail for assault?"

"Well, I had other warrants, too... but yeah. You can do a lot of damage with a crowbar and a bad attitude. Anyway, the bastards deserved it. I have no regrets."

"And you risked your freedom to get Louisa back, for him."

My chest tightened. "Yes. Well, and for Louisa, too."

Seth sighed. "You know, I find it strange you would go to such great lengths for an ex-boyfriend and his sister."

Did I detect a hint of jealousy? "Without Luke, I wouldn't have made it to fourteen."

"That and you still love him," Seth said. A muscle twitched in his jaw.

There was no sense denying such an obvious truth. "I do. But not in a way you have anything to be concerned about. He has my loyalty and my devotion, but he doesn't have my heart." Mushy stuff made Seth squirm and his cheeks redden.

"What kind of damn salad do you want?" he asked, eagerly changing the subject.

"Caesar."

"Fine. Caesar, it is. And… damn it, Lisa, you have my, uh, heart."

What was it about him that made me melt? This older ex-cop with questionable morals and a past that screamed run… The attraction was there, but completely unexplainable.

I leaned in and kissed him, lingering as long as possible on his scruffy face.

"What did I do to deserve you?" he said, swerving slightly.

I laughed. "Pretty much just about everything wrong… that you now get to make right."

LUKE

20

ℕOW ᴵ ᔆEE ᵧOU

THE SOUND OF METAL SCRAPING AGAINST PAVEMENT PULLED ME from a fitful sleep. It grew louder and with it came the smell of lemon. And chicken. And… garlic? I was so tired my body ached and my chest hurt, but curiosity and a very empty stomach insisted I sit up.

I pulled myself upright to see Oliver at the table before a mountain of take-out boxes. The scraping sound was coming from outside. Through parts of the iced-up window I could see the form of a man with a shovel tackling the heavily falling snow. It kept coming, and he kept shoveling. I watched him go down the sidewalk, then back up, over the same spot again and again… He was just doing what he had to do, and so would I—whatever it took to get Kaya back.

"It's a winter wonderland out there. Got about four feet of snow and it still keeps coming," Oliver said, barely glancing up from what he was eating. He motioned me to join him at the table. "Lemon chicken, noodles, and all kinds of sauced-up mystery meat. It's delicious."

In a daze, I plunked myself down across from him in a wobbly chair. It was eight in the evening. I'd slept—or more like had continual nightmares—for thirteen hours. I picked away at something resembling steak and broccoli in one of the containers. I couldn't tell if it was good or not. My mouth had lost all sense of taste, but my body needed the food, so I forced it down.

"I had to use your credit card," Oliver said. He'd showered, and his eyes weren't so bloodshot. "Put a hundred dollars on it for the grub and to bribe them to deliver in this weather. I'm worried my credit card is being tracked, and I'm low on cash, so…"

"Yeah, whatever," I said, noticing my open wallet on the dresser; it was a good thing Seth had set me up with the card. "Obviously you're feeling better?"

"Yeah. Quite a bit. The fever is gone, and my head feels like my own again. Anyway, I figured we'd let the highways get cleared and rest some more tonight, then get back at it in the morning."

I choked down a piece of steak. "Why don't we go now?"

Oliver shook his head as if I'd asked a dumb question. "Cause that's the plan."

"Your plan."

"Yeah, that's right. My plan. You got a problem with it? You'd rather drive through a storm aimlessly and risk hitting the ditch?"

"You would have a few days ago," I said.

This made Oliver flinch. His eyes narrowed on me. "Listen kid, I know what's best right now, and I have no problem slapping some sense into ya to prove it."

"Stop calling me kid," I said, shoving the food away.

Oliver's nostrils flared, and he straightened up in the chair as if ready to fight—but I could tell his anger was forced. He was looking at me the same way I'd looked at him for the last seventeen days—with sympathy and understanding.

"You wanna have another go round?" he snarled.

He was a bad actor.

"Now that I'm better?" he continued. "Shall we just battle to the death and get it over with?"

This hit my exhausted mind the wrong way, and I laughed out loud.

Oliver's eyes grew wide and he feigned being offended...then he laughed, too. A boisterous roar came from him, the sound of it so strange compared to his near death-bed moaning and groaning I'd come accustomed to. I'd been so worried. Now that he was better, a massive weight of responsibility lifted from my shoulders.

"I still don't like you," he said, grinning.

"Good," I said. "Because I can't stand you."

Oliver wiped at his eyes. "Ya know, I'm supposed to want to beat you senseless for stealing my girl and all, but I kind of want to thank you for saving my life."

His eyes were dark, deep, and kind. All the anger and craziness that had been swirling around in them before... was gone. "You already did thank me."

"I did?"

"Yeah. Before—or after, I don't remember—you told me all about your pitiful self. Your dog Marvin or Marfin, the goldfish that ate your other fish, your desire to be a hockey player, how much you like Kaya's butt in yoga pants, and—"

"It is exquisite," Oliver said with a sly grin.

I nodded. "And... you told me about your family and what happened to them."

His jaw dropped, and he stared at me in stunned silence.

"I told you about my family?" he said after a moment, in barely a whisper.

I could have kept that to myself, but I wanted Oliver to know I understood him, that I knew a part of his past. "Yeah," I said softly. "I'm sorry for your loss, Oliver."

"I've never told anyone, ever," he muttered.

"You weren't in control when you did, so don't beat yourself up over it."

He was quiet now, biting his lower lip and staring at his hands. Then he shoved a container of food at me.

"Eat," he said, but I knew what he meant.

I grinned at the big lug. "Yeah. You're welcome."

Oliver cleared his throat. "Anyway, we rest for now. In the morning, we'll start up the search again. We've still got two names to check out. We can hit the closest one first. There's a Ben Smith just outside the town of Radville. It's about an hour from here."

"There's a hundred Ben Smiths," I said dismally.

"Listen, Sindra managed to find Kaya, so we can, too. Have faith, Luke," Oliver said.

Faith. I'd held on to that for so long when Louisa went missing. Prayed, searched, and came up empty handed after following every single crumb left behind. It never really did much for me. How could Oliver have faith after everything that had happened? How could he still chase after a girl that wanted nothing to do with him? Where was he mustering up all this strength from? I wouldn't quit until my heart stopped, and I would search for her until I died trying. Nothing would stop me. But faith? I didn't have much of that left.

"What if when we do find her?" I asked tentatively. "If she took off to protect us and there is no other guy, what then? Do we come up with an agreement to divide our time with her? You get her on weekends, and I get weekdays?"

Oliver put down his fork. I could tell that he'd given this a lot of thought. "I don't expect to get her back. She's in love with you."

His statement hung so heavy in the air I could barely breathe. There was no anger about it, either. He was only stating the facts.

"Then why all this?" I asked after I'd found my voice.

"Because no matter how she feels about me or you, she's... Kaya. I love her. All I care about is her being safe and living a long and happy life. If she chooses you to do that with... then so be it. I've come to

HEATHER McKENZIE

terms with where I stand. I know I don't... uh... own her. That said, though, I am still committed to her completely."

I was taken aback by his selflessness. And impressed. There were no words. So we exchanged a nod of a deep, mutual understanding instead.

WHEN SETH AND LISA BLEW INTO THE MOTEL WITH THE STORM RAGING behind them, my knees practically buckled in relief at the sight of their familiar faces. After a friendly hug from Seth, and a squeeze I had to pry myself out of from Lisa, they both stood, blinking rapidly and taking in the view of the shabby room—and my supposed arch enemy taking up wall space next to the bathroom.

Oliver didn't say a word. Or move. He just stood there, expressionless and foreboding, while my friends dusted snow from their coats.

"Wow, what a dump," Lisa said, warily noting Oliver in the corner.

I took her coat and draped it over the back of a chair. "This is a palace compared to the last place we were in."

Lisa's eyebrows drifted up into her hairline. "We? As in you and..." She eyed Oliver carefully. "Him?"

Seth's hand was hovering over the gun at his waist. He assessed the table covered in empty food containers, the bed that had been slept in and the other that hadn't—and I wondered what he was thinking.

"Oliver and I are on the same side. We're working together," I said.

Lisa's eyes widened. "What?"

"We..." I couldn't say friends, so I said, "We're not enemies anymore."

Lisa was momentarily stunned into silence—which for her was rare. Seth's hand dropped from his belt and he lazily took off his coat, tossing it over Lisa's. "Well, all right then. Apparently, we've got some catching up to do," he said, intrigued.

"You're not kidding." Lisa removed her wool cap, and shook out her honey-blonde hair.

Oliver straightened up; Lisa was stunning. A tight black sweater hugged her ample chest, and a pair of faded jeans made her long legs look even longer. She was a natural beauty, pink flushed cheeks, full red lips... like Kaya's.

I clicked off the TV that was mindlessly droning in the background. "So, Lees, why are you here? And where is Louisa?"

She gave Seth a look that lasted too long—obviously, they hadn't driven two days through a snowstorm just for the hell of it. "Louisa is

163

fine, Luke. I promise. In fact, she is more than fine. She's with Ellis and Regan, and they are taking the best care of her. She is doctoring Regan, and it's really helping her to heal."

Seth shifted uncomfortably.

Lisa continued. "Seth and I came, because we thought you might need us."

"And why is that?" I asked.

Oliver moved from where he was leaning against the wall, on edge now, and that protective instinct of his in high gear. Lisa eyed him with alarm, unsure if she should continue.

"Trust me, Lees. Oliver is one of the good guys. All right? He's my..."

"We're friends," Oliver said without hesitation.

And there it was. Friends.

"Whoa." Lisa shook her head in awe, and took a minute to process it. After a dissecting stare to determine if either of us were high or drunk, she pushed a lock of hair behind her ear and took in a deep breath.

"Seth and I tracked you here from your credit card purchases. By the way, what the heck is Pinky's Pork Palace? And should you really be eating anything from a place with a name like that?" She cast a look of disgust toward the food containers. "Anyway, we know Rayna is tracking you, too. She's going after Kaya—who is where exactly? Please tell me she has her own room and isn't staying in here with you two blokes because Lord help her if that's the case. Anyway, Rayna broke into Seth's place when we were out. She hacked Seth's computer and found the credit card statement. She knows where you are... except for maybe here because this motel purchase is recent and she wouldn't have access to this current information." Lisa took in another deep breath. "Not only did she thrash Seth's house and spread mutilated bunny guts all over the place, but the bitch also cut off two of Regan's fingers."

Lisa paused for a reaction, but before I could even get in a shocked inhale, she continued.

"Louisa saw nothing and was with me. Like I said, she's fine. I promise. But Regan—the poor guy—he has endured so much with the leg, and now this. He's holding up well, though. We were at the hospital for hours. He's pumped up on all kinds of painkillers which is great for Louisa because it has made him the most agreeable patient. Anyway, we are pretty sure Rayna is headed this way. Positive, actually. And I tell ya, I can't wait to come face to face with that nasty woman. When I get my hands around her skinny neck I'm going to have the time of my life choking hers right outta her—"

Seth reached for Lisa's hand, clearing his throat. "Putting what Lisa is trying to say into a nutshell, Kaya is in huge danger. We've got to get her someplace safe. I have a buddy in Winnipeg who will let us stay for a couple of nights while we come up with a game plan. He will keep her hidden, so I can go hunting for my ex-wife."

Lisa nodded eagerly in agreement. "So, where's Kaya?"

Oliver and I were unable to muster up the words needed to explain we had lost her. By the shocked inhale Lisa made and the widening of Seth's eyes, they'd figured it out pretty quick.

Seth spoke through gritted teeth. "You've got to be kidding me."

Oliver stood. "No. She ran off on her own accord to protect us. We have no idea where she is, but we have been assured she's safe."

Seth was completely unimpressed. "By who?"

"Someone I used to work for. She found Kaya and showed us ... uh, evidence she is alive and well."

Seth scratched his stubbled chin. In a movement I could tell was utter irritation, he raked his hand through his salt-and-pepper hair. "How did this someone find her? Because if Kaya can be found, then she is not safe. Get it? Luke was easy to track down. Frankly, I'm not sure why Rayna didn't get here before me. That woman has resources. She has friends in high places. She has people willing to do whatever she wants with no questions asked. So, if you still care about Kaya—and I'm pretty sure you do—then we better find her before Rayna does."

I thought of Dustin and Marie. Of running up those stairs and opening their door at the Lemon Tree Motel to find them all dead. Even those groupie girls and Rusty—all dead. They weren't even connected to Kaya. They were just... there.

I knew what Rayna was capable of.

So did Oliver. And I could see we were sharing the same memory.

"Rayna found us once already. That's why we headed out this way. That's why..."

"That's why Kaya ran," Oliver said. He wiped at the sweat now beading on his forehead. The truck keys went from the dresser to his hand. His eyes met mine. With a quick toss, they were flung in my direction.

"Guess you're driving tonight after all there, golden boy. First stop—Radville."

KAYA

21

Run Baby, Run

The raging storm had finally let up, but left in its wake was a blanket of thick, white snow. I thought of Stephan as my feet pounded the earth, slipping and sliding on the freshly plowed country road. What would he be saying to me right now? What advice would he give?

First, he'd tell me I should be wearing a scarf, and the risk of frostbite on my bare hands was all too real. He'd give me heck for leaving without telling anyone in the ranch house where I was going, and he'd probably mention something about the possibility of coyotes wanting to eat me. Of course, he'd nag about having breakfast and stretching first before running, but when I bolted out of bed at five, all I could think about was getting outside. This morning, I wasn't running away from anything, or running from someone, I was just plain old running.

And as I ran, I realized I could think of Stephan without crying.

I savored each icy breath that cut into my lungs. The sky was still filled with the odd rogue snowflake. Occasionally, one would hit my cheeks and linger. Some had collected on the red wool toque I'd snatched from the closet, and my eyelashes were crusted with ice… nose hairs, too. Damn, it was cold. My numb body matched my emotions. I shivered, but didn't care.

The flat farmland was sparkling crystal white and where the pasture met the sky in the distance it morphed into a stunning, blue-grey. Breathing hard and legs aching, I headed toward that line. I kept in tune with my heartbeat as the adrenaline rush started to overtake my exhaustion. I sped up, running as hard and as fast as the slippery road would allow, until I came to a wall of snow. The plow had left behind a mountain of it at the dead-end. I had no choice but to turn around and go back.

I'd run a long way, and it felt good. Out here on my own, I could drift into conversations in my head with Anne. I could think of Stephan and the comfort of his arms. Get over what Ben had done and erase the guilt on his face when he begged me to come back home with him. I could plot ways to get back at Henry. Remember all the people I'd lost in my life. I could think of Oliver. Davis. Angela. And Rayna… my mother. There were no tears. No nagging chest pains. Nothing.

I had found a new strength, and turned everything off.

But I hadn't given myself the true test yet. I hadn't allowed myself to think of the one person who could turn me into a quivering mess.

Luke.

Testing, I let a vision of his sky-blue eyes trickle in—and an ache pinched the corners of my ribs. I ignored it and continued to imagine his smile, his touch… and that ache threatened to become a dizzying pain. Blocking out the imagery, I instead tried something else. I recalled the timbre of his voice, how it sounded when my head was against his chest, mixing with the comfort of his heartbeat when he said my name…

My knees buckled, and I almost landed flat on my face.

I was strong, but not that strong.

I would have to train my brain. Every time I thought of Luke, I would have to instead think of getting revenge against my father—that was the only way I was going to survive. Stopping whatever Henry was up to and gaining control of what he would kill for, got my legs back up to speed again. That got the fire back in my blood. I pushed ahead until my lungs were screaming in agony and cheeks burning from the cold.

The silence of the pristine morning was soon broken by the roar of a diesel engine. A truck slowed as it approached. The massive letters on the side were impossible to miss. Carlson Farms - Best Angus Beef in Canada was as clear as the wind-whipped white hair of the driver. Red cheeked and bright eyed, Mr. Carlson stuck a bare arm out the window as if the wintry weather was a balmy Florida breeze.

"Aha. Thomas was right we'd find you out here. What the hell ya doin'?" he yelled, pulling up next to me.

I slowed to a jog, forcing him to put the truck into reverse and amble backward alongside me. "Running," I said breathlessly.

"I can see that, but why ya wasting all that precious energy? I can give ya lots of chores if ya need exercise."

I looked up to see Thomas. He was sleepy-eyed in the passenger seat with freshly washed hair. Marlene was in the backseat, scowling. Neither of them looked happy.

"We're going into town. Got errands to run," Mr. Carlson said, his booming voice waking the dead. "You and Marlene are in charge of groceries so get in."

The truck came to a stop, and I bent over to catch my breath. "I can't… go into town today. I have to…"

Mr. Carlson wasn't giving me the chance to come up with an excuse. "You have to nothing. The missus don't want you in the kitchen after what you did to the spaghetti sauce last night, and there's shopping to be done. You know the deal, Kate; I provide room and board and don't ask any questions about why you're here and who you are, and you work for me between seven and five." He looked at his watch. "Now, it's five minutes after seven. Get in. No reason to be lazy."

Thomas's eyes met mine. He knew my desire to avoid public places had nothing to do with being lazy. Worry for my safety was written all over his face.

Mr. Carlson was impatient. "Hurry up. Princess Penny has a sore tooth and needs to get to the vet."

I found myself reluctantly squeezing into the front seat next to Thomas. In the back, next to Marlene, was Princess Penny the potbellied pig, and she squealed like she was dying if I went anywhere near her. I leaned back, still catching my breath, and realized I was sweaty and hot and cold all at the same time. Thomas pulled the seat belt across my chest and clicked it into place, then caught my hands in his.

"Damn, you're frozen, Kate," he said.

My skin had turned an angry red. As much as I wanted to pull away, the heat from him was blissful.

"Happen to see any strays this morning?" Mr. Carlson asked, switching on the radio as he turned the truck around to head for the highway, carefully avoiding the steep ditches.

He was referring to cattle. "Nope," I said.

"That's cause they've all froze to death in this stupid weather," Marlene said. "Why do we live in this God-forsaken province anyway?"

Marlene was ignored.

Thomas kept hold of my hands. I glanced at him, noticing the tiniest shaving cut on his cheek. It reminded me of one Luke had on his chin one day, and how it had gnawed at me to tend to it.

Henry… Revenge…Henry… Revenge….

"Cheap razor." Thomas grinned, catching me staring.

He was rubbing my fingers, making them thaw. From the corner of my eye, I watched the concentration on his face, just like I'd watched him sleep this morning before I snuck out of the room. I couldn't help but wonder why he was going through so much trouble for me. He'd quit his job with Ben, took a pay cut to work for Mr. Carlson, shared a basement bedroom in the Carlson house with me in a cold room that felt like a dungeon, yet he never crossed the 'line' ever. Our beds were on opposite walls. Our eyes in our own heads as we dressed. If I could just ignore the sparks that shot up my spine when he laughed, he'd be the perfect roommate.

"Everything all right?" he asked.

"Of course," I said a little too tersely. "Why?"

He spoke quietly. "Cause you seem a little, uh, different, this morning."

I felt different. "Huh," was my only reply.

He rubbed my fingers a little harder, turning the skin from red to light pink. "I'm glad Jeb let me tag along so I can keep my promise of… uh, buying you a winter jacket," he said, but I knew what he actually meant; he had begged to come along so he could watch over me.

"Thanks," I said.

His thumb was circling the palm of my hand now, and his touch was becoming euphoric. He was acting casual, pretending this act of warming me up was purely out of necessity, but I could tell he craved the touch of another human being as much as I did.

"You girls make sure you get lots of snacks. Chips and pretzels. And not that unsalted healthy crap," Mr. Carlson said. "And Kate, get some of that vegetarian stuff you like to eat. I'm tired of watching you squirm whenever there's meat on your plate. I don't understand it, but to each his own, I guess."

Marlene piped up from the backseat, her tone bitter. "Maybe Thomas could do the shopping and us 'girls' will look after the pig," she spat.

Her irritation rolled off Mr. Carlson like rain off a duck's back. "Maybe. But girls like to shop," he said.

"Ya know, Dad, not every girl likes to shop," Marlene said, vehemently opposed to being put into any female role. "Some would rather do chores like shoveling snow, shit, or pretty much just about anything else."

I turned to face Marlene, using this action as a means of pulling my hands free from Thomas's—his warmth was getting far too comfortable, and I was starting to crave more. I focused on her face instead. Her birthmark was such a royal blue in the bright, snow-lit light, and her hair a perfect golden amber. The colors were beautiful together. "It might be fun, Marlene," I said.

She snatched the hat off my head before yanking it over her own. "If anything, at least I can help you find your own hat. This one, my gran knit for me. And besides, red is not your color."

I nodded, letting her be crabby, and stared ahead—snowy fields, miles and miles of barbed-wire fences with the odd blackbird resting on them, and the occasional lights of an oncoming vehicle. Music filled the cab of the truck—something soft and lilting—and I found my head resting on Thomas's shoulder. I hadn't run for a while, and my energy was sapped. As green signs plastered with sticky snow went by naming town after town that didn't seem to be more than four buildings, I dozed. The heater pumped out warm air across my thighs and the vibration of the engine lulled me into a cozy half-awake feeling. I watched as the snow started to fall again. It was light at first, just big, fat flakes drifting through the grey sky, almost hypnotizing. Then it alarmingly increased. Mr. Carlson slowed the truck and swore under his breath, carefully keeping the vehicle going straight on the treacherous highway.

"Town is only ten minutes away, kids," he said as if to reassure those of us who were worried.

The snow suddenly became a blinding whiteout. Wipers swung furiously to keep the windshield clear, and Mr. Carlson slowed even more. I felt that nagging hint of anxiety over the weather. It threatened me for a moment, pulling at my eardrums and pulsing angrily through my veins. But it was only for a moment. When I gulped, to my surprise, my throat was not dry. My head was not pounding. My eyes could focus on what lay ahead and around me with extreme clarity; I'd conquered one of my biggest fears. As the wind howled and pushed and pulled the snow into mad swirls, it gave me confirmation I had beaten my anxiety into submission. I had control over it now.

Well, at least something good came from losing the necklace.

Lights came up behind us. In the rearview mirror, I could see the massive grill of a semi-truck tight on our bumper. It pulled out from behind us to pass, causing Mr. Carlson to drive as close to the ditch as possible without landing us in the rhubarb. "Can you believe these idiot drivers?" he yelled.

The road was sheer ice and the snow was coming down in buckets, so it was nearly impossible to see what was up ahead. The semi driver was taking a huge chance passing us on the treacherous road. As the truck moved past I caught a glimpse of the driver. Grey hair caught in a ponytail beneath a baseball cap and a plaid jacket. Jeb Carlson shook a meaty fist at him.

The driver gave him the middle finger back.

"Geez, it seems like anyone can get a license these days," Thomas said when the semi had finally pulled in front and began speeding ahead.

"If you're referring to me, I'll have you know I'm an excellent driver," Marlene snapped from the backseat.

Thomas sighed. "It's not always about you, Marlene. I was just saying—"

"I don't care what you were 'just sayin'. You're implying that because I am a girl, I'm a bad driver."

Thomas tensed. "Whoa, it's got nothing to do with being a girl. You're just a bad driver!"

"Hey, how the heck would you even know? Last time you were in the car with me, you were too busy admiring yourself in the rearview mirror to even—"

"That's enough," Mr. Carlson roared, turning up the defrost setting on the heater. "Just settle down now and relax. If it were sunny out today, you wouldn't be getting on each other's nerves like this. It's just this dang weather. It puts the poker in the party pig."

"No, it's…" Marlene was about to argue but suddenly changed her mind, her voice taking on a completely different tone. "Hey Dad, uh… speaking of pigs, you should pull over. I think Princess's butt is about to explode."

An odor confirmed Princess the pig was about to do her business in the backseat. Squirming and starting to squeal, she began warning us.

"She's gonna have to hold it in until it's safe to pull over—"

The words had no sooner left Mr. Carlson's tongue when the semi-truck ahead seemed to start to drift all over the road. Fishtailing as if in slow motion, we watched as the rear moved away from the front, swinging out to the side, and then horrifically twisting and beginning to turn over. Mr. Carlson slammed on the brakes, and snow pounded our windshield as we hit the ditch. In a sudden jolt, before anyone could fully comprehend what was happening, we came to a sudden stop. My body lurched forward, but was restrained by the seat belt. Thomas's lap belt didn't hold the top of him, and his body was violently yanked from mine.

And then there was blood. Lots of it.

Thomas slumped back next to me. My ears rang. I was too stunned to move as I processed what just happened. Thomas was limp against me, and that got my hands frantically fumbling for the seat belt.

"Everyone okay?" Marlene asked.

Mr. Carlson said he was fine, but there was no reply from Thomas. I said his name, but it barely came out as a squeak. My heart pounded, pulsing in my ears dramatically, sending my anxiety into overdrive for one full insane, freaked-out minute…but then I reeled it in. I got the belt undone. There was no time to waste. Thomas needed me.

"Thomas?" Marlene softly asked.

Mr. Carlson was in shock. His hand flew to the radio to turn it off, but he accidently cranked up the volume instead. Hank Williams blasted our ears, and time stood still until his shaky hand found the power switch.

"Thomas?" I took in a deep breath, gathering my wits about me. Blood was pouring from his forehead where it had hit the dash. "You'll be okay," I said, needing something I could press to his head. His hands were limp on his lap. "Can you hear me? Please answer me. It's gonna be okay."

I lifted his chin to peer into his eyes. If anything happened to him...

Suddenly, how much I cared about my new friend hit me harder than we had hit the ditch.

"Please talk to me. Look at me, Thomas," I begged.

His eyes fluttered open. His gaze was unsteady, but at least he was conscious. I got one of his gloves and pressed it against the blood seeping from his wound. This seemed to fully bring him around.

"Holy shit... what happened?" he asked.

"We hit the ditch. Are you—"

"I'm okay," he said quickly, wincing. "Everyone else?"

I nodded. Marlene and Mr. Carlson muttered they were okay.

Thomas's face was soaked with blood. I wiped at his eyes with my sleeve. "I'm gonna have one monster of a neck ache in a few hours," he said. "And if there's a scar on my face, I'm gonna be pissed."

I exhaled, realizing I'd been holding my breath. "Even if there is, you'll still be pretty," I said, feeling my arms start to shake.

"The snow gave us a soft landing at least." Mr. Carlson, whose cheeks had paled to match his beard, was still clutching the steering wheel.

"Are you okay?" I asked.

"Uh, yeah..." But then his face paled even more as he pointed forward. "Oh, shit. This isn't good."

The view out the windshield showed the semi's red brake lights gleaming through the storm. It was ahead, but the wind was lifting the snow and whipping it around, giving us a sudden moment of visual clarity. The semi had jackknifed in half and was on its side. The warning signs, even blurred from such a distance, glowed ominously; the semi was hauling gasoline. The round tank was on its side, stretched across the highway just waiting to be piled into...

As if on cue and right out of a waking nightmare, we watched as lights from a vehicle came up from behind us on the road, going too fast to stop. A blue minivan swerved, but too late. Hitting the brakes, it spun around on the road and then slammed into the tank on its passenger side.

Instantly, there was smoke.

"Oh my God," Marlene yelled.

I pushed on the truck door, but the snow was packed up tight against it. Mr. Carlson was frozen in place, stunned and possibly in shock, and Thomas could barely hold up his head, let alone move.

"Does your door open?" I yelled to Marlene, desperate as I imagined the person in the minivan would be if they couldn't get out either. If the tanker caught fire…

Marlene had her door kicked open, and I scrambled across Thomas into the backseat to get out. Another car had come up behind us, but managed to come to a stop; in seconds, the driver was screaming into his cell phone for help.

I made my way out of the ditch, Marlene close behind me, and we got onto the road. I started running toward the crash, smoke increasing from under the bent-up hood of the van. Keeping my eyes ahead, I re-minded myself anxiety was nonexistent. I was in control.

It took forever to get there. Marlene was fast, keeping up with me and practically throwing herself at the driver's door when we finally got to the crumpled wreck. She yanked on it with all her strength. I tried the sliding rear door.

"It's jammed," I said, winded.

"This door is stuck, too," Marlene said, panic in her voice.

We could see a woman at the wheel, unconscious. Blond hair draped over her face as her head rested on the steering wheel. Now the flames were visible, and the smoke started to become thick as mud—we had to get her out.

"Look out," bellowed a gruff male voice. In a blur, a plaid-covered arm was swinging at the window with a crowbar. The driver of the semi had smashed the window and cleared away the glass. He then leaned in to wrestle off the woman's seat belt, and the three of us began ma-neuvering her through the window while panicked voices from far off began to fill our ears. Someone was yelling Marlene's name. Thomas was screaming mine….

Now the driver had the woman in his arms. Her eyes fluttered as he began running with her, Marlene and me next to him. We ran for our lives, and when we were almost back at the group of people now gathered on the road, I heard the woman mutter something. It was the worst thing in the world to hear in a situation like this. My baby…is in backseat…. My baby is in there….

Marlene heard it, too. "Kaya, oh my God…"

Without second thought, I turned and started running back toward the minivan.

"No! Stop! It's gonna blow!" someone yelled.

I forced my wits to stay about me, praying to God for help while willing my feet to remain glued to the slippery road. I noted the flames, felt the increasing heat, and ignored the yelling of panicked voices from behind me. As I approached, my legs instinctively slowed in fear, so I sped up. I pushed it as hard as I could until I entered a cloud of smoke and came to the crumpled metal of the minivan. I couldn't see a thing now, so I felt around for the window opening and dove in. Something cut my thigh, the heat increasing. Ignoring the pain, I scrambled into the back. There was still a tiny bit of clean air left. I inhaled it as the soft flesh of an infant met my fingers. Tiny, bare arms flailed as the wind outside whipped the smoke away from the van, giving me a moment of clarity. Peering up at me, wide eyed and scared, was the face of a baby girl—the spitting image of the one I'd seen when I'd almost drowned in the rapids.

The vision hit me again with lightning force; I was near death when the baby girl with the blue eyes had drifted out of my arms, floating away with what I thought was my last breath. The vision had been so real. I thought I even felt her.

I knew, in my heart I just knew, this was the baby I was meant to save.

She started crying as I fumbled with the belts keeping her in the car seat. I managed to get a blanket around her, covering her face. Thick black smoke filled the van, and I held my breath. Even yanking with as much force as I could, the slide door wouldn't budge. I had to get back into the front seat. Holding the infant to my chest, I struggled through failing vision. Maneuvering past the steering wheel became a test of will. I knew what I was supposed to do, but my body was failing me and my weak arm holding the baby threatened to give out. Finally managing to get the top part of my body out the driver's window, I realized I couldn't get the rest of the way out without landing on the child or dropping her. Now panicking and unable to swallow or think clearly, I thought for a moment that this was it. My life was over. Me and this tiny brand-new person in my arms who was depending on me to survive. All seemed hopeless until firm hands were suddenly jammed under my armpits, pulling me out the window and leading the way out of the smoke.

"Run," demanded Marlene.

So I did. Full on and as fast as my body would allow, clinging to the baby, spurred on by the fact it had started to scream. I ran hard. Eyes streaming with tears and barely able to see, I strained to keep focus on

Marlene's red hat as it led the way like a beacon to safety. Thomas and Mr. Carlson had started moving, too, as far from the collision as possible as the snow fell harder and the wind raged across the road. Marlene had caught up to Thomas, and I felt a sense of relief as she took hold of his arm and urged him away from the inferno behind us. My lungs were burning and my legs close to collapsing, but I kept going... I kept running... until an intense heat hit my back and lifted my feet off the ground.

I was thrown into the ditch, deep into the snow. I had no choice but to close my eyes and curl around the child as the world began blowing apart around me. Intense heat... the sting of something hitting the back of my head... the ground shaking and rumbling... the world disappearing... and then nothing, not even the sound of my own heartbeat. Silence.

The baby stopped moving.

Then voices trickled in, growing in volume, frantic, Thomas's in particular screaming my name. When I finally got my eyes back open, the sky was a sickly orange. Black snow fell onto my face and the cheeks of the now-whimpering baby girl against my chest.

OLIVER

22

BETTER SAFE THAN SORRY

YESTERDAY, I FELT AS IF I'D COME OUT OF A VERY LONG DREAM. The drug fog taking over my mind had completely cleared, and my head felt like it was my own again. Although my body was weak for the first time ever, at least I could see clearly now. Specifically, I could see what I'd done wrong that cost me the love of my life.

Thinking I owned her was one of those things. Thanks to Luke, I realized how insane that was. And thanks to Luke, I was alive.

I owed him. The man whose throat I had fully intended to slit open had stuck by me for weeks when he could have thrown me to the wolves. Even Davis—someone I thought of as a brother—had left me when things got heated. When I was hell-bent on going after Kaya, Davis headed for the hills. He abandoned me. Not that I blamed him, but... I thought we were closer than that. I thought we had a connection. Luke, however, was someone I'd openly detested, and most certainly tried to kill. Yet, while I was sick he never left my side—not once. Damn it, I couldn't even try to pretend to hate him anymore.

He pulled the truck off the highway into a gas station, Lisa and Seth following close behind.

"Huh," I said without even realizing it.

He glanced over at me, unable to hide his concern; he was so horribly on edge, worrying about Kaya, and worrying I might be sick again. "What?"

"Doesn't anyone drive cars anymore?"

"Really? Is that what you're thinking about?" He shook his head.

It wasn't. But telling him I was grateful for him, and that I understood what Kaya saw in him, weren't words that would come easily. "That and I'm, uh... glad you're driving," I said.

Luke was perceptive. He could read between the lines. "C'mon Oliver, don't get mushy on me. I've got enough to worry about without you turning into a puddle of muck." Emotion sparkled in his eyes. "But yeah, I don't mind driving," he added.

With all he'd done for me, I had to try and comfort him. "Hey… we'll find her," I said, but the worry I also had for Kaya was obvious in my voice.

All Luke could do was gulp and nod his head, hand trembling slightly when he put the truck in park. He didn't have to say anything. I knew how he was feeling. I wasn't the only one shouldering the intense feelings of responsibility for Kaya anymore. My mission was the same as his, and so were my fears. The only difference was I knew in the end, in the very, very end, he would be the one to get the girl.

And I wondered if there was any better man.

Seth and Lisa pulled up to the pump behind us. The snow was falling again and so was the temperature in the air. In the rearview mirror, I watched Lisa get out of the truck and pull her cap snug over her blonde hair. Shivering, she shook a fist and swore at the sky, loudly proclaiming her disgust of the weather. She was feisty, blunt, and ballsy. I'd never met another female like her, and I wasn't surprised to see her take on checking the oil and gassing up the vehicle.

Seth headed toward the store, yelling back to Lisa to make sure and fill it up, and the scars across his cheeks from Kaya's fingernails glowed white against his ruddy skin. Something about him rubbed me the wrong way. I couldn't put my finger on it. I just always had the feeling he couldn't quite be trusted.

I gassed up while Luke followed Seth inside. He pretended to not hear Lisa let loose another bunch of expletives, now at the cold, metal pump in her hands. The prison mouth on her made me blush. As the meters clicked away, I avoided her eyes. Instead, I watched her delicate petite hands alternate to keep from freezing. Before I could stop myself, I was hanging up my pump and moving toward her.

"Give it to me."

I hadn't meant to sound quite so demanding.

She glared like I was a maggot on a French fry. "I'm not some damsel in distress. I am perfectly capable of—"

I stepped in and got my hand around the pump, practically shoving her out of the way. Watching her shiver was making me crazy. "I know you're capable, but your cold and I'm not. I got this."

"Geez, you're an asshole," she said before marching off and into the store.

I couldn't argue with that. From what she knew of me and how I'd acted—she witnessed my drug rage when I shoved Kaya down the stairs—it was accurate. What she didn't know was I'd kicked the pills. I was in control again. I could… breathe.

I waited for what seemed like forever until the tank was filled. Then I finished filling Luke's truck, whistling at the quiet night to ignore the stinging in my fingers. The highway was desolate. Not another vehicle went by, not another soul in sight. At the far end of the parking lot, a few lonely lampposts lit up a collection of rusted-out vehicles and a massive tractor. Behind that there was nothing. Just snow-covered fields. Flat. Empty.

This place was depressing. Smack dab in the middle of nowhere. As I noticed the second level of the store to see a small balcony and tiny windows flanked by lace curtains, I wondered who lived there. Who peered out that window at the highway and what kind of life did that person have? Was it as dreary as it seemed? I pictured myself up there for a moment. Then Kaya beside me; if she were there standing next to me, green eyes shining like they did when she smiled, the whole place would have been lit up like a Christmas tree—she could do that. If she was next to me, I wouldn't care where I was.

God, I missed her. So much it hurt. I had to find her. So I could lose her to—

"Oliver, get in here!" Luke bellowed from the store.

Luke.

I was going to lose her. To Luke.

I stomped up the creaky steps, the bell on the door ringing as it swung open into the overstocked store. The air was warm, but I shoved my frozen hands into my pockets. Behind the counter, an older lady with granny hair eyed me carefully as I headed to a table set by the window where Luke, Seth, and Lisa were all seated. The tension in the air was thick.

"Tea?" Luke offered tensely, nodding to a hefty mug of brew before an empty chair.

Seth and Lisa stared wordlessly. I wondered if maybe I was about to be poisoned. "Uh, we don't have time for tea," I said, still standing.

Luke cleared his throat. It was obvious he was fighting to maintain his composure, but I wasn't sure why. "We talked to the lady who runs this place, but she doesn't know of anyone named Ben Smith around here. She also said the highway going east has been blocked off—cops are turning traffic around due to an accident. And since that's the only way to get to Radville, we are going to enjoy some tea and quite possibly some microwaved pizza."

Golden boy jittered like he was about to explode, and Seth and Lisa were obviously waiting for me to do the same. They didn't know I wasn't that guy anymore. I could handle bad news like a champ, thinking clearly and calmly without my jaw aching from gritting my teeth.

Luke, however… he was vibrating and white-knuckling his mug. I patted his shoulder. "The store lady wouldn't know everybody around here, Luke. We'll figure it out," I said, taking a seat between him and Lisa.

Both Seth and Lisa had to pick their jaws up from the floor.

"Four sugars and one cream, right?" Luke said absently, eyeing the mug in front of me.

I stirred the brew. "Yeah. Thanks."

Lisa couldn't contain her shock. "What the hell, Luke? You even know what the big guy takes in his tea?"

I stifled a laugh. "Don't worry there, Blondie, we still hate each other."

"Detest," Luke corrected.

"Despise," I added.

"Yeah. That, too."

Lisa eyed me suspiciously, the storm outside shaking the window behind her.

"Did the lady give any idea to how long the highway would be closed?" I asked, ignoring Lisa's scrutinizing stare.

"Nope," Luke said. "She says her hubby is out there helping tow vehicles out of the ditch. He's going to call her when the road is open. Apparently, someone ran into an overturned semi hauling gasoline and it blew up."

"Whoa. That sucks." The mental image was horrific.

"Yeah. It's a bloody mess."

Wearing a homemade pink sweater tight down to her knees and plastic beaded jewelry dangling from her neck, the lady shuffled over to us. She plunked some steaming pizzas down onto the table.

"My name is Arlene. I'll turn the TV on for you kids, and y'all can stay as long as ya need to," she said kindly.

Seth began stuffing his mouth immediately. I thanked her. Luke stared at his hands, and Lisa turned up her nose at the pizza and fumbled with a granola bar instead. Next to a round security mirror, an old television dangled from the ceiling in the far corner of the store. Arlene fumbled with the buttons and cranked the volume to an uncomfortable level. I imagined her sitting on her stool behind the counter, eyes darting between the television and the mirror, waiting for customers…

"Okeydokey, here's the news," she yelled, finding the channel she was looking for. "Ah, local. That's us."

I reached for a slice of pizza before Seth inhaled the whole pie, but yet again, Luke didn't eat. I shoved the plate toward him with a demanding stare. Sighing and picking up a piece, he forced some into his mouth. Lisa was about to comment, but instead shook her head.

"So, Ben Smith…" Seth said, wiping sauce from his chin. "That's our guy?"

I chewed my way through overcooked crust before replying. "Yeah. There are two around here. One outside of Radville where we're heading and another about an hour and a half north. If we don't find her there, then…"

"Then we might not find her," Luke said dismally.

Lisa's eyes widened. "We have to find her before Rayna does or—"

Luke erupted. "Tell me something I don't know, Lisa!"

Lisa flinched back from Luke's outburst, then reached across the table and affectionately gripped his arm. "Yes, it might feel like finding a needle in a haystack. But, it can, and it will be done. You gotta relax. Have faith."

Luke's eyes rolled and then drifted down to the food in his hand. "Yeah, I know. I'm sorry, Lees."

"It's okay, luv," she said sweetly.

Seth couldn't hide the jealousy making his nostrils flare. He cleared his throat. "Let's look at a map and see how we can get around the accident. There must be an alternate road or something. We gotta think smart. Check out this lead as fast as possible, and then move on to the next."

We agreed.

Luke put his food down and shoved away his tea. He was really struggling to stay calm. "Maybe that accident will get cleared up soon, and we can head on through. They can't keep a highway closed for too long. By the time we drive in circles to get around it—"

He didn't finish his sentence; a car had pulled up outside at the gas pump opposite his truck, and then another right behind it. They were both identical black SUVs with blackened windows—not the sort of vehicles farmers would drive. The hair rose on the back of my neck and Seth froze, pizza midair. The television was blaring out hockey scores, the phone was ringing behind the counter, and nobody was exiting the cars outside.

Then the backseat driver's side window of the second car started rolling down…

"Get down!"

Seth hit the floor first, then Luke followed, realizing a little too late that Lisa was too engrossed in her granola bar ingredient label to know what was going on. I lunged for her, getting hold of the first thing I could—which was a handful of blonde hair—and pulled her to the floor with me as gunfire shattered the window.

Arlene started screaming. Seth scrambled in her direction, getting to the counter while food packages blasted apart around him. I ignored Lisa's struggles as I shielded her, covering every inch of her petite body with mine as bullets ripped through the air. I pictured Kaya, the day of her birthday in that restaurant, and the moment I lifted up to see her bleeding out from a massive gash to her neck, so deathly pale as she lay there dying…

The gunfire stopped. Arlene was silent. I looked down expecting to see those emerald eyes and thick black lashes—but instead of Kaya, it was Lisa. Glaring and perfectly fine.

"I'll bloody well kill you if you don't get off me," she hissed.

Chips were in her hair and scattered around us. I tentatively rolled off, staying low, and got my gun from the back of my pants. I backed against the wall under the broken window, and felt something slice at my back. I'd cut myself, that unmistakable warmth of blood and sting of a fresh wound caught my breath, but I had to put it out of my mind.

Luke had moved up next to me. We were beneath the window, watching in terror as Lisa decided to crawl on her belly to Seth amidst another round of gunfire.

"Lisa! Stay low," Luke yelled.

Food bags and chocolate bars blasted apart around her while she made her way toward the counter. Seth stood and started firing at the broken window, covering for her until she was safely next to him.

And then the only noise was the wind rushing in and the television screaming the weather forecast: more snow.

The security mirror gave a wide view of the destroyed store and Arlene's tiny feet sticking out from behind the counter; I hoped the old broad hadn't been shot.

"Lisa's safe. But we're sitting ducks, and I'm almost out of ammo," Seth warned.

Keeping my eye on the mirror, I saw the figure of a man crouch next to the steps just outside the door. "There's one outside," I said to Luke, pointing at the security mirror. "See him?"

Golden boy had become still. Eerily calm. Whatever happened to him when he was in fighting mode had switched on; I was glad we were on the same side.

"There are two in the first car… and maybe three in the last," he said, ice-blue eyes unblinking, gun in his hand remarkably steady.

We watched the security mirror while the television shouted out the local news. The man outside on the steps was obviously waiting for a signal, and I imagined as soon as we were surrounded he would be tossing tear gas in through the doors.

And then we'd be screwed.

"We gotta take out the guy on the stairs," I said to Luke.

He didn't answer.

"Luke... do ya hear me?"

He didn't. His eyes had become laser focused on the TV, to where a news anchor's hair was being whipped around by the wind. The man was on a highway with the blackened remains of an explosion in the background.

"Authorities have closed the highway just outside of Radville. An overturned semi exploded when hit by a minivan that couldn't stop in time on the black ice. Incredibly, there were no casualties, and that is thanks to the quick thinking of two very brave young women...

And there, on the screen, was her.

"I think there are six of 'em," Seth said, trying not to yell. "Oliver, when I give you the signal, stand and fire out the window just off to the left. I can see on the security camera two went around back. Lisa can take care of them..."

The television blared, but now I couldn't look away either.

Elsie Summers says the unidentified woman went back for her child even though the vehicle was on fire. Three-month-old Caitlin was strapped into her car seat and was miraculously unharmed in the crash. The unidentified woman who saved the child's life had assistance from a friend who helped pull them both from the wreck moments before the explosion. Ms. Summers would like to personally thank these heroines who saved her child, but they left the scene before...

"Okay," Seth was saying. "On my go..."

The television now showed a girl running, and it was Kaya. No doubt about it. I knew by the way her body moved. Smoke billowed out from behind her. The only other thing visible was another girl wearing a red hat, leading the way. The voices around whoever was filming were panicked and screaming at them to run faster. Kaya had a something in her arms wrapped in a blanket... a baby....

Then a massive explosion ended the video.

Luke gasped. "Uh...Oliver?"

"Yeah, I saw it," I said, noting the advertisement for Carlson Farm's Angus Beef emblazoned on a truck in the ditch just as the video feed ended. When the anchorman reappeared to advise of alternative routes, that truck was gone.

"No casualties..." I repeated, mostly to myself.

"No casualties," Luke reaffirmed.

"Boys! What the hell?" Seth bellowed, "Are you assholes even listening to me?"

Luke smiled wryly, ignoring Seth. "Well, Oliver, we found her," he said. "So...whaddya say we get this party started? Ol' buddy, ol' pal?"

I grinned. "Oh, hell yeah."

Before I was even standing, Luke was on his feet firing at the driver of the second SUV. The windows of the car shattered as he sent bullets at our attackers with deadly aim. Even in the low-lit night, bloodshed was visible all over the front seat. We took aim at the second car, but our sightline was impeded by the gas pump. I was trying to get whoever was driving while Luke tried to shoot out the tires—neither of us wanting to blow ourselves up with a rogue bullet. We stood, side by side at the broken window, and kept firing. When we were out of ammo, the car floored it and started to pull away. Our efforts did nothing to slow it down. Soon, it was disappearing onto the desolate highway.

I didn't notice a man get out of the remaining car—but Luke did. His fast reflexes landed a perfect shot to the man's chest, not even giving the guy a chance to lift his arm to aim where his eyes were fixed—on me.

My knees went weak. "Now I owe ya again for saving my life," I said, trembling slightly.

Luke was still calm. Steady. "Hopefully you won't have to return the favor anytime soon."

Seth had shot at the doors, taking out the man crouched by the stairs. Lisa had taken care of the men at the back of the store.

"All clear back here," she yelled. "I got two."

"All clear up here, too," Seth replied.

Snow whipped in through the broken window.

"Why'd that car take off?" Luke said, running his hand through his hair. "We were sitting ducks, and no one even fired back. Why would they just leave and..." He didn't finish what he was going to say. Instead, he looked at me with an expression that made me take a step back. "Oh my God. They saw it too! They know where she is... and they don't need us idiots to lead them to her now."

Luke's eyes were wild. Everything that had been calm about him had disappeared.

"Saw what?" Seth was red cheeked and vibrating. He was searching the body at the door. The man he'd shot had fallen halfway into the store and was bleeding out of too many places to count.

"The news! Kaya was on TV. They know where she is," Luke said breathlessly. He was about to say more, but I shook my head at him.

"Which is where?" Seth asked eagerly, taking the dead man's gun.

Luke's eyes narrowed. His gaze shifted from me to Seth, centering on him with fury. Suddenly, I could see he had the same reservations I did about the ex-cop.

The wind picked up food wrappers, fluttering them through the store in a whirlwind of chaos and confusion. "Or... maybe they stopped shooting at us because of you, Seth. Maybe Rayna didn't want to harm her ex-hubby. Maybe she still has a thing for you."

Seth stood, perplexed, and then a deep laugh erupted from him. "Yeah, I doubt that."

Luke's muscles tensed like a cat about to pounce. "Tell me then... why is Kaya so important to you?"

The grin left Seth's face. He countered Luke's accusation head on, even though he knew the dead man's gun in his hands was useless if Luke decided to strike—he would never even get a chance to aim and pull the trigger. "Luke, you know I'm on your side."

"Yeah, but for what reason exactly? What's in it for you?"

Seth carefully and slowly placed the gun in his belt, then held his hands up in defense. "Listen, you know you can trust me. Haven't I proved that? I don't work for Rayna anymore. And besides... good Lord Luke, you kidnapped someone! Remember? You knew what Regan wanted to do with Kaya Lowen, and you were just as hell-bent on kidnapping her as the rest of us were. You're just as guilty of being a dickhead as I am, but I am not questioning your motives, now am I?"

Luke was speechless. He wavered slightly.

"What if you hadn't fallen for her, huh?" Seth continued, his words having an obvious effect on Luke. "She would have been Dr. Death's pincushion and then handed over to Rayna to be made into mincemeat—"

Luke roared. "Never! I never would have let it get that far. It might have taken me longer to realize what I had to do, but I... I would have stopped it. I would have..."

Luke's voice trailed off. He was visibly shaken by the truth.

Seth stood his ground. "Anyway, now that we have all come to our senses, it's just obvious what we have to do. I want to help Kaya, to make things right." He gave Lisa a nod, then focused on Luke. "That's all I want. I promise you."

Lisa remained quiet. Whatever was going through her mind, she miraculously kept to herself.

Seth sighed. "I've got good intentions, Luke. Really. So let's figure this out, all right? If that girl was on television, you might as well just announce to every corrupt asshole in the world that a billion bucks is up for grabs."

Luke blanched. "A billion bucks?"

According to the sudden nervous tick in his eye, Seth just said something he shouldn't have. "Figuratively speaking, of course," he added.

There was something Seth wasn't telling us, but now wasn't the time to pound it out of him. I'd wait until I got him alone, then we'd chat.

Luke took in a deep breath, calming down. We waited, leaving it up to him to make the next move. An alarm was going off somewhere, and the ice in the air was like knives.

"The Carlson Ranch… find out where it is, Lees," Luke finally said. "And hurry, please. I think that's where we'll find her." He stormed past Seth, stepped over the dead body, and headed outside through the shattered doors.

Seth cleared his throat, relieved. "Yes, you do that, Lisa, and I'll go in the back and disable the security cameras, swipe the tapes, and empty the cash register so the cops will think it was a robbery. I knocked the store lady out, so she won't remember a thing."

He disappeared into the back room. "Cops…" Lisa said with a shudder, eyes leaving him to follow Luke pacing outside. "Probably not a good idea for me to be anywhere near this place if they show up. And Luke, too."

She had a tiny scrape on her cheek and her hair was mussed, but she wasn't crying or hyperventilating like Kaya would be over the blood or the dead men she'd had a hand in killing. There wasn't any weakness about her. I had the weirdest desire to know what made her that way.

She caught me studying her. Her eyes weren't filled with hatred for me anymore.

"Hey, you're bleeding there, big boy," she said, pointing to the increasing dark splotch on the bottom of my shirt.

I'd been ignoring the ooze of blood seeping through the thin fabric. It hadn't hurt… until now.

"You better let me have a look." She marched over and reached for me.

I backed away. "I remember very well the last time you 'had a look.' It didn't end so well for me."

"Right. The Death Race." Her eyes flashed in concern. "Listen, you have every reason to be wary of me. But I'm on Luke's side—which weirdly enough is your side now, too, and how that twisted bit of reality came about is beyond me." A sly grin crossed her face. "Besides, I promise I won't drug you again."

I cringed, remembering the drug she'd slipped into my water that had doctors thinking I had altitude sickness. I was taken out of the race with busted ribs. Lisa... this petite blond standing before me, was the one who had masterminded that plan. "Uh, yeah. I forgot to thank you for that."

"I was just doing what I had to," she said. "We all were."

"Is that your way of apologizing?"

Lisa's face turned to stone. "I'm not sorry. I'm sure you can understand that, Oliver. I think you'd go just as far as I did for the ones you love."

She stood with her hands on her hips, wind pelting her cheeks, staring me down with the ferocity of a tiger. Instinct made me want to argue with her, but she was right.

I reluctantly turned around and let her fumble with my shirt. Her fingertips on my bare skin gave me goose bumps. My spine tingled when her warm breath brushed my shoulder blades.

"It's bleeding a lot, but it doesn't seem too deep," she muttered.

Pressing a batch of napkins over the wound, she lingered longer than necessary. The world slowed down for a moment. I felt a kindness from Lisa that made my breath catch. I could have stood there with her for a very long while, but Seth emerged from the back room, face slick with sweat and now green with jealousy.

"You better find out where this Carlson Ranch is, Lisa," he said, breathing heavy. "Cops will be here any minute. Get on it before the old broad wakes up."

Lisa's hand fell away. "About that, Seth. Did ya have to hit her so hard?"

The old lady in the pink sweater had begun to moan. "I did what I had to," Seth said flatly.

Right. We were all doing what we had to do. All of us were on the same page... but from completely different books.

Lisa headed for the counter, fumbled with a laptop, and then furiously began typing. She looked up to catch Seth and me watching her. "I think I saw a first aid kit in the back, Oliver. Go grab it, and I'll patch you up while we're on the road."

Seth gritted his teeth and stomped out of the store.

"Oh, and uh...thanks for saving my life there, big boy," she added.

If I hadn't grabbed her by the hair—if it had been left up to Seth—she'd have a bullet through her pretty little head. And she knew it.

Our eyes locked from across the room. She seemed to be holding her breath, waiting for my reply, and I think I'd been holding mine; the warmth of her hand still lingered on my skin.

I made myself look away. "Anytime."

STEPHAN

23

OOPS

"COULD ANYONE BE LOOKING FOR YOU?"

Davis didn't reply.

I knew he was awake even though I couldn't see him—it had been days since any light broke into the cell. His breathing was even and the metal bed he was strapped to wasn't shaking from his violent nightmares.

"Davis?"

Silence.

I wished the fire had just claimed me like it had claimed Old Carl. Being locked down here, deep beneath the estate in a damp cell with the rot and the stench of human waste was worse than hell. It had been days since there had been any contact from above, and I wondered where they were; the Labcoats with covered faces that stuck us with all sorts of things, starved us, and probed and prodded our bruised bodies... They usually didn't leave us torture-free for this long.

"Davis..." I said louder, even though he could hear me even if I whispered.

The chains around his ankles rattled against the metal bed frame. "What?" he said irritably.

I swallowed hard, trying to get some liquid into my throat so I could talk. It hurt to use my voice, but I had to know. "Could Oliver be looking for you? Anyone?"

His pause was too long. The steady drip of the rusted sink in the corner was loud. So was the skittering of a bug on the decaying brick walls and his labored inhales. "No."

"You just... left?"

Davis groaned. "I had to. Ollie wanted to follow Kaya, and I figured he'd come to his senses if I didn't join him. I guess that backfired."

"He'd never leave Kaya. Damn it, Davis, I can't believe you came back here," I said, any hope at being found obliterated.

"Yeah. That was probably an unwise decision." The chains holding him rattled. "I didn't think this job would end up being quite so restrictive."

If Oliver wasn't with Kaya, who would protect her? "This guy, Luke, will he look out for her?" I asked, talking quietly because my voice seemed way too loud in the dark.

"Definitely," Davis replied.

"And you're sure she lost the baby? Had a miscarriage?"

"Positive."

"Hopefully she read my email warning her to never come back here. And where she goes, so will Oliver. He'll follow her to the ends of the earth whether she wants him to or not. So, in other words, no one knows we're missing, Davis. No one."

Davis coughed. "That is correct."

Death was knocking at both my doors—I wished it would just hurry up and come in already.

I reached up to scratch my cheek, my shifting skin felt like it was being rubbed with sandpaper. It was a struggle to get my hand to my face. My stomach flipped and twisted tight against my spine—no food had been in there for days. The burns on my cheeks were itching and oozing. When I finally got my fingers there, I forgot I didn't have fingernails to scratch with and agonizing jolts of pain shot through my hands. I quickly put them back down at my side. Mind over matter... mind over matter...

There were at least six others down here besides me and Davis... but they never spoke. Never made a sound. Not even when Davis had been brought in kicking and swinging, and it had taken six armed men to contain him. The Labcoats wrestled him to the ground and injected him with something that rendered him useless, and then they chained him down onto a bed next to mine. All the while, the others—five men and one woman in a cell across from us—didn't bat an eye. Their expressions remained vacant. They were emotionless and horrifically silent as Davis was electrocuted, half drowned, and hit repeatedly while being asked the same question over and over...

Where is she?

He didn't know.

Where is she?

I didn't know.

Where is she? Where is she? Where is she?

They didn't know.

I heard the question in my sleep and in the dark that had become terrifying. It rattled through the walls and chewed on my bones.

I didn't know. And Davis didn't know either. And... even if I had an idea, an inkling, or a thought... all the torture in the world wouldn't make me talk. Never would I help Henry Lowen find my baby girl. Davis, to his credit, said nothing either. He didn't love Kaya like I did, but he had an extreme loyalty to her and Oliver that kept him quiet.

And that would get him killed.

My body hurt too much to sleep, and the ragged breathing of the others chained up in the cell across from us was like nails on a chalkboard. I needed to hear Davis's voice.

"Tell me about this Luke guy."

There was a heavy sigh. "I don't know him," Davis said wearily.

I could hear him shifting around and pictured his sandy-brown hair slick to his head with nervous sweat, feet still bare because the green and neon-orange shoes he loved had been pulled off and tossed in a corner. His Rush T-shirt was probably even more shredded, and his brown eyes—usually sparkling with mischief and humor—were probably rimmed red and filled with hurt; I was glad I couldn't see him.

But I needed to hear him.

I hated to beg. "Please, Davis. I need to know my baby girl is going to be all right. It might be the last thing I hear. I can't see what's going on with me, but I can feel it. The infection—is worse."

Davis had pleaded with one of the Labcoats to do something about my legs, which were covered in oozing sores from the burns that hadn't been treated. The stinging and the throbbing in my right calf and the fever that brought me in and out of lucidity was increasing along with the shiver. I was dying. No doubt about it. And them torturing me hadn't helped.

"He's tall," Davis finally said.

Tall. "Oh. And?"

"His last name is Ravelle. I guess chicks would think he was pretty good looking if they were into dudes with six-pack abs and that kinda stuff. Kinda golden brown or blonde hair—I dunno whatcha call it. He looks like one of those dudes out of a cologne ad. Buff. Blue eyes...not that I really noticed."

A picture was forming in my head. "But what about him? What's he like?"

Davis coughed and spit; I was glad I couldn't see it. "Seems like a cool guy. Tough. He could pound the crap outta Oliver if he wanted to. And he seems pretty forgiving, too; Oliver tried to slit his throat and he just let him walk away. In fact, afterward, he prevented Oliver from cliff diving without a parachute."

I liked what I was hearing. "And Kaya...does she love him?"

Davis gulped loudly. "Hell yeah. It's one of those 'meant to be' kind of things. You can just see it. I never believed in it before, but then... boom... there it was. No denying it. People talk smack about insta-love and love at first sight, but I am here to tell ya it's real. The day of Kaya's eighteenth birthday, something about her changed. I could see it in her eyes. She was different, and I just assumed it was because of Oliver. But now I know the whole story, I realize it was because of Luke. She met him that day. They fell for each other well before this whole kidnapping thing went down."

Davis paused, and I hoped he would tell me more.

"You know," he added wistfully. "She flung herself into a raging river to save him knowing it would probably kill her. She would do anything for him. Anything. I couldn't imagine having someone love me like that. And I couldn't imagine loving someone enough to die for them either."

I could.

And I did; if Kaya found true love and a future that wasn't her being used for Henry's horrific schemes, I would die a hundred times over for that. There was one problem, though. One thing wrong with the whole pretty picture Davis was painting.

"This Luke guy... he's a kidnapper. A criminal."

Davis sighed. "Yeah. Technically, I guess. One of Eronel's drugs killed his mother and left him with his little sister to look after, then some dickheads took the kid from him and held her for ransom. Luke had run out of options when The Right Choice Group offered him a way to get his sister back. Getting revenge for his mother's death at the same time probably made for a sweet deal. I dunno, Stephan. I think I would have done the same. I mean, if that happened to my family—if I had one that is—I would fight for it. And man, if you saw his sister... she is scared shitless of everything now. Who the hell knows what happened to the poor kid. I just hope that—"

Davis quit talking the instant he heard the stairs creak. We both froze. A pin of white light came into the room. For the first time in a long time, I caught a glimpse of the man locked up next to me; I could have cried. Davis's face was bloodied and swollen, and bruises covered every inch of him. His eyes widened at the sight of me, and then he quickly looked away.

"The neighbors are coming for a visit, Stephan," he said, trying to contain the fear in his voice. "Got the kettle on?"

The room quickly became swathed in light and our eyes, after being in the dark for so long, were blinded. I kept mine shut. Listening for the key in the lock, the cell door creaking open…and waited for the pain to come. What would it be this time? An electrical current followed by the same old question we couldn't answer? The whip? Some experimental drug that made every nerve feel like it had caught fire?

I held my breath.

But there was no pain.

Hands were on my legs, the touch light as a feather, and a soothing feeling crept across my burned skin. I inched my head up to see two Labcoats applying something to the wounds. They toweled off my face, then they slapped the back of my hand to find a vein.

"Why don't ya just kill me now and get it over with?" I said, sounding braver than I felt.

"We're not in the business of killing people, Stephan. You know that. This is just antibiotics, painkiller, and something for your upset stomach," came a muffled reply.

The voice made me shudder. It was the girl, her mask giving away nothing of her features but her slight accent and high-pitched voice unmistakable. I instinctively recoiled, trembling head to toe inside. Another Labcoat was injecting Davis with something, and for once, he wasn't writhing in pain. This was new.

"Why'd it have to take so long, huh, Stephan?" the girl asked. "You could have saved yourself a lot of trouble if you'd just gotten us some information sooner."

Information? My mind reeled in confusion. "What are you—"

"Shush now," she said. "The boys are gonna clean you up and get you fed. You just rest and get better, all right? You're no use to us if you're dead."

I had to laugh. "No use? Well… heaven forbid."

The girl let loose with a laugh, too, the same one that would haunt me in my dreams. It made every part of me ache—especially my fingertips—because it was the laugh I'd heard when she'd ripped the nails from them.

"What do you want us for?" Davis asked.

A jab at my other arm with a needle sent something cold under my skin. My stomach instantly quit rolling, and the pain practically disappeared. I could have died from the relief alone. The girl rolled her shoulders and tossed the needle aside. I suspected she was smiling behind her mask when a lock of purple hair escaped from beneath her hood. She carefully pushed it back.

"What do we want with you, Davis?" she purred. A monster disguised as a kitten. "Well, I'm not sure yet, to be honest. But maybe you'll sweeten the bait. If Kaya is even slightly hesitant about coming here for her precious Luke, Stephan will be the tipping point. And you? Icing on the cake perhaps?"

Both Davis and I inhaled sharply; our innocent conversation had just given Henry Lowen everything he needed to control Kaya—all he had to do was find Luke. With him in their clutches, Kaya would do whatever they wanted.

The girl hovered above me, the pink cactus tattoo on her neck pulsing with her heartbeat. "Ah... Luke," she said viciously. "Blue eyed, blond-haired Luke. The man Kaya would die for. I can't wait to meet him. He sounds... perfect."

KAYA

24

CHOICES

THE ROOM IN THE CARLSON'S BASEMENT WAS DAMP, AND THE heat blowing in from the ceiling vent didn't do much to warm the air. A small lamp barely lit the space and cast eerie shadows on the walls. I was glad Thomas didn't question why I needed it on. The dark still bothered me, but I hadn't told him that yet. "How's your leg?" he asked sleepily.

The cut on my thigh wasn't deep, just long and jagged. It was going to be a nice addition to my already ridiculous collection of scars. When Thomas dressed the wound for me, there were tears in his eyes. He took longer than necessary wrapping the bandage around my leg. Warm hands lingering on my bare skin… giving me goose bumps…and with him so close, it was impossible to deny I felt something for him. Three weeks of sharing a room, laughing in the dark, spilling our guts, and sharing our deepest fears and secrets had created a bond between us like no other. The accident only strengthened it. I hadn't realized just how much I wanted him in my life until that horrific moment when we hit the ditch.

I rubbed at the bandage. "My leg is fine. Doesn't sting anymore. Go to sleep," I said softly.

"Uh-huh," he muttered. "But if you need me to have a look…"

I got butterflies imaging his hands there again. "Nope. Just go to sleep, Thomas."

It was almost three in the morning. I tossed around in the tiny bed, exhausted and restless. The accident had me on pins and needles. Not because of the fear or the shock of what happened, or the discomfort of the countless scrapes and the muscle now throbbing in my injured arm; it was the baby I'd pulled from the van. Her small body tight against my chest and blue eyes wide when I tentatively looked to see if she was alive… was the spitting image of the baby I had seen when I almost drowned in the rapids. The baby who resembled Luke. The one who floated away from me before I lost consciousness… That baby was real.

The vision played out. I had held her. I'd saved her.

But I'd been holding on to the idea that the vision of that baby was a prediction of a future I would share with Luke. That it was a heavy hint at least. Now that she had come and gone and certainly wasn't ours, I wondered if maybe I had it all wrong.

"Kaya? Hey, are you awake?" Thomas asked, his voice barely a whisper.

"Yeah," I said, swallowing hard. I turned my thoughts to my roommate. I was so grateful for him. He was the only one able to get me to let go of the baby at the accident. He had dropped down next to me in the ditch, blood streaming across his face as the fire raged behind him, and said whatever I needed to hear to get me to hand over the crying infant. He shielded me from onlookers and the mother who wanted to express her gratitude, and before I knew it, had me in the truck and crouched as low as I could go. Barely able to stand, he ordered Marlene to hook up the winch to get the truck out of the ditch. He prevented what would have been a colossal mess if we would have stuck around until the police arrived.

And I was grateful for Marlene, too. She practically ran people down to get us out of there before the police showed up. She drove like hell was nipping at our heels, steady on the black ice under Mr. Carlson's guidance. She got us through the storm and back home. No one would question Marlene's driving skills ever again.

Or her bravery.

"It's bloody cold down here," Thomas said, startling my racing mind once again.

The space between our beds felt like a hundred miles even though we were only separated by a ratty shag rug, an ancient dresser, and our discarded shoes. I could see the outline of him underneath his blanket, long and lean, toes hanging off the end of the bed. The clock on the wall ticked and he shifted onto his side, eyes meeting mine in the dim light. I shivered, but not because I was cold.

"Just come and crawl in with me. You know you wanna," he said softly.

I did because I felt so alone it hurt. "What about your head?"

He had been dizzy, wobbling on his feet and eyes unsteady all day. "My head is superb," he said. "I think the bandage makes me look mysterious, don't you? A scar might add an element of danger to my otherwise perfect good looks. Chicks dig bad boys. Or at least you do."

I snorted.

"Really though, come crawl in with me," he said.

It was a tempting offer. "I don't want you to get the wrong impression."

"I think it's pretty obvious where we stand with each other, don't you?"

I actually had no idea where we stood. Thomas was everything a girl could wish for in a man. He was brave, smart, funny, and incredibly gorgeous. Our connection was so undeniably real I couldn't question it now if I tried. But he wasn't Luke. I could never love him like that.

"I don't actually know what we are," I said honestly.

"Friends, Kaya. We're friends," he said. "I know you'll fall in love with me eventually, but for now, that's all we are. Besides, I don't think I'm up to the challenge of having you as a girlfriend."

The grin on his face was a mile wide. It was a magnet pulling me out of bed and toward him before I'd given much thought about the consequences. My breath was stolen from the bite in the air, and my heart raced slightly. I stopped once my shins hit the metal edge of his cot. It would be wrong on every level to use Thomas for purely selfish needs, and I didn't want to hurt him by leading him on. But I craved his closeness.

"Quit thinking so hard and just get in," he said, pulling back his blanket and moving against the wall to make room.

I sat down, and the heat left behind from his body warmed the back of my bare thighs. It reminded me Marlene's nightgown was a bit too short, the fabric threadbare, and there was not enough of it covering me. I tugged it down, suddenly tempted to get up and find my blue sweater, but Thomas's hand had moved to my back. The heat of his palm was soothing, gently moving across my spine. I found myself sliding in next to him. Before I knew it, he was on his side, pulling me close and cradling my forehead against his chest. His skin was firm and inviting beneath my cheek and fingertips, and his masculine smell was heavenly. I tried not to notice.

"What's the scar on your neck from?" he asked, moving my hair away to reveal the long white line from my jaw to my collarbone.

I'd told him most things, but wasn't ready for that story yet. "A knife. On my sixteenth birthday, someone tried to slit my throat," I said. "But that's a tale for another day."

I felt his body stiffen. "You've survived through a lot of crap, haven't you?"

"I guess."

"Ya know, if you were my girl, that would never have happened."

I sighed. "Well, I'm not your girl."

A pause. His arms tightened. "Maybe you should be."

His words hung there in the chilly air, the tone of his voice making it almost impossible to swallow. "I thought you weren't up for the challenge," I said, hoping I sounded lighthearted.

Our chests were now pressed together—the friendship barrier certainly being crossed. He drew in a deep breath. "I might have just changed my mind."

He was so serious I had to laugh. But it got me wondering, what would a life with Thomas be like? What if I was his... girl?

"You're thinking about it, aren't ya? Having a hot guy like me around is pretty tempting, isn't it?" he said with a smile.

"I'm thinking about nachos actually."

"Yeah, sure you are."

He vibrated with a laugh. It sent little sparks down to my toes. As his body enveloped mine, knee to knee, I could hear his heart, stable and steady; it made such a beautiful song. So soothing and comforting—although not as magical as the passionately alluring serenade of Luke's. Thomas made a different kind of music. One born of the dark, of the dead of night, of the need and desire to feel the safety and comfort of another human being. It was a nocturne I could lose myself in...

"Don't get the wrong impression," I reminded.

"Uh-huh," he said sleepily.

I basked in his heat. Couldn't help but wiggle in closer to try and feel more of him.

"You know, that was just crazy what you did today," he muttered, breath on my forehead. "I have a lot of respect for you, Kaya."

I fell deep into his sleepy brown eyes. For a moment, I wished I could love him like I loved Luke. Life would be so much easier. I was here, with Thomas, because I wanted to be. For no other reason. He was my choice. I just wished I felt... more.

I closed my eyes and tucked back into him. "You would have done the same thing if you could have."

"You're brave—braver than you think. Stronger than you realize." He placed a feathery kiss on my forehead. "You know we can't stay here anymore, though, right?"

"I know."

"We'll have to leave in the morning. Find some new place to hide. Your face will be all over the internet by now. I couldn't get to the teenagers with their damn cell phones fast enough."

"My fa—er, Henry Lowen made sure I was never photographed so the public doesn't know what I look like."

"Your crazy daddy is the one I'm worried about. And uh… Luke."

I trembled at the sound of Luke's name resonating in Thomas's chest. I placed my hand over his heart beat increasing in tempo, sorry for what I was about to say. "Don't worry. I am leaving tomorrow. But by myself, Thomas."

He bolted upright, fear in his eyes. "Like hell you are! We have a deal. A plan. Remember?"

I had to stay firm. "You have your plan. Mine is to not have you killed because of me."

His face relaxed. He ran his hand through his hair, the jet-black strands falling right back where they had been before. "Ah. You're just worried about me. That's sweet."

I stared up at him hovering over me, so ruggedly beautiful. "It's not sweet; it's practical."

His hand moved to my cheek, and he gave it a light stroke of his thumb. "Without me, you'll end up dead. And without you, I'd probably feel dead. We stick together. That's what friends do. So, in the morning, we'll head out. I have a car at my sister's; we'll go there first, then get out of this province and maybe head east. Since you've never seen the ocean, how about—"

I cut him off. "My mother's men shot six people in a motel room just because I was there. No other reason. My father has no qualms about killing me… His own daughter! I'm not taking a risk with you."

"Mother shmother… motel shmotel… guns and death… blah blah… Whatever, Kaya. You're not getting rid of me. You've already dumped that Luke dude to protect him, but you don't love me like that. Yet. So for now, don't worry about it. I'm along for the ride."

I sat up to stare him straight in the eyes. "No, Thomas."

"Hey," he said, putting his fingers to my lips. "I know you care about me. I can see it all over your pretty face, and that's all I need."

He eased back down next to me, resuming his position and pulling my head to his chest. His hand was moving up and down my back, easing the tension in my aching muscles, creating a strange heat in the pit of my stomach.

"You could get hurt. People around me—"

"Are really goddamn lucky to be around you," he finished.

Was I changing my mind? "It's not worth the risk, Thomas. You know that."

He became still, his hand pausing between my shoulder blades, his breathing speeding up. "How about this?" he said, voice tight. "Why don't you let me show you how amazing I can make you feel, and then you can decide if keeping me around is worth the risk?"

"What are you talking about?"

He cleared his throat, and his voice became a whisper. "Give your body over to me for a little while."

I didn't know what to say. Thomas's version of 'being friends' didn't quite match mine. I fake coughed. "That's rather bold."

"Yes, I guess it is," he said, his deep voice making my spine tingle. "Let me make you forget everything. Forget Luke and your crazy mother, your messed-up dad. Let me take your mind to another place knowing you can trust me. As your friend."

The devil on my right shoulder started yelling at the angel on my left to take a hike. "I didn't know that's what friends did," I said.

He inhaled. "Well, it's usually only reserved for the type of friendship we have. You know, boy loves girl, girl loves another boy."

"Thomas…"

"The morning I saw you covered in flour, standing helplessly in Ben's kitchen, I knew right then there was no going back to whatever life I had before. I tried to stop feeling it, but that was like trying to stop a freight train with a cornflake. So listen, I know you'll never love me like you love him… and I can live with that. Really and truly I can, as long as I can just be with you. I will be your friend, on whatever terms you want."

"I'm sorry, Thomas. I wish…" I squeezed my eyes shut for a moment, wondering exactly what I really did wish for—yes, to have a life with Luke of course—but I'd pretty much made sure that would never happen. With the necklace gone, I had no way of getting John Marchessa on my side. The blue-eyed baby had come and gone, too, and it wasn't Luke's. I'd misread the signs. This, right here and right now, was what I truly had.

"I wish things were different," was all I could say.

"If there is one thing you can count on in life, it's change."

Thomas's warm lips brushed my forehead. I wanted to pull away, get up and get back into my own bed, even pretend to be shocked and insulted by his offer, but my body betrayed me. My heart sped up. The fire churning in my stomach spread downward like wildfire.

"Take me up on my offer," he breathed.

His hand was at the back of my neck now, kisses trailing across my cheek. I wasn't telling him to stop. I wasn't saying no. His touch was making me slip away from all those things I wanted to forget.

"I… I'm not very experienced with this stuff," I admitted.

He couldn't hide the shock in his voice. "That's okay. But… Luke?"

"We never."

"What? Never? Was there something wrong with him? I mean, good God, what the hell?"

"I had a miscarriage," I said quickly.

Thomas froze.

"I guess I forgot to tell you that part. Luke felt that my body—and quite possibly my mind—were too fragile. He also said, that… he…" I fought to breathe. "He said he wanted to marry me first."

A pain in my ribs threatened the delicate threads that were holding me together. I recalled what Luke had said to me in the field of yellow flowers… the way he looked at me… and the way my heart felt like it might burst from my chest…

And then I shut it out.

I had to.

That memory would be the death of me.

"I'm sorry to hear that," Thomas said, breath catching as my fingers roamed over his heart, exploring his smooth skin and the gentle curve of his muscled chest. His voice wavered. "Then whose baby were you carrying if it wasn't his?"

I was incredibly aware of every single part of my body against his. "It was my bodyguard's. Oliver was my first and only time, and although it was consensual, I didn't really want to. I thought I loved him, but I know now it was… something else."

It took a long time for Thomas to reply. His body was pressing harder against mine, his hand leaving my neck and moving to my lower back. "Your first time, and you got pregnant?" he said slowly, bringing his hips to mine. "So, you've never really known the pleasures of friendship."

"No," I replied, the fire raging within me.

We were becoming increasingly wrapped in each other's limbs. I could feel every inch of him against me, tantalizing and terrifying.

"Then use me, Kaya. I'll do anything you want. Please. Just say the word."

My fingertips were on his throat now, grazing the light stubble there that softly spread to his sculpted chin. I couldn't stop my thumb from touching his lower lip. So soft, full, and warm. "Maybe you could just—"

I didn't know what I wanted.

"Just what?" he asked eagerly.

"Make me feel something besides hate and anger and revenge and fear."

He put his mouth on mine. It didn't feel wrong, but it didn't feel exactly right, either. With Luke, that first kiss ignited all my senses. It had lit my soul. With Thomas, it was different; it was purely physical.

And I was perfectly okay with that.

He kissed me softly, being a gentleman and giving me ample opportunity to stop what was about to happen. He parted my lips, his hands starting to roam up under the nightgown, tentatively moving across my ribcage. He was slow, attentive, and I found my back arching to meet his touch. He kissed his way down each arm, then across my collarbone as my desire for him escalated to a dizzying height.

"You still haven't given me the word," he said. A whisper in my ear.

I couldn't speak, so I nodded.

He pulled away and sat up, the blankets falling below his hips. In seconds, he was naked before me in all his incredible male glory.

"Sit up," he ordered.

I did. My nightgown was removed, and a gasp came from him as his eyes moved across my body. In the dim light of the cold room, I let myself stare back. The look on his face was filled with desire for me. It made mine frantic. I took in the sight of him, rippling stomach muscles, perfect unmarked skin, and the length of him he had no reservations about letting me see.

"You think I'm hot, don't cha?" He grinned.

"I've seen better," I teased.

He took my hands and put them on his chest, then guided them over his body and down his stomach. The look in his eyes lost all humor. "Are you for sure?" he murmured.

My blood threatened to simmer over. "Yes," I squeaked.

"Do you trust me?"

I did. For some crazy, unexplainable reason, I did. So I leaned forward and kissed him as a reply. He pushed me down on the bed and then hovered over me, dark hair falling across his eyes. I reached for him, pulling his face to mine, and his mouth moved more urgently, pressing, searching with his tongue as his hand brushed my thighs, caressing my skin, and trailing to that place where he could feel how much I wanted him.

I couldn't contain the moan that escaped from deep in my throat. The feather-light touch of his fingers circled and explored while he nibbled on my lip, my neck, then down across my chest. I ran my fingers through his hair as he kissed a trail down my stomach, lingering there, his hot breath a blissful hint at what was to come. His head dipped lower, below my hips, and his hands were moving my knees apart. He was almost at the part of me that was screaming in agony for him…

"Wait…" I gripped the sides of his head, making him gaze up from where he was positioned between my legs. His beautiful face made me forget whatever I was about to say.

"Trust me," he said with a wink.

And then his mouth was on me. Tongue moving over my most sensitive parts. When his fingers joined in, making their way to the very center of me, I had to grip the sheets and bite my lip to keep quiet.

I'd never felt anything like it, and Thomas, knowing that, took his time. He took me almost to the point of no return, then reeled me in, stopping to move his mouth over my inner thighs, and then my fingertips… sucking on them playfully. He coyed. He teased. He made me forget my own name. I was soon begging, pleading with him not to stop. His reply, accompanied by a soft moan that flowed from him to my very core, was a touch so mind-blowing there was nothing in the world but me and him. When my body let go with a shuddering release, he kept moving his tongue and fingers in a way that made me completely blind with ecstasy.

And then he did it again.

It didn't matter where I was. Or who I was. All I became was desire for his touch as I surrendered to him completely.

It was heaven unlike no other.

I was panting when he grinned up at me.

"So… am I worth the risk?" he asked mischievously.

I mumbled an affirmative reply.

"Then promise you won't leave without me," he said, holding me captive.

"I promise," I breathed. His mouth… his lips. "I promise…." The world disappeared.

WHEN IT CAME BACK, I FOUGHT TO CATCH MY BREATH. HE CRAWLED UP next to me, eyes ablaze as he gazed at my flushed face. I wanted him. All of him. Not just his mouth and his fingers. But he caught my hands when I reached for him.

"Kaya…" he breathed and laced his fingers through mine. "I don't think—"

I kissed him hard, wanting to give him the same pleasure he gave me. "It's your turn."

He gripped my hands tighter, then suddenly let go. "Ok. Turn on your side," he demanded.

The ticking clock on the wall suddenly seemed so loud. Did I really want this? What about Luke? What about…

I did what I was told, facing my lonely bed on the other wall as he shifted around behind me. His arm slipped under my neck, then his body became a cocoon around mine. I thought of Oliver and that time in the woods, his urgency at having me and the way it felt, wanting to say no but giving myself over anyway. Was I doing that again?

"You can relax, Kaya. We're not going to do that until I'm sure you'll have no regrets," Thomas said as if reading my mind. "As much as I want to—and believe me, good Lord above I want to—it just might take our friendship to the next level and I don't think you're ready for that. And besides, I would most definitely wake up the entire neighborhood. When I make love to you, Kaya Lowen, it will be because you are begging me to. And when I show you exactly what it feels like to be loved, I'm going to howl loud enough for the entire world to hear."

I was aroused and relieved at the same time. His hand stroked my hair as his body remained a raging inferno behind me. Somehow, he had the strength to restrain. My heart fluttered.

"It's an interesting friendship we have," I said.

"Yes. Just so you know though, you can love two people, Kaya. There's nothing wrong with that."

I had no reply. I didn't know what I felt for Thomas, but it was something.

We lay silent in the dark. My mind raced.

"What are you thinking about?" he said after a while.

"I'm scared," I admitted. "I'm trying to stay brave, keep it together, but my family... my mother... and—"

"Shh," he said, breath on my shoulder. "I thought I made you forget all that. Guess I'll have to try harder next time."

My heart raced. Next time.

"Hey, it'll be all right," he said, serious now. "You just need sleep. Or maybe some more distraction."

He was still rock hard against me. "What sort of... distraction?"

He cleared his throat, hand petting my head soothingly. "Ever had angel food cake?" he said.

"Uh, what? Good Lord, if that's some sexual thing—"

He guffawed. "Ha, no. Really. Actual angel food cake. It's a bitch to make but if you get it right and whip up the perfect orange cream sauce to go with it, it's awesome."

"Oh?"

He spoke softly, his voice slow and deep, a whisper brushing over my ears while his hand ran up and down my arm. "Well, I'm gonna tell you how to make it. When I'm done, if you're still awake and need more distracting, I'm going to explain to you everything I know about cheesecake. So close your eyes and picture a shiny white kitchen and clean bowls."

His voice started to drift in and out of my ears. I was in a cocoon of warmth as I basked in the afterglow. His touch was soothing now, and my body relaxed against it, limbs becoming limp like jelly. He was listing ingredients and measurements. Explained types of flour.

"...then you have to separate a dozen eggs. Now to do that you have to crack them, pull them apart, then toss the egg back and forth between the shell..."

And for the first time in a very long time, I slept.

25

CATCH MY DRIFT

A SHARP KNOCK AT THE DOOR JOLTED ME AWAKE. I PRIED MYSELF out of Thomas's arms, swung my legs over the side of the bed, and forced my body upright. My head spun for a moment while I got my bearings.

"I want to know what the hell is going on with you, Kate," Marlene barked from the other side of the door. "You've had time to rest, now it's time to start talking."

The clock on the wall said 6:15 in the morning. Thomas glanced at it, stretched his arms over his head, and then irritably told her to piss off.

But that didn't stop Marlene from barging in. There was a scowl on her face and a thousand questions on the tip of her tongue—which quickly gave way to horror.

"Good God, Kate, you're naked! And Thomas is right there!"

Thomas rolled onto his back and burst into laughter. Embarrassment instantly heated my cheeks—not because I was naked, but because I was standing on the nightgown he'd thrown to the floor and was vividly recalling the things he'd done after it was removed.

Marlene, wide eyed, looked at Thomas and then slowly back to me, then realization settled on her face. "Oh," she said, with a roll of her eyes. "At least you made one good decision, because yesterday was a hornet's nest of bad ones."

She stared at the ceiling while I scrambled for clothes. I picked my sweater off the floor and yanked it down over my head, grateful it was long enough to cover my butt. "What do you mean?" I asked, rubbing sleep out of my eyes.

"First of all, taking my hat." She glared at me now. "Don't ever do that again. And running off in the morning by yourself? The weather here can change in the blink of an eye, so… yeah. Probably not such a good idea. And that whole accident thing—"

"I'm so grateful for you, Marlene," I interrupted. "Without you, me and that baby…" I didn't have to finish that sentence. "You saved our lives."

She was angry. "You gave me no choice! Was I going to stand there and watch you get burned to a crisp? Friends have to help each other out. That's an unbreakable law. And, Good Lord, running back for that kid. It was so stupid!" Her gaze softened, and she sighed heavily. "But so brave."

I stared hard at her flushed face. She had put makeup over the birthmark, but the dark color still showed through. It seemed odd she was trying to cover it.

"I'm sorry I put you in that position, Marlene."

"Yah, well, what's done is done. And anyway, I have a feeling you would do the same for me. And apparently for butt-head Thomas, too," she said bitterly.

Thomas had remained quiet, hand propping his head as he watched with a sleepy gaze. The sheet had fallen away from his bare chest, and Marlene had a tough time keeping her eyes off him.

"So," she said, remaining in the doorway, "After all that nonsense, I think that given the circumstances you can give me some answers. Like first, why was Thomas calling you 'Kaya'?"

Her arms were crossed over her chest. There was no way she was leaving until she got what she wanted. I took in a deep breath. "Because Kaya is my real name."

"Ah," she said, still glaring. "And what is your last name?"

"That I can't tell you," I said firmly.

She sneered. "Then what can you tell me? Huh? My mind is racing, and I need an excuse not to hogtie you and haul your ass down to the cops."

I returned her stare and squared my shoulders. She was trying to appear intimidating, but it had no effect on me. I did owe her some sort of explanation, though. "I am hiding from my father, who is a complete psycho and wants me for the sole purpose of providing him an heir, so he can claim my inheritance. And… I am hiding from my birth mother whom I have never met, who wants nothing more than to put my head on a stick and flaunt it to daddy dearest. She's already tried to kill me once and will do so again. I left those I love to keep them safe and wound up here—with you. But I am leaving today so I won't involve you and your family anymore."

Marlene wavered, the anger on her face dissolving. "Huh." She sucked on her lower lip. "The reason Thomas was so desperate to get you away from the accident before the cops showed up was so your mom and dad wouldn't catch wind of your whereabouts? They are that bad?"

I swallowed hard. "You have no idea."

Marlene nodded as if she understood, and the glare she'd fixed on me completely faded. "So, you're not some criminal, thief, drug dealer, or murderer?"

I stifled a laugh. "No. I promise."

She let out a relieved sigh and charged into the room, the smell of something sweet coming from her flannel shirt. "Okay, well thank heavens. So, what do we do now?"

Thomas sat up, thankfully making sure the sheet covered his lower half as he moved to the edge of the bed. "Kaya and I have a plan," he said, reaching for his jeans. He put his feet in the leg holes and tugged them halfway up, keeping the sheet over his midsection. "We are going to—" He stood to get the pants up to his waist, but plunked down on the bed instead. "Whoa," he said, putting his hand to his forehead.

"Are you okay?" Marlene asked, voice dripping in concern, eyes glued to his glowing skin.

He'd become extremely pale. Where he had hit his forehead on the truck dash was now a good-sized lump that looked painful to touch. "Yah. Just have a headache from hell," he said.

"Upset stomach, too?" I knew all too well what a concussion felt like.

"Yeah," he said flatly. "Whatever. It doesn't matter though, I'm fine. Anyway, Kaya and I are leaving today, Marlene. It's not safe for her to be here anymore."

Marlene cracked her neck. "Then I'm coming with you."

"No way. Besides, you have a family here. A wonderful family that loves you. Why on earth would you want to leave?"

She shoved her hands deep into her jean pockets. Her amber hair bounced around her shoulders as she started pacing the ratty rug. "I'm not going to live with Mom and Dad forever. Geezus, I'm not exactly sure what I want to do with my life, but digging holes and shoveling shit certainly ain't it. I need an excuse to get out of here—just like you do— or I'll be trapped forever. That's what happens to people like us, Thomas. If we don't go now, we'll never get off the damned ranch."

Thomas remained oddly quiet.

Marlene cleared her throat. "Helping out a friend is a good reason to blow this popsicle stand."

I readied myself for an argument. "That said, you're still not coming with us. You'll have to find another excuse. Sorry."

Her eyebrow lifted with a confused stare. She studied me as if trying to put pieces of a broken puzzle together. "You're different. Something about you has changed. I can sense it like I can sense a storm coming on."

She was right. And that change made me realize that being mean was going to be the only way to keep Marlene from following me out the door. "Marlene, I don't need you. Understand? I don't want you to come with me."

Apparently, I was in the business of hurting those I cared about to keep them safe. And judging by the look on Marlene's face, I was good at it. It killed me to see her crumple slightly and reel in the shock from the blow I'd delivered.

"Yeah, all right. I get it," she said and turned to head for the door.

I reached for her hand, making her face me. There were tears in her eyes, a sadness that mirrored my own if I'd allowed it to surface. "I've never met anyone like you. Under any other circumstances I think we would be best of friends."

"Oh, piss off, Kate, Kaya, or whoever the hell you are. I don't need friends."

I squeezed her hand, maybe a bit too firmly; there were so many things I wanted to tell her, like how she never ceased to amaze me, her strength was an inspiration, she was beautiful… wise, and someone I wished I could have gotten closer to.

But words failed me.

Marlene saw it, though. My bad acting hadn't fooled her. Squeezing my hand back just as hard and leaning in to my ear, she whispered, "I understand."

I leaned in and choked slightly on my whisper, "Look after Thomas for me."

She let go and gave me a nod. "I'll go tell Daddy you're running away from an abusive ex-husband, some prick of a cop who keeps hunting you down or something. That's what he and Ben figure is going on anyway. Oh, and by the way, he's here." There was no mistaking the disgust in Marlene's voice at the mention of Ben's name.

"Why the hell is Ben here?" Thomas asked, suddenly on high alert.

"He's taking Zander home now he's sober and says he has extremely important info for Kaya. But Daddy won't let him down here unless she says it's okay." She shivered. Something dark—maybe a memory best left forgotten—seemed to rattle her. "Personally, I wouldn't let him anywhere near me."

Whenever Marlene had talked about Ben before I thought it was just hatred. But now, as I watched her shift her weight between her feet and wring her hands, I knew it was something else. Something her and I shared—fear.

I spoke quietly. Carefully. Hoping the question I was about to ask would be met with a shrug or an incredulous laugh. "Marlene..." I breathed, my chest tightening. "Did Ben... did he ever... try anything with you too?"

She froze and stared at me so hard it was like she was trying to will her thoughts into my head. Her teeth gritted, and her nostrils flared. "Let's just say I'm way stronger than you, and today I made my Daddy's best friend a really great cat food sandwich for the drive home."

I felt my jaw hit the floor. Thomas gasped.

"And after what he did to you, I figured I'd go ahead and disconnect the brakes in his truck as well." She kept her chin up, our eyes remaining locked. "Anyway, I'll send the asshole down in about five minutes. I guess you better hear what he has to say in case it's important. Afterward, feel free to let Thomas beat the crap outta him."

And with that, she was gone, leaving my mind reeling in her wake.

"I'm gonna kill him," Thomas hissed, and he stood, letting the sheet drop as he pulled on his jeans. "I'll show him how it feels to—" His words were left hanging, and he promptly sat back down on the bed again.

"Your head is really hurting, isn't it?"

"Man, I didn't feel this bad yesterday, or last night. It's like I got hit with a hammer in my sleep. I'm so dizzy the world disappears when I stand."

"I think you have a concussion." I moved before him, cradling his forehead against my stomach. I ran my hands through his dark hair, wishing I could take his pain away. "I'll find out what Ben has to say, and then you and I will leave here. Don't worry about him, okay? What's done is done. He's not worth your time or energy. I don't want you to talk to him or fight him. Do you understand?"

"You're giving me orders?"

His face was hot against me, hands safely at his sides. "Yes. Got a problem with that?" I challenged.

He shrugged. "Normally, I wouldn't. But... Marlene, my God. His best friend's daughter. How could he? The sick bastard. He's not getting away with this, Kaya. I'm going to beat him senseless—"

"Shh." I felt Thomas's heart rate speed up and knew it would put extra pressure in his head. I needed to keep him calm. "Marlene has gotten back at him in so many ways. Believe me, he'll get what's coming to him. But not by your hands, Thomas. Promise me, not by your hands."

If Ben had done to Marlene what he'd tried to do to me, maybe I'd kill him.

"I don't know if I can make that promise," Thomas said.

I pushed his head back to see his dark eyes; they were swimming in his head, barely able to focus. I had to be the protector now. I had to make sure Thomas wouldn't get in a fight and end up having his brains scrambled completely. I was going to have to use ultimatums to keep him safe.

"If you want to be with me, Thomas, and run away with me, I have to know you can promise me things like this. It's not a huge request. If you can't promise you will leave Ben alone, then we're through. I'll walk out that door and—"

"Okay, okay!" he said quickly, wincing at either the pain in his head or the thought of me leaving him. "I won't touch him. I promise."

I pulled him back to me. "I'll look after everything. You just sit here and rest. Let me handle Ben," I said, caressing his neck, kneading the muscles there and feeling him relax. "It's time for you to trust me now, all right?"

He sighed. "Uh-huh."

BEN'S BOOTS SHOOK THE STAIRS, AND I BRACED MYSELF. HIS VOICE, followed by a knock on the door, made my skin crawl. It brought back the memory of his hands on me, but instead of cowering, I kept my posture as straight as possible and my expression neutral—no way would I allow him to know how he affected me.

The remains of a black eye reaching his temple and the bruises dusting his jaw were bittersweet. He was sweating, his cowboy hat off and in his hands, fingers pinching the edges of it. His eyes were crystal clear and he appeared sober, so at least the man who came down the stairs was the Ben who had rescued me. He eyed Thomas perched on the bed and failed to conceal a cringe of jealousy. "Kate... I... came to talk to you about something private. Could Thomas leave us for a moment?"

"Not on your life," Thomas hissed, ready to leap from the bed and start swinging.

"Just say what you have to say, Ben," I said sharply and cast Thomas a warning look.

Ben uncomfortably cleared his throat. "Well... first, I'm so sorry for what happened. Really and truly I am. It was the alcohol. I drink sometimes and I blackout. I don't remember a thing. But Jeb told me what I did. I swear I would never do something like that sober."

"You need help."

"I know. And I promise I'm working on that." He was full of remorse. Guilt was written all over his face and rightly so. "I never meant to hurt you," he added sincerely.

I knew that. Ben was a good guy, a really good guy. I thought of the morning I'd found him at the holding lot, how he was ready to defend my honor from whatever he thought I was running from. And the gas station… I was about to walk off and die, and he stepped in. And the diner… who knows what would have happened to me if it weren't for him. I wanted to forgive him, but not yet.

I swallowed hard. "What is this essential information you have to tell me, Ben? Get talking or leave."

Ben's face fell when he didn't receive the forgiveness he was hoping for. He glanced at Thomas, then back to me. "Someone called my house again and hung up. I'm sure they were searching for you. Now, after that accident, they will know where to find you. The 'girl who mysteriously disappeared after saving the baby' is big news. Marlene's mug is recognizable—for obvious reasons—and there's footage of her running from the fire with you and then getting into the truck and driving off. The name of this farm is advertised all over that truck." Ben paused and glanced at Thomas. "Should I be saying this in front of him?"

It took a moment to find my voice. "Thomas knows everything about me, Ben. More than you do. So go ahead."

Ben didn't like that. He spoke through gritted teeth. "Well, there are more people looking for you. The mother of that baby is offering a reward and wants to personally thank you, and the police want your statement. Your face is everywhere. Hell, someone even sent me a picture of you on Facebook with the caption anybody know this girl? Jeb's phone has been ringing off the hook with people who recognized Marlene…"

That was why Marlene was wearing makeup. "This isn't good," I muttered.

"Nope. So, pack your stuff and let's get moving. You need to come with me."

Thomas tensed. "And why is that?"

"Because I can look after her," Ben said.

Thomas let out an incredulous laugh. "Do you really think she's better off with a drunk who will rape her the first chance he gets?"

Ben turned beet red and the veins protruded at his temples. Seething, he tried to ignore Thomas to concentrate solely on me. "Thomas here is just using you," he spat, clenching his fists.

"I know." I felt a wry smile tug at the corners of my mouth. "And I am most certainly using him, too."

Ben dug his fingers into the hat bearing the brunt of his anger. "Well, don't say I didn't warn you."

"I appreciate the information, Ben. And…" I stared hard at him. "I appreciate all you've done for me. I truly do. I just hope you do seek help. You've got a demon on your back you need rid of."

His eyes welled up, and he choked back a rolling boil of emotions with a nod. "Should I be worried about my friends upstairs? Are they in danger too?"

"Absolutely," I said without hesitation.

Ben took his wallet out of his back pocket, and produced a thick wad of cash. He extended his arm to me, and I instinctively recoiled; the weakness brought on by fear I couldn't suppress. I remained where I was, though, even though my feet were itching to bolt from the room.

"Take this," he said. "It's your pay, Thomas's too. Now, hurry up and get the hell outta here."

I had no interest in the money, so Ben tentatively took a few steps toward the freezer and set it down. Sidestepping me carefully, he cleared his throat. "I'm gonna convince the Carlsons they need to go on a little emergency holiday for a few days till things blow over."

"Good. I wish you well, Ben," I said formally.

He wavered slightly like I'd shoved him, gaze drifting to his watch. "I'll have the family out in fifteen minutes. Make sure you head east, not toward Radville, all right?"

"We've got it under control," Thomas said.

Ben turned to leave, but paused at the door. "Kate…" he said, giving Thomas a concerned glance. "I hope you're making the right choice."

I bit my lip. So did I.

FIFTEEN MINUTES PASSED IN THE BLINK OF AN EYE. I PUT WHAT FEW belongings I had into a backpack and said goodbye to the room that felt more like home than anyplace else had in a long time. By the time I zipped up the pack, Thomas had fallen asleep.

He was hurting more than he admitted, and I was torn between leaving him and taking him with me. If I left him here and Henry showed up…I shivered. But if he was with me in the line of fire…

I snuck out of the room and quietly made my way upstairs, tiptoeing even though I knew everyone had left. I would give Thomas a few moments to rest and get him some aspirin. Hopefully, he'd be better upon waking. In the bathroom medicine cabinet, I found something for his pain and something I was all too familiar with—sedatives. When my anxiety would reach freak-out level, Stephan would shove a couple of the blue pills down my throat and Oliver would hold me until I passed out. It was a timeout in medicinal form, forcing my mind to let go of everything to drift off into sleep. It was Marlene's prescription. Now I understood why she might need them.

I put a few in my pocket, along with the white painkiller caplets, and then roamed about the empty house. Family photos on the walls surrounded an ancient dining room table with half-eaten plates of food, and the crocheted lacy things covering the couches and tables in the living room were slightly mussed; there wouldn't be a thing out of place if Mrs. Carlson was home. This house, filled with baked goods, home-made blankets, and gleaming white walls, had been left in a hurry.

I put a velvet cushion back in its place, then stared out the living room window at the miles of ranch land. Vast and stunningly white. The elm tree, focal point of a winter scene, dropped piles of white snow to the ground. Beneath its branches was the place Thomas had made me dance with him. It was the first time in ages I'd laughed. I'd pushed aside everything messed up in my life and just for once, lived in the moment. Free. Happy. Safe. It was a memory that would never leave me, sweet and perfect. Easy and uncomplicated. And all because of Thomas. We were just two people dancing, and strangely enough for a brief second, I hadn't wanted to be anywhere else...

A blackbird soared through the cloudless sky. Hills rolled away like waves. Cattle wandered in the distance. And I felt the most intense sense of longing for this kind of life. Simple... honest... Maybe I could have that someday. Maybe Thomas was the one to make that happen...

"Aren't you supposed to be leaving?" said a voice from behind me.

I damn near jumped out of my skin, spinning around to see Ben standing in the archway between the kitchen and the living room. I cursed him for shocking me.

"I thought you'd gone." I kept my voice steady, but my hands shook. "Thomas is just..."

I didn't finish. Ben took a few large steps toward me and damn it if the fear of what he could do to me made my heart race. I wondered if Thomas would hear me if I yelled. I wondered if Thomas could even help me if I needed him.

"Why are you still here?" I asked.

Ben blinked in the sunlight. "Someone has to stay behind and look after the animals."

That wasn't the only reason. "And look after me, right?"

He was quick to reply. "Well, yeah. How are you going to get out of here? Huh? You can't drive, and judging by the look of Thomas, he can't either."

"I don't want your help."

"Well, you might not have a choice."

Ben's voice trailed off when our attention was caught by something out the window. A white van, matching the color of the ground, was rolling up the drive. "Ah crap. Someone's here. Get into the kitchen."

I stood where I was, not about to take orders from him.

His face became terrifying. "Now," he yelled. "I don't give a shit if you're pissed at me or not, get the hell away from the window and into the kitchen!"

His anger jolted me into obeying. I bolted for the kitchen, almost tripping on the polished tiles, and backed up against the fridge. The marble island in the center of the room where I had first ruined pie dough stood between me and the back door; my escape route if I needed it. If Henry or Rayna were here, I could bolt through that door, head straight across Marlene's snow-covered garden, and into the stand of birch trees. And then what?

I looked down at my bare feet... Great.

A knock at the front door shook the walls. The door squeaking open was loud enough it could have been right next to my head. I remained in the kitchen, staring out at the vast expanse of land through the window. What would I do about Thomas?

"There's no girl who looks like that here. I can assure you," Ben was saying to whoever was at the door.

I pulled open the cutlery drawer. A gleaming silver knife the size of my forearm was cold beneath my fingertips. I withdrew it as the voice of a man who had identified himself as a reporter boomed through the house. It was deep and husky like he'd smoked a pack a day.

"Are you sure?" he was saying. "We've spoken to a few people. They say she got into a truck advertising this ranch. We just want to interview her. The mother of the child she rescued is desperate to thank her as well. I hear there's a reward, too. Maybe you'd get a cut—"

"Oh, piss off," Ben said angrily. "There's no girl here. I got nothing to tell ya so be off now."

Was it really a reporter at the door? Why wasn't he asking about Marlene? She was just as much a part of the rescue as I was.

"Oh, come on now, no need to be rude," the husky-voiced man said. "Why don't you have us in? We can talk about things going on in town and the accident. Wouldn't you like to be on television?"

Ben growled. "Listen, I got a house full of guns and enough hands on deck to put 'em all to good use. Unless you want to interview my pistol pointing at your forehead, I suggest you leave."

I knew Mr. Carlson had guns in the house; his favorite shotgun was under the couch in the living room, and he had a collection in the basement. But I wouldn't be able to get to either without being seen by whoever was at the door.

I held my breath until I heard the door slam and the sound of an engine starting up and fading away.

Ben called out to me. "It was just some nosy prick from town, Kate. Nothing to worry about."

Still, I held the knife. The weight of it was comforting. Ben had come into the kitchen, and I tightened my grip.

"Geezus, whatcha think your gonna do with that?" he said, eyeing my weapon.

I noticed a shift in the light behind him. Something wide darkened the snow for a mere moment. I used the knife to point to the window. "Someone's out there. Outside."

He spun around to peer out between the lace curtains. "Uh, nope. Nothin' but snow and horse crap."

I followed him into the living room where he gave a good solid scan to the front yard. "Nothing here, either. That van is gone." He swung around to face me, eyeing the knife still in my hands. "Now put that down before you hurt yourself."

Before I could back up, he was before me, fingers closing around my wrist. I froze. The memory of being completely at his mercy in that bunkhouse came back with blinding panic. I was so helpless… so weak… but Ben was sober. When the knife was removed from my fingers and placed on the coffee table, I reminded myself of that. He respectfully stepped back and put his hands up—I hoped he'd walk away, but he stayed put.

"I need to tell you something," he said.

I shook my head, barely keeping together. "And I need to leave."

"Just sit a moment, Kate. All right?" he said, motioning to the cream-colored couch where Marlene liked to do her crossword puzzles.

"I really need to leave, Ben. You said so yourself that—"

"I know. But I just need a minute." He put his hands together in mock prayer. "Please."

I sat and hugged an embroidered pillow while he paced in front of me. He rubbed his chin, taking a moment to find his words.

"My wife left me six years ago," he said sadly.

"Sorry to hear that," I offered.

"I don't blame her. I was an asshole."

"Oh?" I wasn't sure what sort of reaction Ben was looking for.

"She was a teacher, wanted kids… I didn't."

I stayed quiet, wishing Thomas would wake up.

"It started pulling us apart, and I discovered that drinking was easier than talking. I started getting angry at her. I may have… hit her. Once or twice."

I couldn't contain a gasp of shock. "You… hit your wife?"

Ben nodded. "When she left, the booze flowed harder. It got me through the lonely nights and made forgetting what I'd done easy. I did some shitty things. And you know what? I didn't even care that I did them. Until… until you came along."

I didn't want to hear what was coming next. "Ben, I—"

He shook his head and kept pacing. "No, it's not like that. I'm not… delusional. I'm probably twice your age. I realize now you and me would never have happened."

He took his hat off and placed it next to the knife. Where he stood, the outline of the sun shining in through the living room window was like a golden halo bathing him in light. When he ran his hand over the top of his head and swallowed hard, his lip quivered slightly. I was grateful the light, enhanced by the blinding snow outside, made it difficult to fully focus on his face.

"I guess what I'm trying to say is you woke me up. It took doing something horrible to someone I—well, someone I thought I might have a future with to make me realize what I needed to change in my life. Because of you, I am going to put away the bottle and work on getting some emotional things in check. And I am going to apologize to my ex-wife. And others I've hurt along the way."

"Make sure one of them is Marlene," I said bitterly.

Ben appeared confused. "Marlene?"

"Yes. You attacked her. Like you attacked me."

His hand flew to his mouth, and he spun away from me. His shoulders slumped. "Oh my God," he muttered. "Jeb's daughter? Oh my God… no…"

I gave him a moment. When he turned back to face me, there were tears on his cheeks. "I never… I didn't mean to… Is that why she hates me so much? I never meant—"

"Regardless of what you meant, you did it. You took advantage of someone weaker than you, and whether fueled by booze or not, there's no excuse for that. So own it and do something about it. And hitting your wife?" I felt fire in my veins. "That's about as low as you can go."

He stood still, staring at the floor.

"I can see that deep inside you're a good man, Ben. I believe you when you say you're going to get help. For your sake and the sake of others, I sure hope it works for you." I forced my own emotions back to where they were trying to explode from. I feared him. And I hated he instilled that feeling in me. So I twisted it into strength, because facing him on my own meant I was strong. "I know from now on you'll do the right thing."

He gave me a subtle nod. "I will. I promise. Can you forgive me? Please?"

Could I? People made mistakes. Lord knew I had. And given the circumstances, given it wasn't pre-meditated, and the pain of remorse and guilt were so obvious on his face, Ben's mistakes could be forgiven someday. But not today.

"I think in time I can, but not quite yet. You… hurt me," I said.

"I'll work hard for your forgiveness, Kate."

The sun grew brighter in the quiet room. "It's Kaya. My real name is Kaya," I said.

A smile came over his face, and his hands dropped to his sides. "Well, thank you for sharing that. You never really seemed like a 'Kate' to me—"

A strange whizzing sound interrupted us. Suddenly, his body jerked and his eyes grew wide. He went to say something, but his face contorted in shock and his hands flew to his chest.

Then he dropped to his knees.

"Ben?" I said tentatively.

An icy wind hit my cheeks. I noticed a hole in the picture window directly behind him.

It took a stunned second to put two and two together.

Blood poured from Ben's chest as he fell forward onto his stomach. In the second it took me to get from the couch to where he'd fallen, there was already a pool of red on the hardwood floor. I shook him, shoving him over onto his back. "Ben?" I said again, feeling dizzy as I stared down; there was a gaping wound at his chest. A bullet from outside had gone straight through the window and him. I glanced at the back of the couch; inches from where I'd been sitting was a red-stained hole.

"Thomas," I screamed at the top of my lungs. "Stay where you are… they're here!"

The only reply was the furnace kicking in.

I shook Ben. "C'mon, open your eyes, Ben, please. We have to get out of here." I stayed low to the floor in case the shooter was still outside. "You'll be all right. I'll get you to a hospital. You'll be okay."

His eyes flew open and focused on mine. He stared, unblinking, holding onto my gaze for dear life. "I'm sorry," he said.

I cradled his head in my hands. "It's okay... I forgive you... I truly do..."

And then the light left his eyes. I saw it flicker, dim, then fade completely. He wasn't seeing me anymore. He was staring. At nothing.

Hearing a cracking sound from outside, I dove for the couch. I pulled out Mr. Carlson's shotgun from underneath. It was loaded, heavy, and my wounded arm shook like a leaf trying to aim it. "I'll blow your goddamn head off," I yelled to whoever was outside, then for good measure fired at the already-broken window and into the yard. The pane shattered completely, and the kickback from the gun sent me reeling backward.

My ears numbly buzzed as I scrambled back to Ben, who had gone completely white.

I grabbed a pillow and placed it on his chest. Pushing down, I put all my strength into my arms. I had to slow the bleeding, then he would be all right. I just had to keep pressure on the hole that was directly through his...

Chest.

I listened for breathing.

Nothing.

I put two fingers to his neck and checked his pulse.

Nothing.

I pushed down harder. Called his name. I squeezed my eyes shut, hoping for a moment I was in a bad dream.

But I opened them to see the cowboy who had saved my life was dead.

White noise filled my ears. My chest rattled, and my lungs felt ready to burst. Anger, hate, revenge, fear, sadness, and heartbreak... it surfaced all at once, creating an unbearable mountain of emotion that clawed at every single fiber of my very being.

And then... I felt nothing.

Wind whipped through the room, fluttering the curtains, knocking over a picture of Marlene on a skating rink. The world around me became silent. Still. The only warmth left in it was Ben's blood as it seeped through the pillow and oozed between my fingers.

I shut his eyelids. I bit my lip so hard my own blood poured onto his forehead and left behind little drops of red on his tanned cheeks.

He was gone, so I released pressure on his chest and let him go.

Then, I let everything go.

26

A Lil' Somethin' For The Idiots

THOMAS HAD MADE HIS WAY UP THE STAIRS, AND WAS CROUCHED in the safety of the windowless hallway. He was breathless as he spoke, asking the same question over and over. I could see him crystal clear in the corner of my vision even though the sight before me demanded my full attention. Ben—lifeless, grey, dead. It took a minute to reply and understand what Thomas was asking.

"Kaya, are you okay?"

Was I? I pulled my gaze away from Ben and turned to Thomas; whatever expression I wore made him jump.

"Are you okay?" he repeated.

I nodded.

"Good. Just stay low, all right? Make your way over to me." His voice quivered with worry.

"Ben is dead." I crawled across the cold floor.

"I know. Just come here. To me. Stay low!"

"He said he was sorry. That was the last thing he said before a bullet went right through his chest. He died in my arms. I forgave him for what he did, but I don't know if he heard me."

"Don't think of that, right now. Just make your way here, carefully."

I focused on Thomas's beautiful face as he nervously tracked my every movement. He had a gun in each hand and waited until I was inches from him before putting one down and throwing an arm around me. I inhaled his scent, allowing him to hold me tight while I rested my head on his shoulder, kneeling before him as he tried to comfort me.

But I didn't need comfort.

I pulled away. "Got extra ammo?" I asked, and there was a calm aloofness to my voice that sounded foreign even in my own ears.

Thomas eyed me curiously. He was expecting me to be a crying mess, not cool and collected. "Uh... yeah."

"Hand it over," I demanded.

His eyes were swimming in his skull. "Do you even know how to use a gun?"

"Doesn't everyone?"

I picked up the one he'd placed on the floor, confidently opened the cartridge, and then locked it back in place. Without argument, he handed me the ammo he had stuffed into his pockets. I put two cartridges in my jeans and another in my bra.

"Good place to keep your stuff," he said, trying to force a grin through chattering teeth. "What else you got in there?"

I had no time for jokes. "Do you know how to use a gun?" I asked.

He nodded, cheeks getting paler by the second. I could tell he was in a lot of pain, his head probably throbbing with every movement. He was barely able to sit up, let alone hold his hand steady and take aim. In a confrontation he'd be dead before he could even pull the trigger.

Our survival was up to me.

"Listen Thomas, I need you to go back to the basement and barricade yourself in the bedroom. Stay there until you hear my voice on the other side of the door telling you it's okay to come out. I'm going to go outside and take care of this. Don't let anyone near you for any reason unless I say so. Got it?"

An anxious laugh escaped him. "No goddamn way. You're not serious."

"Listen, you can't even stand. You've got a concussion. You are no match for whoever we're up against. The only way I can protect you is to get to them first." I clutched the shotgun; there were two rounds left in it and the range was better than the handgun—I just wish I knew how many I was up against.

Thomas, realizing I wasn't kidding, latched onto my forearm in an unbreakable grip. "That's crazy! You don't have to protect me. You aren't doing this on your own, Kaya! Good Lord, who knows how many are out there. I mean—"

"Stop. If anything happens to you, that will be the end of me. Not because I am weak, but because I want you in my life. Understand?"

Thomas's dark eyes glittered. They were priceless jewels. They were a reason to go down fighting and not run away or hide. He blinked, trying to find the right reply, and his breathing speeding up warmed my cheeks. "I'm not letting you do this alone," he said adamantly.

I sighed and dramatically tossed my hands up in defeat. "All right. Damn you're stubborn." I fished the blue pills I'd gotten out of the medicine cabinet from my pocket. "Well, at least take these painkillers so you're not hurting and so dizzy, okay?"

He was quick to swallow the pills that he'd plucked from my hand, desperate for relief. I waited until I knew the meds were making their way into his bloodstream, then I clutched his face with my blood-covered fingers. I put my nose inches from his. "I'm sorry. Please trust me," I said, gently putting my forehead to his.

"Sorry for what?" he asked.

Wind rushed in through the living room window carrying the metallic smell of Ben's blood, surrounding us with the reality of death. I kissed Thomas. I poured as much affection mixed with an apology into the kiss as I could. I let it linger, savoring each moment. His hand met the back of my head and wound into my hair, holding my mouth tight to his… and then he pulled back in confusion. His hand dropped away. I felt his body weaken.

"What the hell…did you…drug me?"

His eyelids were fighting to stay open and his words were slurring; the drug was doing its job a little too fast, forcing him to collapse against me. I hoped I hadn't given him too much.

"Kaya, please don't go out there…not on your own… I can't—"

"Shh," I said, holding him tight. "You'll only be out for an hour. After that, just miserably groggy."

And then he was asleep in my arms.

THOMAS WAS HEAVIER THAN I'D IMAGINED. I WOULD NEVER HAVE GOTTEN him down the stairs and into our room without breaking his bones, so I dragged him to the next best place—the kitchen. Getting him there wasn't easy either, though, and I had to work fast, being careful not to bump his head. Sweating from my ears to my toes, I dragged him between the fridge and the island, hoping the appliances would protect him from any stray gunfire. I had no regrets knocking him out, but I did feel a wild sense of relief when he moaned.

Moving as fast as I could into the living room on my belly, I crawled to Ben's dead body and took the pillow off his chest. It was soaked with blood—perfect. I was careful not to leave a trail of it as I took the pillow, the knife, and Ben's cowboy hat with me back to the kitchen. When I lifted Thomas's arm, it was so limp I worriedly checked his breathing to make sure he was still alive. Thankfully deep, even breaths filled his lungs. Rolling him on his side, I smashed Ben's hat a bit before carefully placing it under Thomas's head, hoping it would act like a pillow but look like it had just fallen beneath him. I adjusted his legs, getting them in a more unnatural position, and placed the knife in his open palm—a weapon if he woke and needed it. Trying not to gag, I then squeezed the pillow, pouring Ben's blood onto Thomas's chest and the floor around him. He looked dead. And I hoped that would keep him alive.

"Just lay here and rest," I whispered close to his ear. "Don't move, no matter what you hear. Just play dead."

I hoped some part of his drugged-out mind would hear me and comprehend what I'd said. The only problem now was there were two bodies in the house and the gunman outside had only fired one shot.

I grabbed the broom leaning in the corner next to the fridge, then the fruit basket off the counter and dumped it upside down. Balancing it on the end of the broom, I got low and headed for the kitchen table to where another large window faced the yard. The curtains were closed, but if someone was outside they would see a shadow that might look like a person's head…

I pushed the broom toward the window, slowly, as if it was someone peeking out of the side of the curtain. Nothing. I moved it a little more, raising it higher as if it were a person standing… and this time, I barely had time to flinch from the whizzing sound and the window breaking when the damn thing blew out of my hands. There was a whoosh of winter air invading the house and I trembled, but only because I was cold; fear was nothing but a four-letter word to me now, one I had no use for.

I smiled as I got on my hands and knees and smeared blood from where I'd held the broom to where Thomas lay. It would look like he was hit and dragged himself into the kitchen. Feeling pleased with myself, I now knew there no less than two gunmen and they weren't sent by Henry because he would want me alive. So, that meant this was Rayna. And I felt eager, giddy almost, at the prospect of meeting her face to face and blowing her fucking head off.

I laughed out loud, and then I laughed at myself for laughing as I got into the hall and made my way upstairs to the bedrooms. Each step creaked under my feet as my hearing started to fully come back. I noticed a high-pitched sound, like an alarm going off. Was it coming from outside? Was it in my head? It didn't matter. All I had to do was focus on luring the gunmen away from Thomas and gaining the upper hand.

The first room I came to was Marlene's; forest green walls, black curtains, and dark-painted furniture decorated a space without a hint of femininity. The bed was unmade, and clothes were all over the floor. I quickly yanked on a pair of her socks and hiking boots and tightened the laces. They were a bit big, but better than heading outside barefoot.

The black cargo jacket she'd worn yesterday was on the edge of the bed. I put it on, the smell of her heady on the collar. I got the ammo Thomas had given me, fishing a cartridge out of my bra, and stuffed it in one of the deep pockets along with a pair of Marlene's gloves. I stood tall. Cracked my neck. And I caught a glimpse of myself in the mirror and did a double take. The person staring back at me wasn't weak anymore. She was fierce. Those men outside, Rayna, Henry, and John Marchessa, they should all be scared… of me.

A strange silence filled the room; the furnace that had been roaring suddenly quit. So did the weird alarm sound. According to the blank screen on the digital clock, the power had gone out. Now I could hear a pin drop as the unmistakable sound of heavy feet trying to walk softly crept over the hardwood floor downstairs.

I put the shotgun under the bed and retrieved the pistol—it was better at a short distance—and hunkered down next to the bed. Straining my ears and listening carefully, I deduced there were two men in the house. Then I started to cry—well, not really cry, because I was certainly far from sad—but I made an Oscar-worthy, pathetic whimpering sound I lightly muffled by putting my mouth against the edge of the bed. I held my breath occasionally, pretending to stifle my sobs. When the stairs creaked, I knew at least one of the idiots downstairs had fallen for my trap.

I tugged at the neck of the tank top I was wearing, stretching the fabric to display as much of my ample cleavage as possible. Fluffed up my hair. I bit my lips and pinched my cheeks. Then, with only the bed between me and the open door, I slipped the handgun under the covers and held it sideways. If I was lucky, both men would be together and that would make getting rid of them that much easier.

"I know you're up here," a male voice said. It rang through the silent house, and I recognized it as the voice of the reporter who had come to the door. I took in some deep breaths, and the incredible calm that came over me was almost blissful—I had to remind myself I was pretending to be scared and sad.

"Don't hurt me, please," I said. "I'll do anything you want… Just please don't hurt me."

The man's shadow came first, then his hands, armed and gloved, and then exactly what I pictured stepped into the doorway—balding, fat, dressed in a suit with horrible blotchy skin and eyes so small I wondered how he could see. Had Ben really thought this person was a reporter? There was no way.

"I'm unarmed, don't shoot," I said, wide-eyed and innocent.

The scowl on the man's face changed to intrigue when he saw me crouched behind the bed. A sick grin pulled at the corners of his mouth. "Well, you are a pretty one, aren't ya? You look like your mother, same dark hair and green eyes," he said, oozing with repulsiveness. "I was expecting a bratty kid… not—" He paused and stared directly at my cleavage, choosing his words carefully. "A pretty young girl."

Depravity clogged his repugnant pores. I wanted to shoot him right there and then, but I needed info. And I needed to know where the other man was.

"You know my mother?" I stifled a sob.

This disarmed him. The gun in his hand lowered slightly.

"Sure do, girlie," he said, grinning.

Girlie? It was what Seth always called me. I spoke in the saddest tone I could muster. "My mom, is she here?" I asked, and raised up slightly so more of my cleavage was visible. I put my free hand to my chest, drawing his eye there again, and the disgusting prick actually licked his lips. Fondling the trigger warming up under the blanket was becoming immensely satisfying.

"Well, as a matter of fact, your momma is here. You'd like to meet her, wouldn't ya?"

I batted my eyelids. "More than anything," I said truthfully, faking a sniffle.

A new set of footsteps creaked the stairs. A shadow grew behind the reporter, and then the second gunman appeared in the doorway. Tall. Lean. A face completely forgettable. He developed the same disgusting look in his eyes as the reporter had when he noticed me.

My mother sure kept questionable company.

"The house is empty. All clear," the tall man relayed.

"Ah, good. It's just us then," the reporter said. "We have a few minutes to kill…"

The tall man grinned maliciously and exchanged a mutual look of understanding with his pal that wasn't lost on me. But they were messing with the wrong girl.

The reporter cracked his neck. "Me and Gill here are tired. It's been a long day. So, no running or freaking out, all right? You be a good girl and do as we say, then we'll take you to see your momma."

This was my lucky day; two idiots for the price of one. I reminded myself to pretend to be sad and play dumb. "But are we… all alone?" I asked. "People are after me you know. Whoever shot my friends could still be down there." I fake sniffled.

The reporter grinned and gave his pal Gil a 'boy is this chick stupid' look, while Gil stared at me like I was a cold beer in the middle of a dying man's desert. Getting tired of the chitchat, the reporter dropped his gun to his side. Gil followed suit. And now both idiots were lined up like dominos.

"Promise, it's just us. Your momma is just down the road. She's waiting for my call. She wanted to make sure it was safe before she came in the house to see your—" the reporter faltered, and I knew he stopped himself from saying dead body. "Your pretty face. So yeah, it's just you, me, and Gill on this godforsaken ranch. So we might as well have a little fun."

He smiled.

I smiled back. "I like fun," I purred.

And then I pulled the trigger.

"Sorry for the mess, Marlene," I muttered after a perfectly aimed bullet ripped a hole through each man's chest, sending both idiots dead to the floor.

A BLACK CAR COMING UP THE DRIVE HAD ME RUNNING DOWN THE STAIRS to check on Thomas. He was still out cold, but his pulse was even, his breathing fine, and shaking him slightly and calling his name only got subtle moans. Good. I covered him with a blanket and checked the shotgun. Only two bullets left, but both handguns were loaded. I slipped out the back door, rounded the house and got in full view of the drive. On one knee in the wet snow, I readied the shotgun, hoping to get the attention of whoever was in the car, so I could lead them away from the house. I aimed, fired a shot at the windshield, and watched the car come to a screeching stop. I'd hit my target. With ringing ears, I ran for the bunkhouse and flattened against an outside wall. Gathering my breath, I waited for my hearing to come back, ignoring the pain in my shoulder as I checked the gun. A female voice crept through the void in my hearing… a car door was slamming… a man was yelling orders… Was Rayna here? I couldn't wait to meet her.

I headed for the barn, careful to not trip in the muck and mushy snow while leaving behind easy-to-follow tracks. Wrestling with the heavy door, I got inside and was greeted with the smell of horse crap and hay. The big Clydesdale at the back of the barn lifted his head and stomped its feet, making others follow suit. Clouds of horse breath filled the air. I was glad to see the wide doors on the other end of the barn were shut.

"Oats?" I said softly.

I'd heard Marlene use that word to quiet the horses. I said it again, scooping up handfuls of food pellets from a sack on the floor. The horses waited patiently for me, their heads hanging over the gates, ears turned forward as I tossed oats into their feed boxes, undoing each latch to their pens as I did. The gates could swing open easily now, but the horses were too busy munching on their favorite treats to notice. They were oblivious to their freedom and me trying to find a place to hide. Except for one—a familiar black horse in the last stall. His ears were perked forward, eyes on me, following my every move as I approached him carefully. He seemed to just know what I was up to. Tossing his head, he avoided my peace offering and shifted his body back and forth irritably. I hesitated to open his gate. He was certainly scarier than the idiots outside and didn't give two hooves about oats. But now I had to hide and had no time to be choosy; the barn doors were being forced open. So with trembling fingers, I undid the latch of Zander's pen and got in next to him.

"I need your help, horsey," I whispered. "Be nice to me, all right? Ben would like that…"

Even though I asked nicely, Zander was having none of me. He swayed, scattering the grains in my hand as I invaded his space. His massive body pinned me to the side of the stall, making it impossible to ready the shotgun or even turn around. I was worried for my life until he decided the doors opening at the back of the barn were far more interesting than me. At the groan of the wood, he grew still. His attention was caught by a man marching into his barn, and he wasn't happy with the intrusion. I crouched next to him and steadied the shotgun.

The unmistakable smell of pig manure wafted in with the man, fresh on his shoes, and his legs covered in muck were visible through the spaces in the gate. I laughed, imagining him falling in the pig crap outside. I strained for a better look; he was dressed head to toe in a black suit—which just seemed ridiculous—and his head was shaved. With his back to me, his kneecaps were lined up with my gun. The huge Clydesdale in the pen across from Zander neighed, clearly agitated as well.

"C'mon out, Kaya. No sense hiding," the man in the suit said, peering into the Clydesdale's stall.

I heard more footsteps. The wooden heels of expensive shoes on concrete. It reminded me of Henry walking through the lobby at the estate, and hatred ignited every part of me that felt tired, sore, or fragile.

"We'll be quick about it if ya don't waste our time," a male voice said. The owner of the shoes, I assumed.

"Yep. No sense playing games. There's three of us and only one of you," another said.

I almost laughed out loud; these idiots were making it way too easy for me.

Zander neighed and caught the eye of the man in the suit. He spun around to face the stall I was hiding in. He took a step closer, then stopped, only seeing the top of my head and not the shotgun still aimed at his kneecaps.

"Found her," he said. Zander tossed his head up furiously, keeping him from getting any closer. I fought to keep aim next to the ornery horse. "She's in this stall…" he yelled to his buddies, then lowered his voice and directed it at me. "Just come out of there," he said icily, "so I don't have to shoot the damn horse."

I waited until I heard those expensive shoes approaching… and then I fired.

Terrified horses reared up and violently slammed into the gates of their unlatched pens, crashing into each other and clamoring to get out any exit they could get to. I fired again, and could hear the shocked and terrified voices of the men as the beasts trampled them in chaos. Zander was on high alert, but for some reason remained still. I stayed safely beside him watching as the big Clydesdale was the last to charge through the barn, and, as if on purpose, danced on the man I'd shot before bolting for the open doors.

Then all that could be heard was moaning, and that meant I'd have to use the handgun to finish them off. I hated using the handgun.

I made my way out of Zander's pen to see the carnage left behind. Bloody and in shock or dead, the suited man lay on his back staring vacantly at the roof. He didn't flinch when I gave him a nudge with my foot. Another, just feet away, was twisted, broken, and barely breathing. His eyes were shut. I didn't even bother to nudge him. The third was bleeding from everywhere, leaving a trail of muck as he tried to crawl to his discarded gun. I marched over and gave him a good swift boot to the belly. He gulped for air as blood spewed from his mouth.

"Where is she?" I asked, kicking away the gun he was trying to retrieve.

Face contorted in pain, his eyes were pleading when they met mine. I expected to feel some sympathy… but nope. Nothing but ice chips tumbled through my veins.

I kicked him again, then pointed the shotgun at his forehead—to hell with the handgun. This was meaner and messier, and it matched my mood.

"I'll ask you again." I tapped his forehead with the tip of the barrel. "Where is she? Where is Rayna?"

"Outside," he muttered.

"And how many more of you are there?"

"Two."

He wasn't lying. I found that odd. His sleeve had lifted around his wrist. On it was a tattoo—RCG in thick, black script. "Why does she want me?" I asked.

"Revenge."

"And why are you working for her? Money?"

This question pulled his eyes away from the ground and up to meet mine. They were blue. Like Luke's. He wore a necklace—a thick gold cross—and he was clean shaven. He sat back on his heels and stared at me. I had to remind myself this man wanted to kill me. No sympathy.

"Really?" he said with a slight accent I couldn't place. "You have to ask? Because of your father. I hate him just as much as Rayna does, and just as much as every single person working for her does. He killed my wife. I lost everything because of him." Venom in his voice made the spit foam in the corners of his mouth. "There is nothing to lose and everything to gain by making Henry Lowen suffer. The pay cut I'll get when you're dead is just a bonus."

I pretended his words didn't bother me. "You are prepared to kill an innocent person for revenge and money?"

A smile crept over his face when he caught me noticing the tattoo. "We all are. The guy you're in love with… Luke, right? Yah. I heard all about you and him. He's a part of us, too, ya know—The Right Choice Group. He took orders from Rayna. He was fully prepared to kidnap you and hand you over knowing it would be the death of you."

I felt like all the wind had been knocked from my lungs. "You don't know him," I said, voice catching in my throat.

"No. You don't know him," the man sneered.

For a brief second, we stared each other down. "My wife didn't deserve to die," he said. "She is what I am fighting for."

He dove his hand into his jacket pocket.

I pulled the trigger.

The kickback tossed me into the pellet bag. When I righted myself, I saw that in his hand was a photograph. Worn. Edges frayed. And now becoming soaked with his blood as it ran out from his lifeless body. It was a picture of a woman. A pretty woman with blonde hair. He'd been trying to show me a picture of his wife, and I'd shot him.

I realized as I stepped across the barn floor littered with gore that, apparently, I wasn't bothered by that. Or the sight of blood anymore.

Huh.

27

HELLO FROM THE OTHER SIDE

RIDING A HORSE WAS NOT ON MY BUCKET LIST. THE GIANT BEASTS had minds of their own and no brake pedals. I'd been on one with Thomas, but he was in control. Riding one on my own? I didn't dare it. Zander would only be used as a shield and a distraction, so I could get out of the barn. There were at least two men and Rayna waiting for me to make a move, so the horse would cover me as I headed for the trees and led them away from the house.

I thought it was a good plan. Zander didn't. We had some very heated discussions until somehow, I won the argument and got the bit in his mouth. Once the reins were clipped to his bridle, I coaxed him out of his stall as his ears flipped around in agitation. He could feel the tension in the air and started pulling back on the reins. I stayed calm, leading him toward the bodies on the barn floor while speaking gently. He reluctantly fell in step beside me only to stop so suddenly my feet almost left the ground; the onslaught of gunfire erupting from outside made him violently toss his head up, knocking the shotgun from my hand. As I struggled to get a hold of his reins, rapid gunfire went off like fireworks. It was a call and answer, but I had no idea who was shooting at who.

Then it stopped. The eerie silence that followed was just as unsettling. Gathering my breath, I fought to contain blind panic about Thomas's safety.

Zander settled down. "Good horsey." I patted his muscled neck. Heavy breathing from me and him was the only sound for what seemed like miles and minutes until a lithe shadow appeared in the barn entrance. Then the air crackled with tension. I knew who it was. And I was ready.

The woman in the barn entrance, light streaming in around her disguising her as an angel, hissed my name. "Kaya," she said.

My knees almost buckled, and I clutched Zander's reins tighter… Some memory deep within dragged her voice into my ears and held on to it for dear life, even though I knew it was poison disguised as the sweetest candy.

"You must be… Rayna." I was barely able to get her name past my lips. I was shaking. The child in me wanted to run to her, but the adult in me held back. She wanted me dead. Dead. I eyed the shotgun, now out of my reach. After a moment of panic, I remembered I had two handguns at my waistband. Without giving myself a chance for a second thought, I readied one in my hand. But I pointed it at the ground.

"Well, well, it's nice to finally meet you Miss Kaya Lowen," Rayna said coldly, and I knew her silky voice would remain stuck in my ears for as long as I lived. She put her hands up in defense, eyeing the gun in my hand. "I came to you unarmed."

She moved slowly, assuredly, completely unfazed by the intermittent exchange of bullets erupting outside, solely focused on me.

"Just stop right there…"

She ignored my warning, stepping over a puddle of red on the ground, not even glancing at the man dead at her feet. She reminded me of that cougar on the mountain, deadly, ready to pounce…

Zander swayed. I held his reins tightly. "I mean it. Don't come any closer or I'll shoot you." I aimed at her head. A pigeon flew madly through the rafters. The hay and blood scented air grew colder. Then Rayna laughed, and every hair on the back of my neck stood on end—I felt like I might vomit.

"You won't shoot me, darling," she said sweetly. "I am your mother."

And there it was. Confirmation. The words spoken aloud stabbing me like razor-sharp daggers, finding their mark to pierce the last remaining piece of my heart.

My mother.

She took another step closer.

"What do you want with me?" I asked. Already knowing the answer but needing to hear it.

I could see her face more clearly now. Bright green eyes and the same bone structure as mine, black wavy hair and fine-boned hands—the resemblance was disturbing. I felt like I was looking in a very cruel mirror.

"I just want to save you from your horrible father," she said bitterly. "You know what he's doing, right? His research is deplorable. Unethical. Drug testing on human beings with his vile—"

I cut her off. I didn't need encouragement to hate Henry. "And you think killing me is the answer?"

Zander huffed when Rayna sidestepped the body of the man I'd shot—the one with the cross around his neck. She glanced down, noting the photo in his hand, then shrugged off whatever emotion it briefly aroused. "Listen, I don't know what lies your head is filled with, but these men…" She motioned to the three dead on the barn floor. "They don't work for me. They kidnapped me. I was just trying to get to you, to save you. I would never harm my own child."

Lies, lies, lies… The gun shook in my hand. Lies. Those were things I could still feel. But…

"Put down the gun, sweetheart. Come closer so I can see your pretty face," she said sweetly.

And my arm dropped to my side. I didn't want it to, but logic defied me. I felt like I'd fallen under a spell.

"That's a good girl," Rayna said. A cat grinning at a mouse. "I've missed you so much, Kaya."

My head spun with the sudden reasoning that maybe this woman didn't want to kill me. Maybe upon seeing me, she'd changed her mind. A ray of hope started to shine that maybe, maybe we could be family… I remained glued to the ground, emotions racing. The horse next to me tossed his head up and down, clearly uneased by her presence. Rayna glanced quickly around, making sure we were still alone. "Guns terrify me darling. Please put yours down."

As if in a dream, I tossed it into Zander's stall.

Rayna's eyes narrowed on me, and her graceful hand gathered her thick hair behind her shoulders. I noticed blood on her neck and a wound on her wrist; she wasn't unarmed on purpose. She was hiding in here, like I was, from whatever was going on outside.

"Aw, my poor baby girl. Stolen from me when you were only two weeks old. You've no idea what I've gone through," she purred, and now she was mere feet away.

I felt like my adult skin had shed and beneath was a child again. Her hands reached for me. My mother's hands reached for me… Her fingernails were polished to a diamond shine. Her clothes form fitting, black pants with a tight black sweater down past her hips and a wide belt around her tiny waist…were inviting me to come closer. The overwhelming thought I could touch her and put my head against her chest numbed all sense of reality. She might lovingly stroke my hair… because she was real…because she was my mother.

"Now, come here sweetheart."

But when her eyes bore into mine, what I was expecting and hoping to see wasn't there. Something vicious danced in her pupils. They were dark stars, raging fires fueled by revenge. "Finally," she breathed, "I have waited so long to do this…"

Before I understood what was happening, a knife appeared in her hands and she lunged at me, aiming for my heart. Only because of Zander was I alive. He reared up, throwing his front legs at her and blocking a fatal plunge. Rayna stumbled back before Zander's hoof connected with her head.

"Oh my God," I stuttered in shock of my stupidity; this woman wanted to slice me into pieces. Such hatred poured from her it almost doubled me over.

"I'm going to mess you up so bad," she said with an ecstatic smile, and the blade gripped in her hand shone. "Henry won't even recognize you when I'm done."

I pulled the other gun out from the back of my waistband and aimed. Upon seeing it, her momentum for killing me was put on pause. I pointed the barrel at her chest because shooting her in the head would be too merciful.

"You won't do it. You're weak," she spat, and cherry-red lipstick clung to her front teeth.

Weak... there was that word again. It brought me fully to my senses. I steadied the gun, knowing the bullet would land dead center of her black heart. She deserved to be killed. Dustin and Marie, our friends... that innocent man at the motel... she deserved to have her brains blown out, just like her minions had done to them, just like she had tried to do to me, just like the man with the cross around his neck did who said he was fighting for his wife...

But I froze. I couldn't pull the trigger. I wasn't weak... and I wasn't a murderer.

Rayna smirked. Backing away and heading toward the doors, she began laughing like I'd told her the best joke in the world. "Oh hell, don't look so bummed out, sweetheart. It will all be over soon. I'll make sure of it. I'll get rid of the annoyances outside first, then I'll come back for you and we can have another heart to heart."

"Stop..." My voice sounded pathetic and high pitched. I still had my aim on her, but my hand was shaking so violently I doubted I'd hit my mark.

At the doors, she turned around, her head tilted as she studied me. "You remind me of him..." she spat. "And it's disgusting."

Then she disappeared out into the sunlight.

I didn't move for the longest time. Chaos continued outside, and Zander stood patiently next to me. I wondered if I'd become nothing more than skin and bones. Because left in my mother's wake, I was now just an empty shell with only a single thought—kill her.

IT TOOK A MINUTE TO ADJUST MY EYES TO THE LIGHT. THE SKY WAS almost white and the snow-covered ground the same blinding color. Zander's massive body flanked mine as we left the barn and headed outside past the bunkhouse. I hoped that among all the other horses scattered about, no one would pay attention to him or notice me taking cover at his side.

I held the gun in my right hand and Zander's reins in the other; I'd like to think I was the one in control, but essentially, he was leading me and only allowing me to tag along. He was heading for the house, not even remotely affected by me trying to direct him toward the trees. Now out in the open, I had to stay glued to his side. Why wasn't he running off like the other horses? Why was he so determined to go to the house?

Then it hit me. He wanted Ben.

Gunfire erupted again, and Zander reared up, but I was ready this time, not letting go of the reins. Between his lifted hooves, I caught a glimpse of a man crouched behind the black car in the driveway as he fired at a truck parked on the road. Who was in the truck? Had Henry found me? Was this my luckiest day ever and the family reunion of my dreams was about to commence? I hoped someone brought the potato salad…

Zander's body was a barrier between me and the black car as he practically dragged me to the porch steps of the house. I ran to keep up, only to stop dead next to him when the front door flew open. Without hesitation, I took aim, but it wasn't who I'd expected. Thomas stood there with the knife I'd left in his palm now at his neck and held there by a burly man with tattooed cheeks. I was hoping for Rayna, eager to blow her head off. I eased my finger off the trigger.

"Toss the gun or I'll cut him ear to ear," the burly man said. Sweat clung like raindrops to the end of his nose. His cheeks were covered in cartoon characters, so were his hands. Aiming at a grown man decorated in Pokémons seemed wrong. Until the knife he held to Thomas's neck produced the tiniest drip of blood…

I steadied my aim.

Thomas's eyes were bleary, but he was conscious. After assessing his well-being, I studied the burly man, picking the best spot to aim. I could hear someone far off in the distance, a female voice perhaps, calling my name, but I couldn't let it cloud up my head. I shut every sound out of my ears—horse's hooves, bullets firing, the icy wind, the squeal of a mini-pig from somewhere by the barn… Instead, I watched the burly man's heartbeat pulsing at the base of his throat. He bared his teeth.

"Put it down," he growled.

Thomas didn't struggle against the blade held to his throat. I knew this scene; I'd had the starring role in it once and the scars to prove it. If I miscalculated, Thomas would be dead.

"Run, Kaya," he said softly. "Don't worry about me… just run."

Run? Nope. I wanted more moments with him, dancing under trees, swimming in lakes, laughing by fires, and savoring the warmth of his body in my bed at night. No way would I leave him.

I smiled. "Nah, I kinda like you, Thomas."

The big man's attention momentarily drifted to whatever was happening behind me; the gunfire had stopped, and Zander grew stone still. I gave Thomas a slight nod, hopefully alerting him to what I was about to do, and he closed his eyes. I focused on the man's wrinkled forehead, and the small mole there between Pikachu and Bulbasaur dead center like a bull's eye… and then I shot him.

My aim was true.

Thomas now stood on the porch steps, the knife at his feet and the burly man missing a substantial portion of his head on the ground behind him. I dove forward, getting my shoulders to Thomas's chest before he fell. "You have to get off these steps…" I said, guiding him away from the porch.

"You're one scary chick. Where did you learn to shoot like that?" He was wobbly and barely able to stand, his weight too much for me to keep holding up. He rubbed at his neck and almost fell backward.

"Get on the horse," I demanded.

The world around us had grown quiet. Where was the man who had been behind the black car? Where was Rayna? I cupped my hands together to give Thomas a leg up. When he was on Zander's back, I grabbed the reins and led the way around to the back of the house. Across from Marlene's garden was a band of trees. Thomas could head there and hide.

"Can you ride?" I asked breathlessly, ankle deep in fresh snow. Zander huffed and tossed up his head. I struggled to restrain him.

"Of course I can ride," Thomas said quickly, but the tremor in his voice said otherwise. "I can do that half dead and in my sleep. But of all the horses to pick … this one?"

Gunfire. Again. Bullets ripped through the air and a female voice was yelling, strangely familiar, and yet I had to ignore it. I had to get Thomas out of here. "Get to the poor man's sauna. I'll come get you as soon as I can."

Thomas leaned forward on Zander, and he latched onto my hand when I offered him the reins. "Nope. I'm not leaving without you. And if you drug me again, our friendship is over."

"I was just doing what I had to do," I said coldly. "Just get somewhere safe. I'll take care of this and make it all up to you later."

Thomas forced a laugh. "Make it up to me, eh? I can't wait for that."

He was so unsteady I thought he might fall off the horse. When the gunfire ceased and silence gripped the air, his fingers tightened around mine. "Or you could make it up to me now," he said quickly.

He could barely sit up, was hurt, confused, still drugged, and trying to hide his fear; I couldn't send him off alone. I had no choice but to get on the horse with him. As much as I wanted to find Rayna, Thomas had to be my priority.

Zander stayed remarkably still while I got on and in front of Thomas. With one arm around my waist and the other holding the reins, Thomas issued a command and Zander was trotting. With every ounce of strength I could muster, I squeezed my legs tight, desperately holding on to keep balance for the both of us. Once in the thicket of trees, cattle trails snaked off in many directions. I felt Thomas slipping and barked at him.

"If you fall, I fall."

He jolted upright and started to shiver. "Sorry. I'm good."

I wound my hand tightly in Zander's mane. "Will this path take us to the lake?" I asked, needing to get him warm soon. He was only in a T-shirt and jeans, thankfully not barefoot.

"Yeah. It just takes longer."

Zander slowed beneath the canopy of low-hanging branches. The barn, the bunkhouse, the road, and pretty much everything at the back end of the ranch was coming in and out of view alongside us as we rode. When I heard my name on the wind again, shrill and desperate, I knew Thomas heard it, too, because he gave Zander a kick to the ribs. We moved faster into the thicket and onto the trail that twisted between the stand of birch trees.

Thomas was trembling. Twice, I had to smack him when I felt him falling asleep. He leaned so heavily on me my muscles were aching for release. "You all right, Thomas?" I asked when I felt his arm loosen and his body shift behind me.

He cleared his throat. "I'd be better if I could see straight, my head didn't throb, sleep wasn't knocking at my door, and a bunch of dudes weren't trying to kill the chick I'm into."

I took the reins from him and put the gun in his free hand, then pulled his arm around me tight and held on to it, pinning him to me.

"I'll make this all up to you someday, I promise."

"Just don't cook for me," he said, as always trying to lighten the situation with humor.

Thomas was slipping. I held him as tight as I could, muscles screaming in my back as he leaned forward. Zander moved fluidly through the trees. "But you love my pancakes and—" I didn't finish. I thought I saw something move up ahead; a shape, low to the ground, shifted across the trail.

"And what?" Thomas said, his breath hot on my neck.

"Shh."

Zander sensed it, too. Thomas held the gun close to me so I could grab it if I had to, and we grew silent while the horse kept moving... but there was nothing ahead. Just the thick silver trees and snow covered overgrown bushes. Whatever it was—coyote, rabbit, or maybe even wolf—was gone. We rode in silence for a while, Thomas holding the gun while I held on to him.

"I hate to be brutally honest, Kaya, but I really don't love your pancakes," he said out of the blue.

I laughed. A flock of geese heading south squawked over our heads. "I'll make it up to you another way then."

Thomas coughed. "Good Lord, please don't say spaghetti. Never again will I look at pasta the same way. How does someone burn noodles? I mean.... you just boil them."

He was shaking so hard he was stuttering. But talking was keeping him awake.

"No food then. How about I buy you your own ranch? Make you ridiculously wealthy?"

I felt the breath catch in his lungs. "Is that what you think I want you for?"

Easy question. "Yes. That's what everyone wants me for. Money. Thing is I've decided I will be the one in control of who gets it."

The chill in the air deepened. I could feel every muscle in Thomas tense. "You misunderstand me, Kaya," he said.

Silence fell between us. The horse kept an even gait, moving out of the birch stand and finally into the thick brush and trees that flanked the path to the lake. Soon, we could see the shack and the gleaming expanse of icy blue water. If I wasn't so hell bent on killing my birth mother, I might have appreciated the view.

"You have to know, what we have between us... it isn't about money for me," Thomas said when we came to a stop at the snow-filled fire pit. He slid off Zander then reached for me, hands circling my waist and lifting me carefully to the ground. His dark eyes were filled with sadness when his freezing fingers grazed my cheek, and he swallowed hard like there was something important he wanted to tell me. But there was no time for whatever that was—he was practically blue.

"Let's warm up in the shack." I pretended I was cold, too.

He nodded, letting his hand drop. "Listen Kaya, I—"

I shook my head and cut him off. "No time for chitchat, Thomas. We need to get a fire lit."

"Right."

His legs gave out, and he slumped to the snow. I fumbled with the latch of the shack door, wondering how I was going to lock him in there once I got the stove going, and hoped no one would notice the smoke.

LUKE

28

Only You

I'D LOST SIGHT OF OLIVER. HE'D GONE SOUTH, INTENT ON MAKING a wide arc to approach the Carlson ranch from the far side while I circled around back and headed into a stand of birch trees. Seth and Lisa were supposed to be creating a diversion by sticking to the road and approaching head on, which, judging by the sound of gunshots rippling across the fields, they were doing a decent job. Every time it grew silent, though, I felt my heart in my throat. What if I got there too late?

I fought to keep my wits about me as I stumbled across roots and weaved through gnarled branches heavy with snow. Birds chirped, sticks cracked under my feet, and every sound made me jump. I couldn't move fast enough, feeling desperate when I realized I'd misjudged the distance to the house by going this way. This was slow going and taking too long. I had to find a way to get to her faster…

At least once I was on the animal trail, walking was easier, but being in the trees was still slow and had become a bad idea. I needed to head back. I turned to go, but the sound of horse's hooves thumped from not far away. A man's voice followed, calm and talking softly, and I had barely enough time to dive behind a thick patch of trees before it was upon me. I dropped to my knees and peered between tree trunks, staying low so I wouldn't be seen. The dark browns and muddy blacks of fall blended with my jacket, the snow deep enough to cover my lower half as shadows of light kept me hidden. The horse approached. I held my breath, wondering if I should reach for my gun—and then I saw her.

Kaya.

On the horse in front of a dark-haired man with his arm around her waist and a gun to her chest.

I could barely breathe.

Her cheeks were flushed, and I caught a glimpse of her mesmerizing green eyes as they briefly scanned over my hiding place. I didn't move. I was enthralled beyond imagination just as I was that night in the garden, her beauty holding me completely captive and momentarily disabling my ability to function. As the horse brought her closer, I noticed an intensity on her face I had never seen before; her jaw was set in stoic determination, and there wasn't a hint of fear about her. She was calm even though the man behind her was holding her at gunpoint. This caught me off guard. It suppressed my urge to lunge from my hiding place. Because of the look on her face and the rigidity of her spine, I held back.

I would wait. Follow and wait. Make sure I wasn't putting her life in jeopardy before I beat the man holding her at gunpoint into a bloody pulp...

The sound of the horse's hooves quieted as they moved away from me, heading farther down the trail. I started following, keeping a safe distance. I was so close... She was there, ahead of me... I was so close... My heart pounded with the thought of holding her in my arms again, of feeling her body against mine.

I moved quietly, carefully, and it took a moment to register the thing buzzing in my pocket; Lisa had given me her cell phone, and I felt as if in a dream fishing it out of my pocket.

"Luke, we saw her. She took off on a horse," she said as I put the phone to my ear.

I whispered. "I know. She just rode past me."

Lisa sounded breathless; I could tell by the lack of background noise she was in a building and moving fast; at least the gunfire had stopped. "I called out to her, but she took off anyway. She seems... different."

I stepped over a fallen tree. "I'm following her as we speak," I said, confirming it to myself as well.

"Good. Be careful, though. Rayna is still out there somewhere. That nasty, two-bit skank. I can't wait to get my hands around—"

I had to cut her off. "Not now."

"Right," Lisa muttered. "Just remember what we talked about, okay? Kaya broke your heart to save your life. No matter what you see or find, please, Luke, just remember that." Footsteps echoed in a quiet room. "And... oh my God... now I've got proof of that."

"Oh?"

"In my hands, as we speak, I am holding one of your shirts. I know because it's one I bought for you, and it, uh... smells like you. I'm in the house. In the basement. It was under a pillow in a place I'm pretty certain she was sleeping. Do you understand what this means?"

I felt a wave of relief so deep it almost buckled my knees. Lisa's words meant more than she would ever know. "I do. Thanks, Lees," I choked out, picking up my pace. "Listen, I'm in that stretch of birch trees we saw on the way in, heading east. Get a hold of Oliver and let him know where I am. Tell him I'm following her."

"I don't know where he is, and he's not answering his phone."

I ducked from a low branch. "Okay. I'll handle this. There's only one guy with her, and I can take him."

There was a pause. "Uh, I would advise against that," Lisa warned.

I stopped dead in my tracks. "Why?"

"From what Seth and I saw, she's intent on preserving this guy's, um… well-being."

I clicked off the phone and dropped it back into my pocket. Of course. My eyes weren't relaying the truth of what I'd seen when Kaya had ridden past; the man was leaning on her, not holding her captive. She was the one leading the horse. She was the one in charge. And he was the man in the video. The one who had lit up her face… laughing and in his arms, falling to the sand in fits of giggles with him next to her…

Whatever reassurance Lisa had just given me flew out the proverbial window. That gut-churning, soul-stealing question came back; what if Kaya truly didn't want me?

A crushing feeling in my chest made it hard to get going again; I guessed I would soon find out.

OLIVER

29

DISCONNECTED

"**ARE YOU GOING** TO ANSWER THAT?"

The cell phone was vibrating incessantly in my hand, but the woman standing before me in braided black hair and an army-green leather jacket seemed far more urgent.

"Oliver?"

I'd never seen Sindra dressed for combat. No matter what was happening or where she was, her style was business glam, done up and polished to the hilt. For once, she seemed to fit the situation in her camo clothes and gun belt, and I found that extremely unsettling. Her cheeks were pink from the cold. She'd been outside for a while now, alone, and how she'd found me on this desolate country road, in the middle of nowhere, defied imagination.

"It can wait," I said.

"I thought I warned you to get as far away from Kaya as possible." She stared me down, hands on her tiny hips.

I gulped hard. I wasn't scared of anyone, but I feared this woman and there was no logical reason why. "Where's your backup?" I asked, changing the topic.

She looked over her shoulder—the road an empty icy line reaching out into the distance before fading into the pale sky. There wasn't a sign of life anywhere except for us and the cattle grazing on a ridge behind a barbed-wire fence. "I'm on my own."

"And why are you here?"

"I still have a job to complete. I am trying to make sure this whole situation doesn't turn into a bloody nightmare. And you, Oliver, have just made it even more complicated and difficult."

I tucked my freezing hands into my jacket pockets. "How's that?"

"Just by being here," she said angrily, then started walking in the direction of the ranch house. I fell in step beside her. "I was going to try and clean up the mess before Henry caught wind of it, but I'm too late. That stupid girl... saving a baby for God's sake! Does she realize she's exposed herself to half the world? Now Henry is on his way to make sure I am doing my job—which, obviously, I haven't been."

There was something in Sindra's voice that caught me off guard. "And why is that?"

She stopped and turned to me, her braid whipping around over her shoulder. Somewhere off in the distance, a coyote howled, but it didn't register in her dark eyes. "So many questions. Are you daft? Because I don't want you to end up dead," she said angrily.

Right. Dead. "Okay... well, thanks for that."

"Yes, well, I am running out of lies to feed Henry to keep you that way. You need to disappear, Oliver. You must leave Kaya. If you continue to fight for her, I won't be able to look out for you anymore."

I laughed at her ludicrous suggestion. "I can't leave Kaya. You know that."

Sindra shifted, seeming uneasy. "Considering the fact you've been programmed to protect her at all costs, I guess that's understandable."

My legs suddenly felt like jelly... The word 'programmed' gave the sensation of dogs gnawing on my bones. There was some distant memory of why there was truth to the word, and it was fighting to surface. I shut it out as my stomach lurched.

"Why are you looking out for me, Sindra?" I asked, changing the subject yet again.

I was expecting a verbal dismissal, or a gesture with the back of her hand signaling that the conversation was over. Instead, her gaze met mine. It was clouded with some emotion I couldn't read; was it sympathy? Kindness? Adoration for another human being besides Henry? That was what it looked like, but that was impossible. The mighty Sindra didn't have feelings. Maybe there was just makeup, or a rogue wind pestering her eyes.

"I'm pretty sure you know what it's like to be in love with someone you will never have," she stated.

I nodded.

"Well, I know what it's like, too."

Did she mean Henry?

Nope. In a display of affection, her hand reached for my arm. She stared straight ahead, her eyes on my chest to avoiding meeting mine as she continued with what felt like a confession long overdue. "It would just feel good knowing this person that I... care for, is..." She paused, her hand dropped, and whatever she was about to say was dropped with it.

I studied her bowed head. This fierce and beautiful woman was trying to say she had a thing for me? I wasn't quite sure how to process that. Or what she thought she might gain by admitting it.

"Sindra… I—"

She flung up her hand, palm out, blocking whatever was about to come out of my mouth. "You should just keep yourself alive, Oliver. That's all I want." She straightened her shoulders and became all business again. "Your capture is just as important to Henry as Kaya's is, and once he's used you for what he needs, he'll kill you. I won't be able to stop him. Do you understand me? You and Kaya can never be together. So it's in your best interest to stay away from her."

I started walking again toward the ranch house to where I'd find Kaya; my mission of protecting her hadn't changed just because Sindra decided to 'care' about me, or because there was a threat to my life. "You know I can't do that."

"I could simply command you to stay away from her," she said, jogging beside me.

I moved faster.

"Or I could command you to turn off all your feelings for her."

That was so ridiculous I laughed out loud and sped up.

"Oliver, I command you to stop," Sindra said, breathless.

Every muscle propelling me forward seized. I slid to a stop on the frozen road.

"Turn around and look at me," she ordered.

I slid full circle and faced the fiercest person I had ever met. I didn't want to, I needed to keep heading toward Kaya, but something in my brain controlling my free will was shorting out. I obeyed despite my desire not to.

Sindra's eyes turned glassy with whatever power she had over me. "Lift your gun and point it at my chest."

"What? No," I said, arms shaking.

"Oliver, I command you to point your gun at my chest."

And in my hand was my gun. And my arm was lifting it, defying me. I was shakily starting to point a loaded pistol at Sindra's chest. What the hell? I knew she had some control over me, but this? My limbs were defying me. My mind felt like it was caught in a trap, unable to break whatever spell she had cast. I struggled against it, my arm shaking as I tried to lower my hand, but it hurt to disobey her. My skin felt like it had caught fire, my nerves screamed, and bones throbbed for no reason.

Until I did as I was told.

Sindra smiled. "Good. Now, point it at your own head," she said.

This was ridiculous. But I felt my limbs move automatically. In my mind, even though I knew it was wrong, I was suddenly perfectly okay with it. Nothing mattered but the instructions I was receiving from this small woman. Her voice found a part of my brain and locked on, driving me like I was a robot and she had the controls.

"Do as I say, Oliver, or there will be consequences."

Consequences—pain. Horrible, inescapable pain… never ending… worse than death… the only relief to obey… The gun in my hand was now pointed at my own forehead. I stood there completely under her control and perfectly fine with ending my own life if she wished it.

"See? You will do what I tell you. You understand that now. Right. Oliver?"

I was at her mercy. Giving in to it was pure relief. I numbly nodded.

"All right. I command you to put the gun down," she said.

Of course, I did as I was told.

"So here's the thing." Sindra rubbed her gloved hands together while I waited for further instructions. "I could give you a command to leave Kaya and you would comply. But you would be an emotional mess living out your days in misery. I don't want that for you. I want you to realize your own true feelings for that girl. So, I am going to do something for you that I should have done long ago."

The wind picked up, swirling snow around us. I remained fixated on Sindra, hanging on her every word, every breath.

"I command you to remember why it is that I have control over you," she said.

It was like a ton of bricks cracked my head open, and the memories of the past came rushing in. A damp cell somewhere deep beneath the estate… torture of all sorts accompanied by Sindra's voice. It had gone on for years. Electric shock. Beatings. Days in solitude. Days of sleep deprivation and injections all leading to one thing and for one purpose—obey her. Sindra had instilled a fear so deep in me I'd given her complete control of my mind. Why did she want me to know this? I stared down at the woman who had claimed my free will and soul, manipulated my mind and abused my body. She stood patiently. Unblinking. Watching me eagerly with the same expression she'd had the day I'd been stationed as Kaya's guard. That was the day the pain and torment had ended. When Kaya became my sole purpose, I was freed from Sindra's torture and manipulation in return for loyalty and obedience. I remembered feeling like Kaya herself had saved me…

"Ah, you can see the truth now. I'm sorry, Oliver, but you don't love her."

I was frozen in shock, feet planted to the ground. I didn't know what to do, say, or feel.

"In case there is any doubt in your mind, I am going to really let you see the truth. I'll show you why you should leave Kaya." After a long pause, as if struggling with an inner voice, Sindra spoke softly, firmly, and my mind latched onto her words like a fish on a hook. "I command you, Oliver, to know what's real in your heart and uncover your true feelings. You are no longer influenced by anyone's decisions or circumstances past or present. I command you to be released from me, and it is my command that you are no longer under my control. Your mind and body are now free."

If I hadn't been standing on a lonely country road in the middle of nowhere beneath a cloudless winter sky, I would have thought a lightning bolt hit me. The strangest feeling of strength flooded my mind. Sindra's words cut the bonds holding me to her, and I fell away like a puppet freed of its strings. I could see her now for what she was—a monster. A sadistic, heartless, shiny, little monster. Just like Henry.

Reeling backward, staring at her in awe, I felt a shift in the world around me. It seemed to get bigger. Widen up on a massive scale. Become full of... color. The question that had been flooding my mind, keeping me up at night and torturing me to the point of mistrusting my every decision, was suddenly and completely obliterated as the answer became so clear it was stunning; were my feelings for Kaya my own? Was the love I felt for her real?

Oh, hell yes.

I started to run, now desperate to get to her, hoping I wasn't too late.

"Oh my God, it is real? Oliver?" Sindra chased after me, the shock in her voice obvious.

I didn't answer.

"But... she doesn't love you back," she yelled.

I stopped, then turned to face the woman who beat and tortured a child. Was she expecting me to forgive her? Think it was no big deal? Fall to my knees at her feet and profess my love for her? She was delusional. I was curious to hear what she would say about Kaya, so I stared hard into her wide-eyed, desperate face, waiting for her to continue.

"Her feelings were 'enhanced,' Oliver. That birthday party? Her sweet sixteen? The waiter at the restaurant? All set up by Henry himself. I'll be damned if it wasn't risky—Kaya lost so much blood I'd thought we'd lost her—but Henry was willing to take the chance. He knew that every time you rescued her, she would become more attached to you. And he was right. I am sorry to say her feelings for you... aren't real. They were manipulated, too."

"Oh!" I laughed. "But I suppose that yours are?"

Her dainty face lit up with hope. "Yes."

I felt a growl come from deep in my throat. "You have a horrific way of showing it. Tell me, Sindra, what other events were 'staged'? What other things did you and Henry do to push Kaya toward me?" I took a stab at the dark, hoping I was way off the mark. "How about Annie? Was her death all part of this too?"

"Yes. Poor old Anne was the icing on the cake. That completely broke Kaya down so you could pick her back up. I wanted her to have a fall and just break a few bones, but Henry knew her death would send Kaya over the edge. And he was right."

The vivid memory of that hospital room filled with yellow daisies to make us all think John Marchessa was behind the attack, and old Annie with a bullet hole through her chest—made my blood boil. Good people died that day. All so Kaya would fall for me. "I can't believe you had a hand in that."

"Well, not directly. But I knew about it," Sindra said flatly.

Anger surged through my veins. It wasn't an artificial drug-related anger either or the part of me I was trained to use when commanded to—it was real. It was my own. I thought of Davis and his warning words about Henry that I refused to listen to. He'd known. He'd tried to tell me something wasn't right, and I'd brushed him off. Suddenly, I had a horrible feeling of worry for him and everyone else I knew at the estate.

"Where's Davis?"

"Listen, Oliver, I have orders to follow. Davis is being re-purposed," Sindra replied. "You'll have to forgive me, but it has to be done."

I charged at her, grabbing her by the shoulders. She stood stick straight, trying to remain cool and in control, but her eyes filled with tears as I shook her like a dog might a chew toy. "It has to be done?" I raged. "Forgive you because you have no backbone of your own? If you hurt Davis, I will tear you to pieces. If you want even the slightest for-giveness from me, you'll let him go. Know this; I don't ever want to lay eyes on your vile face again. You say you have affection for me, but you wouldn't know affection if it bit you on the ass. You horrible, twisted, disgusting woman."

"Oliver, I showed you the truth. I'm looking out for you… I'm—"

"Sick!" I yelled, digging my fingers in to her tiny shoulders. I shoved her away when a tear rolled across her cheek because all I wanted to do was crush it against her face. "You're sick. And if you come anywhere near me again, or anywhere near Kaya, I will rip your head from your body."

I took off at a full run toward the Carlson Ranch, not looking back. Rayna would be standing there for a long time wondering how her plan of 'releasing me' had gone so terribly wrong. I guessed one thing she'd never accounted for was true love.

KAYA

30

CONVERGE

THE TINDER IN THE SMALL WOOD STOVE CAUGHT FIRE AND WITHIN minutes the shack was warm. Thomas's tanned cheeks were pale even with the orange glow lighting them. Through heavy eyelids, he watched my every move. On edge as if I might bolt from him and disappear forever.

"So what's the plan?" He clutched a dusty blanket around his shoulders.

My thoughts were clear and my mission completely black and white; protect Thomas. Kill Rayna. "You're going to stay here and keep warm while I attend to some matters, and then we're leaving."

"Matters?"

I sat down opposite him and checked the cartridge in the gun; still plenty of ammo for what I had to do. "I am going to go, uh…hunting. When I'm done, we will head back to the ranch, get a vehicle, and head east."

Thomas grinned. "Hunting, eh? You're kinda hot when you're doing the chick Rambo thing," he said, rubbing his hands in front of the stove. "Listen, Kaya, just make sure that whatever you do, you can live with yourself afterward."

Live with myself afterward…. I blocked that piece of advice out of my head. There would be no afterward for either of us if I didn't kill now and worry about the consequences later. "I want my life back, Thomas." I took in a deep breath. "And I am going to get it."

I moved for the door. He reached for me, his hands still cold, his voice full of concern. I had to keep going, keep moving, not stop and think too hard about what I had to do.

"Look at me," Thomas insisted.

I did. His dark hair, perfectly disheveled, and the dried blood all over his face and neck did nothing to distract from his good looks. His gaze, still shaky with concussion, managed to put me on pause for a moment. There was something he was working up the courage to say, but what came out of his mouth was not what his eyes were saying.

"You don't have to figure out some way to keep me in here. I'll stay. All right?" he said, wobbling on his feet. "I'll wait for you. I promise."

I breathed a sigh of relief. I'd dodged some deep conversation I wasn't ready for, and I also didn't have to figure out how to barricade him into the shack.

"And whatever happens, I've got your back. And..." he continued. "We need each other, so don't... don't..."

I finished his sentence. "I won't leave you, Thomas."

Now he looked away, because he was either at a loss for words or dizzy and not wanting me to see. Probably both.

He eased down to the bench, pulled his knees to his chest, and tipped back his head. When his eyes closed, I knew it was okay for me to leave.

"Just be careful."

"Of course." I left the warmth of the shack, shutting the door firmly behind me.

Now alone on the beach, I was faced with either walking back to the house or riding Zander, who was shifting around uneasily from where I'd left him rustling the trees. Robotically and not scared or feeling any sense of fear—in fact, not feeling anything at all—I untied him. I was fueled with the one thought repeating in my head. Find Rayna. Kill her.

Nothing else mattered.

I embraced the powerful, ugly feeling that was keeping me on course. The lake, the birds diving in, and the untouched white snow were just a muddy grey with my mind clouded with so much hate. I knew nothing but the task ahead. Nothing but the urgent need to kill my mother before she killed me...

Until a voice—familiar and smooth as butter—almost brought me to my knees.

"Kaya?"

It was the most perfect sound my ears had ever heard. It caught my breath, pulling at every single string attached to my heart.

"Kaya," he said again, as if my name were priceless.

I was yanked out of my dismal shell of skin and bones. In one blinding second, all of me poured back into place and I was simply a girl staring at the love of her life. Luke was here, on the beach. Water sparkling behind him and blue eyes dancing in the light—the most beautiful human being I'd ever laid eyes on. I wanted to run to him, but was it too good to be true? Maybe I was just seeing things.

"I found you," he muttered in awe.

I felt his voice in my chest. It resonated down to my soul. Everything that mattered to me, everything I wanted to hold dear, protect, and give the world to, was standing right before me. I tested his name with barely any air in my lungs, hoping my legs would hold me up if he answered.

"Luke..." It was barely a whisper.

"Yes. It's me." He nodded, a confirmation what he was saying was true, and that glorious, mind-melting smile came over his face.

My God. It really was him.

My feet were moving, but I could have been floating as I was pulled to him like a magnet. Intensity and longing shone in his eyes as he barreled toward me. I hadn't even realized I'd dropped Zander's reins until Luke's hands were on my cheeks, and I was reaching for his face. I thought I might crumble right there and then from the trembling surge of relief and love sparking madly between us. My soul felt whole again. He put his mouth on mine. His hands wound into my hair. The sweet taste of him, the feel of him, real... here... now.... overloaded my senses. I pulled away to scrutinize him, needing to confirm there was no need to pinch myself out of a perfect dream.

"Are you okay?" he asked.

I was shaking so hard I could barely get any air back into my lungs. "Yes." My heart was close to bursting. I could have died from the look in his eyes, such love for me... and such hurt.

"I've missed you so much," he said, hot hands holding me gently, searching my eyes.

That part of my heart I'd locked away burst open. "How did you find me?" I asked, falling into him, feeling my spine tingle as I watched his mouth for an answer.

"I saw you on television... the fire, the accident... I watched it all. The truck you left in advertised this ranch. It wasn't hard."

I stated the obvious. "Then Henry could be here, too."

"I don't know about him, but Sindra probably is." Her name caught in his throat. "She's been... watching you for quite a while."

I backed away, almost into a wave, and his hands fell from my face. My heart sped up, crashing against my ribs. It was as if the world fell upon us; the guns that had been pointed to Oliver's head that day in the meadow, the knife held to my throat on my birthday, Anne—dead because of me. It would be history repeating itself... repeating... repeating... If Sindra were here, then Henry wouldn't be far behind, and Henry would leave no one alive but me.

"Is Sindra... here now?" I asked.

"Maybe."

I scanned the beach, eyes locking on to the place where Thomas and I had slept. That night I had assumed it had been him undoing my jacket and then zipping it back up, but now I realized it was Sindra. She'd taken the necklace. She held the key to my freedom—the one thing that would let me live my life in the arms of the blue-eyed man standing before me—which was all I wanted.

My head spun.

"The necklace," I said, and a frantic awareness of the pendant that wasn't there anymore rushed through me. "She took it. I have to get it back!" I was ready to tear apart the world to have Luke again. I felt wild, crazed... I flung around in a circle, unsure what to do, where to go to find Sindra.

"No. Kaya, stop." Luke's hands gripped my shoulders. He had that calm about him that usually set me at ease, but not this time. "It's gone."

And just like that, in the blink of an eye, he became a target again. "Gone? What do you mean?"

"Sindra gave it to Oliver..." he said carefully, as if his words might send me over the edge. "Oliver was sick. He didn't mean to, but he destroyed it in a fit of rage."

"It's really gone?"

"Yes."

I felt my sanity slip away.

"Kaya," Luke said, studying my face, digging his fingers in slightly to bring me back to him. "The note you left... did you mean it?"

I was swaying slightly, feeling like I might tip over. "I'm so sorry. I had to—"

My apology was left hanging when out of the corner of my eye, I noticed the shack door open. Thomas slowly stepped out. He'd promised he wouldn't, but there he was, shivering in the icy air, taking tentative steps toward Luke and me. I felt sick.

"You had to what?" Luke asked, remaining completely focused on me even though I knew he saw Thomas heading our way. Even though the waves were threatening to soak his feet.

Confusion began to swirl madly—kill Rayna, hide from Henry, protect Thomas, above all... protect Luke. "I... I'm sorry," I repeated.

"So, you didn't mean it?" he said hopefully.

I could see his heart pounding at the base of his throat—his glorious throat—and while I stared at the place I wanted to put my lips against, a familiar sound roared in the distance. I knew what would follow; a helicopter was near, no doubt filled with Lowen Security. If it was Henry, he'd kill anyone around me. He'd kill the man I loved.

Protect Luke. Protect. Luke. Protect Luke.

"No. I'm sorry… I did mean it," I said.

Luke blinked like he hadn't heard me correctly. When my expression didn't change, he stumbled back slightly. He glanced at Thomas and clenched his hands into fists.

"You're joking, right, Kaya?" he said painfully, searching my face for the truth. "You were just trying to protect me. Tell me that please. This isn't because of someone else, is it? Because of him? Tell me that you were just trying to protect me. Please, you're tearing my heart out."

His pain was pure torture, but the sound of the helicopter approaching reminded me why I was hurting him. Lowen hellfire was about to reign down any moment, and Luke barely paid any attention to it. He was more concerned about what I had to say than the death sentence looming over his head. That only reinforced what I had to do.

"I don't want you," I said, making myself back away.

He doubled over like I'd hit him. The roar in the air increased. Zander reared up and took off into the trees like a bullet. I choked back the bile rising into my throat.

"You're nothing but a lowlife criminal," I continued, using that meanness I'd been fueling up with just moments ago, calling it up and slinging it like mud. "You worked for Rayna, for The Right Choice Group. You knew I might end up dead, but you kidnapped me anyway. Whatever your reasons were, they don't matter anymore. I don't want to be with someone like you."

His perfect face crumpled, and he dropped to his knees. "You don't mean this. Please, Kaya… you're killing me."

I dug deep. "Yes. Yes, I do!"

I hadn't realized tears were streaming down my face until I tasted them. Thomas was telling me to make sure I knew what I was doing as the sound of the helicopter grew louder, but I knew exactly what I was doing. "Luke, I don't love you," I hissed.

It was the biggest lie to ever come past my lips. The expression on his face when I said it was like he'd died right there and then. Was I doing the right thing? Was I really protecting him by breaking his heart? I'd sunk so low I couldn't breathe. Tears stung my skin in the chilly wind. I wanted Luke to get up and run. Wanted him to get angry. Call me names and get moving as far away from me as possible before the whole beach started crawling with Henry's men. But he just sat there, staring up at me while water from the lake licked at his boots and snow-covered knees.

"I'll always love you. No matter what," he said.

He meant it. Without a shadow of a doubt, he meant it.

Thomas started pulling me away. He was yelling at Luke to get up and run. Warning him his life was in danger if he stayed on the beach... but Luke didn't even blink. His gaze fell to his hands, limp in his lap as he sat hunched like he'd been shot through the heart. The trees shook. My feet were dragged across the beach as the helicopter drowned out every sound around us, including me yelling. "Maybe I did the wrong thing, Thomas. I have to go to him..."

If Thomas heard me, he wasn't letting go. My voice was lost in the wind, the words mangled and carried away. I fought futilely against Thomas, incensed by the realization I'd made the biggest mistake of my life. "Let me go, Thomas," I yelled.

But Thomas's grip was unyielding. He was intent on getting us under cover. We were almost at the trees when I reached for the gun at my belt. It was in my free hand, and if Thomas didn't let me go....

Suddenly, the helicopter changed direction, the noise was gone, and the air breathable again. My heartbeat hammered in my ears, then almost stopped when I realized I was holding my gun and pointing it at Thomas's head.

I quickly lowered my arm.

Thomas's jaw dropped. His fingers unwound from my wrist. He stared at me, stunned, with the most horrific look of hurt and confusion. Did he think I would shoot him?

Would I have if he hadn't let go?

It didn't matter. I had to get to Luke, apologize... tell him I'd been lying to protect him... beg his forgiveness.

I spun away from Thomas, got two steps from the trees, and came face to face with Rayna.

"Where do you think you're going?" she hissed.

She stood between me and what I wanted most, and our eyes locked. Our guns aimed at each other's hearts. Now in full light, I could see what I hadn't before—bloodshot eyes, dark circles, and heavy lines around her mouth. Her makeup was packed into her skin like she'd pressed it in with a putty knife; she was an ogre dressed up as a woman. No. She looked nothing like me. My finger feathered the trigger.

"Think carefully about that, Kaya," Rayna said, and she gave a chin nod to where Thomas stood next to me.

I was so focused on her I'd failed to notice his hands were up in self-defense while a man in a suit held a gun to his head. Two of Rayna's idiots marched toward Luke, and I bit my lip to keep my aim steady.

"Geez, how many cockroaches do you have working for you?" I

asked, not faltering or shaking even the slightest. "Did I miss the cereal box coupon for ugly buttheads in cheap suits?"

She grinned. "Let's just say your father has pissed off enough people to give me an endless supply." She glanced at Luke, who hadn't moved or even lifted his head in the slightest. "Ah, Luke Ravelle. A traitor to The Right Choice Group. It's such a shame you had to let this female compromise your mission. She's not worth it. I can guarantee you that."

Luke remained quiet. Eyes cast downward. Broken.

"Secure his hands and feet," Rayna ordered the idiots who were wisely tentative to approach him. "You know what he's capable of."

I kept my eyes averted from him as her orders were carried out, my gun aimed at her heart—I couldn't waver. I couldn't let emotions distract me. Not now.

"Henry's here, too, isn't he?" she said. A crazed grin pulled at the corners of her mouth. "I had planned to slice you up and send parts of you to him in those nice little blue jewelry boxes he likes so much. But I guess I can just shoot a hundred holes in you instead and save myself the postage."

Luke exploded from where he'd been kneeling. The two men flanking him were spared only because of his restraints. They had the advantage, one slamming the butt end of a pistol to the side of his head, the other giving him a swift kick to the abdomen. Luke was pushed back down to his knees, and now there was a trickle of blood on his temple. I could barely look away from it.

Rayna noticed. "Hm…what if I just shoot him first?" she said, and then her aim shifted from me to Luke.

The air involuntarily caught in my lungs. I fought to breathe. When Luke lifted his hanging head, his eyes were void of any light and filled with nothing but rage and hurt. The amount of pain I'd caused him was obvious, yet after all I'd done, he still wanted to fight for me.

As I'd fight for him.

I kept Rayna in my sights; I could shoot her now. I wouldn't miss. But what about the man next to Thomas, and the two men flanking Luke? I could take out one, but not all three…

"I don't care what you do to him," I said, motioning to Luke. "He's nothing but a lowlife kidnapper."

Rayna's eyes lit up. "Oh, really?"

Clearly, she wasn't buying what I was selling. The beads of sweat breaking out on my forehead were giving me away, along with the shaking in my legs.

Her eyes glowed acid green. "He is gorgeous. No wonder you've fallen for him. It's such a shame to let a man so beautiful go to waste. I was going to try to rehabilitate him. Remind him why he joined forces with The RCG in the first place, but…" Her eyes lowered, and the veins protruded at her temples. "I don't feel like it."

The unmistakable sound of a trigger clicking into place brought me to my knees. She was going to kill him. My whole body went into complete panic.

"No! Don't hurt him, please!" Without further thought, I dropped my gun to the snowy beach and put my hands up in defeat. I would beg for his life. "Please, it's me you want. Don't hurt him. Let him go. It's all my fault. Just focus on me, all right?"

Rayna was delighted to see me beg. "Gladly," she said, and returned her aim to my chest.

Luke bolted to his feet again, valiantly trying to shake off the men holding him, but a blow to the stomach doubled him over. Another hit to the head sent him unconscious to the ground. My stomach came up in my throat. Our lives were about to end, and all I could think about was that he would never know how I truly felt. He would never know I'd been lying to protect him. And that I had failed.

Thomas was saying something, but I wasn't listening. I took in a deep breath, hoping my death would be quick and painless but knowing in my heart that was wishful thinking. I braced myself, closing my eyes.

"I have waited so long for this," Rayna said, and a shot was fired. Then three more so fast they were almost indiscernible.

But I felt… nothing. No pain.

I tentatively opened my eyes; Luke was still unconscious, but the idiots next to him were dead and bleeding out into the snow. Thomas was still standing, appearing unharmed, but Rayna… she was on the ground before me in agony. The gun that had been in her hand was now a few feet away, and so were her fingers. She was staring, mouth agape in a choked scream, at her mangled hand.

Thomas stumbled backward. "What the—?"

The man in the suit next to him had dropped to the ground, too, and there, marching toward us appearing annoyed with a gun in her hand, was Sindra. She barreled out of the trees, slightly flushed and completely in control. Not even remotely breathless, she thrust out a hand and pulled me upright.

"Here I am cleaning up after you again," she said bitterly, but her eyes weren't digging in to me like daggers. There was something else there I'd only caught glimpses of when I was a child. "Are you hurt?" she asked.

I was in shock at her appearance, her aim, and by the tone of affection in her voice. "No."

Sindra seemed relieved. She moved to block Rayna, who was squirming toward the beach and making distressed whimpering sounds. The snow around her had become a gruesome red from her mangled hand, and her makeup-streaked face contorted in agony when she stared up at my petite, bronze- skinned rescuer.

"Geez, you've sure been a pain in the ass, Rayna," Sindra said, not displaying a hint of sympathy for the woman cowering at her feet.

Rayna gasped for air, cradling her mangled hand while slithering toward her discarded gun.

"You bitch," she screamed when Sindra kicked it out of her reach.

Sindra scanned our surroundings, then checked her watch. "I can't believe you would hunt down your own child, Rayna. I thought you'd have given up this revenge crap by now."

Rayna's lip curled into a sneer. "And I thought you'd be way prettier."

Sindra shrugged her shoulders as if it was a waste of a breath to even reply. She turned to me, eyes darkening, and I could tell I was about to get a scolding. "Rescuing a kid from a fire? Really? That's not smart, Kaya. It's got you into a huge mess. That little act you pulled was on television, you know. Broadcast all over the world. That's how this trash," she motioned to Rayna, "found you. That's how he found you." She pointed to Luke. "Good Lord, child. Now everyone this side of the equator has seen your face. Thank heavens your father was diligent about not letting you be photographed so the public doesn't put two and two together. But John Marchessa? He'll know it's you."

I was too numb to reply. Thomas was motionless by my side, incredibly steady considering the amount of sedatives in him and the fact I'd pointed a gun at his head. He reached for my hand.

Luke moaned. He sat up, leaned back on his heels, and blinked the world around him back into clarity. When his blue eyes fell to Thomas's hand possessively over mine, I quickly pulled away. Luke's gaze softened. He looked at me like he knew, like he understood everything. Like my words and apologies weren't necessary. Like everything would be okay...

"Anyway, do you want to end her, or shall I?" Sindra said, patiently waiting for me to take the gun from her outstretched hand.

All I wanted to do was run to Luke, but I would finish this first. I pointed the gun at Rayna's forehead while she sat on the snowy beach, bleeding and in torment. I was hoping to see some desperation or hear her beg for forgiveness... anything... but there was only pure, gut-churning hatred in her eyes. There was nothing there redeeming.

Nothing there worth saving. I knew what I had to do.

Thomas's hand was on my back, either leaning on me or supporting me. I couldn't tell which. His words echoed—make sure you can live with yourself afterward.

I tried to pull the trigger. Damn it, I tried… but I couldn't. My hand just shook. I was pointing a loaded pistol at the woman who had tried to kill me, and all I could see… was me. Not the physical resemblance, but someone once innocent. Someone molded by the circumstances forced upon her—someone poisoned by Henry.

I couldn't do it.

"Ah. That's why I adore you, Kaya," Sindra said, her voice tinged with pride. "You're good inside, despite your Lowen upbringing." Her hand reached out and gently took back the gun from me. "You have solid morals." She aimed at Rayna, not even blinking as she shot her in the head. "I, however, do not."

31

EVIL GETS HIS FEET WET

AN ARM AS BIG AS A TRUCK CIRCLED MY WAIST. MY FEET WERE
lifted effortlessly off the ground. My desperate call to Luke was
blocked when a hand with an iron grip clamped over my mouth.
I didn't even have to look to know who was dragging me off
the beach and into the trees. I knew his smell, his touch, and
everything about him. And I fought like the devil was dragging me
to hell.

"Quit it, Kaya. He's here…" Oliver said in a breathless whisper. "And
if you call attention to us, we'll all be dead."

All? He meant Luke, still kneeling by the water's edge, and Thomas,
still stuck like glue to my side.

I quit struggling.

The birds that had returned to the shoreline took to the sky. The
wind disappeared. Not one living thing made a single peep. Not even
the leaves rustled in the presence of such evil. Oliver sought cover, the
thick brush enveloping us and his hand remaining over my mouth.
"Don't move and don't say a word," he whispered. Next to me, I saw
Thomas nod obediently.

Sticks and thorns dug into my knees, and the air making its way
into my nose smelled of whatever soap Oliver had used last. In seven
heartbeats, the beach became overrun with Lowen Security. The badges
on their army-green jackets gleamed gold. Luke was surrounded, then
the man I hated most in the world walked by him, smoothed his silk
suit, and carefully avoided getting muck on his expensive shoes. He
strode to where Sindra awaited him, diamonds dripping off his hands,
and glossy jet-black hair catching the waning sun. His eyes scanned
the dead. When they fell on Rayna's body, a slight grin came over his
imperial face. It made me hate him even more—if that was possible. I'd
been the recipient of that grin… the day he'd placed the tracking device
around my ankle was one of those times. That gleam in his eyes that said
'gotcha' was hollering now, even though "where is my daughter?" was the

first thing out of Henry Lowen's disgusting mouth.

I was waiting for Sindra to point and give us away. But, to my surprise, she lied.

"No idea at the moment. She must have taken off this morning. There is no sign of her here. I've checked the entire perimeter."

"And Oliver?" Henry asked, noting the top of the shack where smoke from the fire had sputtered out. With nothing but a hand signal from him, four armed men stormed the small space.

"Gone, too," Sindra replied, her tone rigid. "I haven't been able to contact him in a while, but I would imagine he knows exactly where Kaya is. He will report back to me as soon as he has her. He's still under my complete control so you have nothing to worry about."

Oliver flinched, and every muscle in his body tensed. His hand tightened even more over my mouth. My teeth cut into my lip.

"This is a mess," Henry said. "Get it cleaned up immediately."

"Yes, sir."

Henry stared long and hard at Sindra, as if trying to figure out what was different about her, because, indeed, there was something.

"What aren't you telling me, Sindra?" he asked intuitively, and the two guards flanking him became even more alert.

I couldn't see Sindra's face, only the back of her head, but her expression wouldn't have changed. "I don't keep things from you, Henry."

Henry continued to analyze her with intense scrutiny. "Right. Then find my daughter. This has taken long enough. I shouldn't have to come out here to check on you. Do your job or else…"

Sindra nodded. "Of course."

Henry turned to leave, guards in tow, and took a few steps past Luke before stopping. He stared down to where Luke sat, still hunched over, bleeding at the temple, and studied him while the world became even quieter yet. Luke's eyes lifted, his baby blues staring at Henry like he was nothing more than a pestering mosquito. The disgust Luke had for Henry was clear on his face, and a pin drop could have been heard while the wheels in Henry's evil mind spun. I prayed Luke would look away, and I desperately hoped Henry would walk away. I almost breathed a sigh of relief when Henry shook his head and turned. But instead of going back to the hole he came out of, he spun around to face Sindra where she remained cemented to the snow.

"Who is this?" Henry asked, pointing a manicured fingernail at Luke's golden head.

"Just one of Rayna's employees. I'll take care of him," Sindra said, but her tone was far too casual.

Oliver was squeezing me so tight now I could barely breathe. He didn't have to—I was frozen in fear.

Henry's head tipped to the side, still studying Luke as if he were a piece of a puzzle close to coming together. "Who bound his hands and feet?"

"Rayna," Sindra replied.

Henry cracked his neck. He always did when his curiosity was aroused. "Why would she cuff her own man?"

I could tell by the way Sindra shifted from one foot to the next that she had become nervous. I'd seen her do this when Henry confronted her about things she'd let slip when I was younger... Who gave Kaya candy? Why does she only have one guard with her? Who said it was okay for her to have a pet? Except this time, Sindra shifted back to the other foot, which meant she was extremely nervous.

"I'm not sure," she answered.

Henry bent down before Luke. "What is your name?" he demanded.

Time stood still while Luke stared stoically at Henry, completely disregarding his question. Henry waited, his patience only good for a few seconds, then he abruptly stood and turned to Sindra.

"Shoot him," he ordered.

I couldn't contain the scream that gurgled in my throat. Oliver's hand tightened, but I'd made some sort of noise. I fought against the arms holding me, shaking the branches around us in the process. Every armed man on the beach pointed their guns in our direction.

"You're going to get us all killed," Oliver hissed in my ear.

Thomas bolted upright. I felt the effects of panic and lack of air taking over my head as he walked slowly out of the protection of the shadowy leaves toward the beach, hands in the air. Now I quit struggling. Quit making any sound as all the guns on the beach were trained on him. Sindra gave the order for the men to stand down, but her eyes had momentarily widened in what seemed like horror when she saw Thomas. Quickly regaining her composure, she gave a casual yet irritated nod to where he stood.

"Sir, that is just Thomas. He's a recruit in training."

The guards relaxed, but my mind spun... How did Sindra know his name? Why was she protecting him, too? There was a second of silence while Henry regarded Thomas—only a second—but it felt like eternity.

"What happened to your head?" Henry asked.

Thomas seemed confused until he remembered Ben's blood on his face and torso, and the goose bump protruding from his forehead. "Oh," he said casually. "Tripped and hit a rock." Then, he added quickly, "Sir."

Henry's perfectly waxed eyebrows arched in disbelief. "Has he been sniffing around this place as long as you have, Sindra?"

"Yes," Sindra said, shifting her weight to her other foot.

"Well then, Thomas, do you know who this man is?" Henry made a sweeping gesture to Luke. Fighting to remain upright, Thomas stared hard at the love of my life, then cleared his throat. "I think I heard someone call him Luke."

Henry's eyes lit up. "What?" With an incredulous look, he let out a laugh that made my skin crawl. "Are the Gods smiling down upon me today?"

"Sir?" Sindra said, as confused as I was. Thomas wavered as if realizing he'd made a huge mistake.

"Oh, I know all about Luke. And it would make sense to see him out here, where Kaya apparently was," Henry said, his sick grin stretching right to his earlobes.

Sindra balked. "I don't know what—"

Henry waved a hand impatiently. "Davis gave us some very valuable information. Apparently, Kaya will do anything for one of her kidnappers. She's fallen for the one named Luke—head over heels in love—and right from the horse's mouth that came! Yes. It would make perfect sense he would be here."

The light came back on in Luke's eyes. He glared up at Henry, then at Thomas standing mere feet from where Oliver and I were hiding.

Henry clapped his hands in anticipation. "So, I'll ask you again, boy. And if you know what's good for you, you'll have the right answer." Henry stepped closer, not caring at all now about his shiny leather shoes connecting with a pile of mucky, red snow or parts of Rayna's fingers that were mere feet away. "What is your name?"

Oliver's muscles tightened around me even more. I was screaming in my mind at Luke to not answer. Praying he would lie. Lie like his life depended on it—because it did. If Luke spoke the truth, it would only be to protect me.

Luke straightened up. "I am Luke Ravelle."

Eyes widening, Henry beamed as if he'd won the lottery. "What? Ha! Oh my, this is excellent. Excellent! My daughter's kidnapper—the man she'd die for—is right here, and mine for the taking. Oh, Mr. Luke Ravelle, you have certainly made my day. You are going to come in very handy."

Luke was suddenly descended on by a dozen men. He was lifted to his feet while Henry barked orders. I struggled against Oliver, but he'd completely cut off my air now. Black spots clouded my vision, and I was helpless to do anything. Unable to even breathe as I watched Luke taken away.

The beach was almost empty of Henry's men. He turned to leave, too, then paused and returned his attention to Thomas with eyes narrowed into a deadly glare. "I'd say welcome to the family, but you're rather noisy and apparently quite clumsy. I don't think you are Lowen Security material, boy," he said.

And the last thing I saw before succumbing to darkness was my father pulling a handgun from his coat pocket and sending my best friend off his feet with a single gunshot.

32

Take The Wheel

THE DESIRE TO KEEP MY EYES CLOSED FOREVER WAS IMPEDED with Oliver's persistent cheek slaps.

"C'mon, wake up," he whispered.

I played dead. Opening my eyes meant facing reality. Luke was gone. Thomas was dead.

"Kaya, wake up. Your friend Thomas is dying..."

What? Thomas wasn't dead?

My hands stung from the cold. I brought them to my face and rubbed at my eyes to get them open. Raising my head, I saw Oliver—and was instantly flooded with rage. I flung my hand up to slap him, but he caught it easily.

"Shh.... stay quiet," he said softly. "There is Lowen security everywhere still. There's no time for—"

"I hate you," I hissed.

He nodded as if that was acceptable, and I fumed that what I'd said hadn't seemed to hurt him. He motioned toward Thomas, who was flat on his back in a lovely pool of red, mere feet away, but out of reach. "Good thing your father is a lousy shot."

Thomas... I tried to rise, wanting to go to him, but Oliver held me back. A clump of snow fell from the overhanging trees, and I jumped in alarm. "Be still. We can't be seen yet, all right? Or we will have no chance of getting him out of here."

I pulled in air and remained where I was—in clear sight of Thomas's chest, barely rising and falling with small, labored breaths. There was a Lowen Security man on the beach. His hands were gloved, and he was heading for Thomas to take his body away—if Thomas wasn't dead yet, he soon would be. My only hope was Sindra. I held my breath as she moved quickly to stand at Thomas's feet, blocking the guard.

"I'll look after this one," she said.

The guard was confused. "My instructions were to get rid of all the bodies."

Sindra sighed. "Well, I guess it's your choice. You can follow my instructions," she motioned behind her. "…or end up dead like this one. What'll it be?"

Her legendary wrath wasn't tempting the guard into an argument, so he was quickly marching off down the beach. When he was out of sight, Sindra scanned the area and came to stand mere feet from where we were hiding. She pretended to dial a number on her cell phone. Putting the device to her ear, she spoke, but her words were directed at us.

"I will leave a car for you on the road you ran on yesterday. At the dead end. Do you know the place, Kaya?"

I'd assumed she was talking to Oliver until she spoke my name. "Yes," I whispered through bare branches.

"I'll try and keep everyone focused on the ranch house for a couple of hours to give you some time to get there. If you get caught, there will be nothing I can do for you or Oliver. Got it? You must not get caught, Kaya. Understand?"

"Yes," I replied quietly and glanced at Oliver. Was he gritting his teeth? Why wasn't he doing the talking? "My necklace?" I asked hopefully. "Is it destroyed?"

"Yes," Sindra said, phone to her ear. "That insurance policy has expired."

I glared at Oliver, waiting for him to say something because his arms were practically vibrating, and his jaw was set as if a million words were waiting on the tip of his tongue—but he only watched Sindra with what seemed like revulsion and hate. That was new.

"Why are you helping me?" I asked.

Sindra stared out at the lake. "I care about you, Kaya. Have since you were a kid. I've helped you your whole life so why stop now?"

"Then help me get Luke back," I said, feeling my heart race. "Please."

Sindra began to pace, tiny footsteps in the mucky snow, eyes on the beach and on high alert. "I promise you I'll do what I can to make sure Luke isn't harmed. That's all I can do. And only if you promise me right now that you will get as far away from here as possible—you must never go back to the estate. I'll keep Luke alive, and you disappear—with Oliver—forever. Deal?"

No way in hell. "Deal," I said.

Sindra dropped her phone in her pocket, and then headed off down the beach. That was it—conversation over. Oliver and I waited until we were sure the coast was clear before we lunged to Thomas's side. His eyes were open. He was staring up at me as he lay flat on his back. His black shirt was soaked with blood and lifted away from his waist. There was a gushing hole in him, just above his hipbone.

"Took ya... long enough," he said weakly.

I pulled him into my arms. His body was cold from lying in the snow and losing so much blood. "Don't worry, you'll be all right." I ached to comfort him. He coughed and moaned. I brushed the snow from his bare arms. "You said you'd stay inside. You broke your promise to me," I said, unable to hide the worry in my voice.

"Sorry," he answered.

"I should've locked you in. What you did was the dumbest thing ever."

Oliver was kneeling across from me. He gently moved Thomas's shirt to inspect his wound.

"I would call it incredibly brave," he said.

I wanted to shove Oliver away. "No one asked you."

He ignored me by pressing his meaty hand to Thomas's wound to halt the bleeding. "Thanks for what you did, Thomas. Kaya is lucky to have a friend like—"

I cut him off. "Oh, save it! We both know what you're thinking. And I won't let you hurt him, Oliver."

Oliver blinked as my words cut deep. He swallowed hard. "I'm here only to help," he said.

"Oh, really? You're not going to try to drown him in a few minutes? Or choke the life outta him? Because I care about this guy a lot." I was pushing him. I didn't care. "That's right... I care... a lot."

The hands that had protected me for so many years remained firm on Thomas's belly, but only for aid. There was no anger about Oliver. His eyes were bright and clear and only sadness clouded the edges. "Truly, on my honor, I will not hurt your friend." His eyes bore into mine. "Or you," he added.

Oliver was telling the truth. I had to use hatred to keep myself together. "There are blankets in the shack. Go get them," I ordered.

He flinched, but rose promptly to do as I asked. I tried to hide my shock.

"Keep your hand over his wound," he called back to me.

I placed my palm over the bullet hole, Thomas's taut skin sticky and warm. I held back the desire to scream at the skies. Instead, I smoothed his dark hair back from his forehead, the bump there from yesterday an angry red.

"I'll be fine," he said, sensing my anxiety.

I pushed down harder on his wound when I felt blood seep through my fingers. He stifled a moan. "How did Sindra know your name?" I asked, not sure if I really wanted to know.

Thomas's eyelids were fluttering, and I was amazed he was conscious. Still though, with all the pain registering on his face and the unsteadiness of his pupils, I could see he was about to lie.

"No idea," he said.

"No idea?" I repeated incredulously, and my palm pushed down a little harder.

"She must have... heard it somewhere... I guess," he said between ragged breaths.

Oliver was back with the blankets. I pulled Thomas tighter, shoving away all notions of betrayal and displaying more affection than I felt. Somehow, Sindra knew Thomas's name, so there was a hefty bit of information he wasn't telling me. I wanted to demand the truth, but now wasn't the time. Besides, I'd pulled a gun on Thomas; I didn't want to address that yet, either.

I cradled Thomas lovingly while Oliver draped a blanket over him. I kept Thomas's head against my chest and a watchful eye on Oliver, but that warning look never came over his face. He wasn't vibrating with anger and jealousy or looking like he might take the knife strapped to his waist and slit Thomas's throat like he'd tried to do with Luke. No. He seemed to be genuinely concerned with the well-being of a man I was openly showing affection for. Something about him was different. Had he gotten into some strange pool of Kool-Aid with Sindra?

"Can you stand?" Oliver asked Thomas.

"Of course."

Thomas tried, but his legs weren't holding him up. He remained upright for mere seconds before tipping backward. Oliver caught him before he hit the ground.

"We gotta get you out of here and patched up, boy," Oliver said as he dragged Thomas into the trees and away from the beach. "That bullet has to come out or you won't last long."

Nothing about Oliver made sense. "What are you doing?" I challenged as Oliver plucked a few wide leaves from a low branch. Thomas was flat on his back again, turning the snow around him red.

"Uh, at the moment, I am trying to figure out how to get your pal's wound to stop gushing—"

"No really, what are you doing?" I said, trying not to yell. "I don't want you here. I don't want you. So, why are you trying to help me?"

Oliver pressed the leaves to Thomas's wound, then shredded a strip off the blanket to hold them in place. Satisfied the bleeding had slowed, he then straightened his shoulders and leveled his eyes on mine. "I am here because my feelings for you haven't changed," he said rigidly.

I had no reply. None.

"And… I know you can tell that I'm not lying," he added.

I had nothing to say to that, either.

He looked away uncomfortably. "Anyway, we have to get out of here and get your pal to a doctor. Then we'll figure out what to do about Luke."

His words slammed into my chest and almost knocked me over. "Luke?" I sputtered.

"Yeah. The past might give you a reason not to, but please, Kaya… trust me."

I had no choice. I wasn't getting Thomas anywhere by myself. Nor would I be getting Luke back alone. I stared hard into those brown eyes that used to melt my heart. "Just tell me what to do," I said.

WE ROLLED THOMAS UP IN ONE BLANKET AND DRAGGED HIM WITH THE other. I said we, but I wasn't helping much. I was drained, mentally and physically, and pretty much only assisted by being in awe of Oliver's determination to help my friend.

Once we were in the stand of birch trees, Oliver paused to catch his breath and answer his incessantly buzzing phone. "Lisa?" he said quietly into the device.

My mind reeled… Lisa? As in, Blonde Barbie from the Death Race? The Lisa who let me cry on her shoulder for hours? Luke's ex-girlfriend? The same woman who'd threatened Oliver with a frying pan and called him every horrible name imaginable? Why would they be talking to each other?

Oliver kneeled, breathless. "Yeah, I've got Kaya with me… and a way out. We will meet you at the rendezvous point… No. No, I don't have Luke. Yes, he's alive. But… he was taken by Henry."

Lisa's frantic voice burst through the phone. She was practically screaming when Oliver hung up. He shrugged his shoulders, then grabbed the corners of the blanket and started pulling Thomas again.

"You're talking to Lisa now?" I asked, and I hoped there wasn't a tone of jealousy in my voice—because I certainly wasn't jealous. Just confused.

"Yeah. She and Seth came to help us find you."

"Us?"

"Luke and me."

I thought I hadn't heard him correctly. "You and Luke?" I repeated.

Oliver cleared his throat. "Yes. We've been working together."

This was too much. "You mean you and Luke stayed... with each other? And..." I couldn't finish because I couldn't even imagine what that would have been like.

"He's a good guy, Kaya," Oliver said sincerely.

I almost fell off my feet in shock. "Yeah, I know." I had a million questions, but I desperately needed to think of anything but Luke—the worry for him was so deep I thought I might drown in it.

A half hour passed, and our breaths became white clouds as we tugged Thomas through the bush on the narrower animal trails. The sun was getting ready to leave the sky and not heating up the air anymore. I was sweating and freezing at the same time.

"You all right back there, Thomas?" I said, probably for the fiftieth time in the last fifteen minutes. All I could see was his dark hair, and I wondered if his feet were as frozen as mine. "Thomas?" I asked again.

There was no reply.

I didn't have to ask Oliver to stop; he abruptly quit moving and began unwrapping Thomas from the heavy blanket. Thomas's eyes were shut tight, his cheeks a deathly white. He was unresponsive.

"Damn it," Oliver muttered under his breath as he checked Thomas's wound. "Too much bleeding." He flattened his hand over the bullet hole. "Get some more leaves, Kaya. They are cleaner than this filthy blanket."

I plucked the widest ones I could find, brown from fall, and handed them over. He layered them over the wound and then packed a handful of clean snow on top. "The cold should slow the bleeding." He secured his handiwork with the torn blanket before wrapping Thomas back up. "How much farther to the road?"

I felt my own blood drain from my cheeks, and an odd buzzing in my head.

"Kaya, we gotta get him outta here. How much farther?" Oliver asked again.

I tipped back my head to see the sun in the west end of the sky. "We either keep moving through the trees, the same way we're going—and I'm not really sure for how long that will take us. Or we get out into the field and cross it."

"We'd be in the open then. Sitting ducks."

I moved toward the edge of the stand of trees. Oliver and I could make a run for it, ten minutes tops and we would be at the road. But with Thomas, we'd be moving slowly. Oliver was already exhausted, and there was no way he could carry or drag Thomas across the field quickly, if at all. Thomas's life was slipping away. I felt helpless. The trails through the trees seemed never-ending and bleak. Was there another way? Maybe I could run back to the ranch house, sneak in somehow, find the medicine cabinet and gather supplies, then get back here. But that would take so long.

"C'mon, Kaya, let's keep moving," Oliver said breathlessly, maneuvering a completely unconscious Thomas back onto the blanket and dragging him again.

I felt frozen. Not by the cold, but by everything. I had been so strong, keeping my anxiety away, doing what I had to... Why suddenly was I about to crumble? My legs wouldn't move. My arms felt stuck to my sides.

"Kaya?"

"I can't move," I said stubbornly.

Oliver let out an irritated huff. With a free hand, he grabbed a corner of my jacket and pushed me ahead. "No time for whatever's going on in your head. Get walking."

He wasn't giving up on Thomas or me, so why was I? What was wrong with me? I wouldn't have needed a shove a few hours ago...

I trudged ahead, fighting the buzzing in my head, only to stop short again. Oliver saw it, too. Through the shadowy trees, about a hundred feet ahead, there was a massive shape blocking the light from the field.

"Is that a horse?"

"No, can't be," I muttered, and motioned to Oliver not to move a muscle. I weaved through the bushes and around the silvery tree trunks until I was walking in hoofprints the horse had left behind. As I stepped lightly and not too fast, I knew he saw me coming. By the sheer mass of him and his solid black gleam from tail to nose, I could tell it was Zander.

Strangely, he didn't take off.

"Zander?" I said calmly, and reminded myself to stay firm with him. "Just stay right there..." I was impressed with how well he obeyed, then I realized he was only still because his reins were tangled in a tree.

"Good boy," I said. I untwisted the leather from a persistent branch. He flipped his head up when he was freed, and I held the straps tightly. "I think you're my guardian angel today." I rubbed him behind the ear, and his reply was a shake of his thick black mane. "Ben would be proud."

Thomas slipped in and out of consciousness as we wrestled him onto Zander's back. His arms and legs dangled uselessly while I led the way and Oliver made sure he wouldn't fall off. We hurried into the sparkling white field stretching out between fences like a frozen lake. I hoped I remembered where I was going. The dead-end road was east of the ranch house, of that I was certain, but everything else from my memory was questionable. The field had to end at some point, and the road flanking it would be running east to west, so I headed south hoping to come upon it.

"Damn it. Now I can see the house, and that means they can see us," Oliver said.

The Carlson ranch house was still very far off, but anyone straining their eye would spot the shifting dark spots on the white ground. We walked along the other side of Zander, hoping from a distance it would just look like one of the horses was wandering about.

We picked up the pace when we saw the road. At a barbed-wire fence, we struggled to get Thomas through. I said goodbye to Zander. After I stroked his muzzle, I removed the bridle from his head and thanked him profusely. After a series of horse snorts and head shakes, he took off running. I knew I'd never see him again, and I felt a sting of sadness as I said goodbye to Ben, too.

Oliver struggled with Thomas, dragging him out of the ditch and onto the road. Now, without any cover, we truly were sitting ducks in a white wonderland, on a white road… as obvious as the waning sun. And to top it all off, there was the unmistakable sound of a helicopter firing up. Every square inch of me turned to goose bumps. Terror, cold and stinging, crawled up my back. Oliver turned to me, sweat streaming across his face.

"Get to the car, Kaya," he said, collapsing to the slick road. "Get as far away as you can. Just keep going and don't look back."

I just stared at him.

"Run, please…"

I was frozen. "I can't. I can't leave you here."

He looked at me the same way he had in the Death Race when I was stuck in the mud. His chest was heaving as he gathered a massive lungful of breath. "I… said… run!"

I spun away and dug deep for whatever energy I had left. One foot after the other, I struggled to get my speed up, my lungs burning instantly. I slipped and fought to keep traction as I forged forward, each step as difficult as it was that day in that mud. Oliver had spurred me ahead. His ferocity hadn't scared me into it, nor was it some sense of obedience that got me going forward. It was because I saw something in his eyes I'd never seen before. The same thing that was in Marlene's eyes when she talked about Ben. The same thing I felt when I thought about Luke in my father's hands—fear.

The road stretched on and on... and I could have wept when I saw the car and came skidding to a halt at the black four-door sedan. Hands and legs vibrating, I bent over to catch my breath before I could muster up the strength to even open the door. The keys were already in the ignition. A note on the steering wheel said 'Go Straight. Trust me'. I recognized Sindra's handwriting and looked ahead; yesterday, the plow had left behind a massive mountain of snow at the end of this dead-end road. Now there was a space carved out in the middle wide enough for the car to fit through.

This was great and all... but I didn't know how to drive.

I knew I had to turn the key; when I did, the engine purred to life. There were two foot pedals—I knew one was the gas, and the other the brake, but how to go backward? I had no idea. There was definitely no room to turn the car around. Oliver and Thomas were on the road, in plain sight—one of them dying and the other most certainly dead if found by Henry... and I didn't know how to go backward.

I panicked, pushing every button and knob. Something made the windshield wipers go crazy and the heat blasted on. I felt the anxiety attack that had been at bay ebb in. I couldn't catch my breath. The metal around me closed in. I bolted out of the car and stood on the road.

"I can't do this!" I yelled at the sky.

The chopper was in the air now. I could hear it. It was far off, but wouldn't take long to be overhead. If I didn't do something, my friends would die. I had been so strong, keeping my head up, trying not to be weak, and here it was... anxiety... back again. Why now?

Oliver.

Of course! With him around, I was reverting to my helpless self. I'd relied on him so much in the past I never had to be strong. I never had to take charge or do anything when he was with me. I was reverting to the girl I was before Luke. The one who depended on Oliver for everything...and I wasn't that girl anymore. Now was the time to prove it.

I had to think logically. There had to be something that switched the gears in the motor to make it go forward and backward. I got back in and found a lever beside the steering wheel. I remembered watching Marlene put the left pedal to the floor before going forward or backing up, so I did that, then pulled down the lever until it rested on the letter R. I took my foot off the left pedal, and miraculously the car started moving backward. Shocked, I pushed the pedal down again and it stopped. This was good, I could go backward. I twisted my body around as much as I could to look out the rear window and took my foot off the brake. The car kept going. It swayed, but I managed to get it back going straight. I gave it gas and almost hit the ditch but didn't let up. When I could see Oliver dragging Thomas behind him, I tapped the gas pedal some more, then stomped on the brakes when I feared I might run them over.

The sound of the chopper roaring through the sky could be heard when the back door opened.

"Drive, Kaya!" Oliver roared after he threw Thomas in and jumped in the backseat with him.

"I don't know how to go forward…"

"Foot on the break, lever to the D position."

I did as I was told.

"Push the gas pedal, Kaya!"

He struggled to get into the front seat as we raced toward the dead-end. The road was icy, and Oliver's hands were reaching for the steering wheel, working with me as I drove. At the wall of snow, we sailed through the space carved out just for us, and Oliver ordered me to keep going. He gave directions while the car sped through a field on a freshly plowed path, past a neighbor's driveway, and finally onto an actual road again. I gripped the steering wheel, guiding the car on my own now, keeping the vehicle between the lines while we breathed heavy sighs of relief. Frequent looks at the cloudless sky said the chopper was nowhere to be seen.

"I can't believe we got away," I said, every muscle quivering.

"You can pull over. I'll drive," Oliver said. "We need to get Thomas to a doctor. Not end up in a car accident."

I agreed. "I just can't believe it. If it weren't for Sindra, we'd be—" I didn't get a chance to finish.

"Don't say her name," Oliver hissed. "Just… don't. Ever."

"All right." Now I had a million and one questions. I held them in as I brought the car to a stop on the side of the road, which was just another lonely line stretching from who knows where to nowhere.

"Just know I am not under her control anymore. I am my own man," Oliver said. "I am not following her orders, or Henry's orders, ever again."

Night was falling over the prairies, but Oliver was being cast in a new light. He was here… on his own… for me. How could I hate him? We'd both made mistakes. We'd both been assholes. I glanced at him, now calm, focused, and certainly not angry, and realized he really was different. I could feel it. It was like the blanket of sickness he'd been covered with had been cast off.

"What you see is the real me now, Kaya. Here by my own choice. Just know that."

I gulped. Silence fell between us as we stared at each other. And after a full minute of sharing a wordless and unexplainable level of understanding, Thomas spoke up from the backseat.

"Hey," he said weakly. "Can you finish your heart to heart another time? I'm kinda dying back here…"

LUKE

33

BAST FROM THE PAST

THE ROOM CAME IN AND OUT OF FOCUS—BRICK WALLS, A LIGHT bulb dangling from the ceiling, silver carts covered with shiny vials, and a wall of whips and chains. Through a drug haze, I realized I was in a cell of some sort. My body felt as if floating, not comfortable, but on edge. Was I on a table? Shaking? Cold metal bit into my bones as I drifted between being awake and asleep. Voices rolled over my mind like thorns on a breeze, real or fake I couldn't tell. Regardless, I refused to answer any questions. No amount of threats or drugs would make me talk about Kaya. Whatever pain they would inflict was nothing compared to what I felt when she told me she didn't love me back at that beach…

Jabs to my ribs. Multiple blows to my stomach. No way was I talking. No way was I uttering one word about her, even when the pain became something else—torture. I was pulled upright. Chained from the ceiling. And suddenly, my insides were on fire and my back felt like the skin was being stripped from the bone. A whip was delivering lashes between my shoulders—crack, crack—I gasped for air as it seemed to cut through to my spine. A lashing licked the tip over the back of my ear. Warm blood trickled down my neck. They could cut me to shreds, and I still wouldn't talk.

"Don't damage his face or Henry will have your head," someone said to the girl with the purple hair and neck tattoos.

She was the one enjoying causing me pain. I told her it didn't hurt. At least, I thought that was what I said. Whatever drug was in me had my mind jumbled. My thoughts were jumping from where I was to a serene, flowing river with Kaya standing at my side… smiling in the moonlight…telling me she was just trying to protect me…

I blacked out. I thought I did, anyway. And when the light bulb came back into view, there was only silence. All I could hear was my own heartbeat, which seemed to be alarmingly erratic. Alone in the dim room, I waited, until I could see blurry shapes moving around me again—lunch break was over. White hooded figures hovered over the silver tables. They were readying some sort of concoction to slip into my veins. I fought with everything I had, but the chains holding me were unbreakable. So was the determination of the people in the lab coats.

Soon, liquid fire surged through my blood and seeped into my mind.

Then came more questions… Where is Kaya? Why did you go to the Carlson Ranch? When did Sindra come to your motel? Where is Oliver?

I tried, but couldn't lie. Whatever they injected me with had taken away the ability to hold my tongue. Not one part of me could hold back the honest answers that flowed, my voice sounding nothing like my own as I relayed that I didn't know where Kaya was. They could beat me to a pulp and it wouldn't matter, because I truly didn't know. And the baby she lost… why were they questioning me about that? And why was I answering? Something sharp was diving into my arm again, and my mind wasn't under my control. Questions were followed by pain… the purple-haired girl was demanding answers… Where is Oliver? Do you love Kaya? Does she love you? Would she truly do anything for you?

My muscles felt like they were being stretched apart. Only when I decided that trying to bite off my own tongue was better than talking did they stop the questions.

Then there was nothing. The throb of my heartbeat pulsed through every wounded part of my body, and the taste of blood in my mouth were the only things reassuring me that I wasn't dead. So I welcomed an impending blackout wholeheartedly…

A SURGE OF FIRE SHOT THROUGH THE TIPS OF MY FINGERS TO MY NECK and shocked me awake. I was hanging from the ceiling by my hands. Metal cuffs were digging into my wrists and attached to chains. I straightened my legs to ease the pressure, but realized my ankles were cuffed, too. I fought against the restraints even though I knew it was futile, and even though every part of my aching body screamed in rebellion.

"Struggling is stupid," the girl said.

Her hair was done up in some intricately arranged style, her makeup plastered on masterfully, and a polka-dot dress matching the pink cactus tattoo on her neck had replaced the lab coat. I pulled against the chains, feeling fresh blood trickle down my arms.

"Stop doing that, or I'll make you stop," she threatened.

I obeyed, mostly because I was too exhausted not to. "Nice dress," I found myself saying. Slurring slightly, tongue throbbing but thankfully still intact. "I appreciate you dressing for the occasion. Torturing someone is such a glamorous event."

She laughed. "Ooh, you're good. And those eyes of yours... no wonder Kaya has fallen for you. I don't think I've seen anyone quite so gorgeous. I bet you clean up spectacularly."

Kaya. I allowed my mind to drift back to the vision of her standing on that beach, eyes pouring with tears when she said she didn't love me. I could have died right there...

"Hey, are you listening to me, Luke? What do you say when someone gives you a compliment?"

"Depends, I guess," I said, trying to get some saliva in my mouth to swallow. "If it was from someone I respected, I'd say thanks. But from a sadistic bitch like you? I think I'll just say fuck off."

She laughed. It was a horrifying sound. It gave me the chills more than the metal table displaying shining vials of God knows what ready at her disposal. She caressed a few of the needles, dragging thin fingers across the syringes, but it was the whip that she settled on and picked up with a gleam in her eye.

"You look good with that skin of yours nice and pink," she said. "It sort of takes my breath away."

I couldn't help but shudder. She circled me, running her fingers across my bare arms, then across the welts on my back. Her breath was on my neck as she spoke. "Oh, darling Luke, there's no place in the world I'd rather be than here with you. You see, at first, I fought it. I fought them. But then I realized they were right, and I could have everything I ever wanted if I just did as I was told." She pressed her body against mine, reaching around so the tip of the leather strap rested against my bare stomach. "I have all the pretty dresses I want, make-up and jewelry for miles, and a cozy little suite with twenty-four-hour room service. Plus, now I have a man to play with." She came around to face me and tugged on the waistband of my pants, toying with the button. "My old life sucked. My new life is superb. All I have to do is make people talk—and I'm good at that. When I get my hands on Kaya, I can personally thank her for landing me this job."

There was so much crazy in her eyes it made my stomach churn. She backed up then. With a flick of her wrist, she sent the tip of the whip across my hip bone. This was just a warm up—I knew what was to come.

"Then you owe her," I said, clutching at straws, trying the nice-guy approach. "She would want you to let me go. I can get you out of here and take you somewhere nice, away from all this—"

The girl put her fingers to my lips, dragging a pointed fingernail down to my chin. Her breath smelled of cinnamon, her hands like leather and metal.

"Shh… No, no, no, darling. Soon, you will stand here, next to me, the whip in your hands when you deliver the first lashing to your precious Kaya's back. I wonder… will you break her skin? Oh, I get goose bumps just thinking about it. I can't imagine how she will scream."

I pulled with everything I had against the chains, feeling my head spin with pain. "There's nothing you can do that would make me hurt Kaya. Nothing," I hissed.

"Now settle down, Luke, or I'll light your insides on fire with one of these fancy Eronel Pharmaceutical cocktails.

I growled, baring my teeth with the primal urge to rip her head off.

The girl backed away and smoothed her hair. "Anyway, let's not worry about Kaya for now. We are on a tight schedule. We only have a few minutes of fun before I have to clean you up and fix that messy hair of yours. If you're a good boy, I'll get you something to eat and drink."

Ha. No way in hell was I taking anything she was offering.

She moved to a small mirror hanging from the wall and checked her makeup. "Oh, I've picked out some nice clothes for you to wear," she added. "So don't worry, you'll look good when the camera crew gets here. I'll make sure you're ready for your television debut."

Had I heard this crazy broad correctly? "Camera crew? What are you talking about?"

She licked her lips, cherry-red lipstick glistening. "Oh, you'll see. You're going to cooperate. Right, Luke? Cause if you don't, I'll pump you full of so much dope you'll be crying for your dead mama, and then, when it wears off, I won't be as gentle with you as I'm going to be right now."

She smiled, and I braced myself for what was to come.

Crack…

KAYA

34

CIRCLING THE DRAIN

I KEPT THE HOT WATER TRICKLING, NOT JUST TO RID THE CHILL clinging to my bones, but to drown out the voices incessantly blathering in the next room. The motel walls were paper thin and everything—even Lisa's sniffles—were unavoidable.

The men were arguing about what to do next, where to go and how to hide me, and Lisa was having a meltdown over Luke. She wanted to find him. Now. She wanted to rip the world to shreds and seek revenge tenfold for every hair mussed on his handsome head. And, since her feelings mirrored my own and she vocalized them so well, I didn't have to say a word. I realized—as she ranted and yelled—that she could speak for me while I dissolved in the bathtub.

The whirlwind of the last few days had caught up with me. When we'd found a doctor for Thomas—a well-paid veterinarian, but a doctor just the same—he got the help he needed while stretched out on a metal table too short for a human. It was then it hit me. Full force. All the physical exertion I'd managed to force with the exhaustion I had on every level came at me with a crushing blow. Even my heart was tired. While the doctor dug the bullet out of Thomas's body, then used something like a staple gun to put him back together, my legs dropped out from underneath me.

It infuriated me that my body was failing while my mind seemed to have become stronger, and I was livid when Oliver got Thomas in the car and had to come back for me. I couldn't stop shaking, clothes damp and filthy, clinging to the chair I'd melted into in the veterinarian's waiting room. My legs and arms were limp as rags. Useless. I was angry I needed his help. And now, as my discarded clothes lay strewn across the lime-green bathroom floor, I was angry I had nothing clean to change into.

I sank into the water, my ears filling up, holding my breath and losing myself in my heartbeat and the soothing sound of the faucet running. I stayed submerged for as long as I could, but it was too tiring and required too much effort to keep bobbing up and down for air. So I rested my head against the wall, letting the bubbles from the cheap motel shampoo build up against my skin. I tried to tune out the voices in the next room, but Oliver's—deep and loud—was impossible to escape.

"No… I say we head east. Get lost in a big city for a while. It's most important we get Kaya as far from here as possible."

Lisa was raging. "More important than going after Luke? Are you kidding me? Who knows what Henry will do to him! There is no time to wait. You can take Kaya wherever you want, but I am going to go get Luke back, starting right this second."

Oliver was calm. "Lisa, relax, please. Sindra promised us he wouldn't be hurt, and although she is heinous beyond belief, she would never break a promise. So, we have time—"

Lisa was on the verge of exploding. "I don't give a stinkin' rat's mangy ass about what this devil woman Sindra says! She works for Henry, for God sake. What the hell is wrong with you?"

Seth piped up. "Listen, Lisa, honey, I know you're upset, but we have to think things through. We need a game plan. A good one. Do you realize what we are up against? Luke could be anywhere. Henry has estates and lab facilities all over the country. So, I think Oliver is right. For now, we concentrate on getting Kaya somewhere she won't be found."

Lisa swore. Words I'd never even imagined existed were slung about the room with bloodcurdling fury. They were followed by a moment of stunned silence before Thomas spoke.

"Has anyone asked Kaya what she wants to do?" he asked.

No one answered.

"I mean, it is her life we're talking about. Should she not be included in this conversation?"

I dipped under the water again, holding my breath, letting the bubbles escape from my lungs… Worry for Luke was eating me alive. Thomas knew that. They all knew that. Oliver was talking when I came up for air.

"…at least we only have Henry to deal with now Rayna is out of the picture. Thankfully, that bitch is dead."

There was no mistaking the sound of a shocked inhale, maybe even feet stumbling backward. "What do you mean?" Seth said, his voice catching in his throat.

"Rayna was shot. She's dead," Oliver said carefully.

Seth seemed caught off guard. His voice rose in pitch. "You saw this? You were a witness? It's for sure? She's… dead? No… no… Can't be…

not... yet..."

Lisa's tone was barbed. "What the hell, Seth? We wanted her dead, remember? What's going on with you?"

I sat up a little straighter in the tub now, wanting to hear what they were saying.

Seth was rambling. "I... well, I mean, I just didn't know she was, uh... I just thought... I thought that maybe she—"

"She... what?" Lisa demanded.

"I—uh, damn it, I'm hungry! That is all, Lisa. I'm going to my room."

"Not without me you're not!"

A slamming door shook the walls. I rubbed at my eyes and cranked the hot water all the way open. The bathroom was already filled with steam and the water was scorching hot, but it wasn't taking away the chill in my bones. I drifted beneath the surface again, fading into it, holding my breath. Trying not to think about Luke, or Seth, or Lisa, or Rayna... The running tap hurt my feet, the water scalding, but I was too tired to care. I kept holding my breath. Soon a thick, eerie darkness started to creep toward me. My heart was pounding, but the voices in the other room had finally disappeared. Then so did the sound of the tap running. Everything was quiet. Blissfully quiet. The chill had gone, too. I was fading easily into darkness...

Until I was violently pulled out of the scorching water.

"Kaya, what the hell? Are you trying to drown yourself?"

Oliver had a hold of my arm. He'd yanked it so hard I wondered if my shoulder came out of its socket. It brought my head sharply back to reality as his hands slipped under my armpits. All I could do was fall against him. The blackness wanted to creep back in, but now it wasn't welcome. Had I almost drowned?

Oliver threw a towel around me, then turned off the tap and pulled the plug.

"How did you get in here?" I stammered, then noticed the bathroom door no longer on its hinges.

He sat me down on the edge of the tub, his eyes wide. "Were you trying to cook yourself?"

I didn't know what I was trying to do. Water poured from my sopping hair to the bathroom floor, soaking Oliver's socks. He had a towel in the sink and was running it under chilly water. His eyes were misty when he flattened it to my forehead.

Thomas politely knocked on the doorframe. "Hey, is everything all right in there?"

"It's fine," Oliver and I said in unison.

The cold water on my face pulled me completely away from the darkness now. What was I thinking?

"You could get heat stroke, pass out, and drown! Damn it, Kaya. That water was way too hot... way too damn hot... What the hell?"

I was pink. I was dizzy. And Oliver was frazzled. The big lug, all tough and nothing but muscle, was patting the cloth to my neck and then my cheeks, like he used to whenever I was sick with fever. And now I was just... done. I felt my eyes closing. My limbs evaporating. I didn't even have the strength to put an arm out when I started to slip off the tub. I didn't even have the energy to give him hell for invading my privacy.

"Put this on..." Oliver was saying, and the towel was taken away from me.

Often, Oliver had seen me naked, and I'd never cared. Still didn't. I closed my eyes, unable to keep them open any longer, and a shirt, smelling of his cologne, was pulled over my head. Then I was up and in his arms—as I'd been too many times to count—and carried to bed. The television was on, and the smell of pizza was in the air, but I kept my eyes closed. A pillow was placed under my head and the cloth back on my forehead. Oliver was telling Thomas how careless I had been as he made me drink water. He fanned my overheated body with a magazine, and I peeled my eyelids apart to see that smooth stretch of dark skin over his chest; he had literally given me the shirt off his back.

When my body returned to a normal temperature, Oliver moved to a chair by the window and now sat gazing out at the night. I could hear Thomas shifting around, trying to get comfortable on the other bed. I'd hoped to fall asleep, but a few things were keeping me awake.

"Thomas?" I said after a while, hoping he was up, too.

"Hmm?" he said sleepily.

"Are you all right?"

Oliver sighed heavily.

"Yeah," Thomas said. "Good as new."

"Did you betray me?" I held my breath for an answer.

"What do you mean—"

"Sindra."

"Oh," he said. "I hoped you wouldn't find out. But, well, she made me an offer."

Oliver shifted in his chair. I would have bolted upright if I could have moved. I wanted to know... and I didn't at the same time. "What was that offer?" I whispered.

Thomas's breath caught as he sat up. Wincing, he inched to the edge of my bed. "I wasn't with Marlene when Ben, uh… attacked you in the bunkhouse." Oliver gasped, but Thomas continued. "Sindra approached me in the barn. She offered me a check—three hundred and fifty thousand bucks if I guarded you with my life for two months. All I had to do was say yes and it was mine."

My heart sped up. "And… what did you say?" I would run from the room if he had taken her offer. I thought of our time together, our moment, and the way he seemed to care for me. I cherished our friendship. If he had been paid to do that…

I forced my eyes to open, to stare at him fully while he fidgeted.

"I said yes," he said.

I felt my stomach flip into my throat.

"But…" he added, gaze settling on mine. "I didn't take the check. I ripped it up in front of her. Nobody has to pay me to guard you with my life. That I'll do of my own free will."

Tears of relief flowed. I couldn't stop them. I believed Thomas, wholeheartedly, and when his hand reached for mine, I clung to it.

"I'm sorry I didn't tell you sooner," he said sincerely. "There just never seemed to be the right time. I didn't want to keep it from you, but—"

"It's okay. I understand."

"Thanks."

"Ben's dead," I blurted out.

"I know."

"And I—I shot people. I shot a man. He was just trying to show me a picture, and I shot him."

"It had to be done," Thomas said.

"And… Luke. I failed him. I failed—"

His hand was on my shoulder. "Shush now. It's not your fault, and you know that."

"And drugging you… I'm so sorry for that."

He laughed. "It probably was for the best. And hey, if you can forgive me for not telling you about Sindra, I can forgive you for knocking me unconscious."

I brought up what we were both thinking. "Can you forgive me for pointing a gun at your head?"

He didn't hesitate. "You wouldn't have shot me; we both know that."

I didn't know that. I was ready to do anything for Luke. And that scared the hell out of me.

"I'm sorry you had to go through all this. I wish things were different," Thomas said.

"You know, I thought… I thought maybe if I saw Rayna face to face, that she would change her mind about me. I thought that my mother would want suddenly to be my mother."

Thomas sighed and stretched out next to me, his body a safe distance, his hands folded under his head. "I'm sorry that didn't happen, Kaya. At least you have family, though—maybe not blood related—but people who truly love you."

He was referring to himself. And Oliver. That wasn't lost on my fatigued mind.

"I just... I can't... I don't know..." Words failed me.

"Hey relax," he said. "Take in a deep breath. Now... I haven't told you about cherry angel food cake yet, have I? Well, cherry is great. If you pair it with cream cheese icing and..."

I SLEPT FITFULLY, IF AT ALL. THOMAS'S VOICE WAS SOOTHING AND HAD lulled me to sleep, but dreams of blood and guts and the picture that man in the barn had been holding out to me made me wake in a cold sweat. I'd drift off again, only to jolt awake with the vision of Luke's eyes, so blue, so pained... pleading... Sleep was just not happening tonight.

I was glad the television was still on, the grey light of it allowing my eyes to quickly take in my roommates. Thomas was sound asleep, flat on his back next to me, and Oliver was stretched out on the other bed. The clock on the nightstand said it was four in the morning, and the pitch black on the other side of the flimsy curtains confirmed that.

"Can't sleep?" Oliver murmured.

His feet hung over the end of the bed. He was fully dressed on high alert, blankets flat and unused beneath him.

"No."

"Me neither."

I stood, muscles not happy about doing so, and reached for an empty glass next to the television. My mouth was so dry I could barely swallow, but five feet to the bathroom for water seemed too far to walk. I couldn't decide what to do—bed, water, or just sink to my knees and crumble to the floor.

"Answer me one question, please," Oliver said.

I turned to face him; he'd been thinking about this for a while. "Okay."

"Are you... in love with... him?" Oliver asked with a slight head tilt in Thomas's direction.

I could be honest. "No. I mean, I love him. But not like that."

"Not like Luke."

All I could do was nod; not like Oliver, either.

"All right," Oliver said.

The heater whirred. Thomas snored. I debated sleeping on my feet.

"Bring me the glass, Kaya," Oliver said.

It wasn't a command like the old days. Nor was it a direct order. I slowly padded over to him and he sat up, reaching for something beside his bed.

"In honor of Stephan, I figured I'd give scotch a try." He produced a half-empty bottle of amber liquid with a familiar label.

Stephan. The sound of his name hurt my heart. "I miss him so much."

Oliver filled my glass. Together, we took long swigs, the fire in our throats barely registering among so many other painfully unspoken things. I found myself sitting on the bed next to him, looking through the curtains at the moon that was about to leave the sky. I didn't care that his shirt barely covered my thighs or the dim light barely concealed my tears; it was Oliver.

"I'm going to get Luke back for you. I promise," he said.

I couldn't believe what I was hearing. He truly wanted to help me even though I'd left him.

"He saved my life," he added. "He made me realize a few things about myself."

I could barely swallow. Not from Oliver's offer to help me, but from the startling realization of what it was between us that would never fade no matter what we were faced with. It really and truly was love. Different from what I felt with Luke, different from what I felt with Thomas, but it was love just the same.

"Thank you," I muttered, and I crawled up next to him like I had so many times. Only because I wanted to, I laid my head upon his chest, moving into the comfort of his arms.

"Kaya, I'm—"

I cut him off, shaking my head at him not to speak because I knew what he was going to say... and the familiarity and safety of him, along with his earnest desire to care for me, was obvious. He'd fought his de-mon—whatever is was—and he'd won. What was done was done. The past... was the past. He didn't have to tell me how much he loved me.

I peered up at him. "I love you, too."

OLIVER

35

OPTIONS

I WATCHED THE SUN COME UP, NOT EVEN REMOTELY SLEEPY EVEN with the amount of scotch I'd consumed. I didn't dare move, although every fiber of my being ached to pull Kaya even tighter to me and never let her go. Relishing every single second of her warmth as she breathed, her body warm and soft against mine, I realized I might never have a moment like this again.

"Whatcha lost in thought about, Oliver... pancakes?" she said softly.

I gulped. I hadn't realized she was awake, and I couldn't help but tighten my arms protectively around her. I cleared my throat. "Just thinking that I... really don't want you to run away again."

She lifted her eyes to mine. "I'm sorry. I thought I was doing the right thing. For... everyone."

"I know." I reached across her, my face coming a bit too close to hers, and pulled a corner of the sheet over her bare legs. I couldn't think straight with that glorious skin of hers shining like a pearl in the moonlight. "You have to understand, Kaya, that me and Luke, and Seth and Lisa, too... we are all here and in this with you because we want to be. This whole mess is bigger than you. We chose to get involved, knowing the risks. The sooner you realize that, the better."

She bit her lip. "I do. I understand. I just wanted Luke—and you—to be able to opt out before things got even crazier. Before one of you got hurt."

"If the roles were switched, if Luke was the one in your situation, would you opt out? Would it change your feelings?"

She answered quickly. "Hell no."

"Well, it doesn't change ours either."

Her heart sped up slightly and her body tensed. "Oliver, there's something you need to know."

She pulled away to look me square in the eye. It felt as if her eyes were peering right into my soul. I used to say things to her in my mind, hoping to convey to her all the thoughts I could never get past my tongue. All those years watching her grow into the woman she was now, becoming stronger than I ever imagined, more beautiful than my heart could handle, stirred that part in the center of me that gave me a reason to live. I felt that now, in the dim light, under the steady glow of her remarkable green irises. She was so beautiful my chest ached to touch her. So I told her that—in my mind of course—just like I used to.

"Oliver?" she stammered.

"Uh-huh…" I said, trying to get my expression back to neutral.

"I own it all. The estate, Eronel Pharmaceutical and the sister companies, and a massive trust fund. Henry has only been looking after it until I turn twenty-one, and then I can legally do what I want with it. The reason he wants me back so badly is not to protect me; it's so he can get control of my inheritance."

I wasn't shocked to hear any of what she was saying. It made perfect sense. "And how will he gain control?"

Her eyes drifted to the window, and she suddenly looked uncomfortable. "He needs you and me to make him an heir. He wants… a grandchild. By murdering the three of us, all rights of my inheritance would bypass John Marchessa and land back in his hands. Hence his reason for wanting us to be… together."

I shifted uncomfortably, too, because I wanted nothing more than to make a child with Kaya, and not just for the act of making love to her. I didn't want kids. I hadn't wanted kids—until now. Something had switched on in my head when I pictured the life we created growing in her womb. My child… my baby…was now lost forever. I'd never even mourned it. In fact, I'd been happy about the miscarriage. But now? I allowed myself to gaze at her slim body, stretched against mine, and every part of me wanted it back so bad.

She was holding back tears. "We can never be together, Oliver. Even if I wanted to be… with you… I couldn't. I would be putting your life in danger even more than I am now. Also, technically…" She swallowed hard. Whatever she was about say was difficult. "You and I… are brother and sister. Stephan told me Henry adopted you when you first came to the estate. That's the loophole to claiming my inheritance."

Well lucky me. Torture and adoption went hand in hand, didn't they? "Well, that sucks," I said, barely managing the words.

She quickly changed the subject. "That necklace you destroyed… it held a drop of Lenore's blood. It would have solved all this. A DNA analysis would have proved I am not a blood relation to the Marchessas. I would have been free of all this mess."

I felt the blood drain from my stupid head. "Oh my God, that's why you were so angry with me. Kaya, I'm so sorry—"

"No... No, Oliver. It's okay. Really. You didn't know. And honestly, I have decided it is for the best. I want the inheritance now. I want to use it to make a difference. You did me a favor by making me realize that. I will clean up the mess Eronel has left behind and shut down whatever else Henry is up to. I can't imagine what is so important he would want to murder his own family for, but I will find out. And I will stop him."

I reached for the scotch and unscrewed the lid. Not because I wanted some more, but because I didn't know what to say or do.

Kaya cleared her throat nervously. "Anyway, now you know the danger you face," she continued. "There's a heavy mark on your back as it is, and multiplied tenfold just by being with me. If you're caught, who knows what would happen to you. I won't run away again, Oliver, but I am officially giving you the opportunity to opt out."

Her eyes shone, and her bottom lip quivered ever so slightly. The sun coming up was playing with her hair and lighting up the places where the sheet had fallen away from her flawless skin. I put down the bottle and slowly pulled her back to me. Her body returned to mine, and I had the slightest hope that maybe someday her mind would follow.

We lay together, like we had so many times, for so many years, and I knew she was exactly where she should be. I just wished she knew it, too.

"Sleep now. Everything is going to be all right," I said. "I know what I'm up against. And no way am I opting out."

KAYA

36

EVERYTHING AND NOTHING TO LOSE

Eighteen hours had gone by since Luke had been taken.

I pried myself away from the warmth of the bed. Oliver was asleep now, and I tried not to wake him as I groaned with the ache in every muscle. The floor was ice cold on my bare feet. I clicked on a lamp and the view of the stark, dingy motel room intensified my pains with a sudden sense of despair. How was I going to get Luke back?

"Hey, Kaya," Thomas said sleepily—the light must have woken him.

"It's after twelve," I said. "In the afternoon." I was unable to hide the shakiness in my voice. "We could have been halfway to—"

"To where?" Thomas said, swinging his legs over the side of the bed and wincing. "Listen, I know you're worried about Luke, but think logically. Running around like a chicken with its head cut off isn't going to get him back."

We'd woken Oliver. He stood and then stumbled past me on his way to the bathroom—I caught a whiff of the scotch we'd shared. "Shower first. Then plan," was all he said.

The bathroom door shut. I remained glued to the threadbare carpet.

"Man, I could use a shower, too," Thomas said when the sound of the pipes opening squeaked through the ancient building.

"Who cares about showering!" I was unable to contain the sound of panic in my voice. "We need to put our heads together and figure out where Henry could have taken Luke… and how to get him back." I felt anxiety coming full on when I realized I didn't even know what town I was in. "Car… do we have a car? And money? Ha! Here I am, a billionaire, and I don't even have a dollar to spend. Or clothes even. Damn it, Thomas, I have no clothes, again. Just those ripped and filthy things on that chair. I have nothing. Nothing!"

Thomas was standing in front of me now, and a light smile played upon his beautiful face. It halted my meltdown. "Luckily, you'd look hot in a garbage bag. And you don't have nothing… you have me. Now, deep breaths…" He patted my arm and tugged up the sleeve of Oliver's shirt falling off my shoulder. "I mean, you are super cute with the oversized shirt-off-the-shoulder eighties' vibe. But you could use something a little more in style. Personally, I would have you in a little black dress and high heels—or nothing at all."

He gave me a wink that made me blush.

"But…" he continued as the rush of water from Oliver showering could be heard. "That might be a little inappropriate for the current situation. Hey, maybe that blonde chick could help you with the clothing issue? What's her name… Lisa?"

Within minutes, Lisa was in our room with the contents of her duffel bag strewn across one of the beds. She was helpful, finding me something that would fit over my ample chest. With eyes bruised from lack of sleep and hands shaking with worry, she produced a sweater, soft and black, and it stretched just right across my hips. So did a pair of jeans, long enough when I rolled them down at the ankles. I was grateful for the full coverage and clean smell. Beyond grateful to have a girlfriend in the room.

Lisa shoved everything back in her bag, then started fidgeting with her honey-blonde hair, twisting and coiling it nervously.

"We'll get him back," I said, recognizing her anxiety and trying to be the one doing the comforting.

She only nodded, all yelled out from the night before. She looked beaten. Overcome with worry. But a bit of light came back on in her eyes when Oliver emerged from the bathroom in a cloud of steam. She watched him dig through his bag before pulling a shirt over his head. I was close to reminding her to pick her jaw up off the floor; Oliver's body was incredible, and it was almost comical to see the reaction it caused.

"The shower is all yours, Thomas," Oliver said, completely oblivious to the fact he was being ogled. "Be careful with that wound of yours, though."

"Yeah, no kidding," Thomas said, standing and groaning. "My staples might rust. Why did you and Kaya take me to a veterinarian anyway?"

Oliver laughed. It seemed so odd. "Because that's where most people take their pets."

"Pets?" Thomas said, only slightly offended. He was muttering as he headed for the shower. "Is that what I am? A pet?"

Lisa's eyes remained wide. "I think I'll have breakfast in here," she said softly, cheeks very pink. "You seem to have the room with the view."

My 'room with the view' quickly became a soap-scented meeting place with more boxes of pizza than five people needed in a lifetime. Seth joined us, and the debate over what to do was heated. It seemed everyone had a different opinion, and emotions were escalating. I stayed quiet, trying not to be disgusted by the food; the last thing I wanted to do was eat.

Seth talked between mouthfuls. Thomas and Lisa picked at the cheese. Oliver practically inhaled four pieces in record time. "You better eat something, too," he said to me.

Mine lay flat and untouched in my hand. Grease dripped through my fingers. "I'm not really all that hungry."

Oliver nodded understandably. "Right. You're just like Luke—he can't eat when he's worried either."

It was a nonchalant comment, but it hit both Lisa and I powerfully. The affection he had for the golden-haired love of our lives wasn't lost on either of us.

"What?" he said, catching us both staring at him.

The new Oliver was being painted in a very flattering light. It suited him so well Lisa couldn't look away. "Uh... there's just a little cheese grease on your chin," she said, and then reached across the space between the two beds to dab at him with her napkin.

Seth irritably dropped his half-eaten slice in the garbage can and got back to business. "Well, ladies and gents, I stand firm in my opinion. We know Luke won't be harmed so we have lots of time. I say we get Kaya as far as possible from any place Henry could be, then we gather up some assistance and systematically search for the boy."

This didn't sit well with Lisa. "You have no idea what Luke's going through. Henry is using him as bait to get Kaya back, and if he doesn't get her, Luke will be expendable. We have to contact Henry and barter some sort of exchange. Take Kaya to that estate or—"

"Nope," Oliver said, practically springing from the bed. "We aren't using Kaya for anything. Seth has it right. Our top priority is getting her to a safe place. She can't go anywhere near the estate. It's way too dangerous. We need back up, firepower, and a plan. And that is only after we have Kaya hidden and as far as possible from her father."

"I'll stay with her," Thomas said. "I'll look after her."

Oliver nodded agreeably. "Ah, yes, the loyal guard dog. I've no doubt of your commitment." It wasn't an insult. "Then it's settled."

My stomach rolled.

Lisa stood, her face fierce, her hands in fists. "Since when do the women in this room not have a say in things?" Any affection she'd previously shown for Oliver was gone. Now she bristled like she might scratch his eyes out.

"You do have a say, Lisa," Oliver said calmly, "but this is a man's mission. I'm sure Luke would much rather you be with Louisa May, anyway. That's where you are needed. With us, you would just be—I hate to say it—in the way."

Her eyes widened, and the room grew silent. "Oh, really? You realize it was me who took you out of the Death Race, right? Me and an eighty-year-old man named Wilbur I paid twenty bucks to make sure you got a metal cleat to the chest. Remember that? Me. A girl. I drugged you. I seemed to somehow figure out how to kidnap your precious Kaya right out from under your nose. It was me who made that plan. Yeah. A girl."

Oliver's reaction was not what I expected. "I'm sorry," he said. "I meant no disrespect."

Whoa... he really had changed.

"Saying I would be in the way? Damn, you can be such an asshole," Lisa shot back.

"Me? I'm trying to apologize and you're—"

"You're all assholes!" Thomas said, suddenly angry, standing now with his hand protecting his wounded stomach. "Yeah, that's right. You're all a bunch of stinking assholes—well, not you, Kaya—But you..." He pointed at Oliver, and I felt worried for his finger for a moment. "You are a chauvinistic asshole. I mean, thanks for saving my life and all, but honestly... what the hell is your deal with women? And you two..." He pointed at Lisa and then Seth. "You are kidnappers! You took a girl against her will, drugged her, and dragged her through hell and back... Assholes. I think y'all should just shut up and let Kaya decide what to do."

Seth, with who knew how many guns strapped to his body, was gobsmacked, and Lisa, for once, had nothing to say, either. Oliver blinked, and his forehead creased in utter awe of the cowboy who had the guts to stand up to him—and I thought he might have smiled. And me? I snickered. I couldn't help it, but the slightest snort came from my nose. And it was followed by another. The tension was so thick I could see it wave through the room like heat rising from the asphalt on a scorching summer day. And, because laughter was the only emotion I hadn't let surface in a while, it was unstoppable. The giggles came. I tried to suppress them, and the glare I got from Lisa made them even worse.

Then Oliver grinned, too. There was the slightest sound of a laugh coming from his throat. It reminded me of the lake, of the bears and stomping up the logging road with the entire Lowen army at our sides in their ridiculous camo outfits and army boots... trying not to laugh at them, but not wanting to stop because then all there was to do was cry...

Lisa fumed. "I don't get it. What's so damn funny?"

"Nothing... nothing is funny at all... that's why it's—"

"Funny," Oliver said for me.

He and I shared a memory that would forever bond us together in some way. And it suddenly made me feel stronger than ever. His understanding of me, and his love, fueled me up. I realized that even though I was stronger than I'd ever been it was okay to need him. We all needed someone. That was simply part of being human.

Seth had grown impatient. "Well, girlie," he said. "You haven't given us your opinion yet. So, what is it? What do you think we should do?"

Gone were the giggles. "Well—" A ringing cell phone cut me off.

"Hold that thought," Seth said. "It's Regan. I'll put him on speaker."

The phone was placed on the bed so we all could hear; there wasn't a pleasant hello. "What the hell is going on there?" the redheaded Englishman barked into the phone.

"Well, hello to you, too, Regan," Seth said casually. "We've got Kaya. She is okay, but—"

Regan cut Seth off and was practically yelling. "No, I mean, what the hell is going on? Where the hell is Luke? Why did I just see his face on television? Huh? Louisa came flying into my room this morning, telling me her brother is a TV star now. That she saw him after an orange juice commercial. Well, I thought the kid was delusional, but I just saw Luke in a cold medication ad before the hockey game. So tell me, right now, what the hell is going on? Where is he?"

We were all stunned. Lisa was the only one able to talk. "Luke... was on television?"

Regan roared. "Yeah. That's what I said! And he doesn't look so hot."

"Henry has him," Lisa muttered.

It sounded for a moment like Regan had thrown his phone to the floor. The clamber and crashing were so great we all sat in stunned silence until it stopped. He spoke again, sounding as if struggling to stay calm. "Bloody hell. If Henry Lowen touches one more hair on that boy's head, I will slice and dice him... I will hunt him down and—"

"Regan," Lisa said. "What do you mean by 'one more hair'?"

"Oh, you'll know when you see the commercial. Search 'HOME RX' cold medicine on a laptop or something. Damn it! I can't believe you dumbasses let this happen!"

"Hey," Seth said. "We're not idiots. Luke was protecting Kaya and—"

"Of course he was," Regan interjected bitterly, clearing his throat. "You all better just get back here, like... now. By the time your feet are in this door, I will have figured out something. Kaya, you can hear me, right?"

"Yes."

"It doesn't matter what any of those idiots you are with decide to do. Got it? You have to come here, to me. All right? I'm way smarter than all of them. I know how to get Luke back. I know what we have to do."

"I do, too," I said.

Seth lunged for the phone on the bed and took it off the speaker. Placing the device to his ear, he wandered out the door to start an argument with Regan. I could hear him yelling, going on about my safety this, and my safety that...

"Find that commercial," I said to Lisa.

She was scrambling for her phone and typing 'Home RX' into the YouTube search button. As if in a dream, I went to sit beside her. In moments, there was Luke, his picture frozen on the screen in Lisa's hands. His eyes were rimmed with heavy red, his lip swollen, and he seemed to be in pain.

"I don't know if I can do this," Lisa said, her hand shaking as her fingertip hovered over the play button. "I've seen him at his worse, but this... I have a feeling that this..."

"Just do it."

'What if he's—?'

"Just goddamn push that play button, Lisa," I hissed, and the ice-cold tone of my voice was a shock, even to me.

She pushed play.

A smiley man in a lab coat was standing next to Luke, the wall behind them an obviously fake scene of lush green meadow. Luke was standing awkwardly, his feet bare. Beige-colored pants and a clean white button-up shirt perfectly fit his lean body. The man with the lab coat had a yard stick, and used it to point at Luke as he spoke to the camera.

"Colds. Everyone gets them. Luke here is practically dying of one— stuffy nose, swollen eyes, sore throat, and pounding headache—and it all could have been preventable with 'Home RX'." The man used the yard stick to give Luke a tap to the abdomen, and this made Luke double over slightly. "Even that pesky nausea will take a hike! One dose a day is all you need so you never have to end up looking like poor Luke here. So, hurry. Don't waste any time, run like your life depends on it to your nearest pharmacy, and get Home RX right away! Right, Luke?"

The camera zoomed in on Luke's beautiful face. He nodded. He had been beaten, badly. He could barely hold up his head and his eyes were swimming in their sockets. The scar over his cheekbone was gone, so that meant he had on makeup—which was probably to cover up bruises. "Get Home right away," Luke repeated.

"What's that, Luke?" asked the man.

"Get Home RX," Luke said in a detached voice. It did sound like he had a cold…

"That's right, get Home RX. Listen to Luke! Quantities are limited, so don't tempt fate. If you wait two days, it will be too late!"

Luke coughed as if on cue, and a disclaimer flashed across the screen while a male voice narrated the small text as fast as possible: "Home RX is an Eronel product. Medicine for your family that you can trust. Don't take if you have nut allergies, glaucoma, heart disease, diabetes, eczema, psoriasis, trouble sleeping or difficulty with urination, or a history of cancer in your family or cancer yourself. Emotional unbalances may be enhanced, and risk of infection increased in those with a low immune system. Do not take if you have had the measles or chicken pox or have had pneumonia or…"

I didn't need to hear the rest. Neither did Lisa. She dropped her phone, and her body started to vibrate with anger. "Apparently, your pal Sindra doesn't keep her word."

Seth had returned to the room. Oliver and Thomas moved toward me, no doubt expecting a complete freak out. I put my hands up and backed away, so I could stand my ground.

"The message is pretty clear," I said, completely in control. "I have to get to the estate or Luke dies. They've beaten him—we know he doesn't look like that because of a cold—and Henry is giving me two days max. I know my father. He doesn't make idle threats."

"How could he even assume you would see that commercial?" Thomas asked.

"And when did the commercial come out? How do we know exactly how much time we have?" Lisa asked.

"None of that matters," Seth roared. "He wants Kaya, and I'll be damned if he's going to get her!"

"Since when are you in charge?" Oliver yelled back.

Conflict broke out around me. I headed for the door. I stepped outside into the bitterly cold air, and didn't feel the sting of a single tear. I was worried for Luke. Rattled right to my very core. But I knew what I had to do. I knew what poured into me, fueling me up, charging all my cells and taking over my emotionally ravaged mind, would keep me going forward—hatred, revenge, and love. I would seek retribution on Luke's behalf. For his mother. For Regan's sister and Anne. For Angela and Ben, and Dustin, Rusty, and Marie… even for Rayna. I would do whatever it took to get back at my father for what he'd done. I knew my part in this, but Oliver was right… it was bigger than me.

"Kaya?"

He'd come into the waning afternoon to stand next to me under the motel lamp. Snowflakes as brilliant as the whites of his eyes drifted through the air and fluttered around him. He had that determined look on his face, and I knew what he was about to say. He wanted to drag me off somewhere to hide me so he could look after everything, just like he always had. I turned to face him and swallowed hard, but this time, I didn't have to dig too deep for the courage to speak my mind. This was my life—I was the one in charge.

"Listen," I said, staring into his deep brown eyes as steadily as I could. "If you think I'm going to bury my head in the sand and wait for you and Seth to come up with some game plan, you're wrong. I am not going into hiding. I am not running to keep myself safe. No matter what your opinion is, no matter what anyone's opinion is, I don't care. I am making my own decisions and following my own plan, even if that means doing it all by myself. I am going to face this tiger head on. Because if Luke dies, my life is meaningless and Henry will have won—and I'll be damned if I'm going to let that happen." I felt my heart speed up, but only slightly. "I am going to the estate because nothing, and I mean nothing, matters to me more than Luke. I refuse to live in a world without him in it."

I expected a fight.

"I understand," Oliver said, and he reached for my hand.He was nodding like he'd been in my shoes before… like he completely understood. "And I'm coming with you."

I had to give my head a shake. He wasn't arguing with me? "You could die. Because of me."

He smiled. "You know the way you feel about Luke?" Oliver's eyes glistened as he took in the sky, grey and wide as it stretched across the snowy prairies. "I feel the same way about you."

I left my hand in his and studied the world before me—the big, wide world. With Oliver beside me, I could conquer it. I linked my fingers through his. "Thank you," I said. "For everything."

The base of his throat bobbed. "Anytime. You know you'll always be my girl, Kaya."

He didn't mean possessively. "I know."

The sky darkened, and the snow fell harder. We were going to get a storm. A big one. The wind picked up and brought with it a stinging taste of things to come—but I was ready for it.

EPILOGUE

SHE'D DESCRIBED HIM SO PERFECTLY I KNEW IT WAS HIM THE INSTANT I saw his face. There was no doubt in my mind who the man on the television was, and no doubt he was not being filmed of his own free will.

I'd been questioning my next move, but the answer came to me in the form of a cryptic ad for cold medicine. The message was one only me and a few others might understand; Kaya needed help. This was a sign, a confirmation, and a total affirmation of what I had to do next—which was get off this stinking ranch.

I plopped down on the floor next to my bed, the carpet gone, the blankets brand new, and the smell of bleach still strong even two days later. Whatever happened in our house while we were gone must have been bad. So bad that a massive undertaking to erase all evidence of it had left behind new windows, new floors, and countless tire tracks across the lawn. Couches, pillows, cutlery, and some of my clothes had disappeared. So did every bit of hay and straw in the barn. There was a bank draft for five hundred thousand dollars and a note attached that said, 'Hope you enjoyed your vacation. Keep this quiet or it will become permanent,' taped to the fridge. A warning for sure. A threat most definitely. And I knew who it was from—I knew more than Kaya thought I did.

Daddy had sworn loudly when he'd found the note, and then marched out the door to round up the horses. Mom had just given her head a shake, started to cry, and then headed to the kitchen to bake. That night, not a word was spoken about what might have happened. Not a word was spoken about Ben being missing either. Mostly because saying it out loud meant opening a can of worms not one of us would be able to put back.

It was the next morning, out in the barn, when I'd found the note addressed to me. I recognized the handwriting. I also recognized the floral stationary I'd bought at the dollar store a while back. It was stuck on a nail in Zander's pen, and, oddly enough, the horse didn't spook when I reached for it. He seemed calm, nudging my arm for oats as I pulled the paper out of the thin envelope.

Marlene,
I want to thank you for being there for me and for being a friend. It is rare these days to meet someone like you, and I will cherish every moment you gave me. Things happened at your house—really bad things—and I'm sorry I couldn't have prevented it. People were hurt. Thomas is okay, though. He is with me. Just know I am going to do what I can to make things right. My hope is that you will carry on, forget you ever knew me, and live a long and wonderful life.
I will never forget you,
Love,

Kaya.

I gathered up some clothes and then opened the box I kept hidden under my bed; I had close to five thousand dollars. I never knew what I was saving every birthday cent or paycheck from shoveling snow for. But now I did…

The keys to the truck were sitting underneath my red wool cap; both went into my jacket pocket. So did the handgun I'd owned since sixth grade—a very disturbing present from a very disturbed uncle—along with my favorite hunting knife. Then I wrote my own note, on the same stationary, and addressed it to Mom and Dad. I didn't feel the slightest bit of guilt, remorse, or trepidation about leaving when I set it on the coffee table.

On the way out the door, I could hear Mom softly talking to her pie dough and see Dad wrestling with the stubborn Clydesdale out in the pasture. I stopped to look at them—really look at them. They were beautiful. They'd given me everything, and I loved them dearly… but it was time to go. For the first time in my life, I had a purpose beyond digging holes and staying out of everyone's way; I had a friend who needed me.

ᏗCKNOWLEDGEMENTS

Thank you...

THIS BOOK WOULDN'T HAVE BEEN POSSIBLE WITHOUT THE support of my husband, Byran Bueckert, who kept reality in check and looked after life while I wandered about in my dream world. Haley Bueckert—your encouragement, love, and willingness to dream right along with me was more treasured than you will ever know. Emily Bueckert and Josh Bueckert—your extremely honest criticism was so important and valued—I am grateful for every word you read. Mom—thanks for being there for me, always, and tackling the first mammoth manuscript like a champ. My friend Tammy Wiebe—I felt like you truly believed in me, and that has fueled the fires to keep me going. Thank you for the advice and for being there for me in so many ways. You are my number one! Thank you from the bottom of my heart to everyone at Clean Teen Publishing; I am so grateful for all you do! Rebecca Gober, Courtney Knight, Marya Heiman, Melanie Newton, and Wendy Martinez—your patience, dedication and guidance is so appreciated and I am so honored to be a part of CTP. Cynthia Shepp, you are a rock star! I am eternally grateful for your mad editing skills and in complete awe of your vast literary knowledge. Thank you for everything you've done for Nocturne. Also a huge thanks to Shelley Mckenzie, the best sister in the world, and Reanne and Kieran Averay-Jones, Grant Tarapacki, My bro Brian Vincent, Ross McKenzie, Stan Pietrusik, Darrell Newsham, DJ Newsham, Courtney Whittamore, Kourtney Bueckert, Myrna Bueckert, my incredible Mckenzie family, and supportive Bueckert family. To everyone who read SERENADE and sent me positive vibes, thank you so much! To my musician friends and all the Edmontonians who have supported me musically and have hopped on board my author adventure, I treasure you more than you know. I am wildly grateful for all of you! — HMB

$\mathcal{A}$BOUT $\mathcal{T}$HE $\mathcal{A}$UTHOR

HEATHER MCKENZIE IS A Canadian author and Serenade is her first novel. A professional singer/songwriter with five albums to date, she has been telling stories through music for years and pulls from her extraordinary experiences as a musician to fuel her passion for creating Young Adult fiction. A rocker at heart, a mom of three, an aspiring painter, and a lover of animals, she is kept grounded by her husband at their home in Edmonton. You can visit Heather at

WWW.HEATHERMCKENZIE.COM

CPSIA information can be obtained
at www.ICGtesting.com
Printed in the USA
LVHW02s0025120518
576935LV00002B/3/P

9 781634 223065